高考英语
总复习点击与突破

编者：王志强　陶子萍　宋秀梅
　　　李雪芹　孙奕　张玉芬　魏芳

下册

外语教学与研究出版社
FOREIGN LANGUAGE TEACHING AND RESEARCH PRESS
北京　BEIJING

图书在版编目(CIP)数据

高考英语总复习点击与突破. 下册／王志强等编 .— 北京：外语教学与研究出版社，2008.7
（考试时间）
ISBN 978－7－5600－7704－8

Ⅰ. 高…　Ⅱ. 王…　Ⅲ. 英语课—高中—升学参考资料　Ⅳ. G634.413

中国版本图书馆 CIP 数据核字 (2008) 第 117664 号

出　版　人：于春迟
责任编辑：李小香
封面设计：刘　冬
出版发行：外语教学与研究出版社
社　　址：北京市西三环北路 19 号 (100089)
网　　址：http://www.fltrp.com
印　　刷：北京京师印务有限公司
开　　本：787×1092　1/16
印　　张：21.5
版　　次：2008 年 9 月第 1 版　2008 年 9 月第 1 次印刷
书　　号：ISBN 978－7－5600－7704－8
定　　价：49.90 元
＊　　＊　　＊
基础英语教育出版分社：
地　　址：北京市西三环北路 19 号 外研社大厦 基础英语教育出版分社 (100089)
咨询电话：010－88819666 (编辑部)/88819688 (市场部)
传　　真：010－88819422 (编辑部)/88819423 (市场部)
网　　址：http://www.nse.cn
电子信箱：beed@fltrp.com 或登录 http://www.nse.cn (留言反馈)栏目
购书电话：010－88819928/9929/9930 (邮购部)
购书传真：010－88819428 (邮购部)
＊　　＊　　＊
如有印刷、装订质量问题出版社负责调换
制售盗版必究　举报查实奖励
版权保护办公室举报电话：(010)88817519
物料号：177040001

前言

　　国家教育部颁布《普通高中课程方案（实验）》和各学科课程标准以来，全国先后有十多个省开始新课程实验，换用新课程实验教材。《英语》（新标准）高中教材是外语教学与研究出版社依据教育部制定的国家《英语课程标准》在充分调研和科学论证的基础上，与世界著名教育出版机构——英国麦克米伦出版公司共同推出的我国第一套中小学"一条龙"英语教材——《英语》（新标准）的有机组成部分，是全国使用量最大的英语教材之一。2007年，首批使用《英语》（新标准）高中教材的学生参加了高考，取得了良好成绩。为了帮助今后参加高考的学生更快、更好地掌握《英语》（新标准）高中教材的目标要求，高效率地进行复习备考，我们特聘请高中英语教育方面的专家、优秀教研人员和骨干教师编写了这套与《英语》（新标准）高中教材配套的《高考英语总复习点击与突破》。

　　这套书分上、下两册。上册为《英语》（新标准）高中教材必修1至必修5的总复习，含语法总结；下册为《英语》（新标准）高中教材顺序选修6至顺序选修8的总复习，含两套总复习检测题。

　　全套书充分体现国家《英语课程标准》的目标要求，根据《英语》（新标准）高中教材的特点，结合近年来的高考命题情况，与教材的每个模块同步总结复习要点并设计能力训练题，突出基础性、针对性、提高性和发展性。每个模块由"要点纵览"、"知识梳理"、"综合训练"三部分组成。"要点纵览"揭示归纳总结本模块的复习要点；"知识梳理"主要针对考点和易错内容对"要点纵览"中的重点项目进行讲解，并穿插"真题解析"；"综合训练"针对本模块复习要点和高考命题趋势提供巩固练习题。上册中的"语法总结"结合高考真题对语法重点、难点和考点进行点拨、梳理、巩固和提高。

　　总之，我们力求通过这套书帮助考生夯实基础、开阔视野，在提升综合运用英语能力的同时，提高参加高考的应试能力。

　　本套书适合第一轮高考复习使用。

Contents

高考英语总复习点击与突破

顺序选修6

Module ①

Small Talk

高考词汇	serious, confidently, lack, advance, nod, yawn, sigh, prize, application, form, immigration, visa, tidy, favour, reception, embassy, certain, reply, saleswoman, firm, fax, outspoken, motto, shortcoming, absence, coincidence, customer, mature, awkward, tease, typist, contradict, pregnant, apology, cautious, acquaintance, messy, divorce, fool, clerk, haircut, anyhow, modest, brunch, anniversary, hostess, interrupt, violate, function, successful, imagine, purpose, circumstance, apologise
常用短语	ask a favour, make light conversations, encourage sb to do better, take the lead, lack confidence, make sb a better listener, during a job interview, keep eye contact, in addition, nod in agreement, be aware of, look away from, show off, as a consequence, be cautious about (doing) sth, cheer sb up, discourage sb from doing sth
实用句型	1. Have you ever crossed the road to avoid talking to someone you recognise? 2. That way, you don't damage your confidence! 3. In addition, you need to know how long you should stay, and when you have to leave. 4. Her motto was "Every time I open my mouth, I put my foot in it." 5. "No, I guess they chose you to discourage you from spending your whole career with us," Esther replied sweetly. 6. Imagine a situation where two strangers are talking to each other after someone they both know has left the room, or the café or party, etc.
交际用语	1. Wonderful, aren't they? (They're wonderful, aren't they?) 2. Been here before? (Have you been here before?) 3. Staying long? (Are you staying long?)

◆ 高考词汇

1. matter

n. 1) [C] 事情；2) 情况，事态；3) [U] 物质，材料，东西；

　4) (与 the 连用) 麻烦，毛病

v. 有关系，重要，要紧

It was a personal matter.

Don't do it that way. It will make matters worse.

Marxism sees all matter is changing.

What's the matter with you?

It doesn't matter to me what you do or where you go.

➡ 常用短语：

as a matter of fact 实际上，事实上　　no matter 无论，不要紧，无关紧要

to make matters worse 使不好的情况更糟，更糟的是

2. impress

v. 留下印象，使……明白，印上

The girl impressed her friends with her sense of humour.

He impressed the importance of the work on them.

Henry impressed the design on his T-shirt.

➡ 常用短语：

impress sth on sb (= impress sb with sth) 使某人铭记某事物

> **拓展**
>
> impression *n.* 印象，感觉
> impressive *adj.* 令人印象深刻的
> have / get the impression (that) 觉得
> make an impression on sb 给某人留下印象

3. recognise

v. 1) 认出，分辨出；2) 认为，承认

I recognised Alice on the photograph.

Can you recognise his voice over the phone?

He is recognised as a great writer.

I recognise that he is the best player in the team.

4. lack

n. 缺少，不足

v. 没有，缺乏

I've got dark rings under my eyes for lack of sleep.

They are so rich that they lack for nothing.

What the company lacks is sufficient money to invest in new products.

注意：lack 作名词时，后面常跟介词 of；作不及物动词时，后面常跟介词 for。

➡ 常用短语：

for lack of 因缺少　　lack for nothing 什么也不缺　　no lack of 不缺少，足够

5. reply

n. 回答，答复，答案

v. 回答，回复

I've got no reply to my letter.

I have nothing to say in reply to your question.

He replied that he couldn't attend the party.

He gave me no chance to reply to his questions.

注意：reply 一般作不及物动词，后接介词 to。当作及物动词时，其宾语往往只限于直接引语或宾语从句，此时，其含义和用法与 answer 相同。

➡ 常用短语：

in reply (to) 作为对……的答复　　make a reply to 回答，对……作答复

make (no) reply (不) 作答复

◆ 常用短语

1. in agreement

in agreement 意思是"同意"。

He nodded his head in agreement.

2. in addition

in addition 意思是"除此之外，另外"。这个短语的意思和 besides 近似，是副词性质。

People get valuable work experience and, in addition, employers can afford to employ them.

> **拓展**
>
> arrive at / come to / make / reach an agreement 达成协议，取得一致意见
>
> in agreement with 符合，按照，同意，(和……) 一致
>
> under an agreement 根据协议

辨析

in addition to 意思是"除……之外还"。这个短语是介词性质，后需接宾语成分。

He's now running his own research company, in addition to his job at the university.

3. be aware of

be aware of 意思是"知道，意识到，觉察到"。

Most smokers are perfectly aware of the dangers of smoking.

He was aware of a faint smell of gas.

aware 的其他常见用法：

1) be aware + that 从句 知道，意识到

   Were you aware that your son was having difficulties at school?

2) make sb aware of sth 让某人明白 (某事)

   It's time for you to make him aware of the effects of his actions.

3) so far as I am aware [口]就我所知

   So far as I am aware, this is the first time a British rider has won the competition.

 综合训练

考试时间：45分钟　满分：100分

Ⅰ. 单项选择（共15小题；每小题1分，满分15分）

1. I'm surprised that you should have been fooled by such a(n) _____ trick.

   A. ordinary   B. easy   C. smart   D. simple

2. For students of Senior 3, it is the most important to _____ a good state of mind in face of failure.

   A. keep up   B. keep on   C. keep off   D. keep away

3. Although the teacher did not mention any names, everybody knew who he was _____.

   A. attending to   B. turning to   C. referring to   D. talking to

4. —Why haven't you bought any butter?

   —I _____ to, but I forgot about it.

   A. liked   B. wished   C. meant   D. expected

5. I've worked with children before, so I know what _____ in my new job.

   A. expected   B. to expect   C. to be expecting   D. expects

6. _____ is it _____ has made Peter what he is today?

   A. What; that   B. That; that

   C. That; what   D. What; what

7. The boy said confidently that he would avoid _____ the same mistake again.

   A. to make   B. make   C. making   D. being made

8. —Can I pay the bill next month?

   —Sorry, sir. But it is the rule of our company that all payments _____ be made by the end of the month.

   A. can   B. need   C. will   D. shall

9. —Which share _____ for me?

   —You can take _____ half; they are both of the same weight.

   A. is intended; either　　　　　B. means; both

   C. is meant; any　　　　　　　D. is intended; all

10. His daughter is always shy in _____ and she never dares to make a speech to _____.

    A. the public; the public　　　B. public; the public

    C. the public; public　　　　　D. public; public

11. —The teacher _____ the problem so carefully, I think.

    —Yes, we had learnt it in junior school.

    A. needn't have explained　　　B. needn't explain

    C. shouldn't have explained　　D. mustn't explain

12. A middle-aged man came _____ to the bus stop only _____ the bus had gone.

    A. to run; finding　　　　　　B. running; to find

    C. and ran; found　　　　　　D. running; finding

13. Shortsightedness can be _____ by the use of suitable glasses.

    A. fixed　　　B. improved　　　C. reduced　　　　D. corrected

14. You are really very kind. I'll never forget the _____ you have done for me.

    A. favour　　　B. deed　　　C. help　　　　　D. kindness

15. —I was wondering if we could go camping in the nearby forest at the weekend.

    —_____ interesting.

    A. Sound　　　B. Sounds　　　C. Sounded　　　　D. Sounding

Ⅱ. 完形填空（共20小题；每小题1分，满分20分）

In the city of Fujisawa, Japan, lives a woman named Atsuko Saeki. When she was a teenager, she __1__ of going to the United States. Most of what she knew about American __2__ was from the textbooks she had read. "I had a __3__ in mind: Daddy watching TV in the living room, Mummy __4__ cakes and their teenage daughter off to the cinema with her boyfriend."

Atsuko __5__ to attend college in California. When she arrived, however, she found it was not her __6__ world. "People were struggling with problems and often seemed __7__," she said. "I felt very lonely."

One of her hardest __8__ was physical education. "We played volleyball," she said. "The other students were __9__ it, but I wasn't."

One afternoon, the instructor asked Atsuko to __10__ the ball to her teammates so they could knock it __11__ the net. No big deal for most people, but it terrified Atsuko. She was afraid of losing face __12__ she failed.

A young man on her team __13__ what she was going through. "He walked up to me and __14__, 'Come on. You can do that.'"

"You will never understand how those words of __15__ made me feel. Four words:

You can do that. I felt like crying with happiness."

She made it through the class. Perhaps she thanked the young man; she is not __16__.

Six years have passed. Atsuko is back in Japan, working as a salesclerk. "I have __17__ forgotten the words," she said. "When things are not going so well, I think of them."

She is sure the young man had no idea how much his kindness __18__ to her. "He probably doesn't even remember it," she said. That may be the lesson. Whenever you say something to a person — cruel or kind — you have no idea how long the words will __19__. Atsuko is all the way over in Japan, but still she hears those four __20__ words: You can do that.

1. A. learnt	B. spoke	C. dreamed	D. headed
2. A. way	B. life	C. education	D. spirit
3. A. photo	B. painting	C. picture	D. drawing
4. A. baking	B. frying	C. steaming	D. boiling
5. A. hoped	B. arranged	C. liked	D. attempted
6. A. described	B. imagined	C. created	D. discovered
7. A. tense	B. cheerful	C. relaxed	D. deserted
8. A. times	B. questions	C. classes	D. projects
9. A. curious about	B. good at	C. slow at	D. nervous about
10. A. kick	B. knock	C. carry	D. hit
11. A. through	B. into	C. over	D. past
12. A. after	B. if	C. because	D. until
13. A. believed	B. considered	C. wondered	D. sensed
14. A. warned	B. sighed	C. ordered	D. whispered
15. A. excitement	B. encouragement	C. persuasion	D. suggestion
16. A. interested	B. doubtful	C. puzzled	D. sure
17. A. never	B. already	C. seldom	D. almost
18. A. happened	B. applied	C. seemed	D. meant
19. A. continue	B. stay	C. exist	D. live
20. A. merciful	B. bitter	C. simple	D. easy

Ⅲ. 阅读理解（共10小题；每小题2分，满分20分）

A

The flag, the most common symbol of a nation in the modern world, is also one of the most ancient. With a clear symbolic meaning, the flag in the traditional form is still used today to mark buildings, ships and other vehicles related to a country.

The national flag, as we know it today, is in no way a primitive artifact (人造物品). It is, rather, the product of thousands of years' development. Historians believe that it had two major ancestors, of which the earlier served to show wind direction.

Early human beings used very fragile houses and boats. Often strong winds would tear roofs from houses or cause high waves that endangered travellers. People's food supplies were similarly <u>vulnerable</u>. Even after they had learnt how to plant grains, they still needed help from nature to ensure good harvests. Therefore they feared and depended on the power of the wind, which could bring warmth from one direction and cold from another.

Using a simple piece of cloth tied to the top of a post to tell the direction of the wind was more dependable than earlier methods, such as watching the rising of smoke from a fire. The connection of the flag with heavenly power was therefore reasonable. Early human societies began to fix long pieces of cloth to the tops of totems (图腾) before carrying them into battle. They believed that the power of the wind would be added to the good wishes of the gods and ancestors represented by the totems themselves.

These flags developed very slowly into modern flags. The first known flag of a nation or a ruler was unmarked: The king of China around 1122 BC was said to have a white flag carried ahead of him. This practice might have been learnt from Egyptians even further in the past, but it was from China that it spread over trade routes through India, then across Arab lands, and finally to Europe, where it met up with the other ancestor of the national flag.

1. The best title for the passage would be _____.
   A. Development of the National Flag   B. Power of the National Flag
   C. Types of Flags   D. Uses of Flags
2. The underlined word "vulnerable" in the third paragraph means _____.
   A. impossible to make sure of   B. likely to be protected
   C. easy to damage   D. difficult to find
3. The earliest flags were connected with heavenly power because they _____.
   A. could tell wind direction   B. could bring good luck to fighters
   C. were handed down by the ancestors   D. were believed to stand for natural forces
4. What does the author know of the first national flag?
   A. He knows when it was sent to Europe.   B. He believes it was made in Egypt.
   C. He thinks it came from China.   D. He doubts where it started.
5. What will the author most probably talk about next?
   A. The role of China in the spread of the national flag.
   B. The second ancestor of the national flag.
   C. The use of modern flags in Europe.
   D. The importance of modern flags.

B

Tuvalu, a tiny country in the Pacific Ocean, has asked for help as it will be swallowed up by the sea.

Storms and huge waves are a constant threat and none of Tuvalu's nine little islands is more than five metres above sea level. Salt water is already entering the country's drinking water supply, as well as damaging plants that produce fruit and vegetables. Without urgent help, the country's days are numbered.

But Tuvalu is not the first place to face sinking into the sea. Venice, a historic city in Italy best known for its canals, has sunk about 24cm over the past 100 years. Experts say that it will have sunk another 20–50cm by 2050. A century ago, St. Mark's Square, the lowest point of the city, flooded about nine times a year. Nowadays, it happens more than 100 times. While Venice is slowly sinking into the mud on which it stands, global warming causes Tuvalu's rising sea level.

The average global temperature has increased by almost 0.5 centigrade degrees over the past century; scientists expect it to rise by extra 1–3 degrees over the next 100 years.

Warmer weather makes glaciers (冰川) melt, adding more water to the ocean. The warmer temperatures also make water expand, so it takes up more space, causing the sea level to rise. The sea level has risen about 10–25cm in the last 100 years.

The main cause of global warming is human pollution. Through burning coal, oil and gas, people have been increasing the greenhouse gases in the atomosphere, such as CO_2. This adds to the power of the greenhouse effect, making the planet even warmer.

Many scientists believe that, if the warming is not stopped, there will be huge climate changes. The sea level could rise by one metre this century.

Should this come true, the sea will swallow up millions of homes and the world will be flooded with "climate refugees" looking for somewhere to live?

6. We can infer from the passage that _____.
   A. Tuvalu is in danger of being swallowed up by the sea
   B. all Tuvalu's islands are about five metres above the sea level
   C. drinking water in Tuvalu has been destroyed
   D. Tuvalu is often flooded by storms and waves
7. The author uses Tuvalu and Venice as examples in order to explain _____.
   A. they are the first place sinking into the sea
   B. they are both sinking into the mud where they stand
   C. they will disappear in the future
   D. their trouble is caused by global warming
8. Put the following events in the right order.
   a. Glaciers began to melt.
   b. People burn coal, oil and gas.
   c. The greenhouse effect is growing.
   d. The earth is getting warmer and warmer.
   e. The sea level is rising.

f. More CO_2 is produced.

g. Many places are sinking into the sea.

A. d, f, b, c, a, e, g   B. b, f, c, d, e, a, g   C. f, c, b, d, a, e, g   D. b, f, c, d, a, e, g

9. What does "climate refugees" mean?

A. People who are forced away from their homeland by climate.

B. The climate that has been greatly changed by people.

C. The places that are often threatened by storms.·

D. The bad effects that the pollution caused.

10. Which of the following is not true according to the passage?

A. Tuvalu's nine little islands are less than five metres above the sea level.

B. The average global temperature has risen by 1–3 centigrade degrees over the past 100 years.

C. The warmer temperature causes the sea level to rise.

D. There will be huge climate changes unless the warming is stopped.

IV．阅读表达（共5小题；每小题3分，满分15分）

In recent years, many countries of the world have been facing with the problem of how to make their workers more productive. Some experts claim the answer is to make jobs more varied. But do more various jobs lead to greater productivity? There is evidence to suggest that while variety certainly makes the workers' life more enjoyable, it doesn't actually make them work harder. As far as increasing productivity is concerned, variety is not an important factor.

Other experts feel that _____ to do their job in their own way is important, and there is no doubt that this is true. The problem is that this kind of freedom cannot easily be given in the modern factory with its complicated machinery that must be used in a fixed way. Thus while freedom of choice is important, there is usually very little that can be done to create it.

Another very important consideration is how each worker contributes to the product he is making. In most factories one worker sees only one part of the product. Some car factories are now experimenting with having many small production lines rather than one large one, so that each worker contributes more to the production of the cars on his line. Therefore, it would seem that not only is degree of the worker's contribution an important factor, but it is one we can do something about.

To what extent does more money lead to greater productivity? The workers themselves certainly think this is important. But perhaps they want more money only because the work they do is boring. Money just let them enjoy their spare time more. A similar argument may explain demands for shorter working hours. Perhaps if we succeed in making their jobs more interesting, they will neither want more money, nor will shorter working hours be so important to them.

1. What is the best way to make the workers work harder according to the author? (Please answer within 10 words.)

_____

2. Why can't a worker have the freedom in doing the job in his own way?

_____

3. What is the best title for the passage? (Please answer within 10 words.)

_____

4. Fill in the blank in the second paragraph with proper words or phrases to complete the sentence. (Please answer within 10 words.)

_____

5. Translate the underlined sentence in the first paragraph into Chinese.

_____

V. 句型转换（共3小题；每空1分，满分10分）

1. He is such a good student that every teacher loves him.

He is _____ _____ _____ student _____ every teacher loves him.

2. We have another two cars besides this one.

We have another two cars _____ _____ _____ this one.

3. He should say "sorry" to you for what he said.

He should _____ _____ _____ to you for what he said.

VI. 完成句子（共5小题；每空1分，满分20分）

1. 你没有必要这么早就去那儿。

_____ _____ _____ _____ for you to go there so early.

2. 他将不得不受到老板的惩罚。

He _____ _____ _____ _____ _____ by his boss.

3. 是谁把这个消息透露出去的？

Who was it _____ _____ _____ the news?

4. 你其实没有必要去机场接他。

You _____ _____ _____ _____ _____ at the airport.

5. 从太空中看，表面70%以上都是水的地球就像是一个蓝色的星球。

Seen from space, the earth _____ _____ _____ more than 70 percent of its surface, appears as a "blue planet".

Module ②

Fantasy Literature

📖 要点纵览

高考词汇	heroine, hero, novel, behave, bush, hesitate, doubt, direction, bite, arch, alarm, sniff, edge, square, shape, level, swim, bare, bend, dream, awake, revenge, marry, cottage, punish, appeal, cafeteria, envelope, literary, bond, output, typewriter, gifted, flesh, format, anecdote, draft, burden, swift, stubborn, overcome, adjustment, automatic, target, curriculum, distribute, accumulate, deposit, thus, attain, status, sorrow, ought, power, possess
常用短语	ahead of, play an important part in, put down, hold out one's hands, turn away, no doubt, bend down, look around for, for some reason, be similar to, come up to, keep one's eyes on, in the air, put a spell on, pass by, once again, appeal to sb, be associated with, look back over one's shoulder, be responsible for, be restricted to
实用句型	1. …and he might have gone on to the north, or he might have laid his head on the grass under one of those trees and slept… 2. …keeping his eyes on the spot where the cat had been investigating. 3. It looked as if someone had cut a patch out of the air… 4. But Will knew without the slightest doubt that… 5. It was only in 1997 that she completed the first Harry Potter story…
交际用语	1. Give me a moment. 2. See what I mean? 3. It's your turn. 4. I'm stuck. 5. Look at the time!

◆ 高考词汇

1. hesitate

v. 犹豫，踌躇，迟疑

Harry hesitated a moment before replying.

Don't hesitate to contact me if you need any more information.

2. marry

v. 结婚，娶，嫁

The old man married late and had no children.

➡ 常用短语：

marry sb 嫁/娶某人   marry sb to sb 把某人嫁给某人

be married 结婚 (强调状态)   get married 结婚 (强调动作)

He married a classmate from the university.

He married his daughter to a doctor.

He has been married for 10 years.

He got married last week.

真 题 解 析

My uncle _____ until he was 45. (2006 黄冈模拟)

A. married   B. didn't marry   C. was not marrying   D. would marry

解析：由于 marry 为终止性动词，所以不能用进行时态。根据句意，特别是根据句子的状语成分 until he was 45判断，主句应该用否定形式。答案为 B。

3. appeal

n. 1) 恳求；呼吁；2) 感染力，吸引力；3) 上诉，申诉

v. 1) 恳请，恳求；呼吁；2) 吸引；3) 上诉

The United Nations' appeal for a peace talk has been completely ignored by both sides.

Much of Qingdao's appeal lies in its charming beaches.

The case is on appeal.

The police are appealing to the public for information about the crime.

She appealed to the robbers to set her son free.

Does the idea of working abroad appeal to you?

If you are not satisfied, you can appeal.

◆ **常用短语**

1. play a part

play a part 的主要含义有：

1) 扮演角色；2) 承担任务，起作用，有贡献；3) 参与，参加

Who will play the part of Shakespeare in the film?

They played a major part in the success of the project.

She plays an active part in local politics.

2. in the air

in the air 意思是"在空中，在流传中；未确定的，悬而未决的"。

There is a feeling of unrest in the air.

Our plans are still in the air.

> **拓展**
>
> as light as air / a feather 很轻
> in the open air 在户外，露天
> on / off (the) air (广播或电视等)
> 正在/停止播放

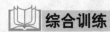 **综合训练**

考试时间：45分钟 满分：100分

I. 单项选择（共15小题；每小题1分，满分15分）

1. —How can I get the main idea of the story?

　—You'd better _____ the book and find it for yourself.

　A. look up 　　B. look for 　　　　C. look through 　　D. look at

2. He was such a _____ person that he will never follow the others' suggestions.

　A. foolish 　　B. stubborn 　　　C. bright 　　　　D. gifted

3. Whoever is found _____ in the forest will be fined at least 200 *yuan*.

　A. to smoke 　B. smoke 　　　　C. smoking 　　　D. being smoked

4. The student left the classroom, with the lights _____.

　A. burn 　　　B. burning 　　　C. burned 　　　D. to burn

5. Don't use words, expressions, or phrases _____ only to people with specific knowledge.

　A. being known 　　　　　　　B. having been known

　C. to be known 　　　　　　　D. known

6. The number 2008 is a special number, _____ I think, that will be remembered by the Chinese forever.

　A. which 　　B. what 　　　　C. one 　　　　　D. it

7. He failed in the entrance examination and only then _____ the importance of study.

　A. he realised 　B. he had realised 　C. had he realised 　D. did he realise

15

8. —Who are the young people gathering at the school gate?

   —Well, if you _____ know, they are all my visiting students.

   A. must   B. can   C. may   D. shall

9. Hospital staff burst into cheer after doctors completed a 20-hour operation to have

   _____ one-year-old twins at the head.

   A. isolated   B. separated   C. divided   D. removed

10. Was it _____ she said or something that she did _____ you were angry at so much?

    A. what; that   B. what; what   C. that; which   D. that; what

11. Bruce was doing a lot of physical exercise to build up his _____.

    A. ability   B. force   C. strength   D. mind

12. She _____ for 15 years, yet she didn't know what kind of man she _____.

    A. had married; married   B. had got married; married to

    C. had been married; had married   D. married; had married to

13. _____ what to do next, they stopped and went to ask the manager for advice.

    A. Knowing not   B. Not to know

    C. Having not known   D. Not knowing

14. The doctor gave us instructions to prevent the medicine from _____.

    A. being abused   B. abusing

    C. being accused   D. accusing

15. —How much of his speech did you think you understood?

    —_____. I wish I had worked harder.

    A. Very few   B. Nearly everything

    C. Almost nothing   D. Not a little

II. 完形填空（共20小题；每小题1分，满分20分）

There are so many different plastic cards that adults have to carry around — library cards, saving cards for different __1__, credit cards, just to name __2__. So why not have one card to __3__ them all?

Scott Barnhill, an __4__ fifth-grade student in the US, has __5__ with an idea for a "Security One Card". The US Patent (专利) Office agreed to give a patent for his idea in April.

Here's an example of how Barnhill's idea would __6__.

Let's say you have the three cards mentioned __7__. Instead of carrying them all, you could have just one by having additional magnetic stripes (磁条) __8__ to it. The magnetic stripes can be added to any plastic card, __9__ a blank one. Companies could add their __10__ to one of the stripes. __11__, you could ask a library to add a stripe to your bank card.

Barnhill has a lot of __12__, including designing websites. He got the idea at the age of 9 when he saw his father using a key card __13__ their hotel room. He thought, "The hotels are __14__ money with the key cards." So, instead of using a hotel-issued key card, guests could use their credit cards — if the hotels added a(n) __15__ magnetic stripe. At checkout, the stripe would __16__ be removed.

__17__ he has got his patent, he is hoping to make money from his patent and has decided it would be __18__ to collect royalties (专利权的使用费) if the idea __19__ rather than sell his patent. "The ATM person who invented that sold it completely, and if he __20__ royalties he'd get like two cents for every transaction and he'd be a billionaire now," Scott said.

1. A. post offices   B. banks   C. hotels   D. hospitals
2. A. many   B. a lot   C. a few   D. few
3. A. replace   B. exchange   C. take   D. change
4. A. 11-year old   B. 11 years old   C. 11-years-old   D. 11-year-old
5. A. come out   B. come along   C. come up   D. come off
6. A. work   B. effect   C. affect   D. run
7. A. over   B. below   C. above   D. under
8. A. adding   B. adding up   C. added up   D. added
9. A. still   B. even   C. merely   D. though
10. A. money   B. information   C. names   D. instructions
11. A. What's more   B. Such as   C. Meanwhile   D. For instance
12. A. jobs   B. chances   C. hobbies   D. gifts
13. A. entering   B. to enter   C. entered   D. enter
14. A. saving   B. spending   C. wasting   D. making
15. A. special   B. particular   C. peculiar   D. exceptional
16. A. quickly   B. usually   C. simply   D. carefully
17. A. As a result   B. Now that   C. Since then   D. As well as
18. A. good   B. better   C. bad   D. worse
19. A. takes in   B. takes out   C. takes off   D. takes up
20. A. chose   B. choose   C. had chosen   D. has chosen

III. 阅读理解（共10小题；每小题2分，满分20分）

A

In 1947 a pilot of a small aeroplane saw nine strange objects in the sky over Washington in the USA. He said that they looked like saucers. Newspapers printed his story under the headline "Flying Saucers".

Since then, all over the world, people have reported seeing similar strange objects. No one knows what they are or where they come from. Some people say that they do not exist, but many others say that they have seen them. Usually people on the ground have seen them but not always. Airline pilots also have reported seeing them and so have astronauts — the men who fly in spaceships.

Perhaps some people saw them only in their imagination. Perhaps some people made a mistake. But airline pilots and astronauts do not usually make mistakes of this kind. Captain Ed Mitchell, who was the sixth man to walk on the moon, said in 1974 that he believed that some "flying saucers" were real. Many other people now believe that these strange flying objects are visiting the earth from other worlds in space.

"They have come to look at us," they say. The American government tried to find out more about these objects. It interviewed a great many people who said they had seen them. But the Government Committee could not decide on what the objects were. It called them UFOs, which is short for "Unidentified Flying Objects".

Some say they have seen people in the flying saucers! In 1964, a driver of a police car in New Mexico saw a UFO landing a mile away. When he reached it, there were two small figures standing near it. They looked like little men. When he reported on his radio, they got inside the object and flew away.

In 1973 two men were out fishing in Mississippi. They said they saw a UFO shaped like an egg. There were three creatures like men but their skins were silver in colour. They had no eyes, and their mouths were just slits (裂缝). Their noses and ears were pointed. They made the fishermen get inside the UFO for a while. Then the creatures photographed them and took them to the place where they had been fishing.

There are many other similar stories. Some are probably untrue but some may be true. No one knows.

1. According to the passage, the name "flying saucers" was first used by _____.
   A. a pilot of a small plane   B. an official in Washington
   C. an editor of a newspaper   D. the man who flies in saucers
2. The American government tried to _____.
   A. look for the flying objects   B. know where the objects come from
   C. learn more about UFOs   D. report more about UFOs
3. _____ took pictures of the two fishermen.
   A. The creatures in a UFO   B. A driver of a police car
   C. A pilot of a plane   D. Captain Ed Mitchell
4. The purpose of this passage is to tell _____.
   A. the shape of UFOs   B. how to observe UFOs
   C. the danger of UFOs   D. what we know about UFOs
5. It is implied in the passage that the author _____.
   A. does not believe at all about the existence of UFOs
   B. believes that UFOs are real objects flying in the sky
   C. is not sure whether there are UFOs or not
   D. thinks UFOs come from other planets

B

Students laughed nervously as they sat in the dark waiting room for the signal. As the clock got nearer to 7:55 pm, the world's attention turned closer to the Affiliated (附属的) High School of Shanxi University in Taiyuan.

Then at 7:55 pm on the night of April 19, 2005, the campus exploded into light. One after another students turned on their flashlights under red umbrellas and the school boiled over with excitement.

It was all part of a worldwide light relay that began last Monday night in the United States and circled the globe via phone calls and emails. The event was organised to celebrate the World Year of Physics and to honour Albert Einstein. The relay began in Princeton, New Jersey, where the great physicist lived and worked from 1933 until his death on April 18, 1955.

"It's great to be part of the relay. Einstein has inspired me to explore the colourful world — physics," said Xie Yuhao, a Senior 1 student in the school.

The light relay, called "Physics Enlightens the World", started its journey in China via an email from Princeton, arriving in Shanghai at 7 pm. The email contained a photo of the famous physicist and statements <u>emphasising</u> the importance of scientists. It also contained a physics test for students.

Then the light was sent to 29 other cities in China, one after another, with five minutes in each stop. It later moved on to India and Russia.

After the short and inspiring five minutes in the Shanxi school, it went to Xi'an, Shaanxi Province.

With great enthusiasm, Shaanxi students sent up their water-powered rockets and flew balloons like Kongming lanterns into the dark sky.

"Our group's rocket reached as high as four floors. It's great to create things using the knowledge we've learnt in physics classes," said rocket maker Li Yang.

"When the Kongming lantern filled with our love for physics went up, I was delighted. It is the Physics Year that gives us the chance to observe, feel and love physics again," said Hu Xiaoxin excitedly.

6. How was the light relay managed around the world?

    A. By using flashlights.

    B. By using red umbrellas.

    C. Via telephones and emails.

    D. Through a beam of light reflected from Princeton.

7. How many cities in China was the light sent to?

    A. Twenty-nine.   B. Thirty.   C. Thirty-one.   D. Thirty-two.

8. What does the underlined word "emphasising" in the fifth paragraph mean?

    A. Stressing.   B. Lessening.   C. Stating.   D. Weakening.

9. What is the aim of the light relay?

    A. To celebrate the World Year of Physics.

    B. To honour Albert Einstein.

    C. To inspire students to learn physics.

    D. Both A and B.

10. What is the main idea of the story?

    A. Einstein inspired students to create things using the knowledge they've learnt in physics classes.

    B. The light relay wandered across China to honour Einstein's great contributions.

    C. Shanxi high school students participated in a worldwide light relay.

    D. The light relay continued from one country to another.

Ⅳ．阅读表达（共5小题；每小题3分，满分15分）

Crime has its own cycles, a magazine reported some years ago. <u>Police records that were studied for five years from over 2,400 cities and towns show a surprising link between changes in the season and crime patterns.</u>

The pattern of crime has varied very little over a long period of years. Murder reaches its high during July and August, as do other violent attacks. Murder, moreover, is more than seasonal: it is a weekend crime. It is also a night crime: 62 percent of murders are committed between 6 pm and 6 am.

Unlike the summer high in crimes of bodily harm, robbery has a different cycle. _____ between 6 pm and 2 am on a Saturday night in December, January, or February. The month with least crimes of all is May except for one strange fact. More dog bites are reported in this month than in any other month of the year.

Clearly our seasonal cycles of knowledge are completely different from our tendencies for crimes. Professor Huntington made extensive studies to discover the seasons when people read serious books, attend scientific meetings and get highest results on examinations. In all cases, he found a spring high and autumn high separated by a summer low.

Possibly, high temperature and high humidity (湿度) cause our strange and violent summer actions, but police officials are not sure. "There is, of course, no proof of a connection between humidity and murder," they say. "Why murder's high time should come in the summertime we really don't know."

1. What is the best title for the passage? (Please answer within 10 words.)

_____

2. Fill in the blank in the third paragraph with proper words or phrases to complete the sentence. (Please answer within 10 words.)

_____

3. What did Professor Huntington discover after making wide studies? (Please answer

within 20 words.)

_____

4. Can you give some reasonable explanations about the murder's high time? (Please answer within 20 words.)

_____

5. Translate the underlined sentence in the first paragraph into Chinese.

_____

Ⅴ. 完成句子（共9小题；每空1分，满分30分）

1. 他梦想成为一名文学方面的专家。

   He _____ _____ _____ an expert on literature.

2. 很久没有收到他的来信，我们决定再给他写一封信。

   _____ _____ _____ _____ _____ for such a long time, we decided to write him again.

3. 思想可以通过音乐的方式来表达。

   Thoughts can be expressed _____ _____ _____ music.

4. 这位年轻老师不知道如何对待这个顽皮的孩子。

   The young teacher didn't know _____ _____ _____ such a naughty boy.

5. 我妻子和我在音乐方面的爱好相似。

   My wife and I _____ _____ _____ in music.

6. 在古典文学知识方面没有人能和她相匹敌。

   No one can _____ _____ _____ _____ classical literature.

7. 他因某种原因没能参加学生会组织的晚会。

   He failed to attend the party held by the Student Union _____ _____ _____.

8. 这本杂志计划吸引二十多岁和三十多岁的职业女性。

   The magazine is intended to _____ _____ the working women in their 20s and 30s.

9. 由于不知道他的电话号码，我不能给他打电话。

   _____ _____ his telephone number, I couldn't ring him up.

Module ③

Interpersonal Relationships
— Friendship

📖 要点纵览

高考词汇	close, trust, chat, note, amount, fair, raise, theft, swing, count, lively, quarrel, regret, sweets, alike, betray, considerate, forgive, loss, scold, hurt, bungalow, pine, worm, cage, swell, walnut, squirrel, ripen, harvest, slide, spray, carpenter, broom, cigar, slip, damp, scratch, heel, tear, underwear, salute, spy, perfect, acute, privilege, rewind, predict, click, flee, pace, couple, partner, mention, bottom
常用短语	get to know sb, chat about sth, get together, lose interest in, in the centre of, tell a joke, burst out laughing, knock…over, from time to time, go through, turn round, raise money, make up, pull out, from the bottom of one's heart, be ashamed of, bring…to mind, lose one's memory, lose touch / keep in touch / get in touch with, be blessed with, be on good / bad terms with
实用句型	1. …, and found Roy going through the pockets of people's coats. 2. But to our surprise, the next morning, we were told that the money had been stolen. 3. I was blessed with a happy childhood, one that most people would want to have. 4. It was here that I discovered that I was allergic to the tiny flies which bit me and… 5. He was a very considerate boy for someone so young.
交际用语	1. It's my guess. 2. We get on very well. 3. From the bottom of my heart, thank you.

◆ **高考词汇**

1. trust

n. 1) 信赖，信任；2) 信心，希望

v. 1) 相信，信任，信赖；2) 委托，托付

I have no trust in him.

They have trust in the future.

You might trust her to do the work.

I can't trust him with my car.

➡ 常用短语：

take sth on trust 凭空相信   trust (in) sb (= believe in sb) 相信某人

2. regret

n. 懊悔，悔恨；遗憾，惋惜

v. 懊悔，悔恨；惋惜

The company expressed great regret at the accident.

It was a stupid decision and I bitterly regret it.

regret 作动词时的主要用法有：

1) regret doing sth

2) regret to tell / say / inform

3) regret + that 从句

　　She deeply regretted losing her temper.

　　I regret to tell you that you failed again this term.

　　I regret that I will be unable to attend the meeting.

◆ **常用短语**

1. burst out doing

burst out doing 意思是"突然发生，突然……起来"。

He burst out crying like a child.

burst 的相关短语还有：

burst into a place 闯入某地

burst into laughter / tears 突然大笑/哭起来

burst with anger / joy 勃然大怒/乐不可支

2. knock...over

knock...over 意思是"(开车) 撞伤，撞死；打翻，打倒"。

Alex was knocked over by a bus yesterday.

Who knocked the bottle over?

He knocked the chair over.

拓 展

knock down 撞倒；拆除，拆卸；减价

knock off work 下班

knock sb flat / knock sb to the ground 撞倒某人

The new stove we bought was knocked down from $300 to $200.

Mary usually knocks off work about 5：30 pm.

He knocked the old lady to the ground and ran off with her purse.

真 题 解 析

Lost in thought, he was _____ by the car in front of him. (2005 苏州模拟)

A. knocked out   B. knocked down

C. knocked off   D. knocked about

解析：这句话的意思是：由于陷入了沉思，他被前面的车撞倒了。只有 B 项 knock down 有"撞倒"的意思。knock out 意为"使精疲力竭，淘汰"，knock off 意为"击倒，敲掉"，knock about 意为"漫游"，这些选项均与句意不符。答案为 B。

3. make up

make up 的主要含义有：

1) 编造，创造；2) 和解，言归于好；3) 弥补，把……补上

The teacher asked the students to make up a poem about Christmas.

Mary and John quarrelled, but made up after a while.

John must make up the work he missed.

真 题 解 析

Everybody in the village likes Jack because he is good at telling and _____ jokes. (2005 江苏)

A. turning up   B. putting up   C. making up   D. showing up

解析：make up 在此题中表示"编造"，而 turn up 意为"出现，露面"，put up 意为"搭起，建立"，show up 意为"使显眼，显现"。只有 C 项的意思与句意相符。答案为 C。

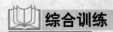

考试时间：45分钟　满分：100分

I. 单项选择（共15小题；每小题1分，满分15分）

1. One way to understand thousands of new words is to gain _____ good knowledge of basic word formation.

   A. /　　　　　　　B. the　　　　　　　C. a　　　　　　　D. one

2. The story is partly true and partly _____.

   A. turned up　　　B. put up　　　　　C. made up　　　　D. shown up

3. In some parts of London, missing a bus means _____ for another hour.

   A. waiting　　　　B. to wait　　　　　C. wait　　　　　　D. to be waiting

4. Tom, _____ yourself. Do you forget the school rules?

   A. behave　　　　B. believe　　　　　C. perform　　　　D. conduct

5. —How do you deal with the disagreement between the company and the customers?

   —The key _____ the problem is to meet the demand _____ by the customers.

   A. to solving; making
   B. to solving; made
   C. to solve; making
   D. to solve; made

6. Although Linda tried hard in the exam, she did _____ than her brother.

   A. more badly　　B. much better　　　C. much badly　　D. much worse

7. It took _____ people as well as _____ time to build the pyramids.

   A. a large number of; a great many
   B. a great many; a large amount of
   C. a great many of; large amounts of
   D. a large amount of; a great deal of

8. —Do you like the material?

   —Yes, it _____ very soft and smooth.

   A. is feeling　　　B. felt　　　　　　C. feels　　　　　D. is felt

9. He hasn't slept at all for three days. _____ he is tired out.

   A. There is no point
   B. There is no need
   C. It is no wonder
   D. It is no way

10. _____ such heavy pollution, it may now be too late to clean up the river.

    A. Having suffered　B. Suffering　　　C. To suffer　　　D. Suffered

11. All these gifts must be mailed immediately _____ in time for Christmas.

    A. in order to have received
    B. in order to receive
    C. so as to be received
    D. so as to be receiving

12. He has got himself into a dangerous situation _____ he is likely to lose control over the plane.

    A. where　　　　　B. which　　　　　C. while　　　　　D. why

13. —Why does she always ask you for help?

　　—There's no one else ＿＿＿＿＿＿, is there?

　　A. who to turn to　　B. she can turn to　　C. for whom to turn　　D. for her to turn

14. You didn't let me drive. If we ＿＿＿＿＿＿ in turn, you ＿＿＿＿＿＿ so tired.

　　A. drove; didn't get　　　　　　　　B. drove; wouldn't get

　　C. were driving; wouldn't get　　　　D. had driven; wouldn't have got

15. —Why did Mr Black hurt his forehead?

　　—He was so careless that he ＿＿＿＿＿＿ a tree while walking in the street.

　　A. knocked over　　B. knocked into　　C. knocked down　　D. knocked on

II. 完形填空（共20小题；每小题1分，满分20分）

　　Roger Crawford had everything he needed to play tennis except two hands and a leg. He had no palms. His arms and legs were shortened, and he had only three toes on his right foot and his left leg was cut off.

　　The doctor said Roger ＿＿1＿＿ from congenital malformation (先天性畸形), a rare birth defect affecting only one out of 90,000 children born in the United States. The doctor said Roger would probably never be able to walk or ＿＿2＿＿ himself. Fortunately Roger's parents didn't ＿＿3＿＿ the doctor.

　　"My parents always taught me that I was only as handicapped (残疾的) as I wanted to be," said Roger. "They never allowed me to feel sorry for myself or ＿＿4＿＿ advantage of people because of my handicap. Once I got into trouble, my school papers were continually late," explained Roger, who had to hold his pencil with both hands to write ＿＿5＿＿. "I asked Dad to write a note to my teacher, ＿＿6＿＿ for a two-day extension on my assignments. Dad never did that. ＿＿7＿＿, Dad made me start writing my paper two days early!"

　　Roger's father always ＿＿8＿＿ him to get involved in sports, teaching Roger to catch and throw a volleyball, and play football after school. At the age of 12, Roger ＿＿9＿＿ to win a spot on the school football team.

　　Before every game, Roger would ＿＿10＿＿ of scoring a touchdown (持球过底线得分). Then one day he got his ＿＿11＿＿. The ball landed in his arms and off, he ran as fast as he could on his artificial leg toward the goal line, his coach and teammates ＿＿12＿＿ wildly. But at the 10-yard line, a guy from the other team ＿＿13＿＿ up with Roger, grabbing his left ankle. Roger tried to pull his artificial leg ＿＿14＿＿, but instead ended up being pulled off.

　　Roger's love of sports ＿＿15＿＿ and so did his self-confidence. But not every obstacle (障碍) gave way to Roger's determination.

　　Roger went on to play college tennis, finishing his tennis career with 22 wins and 11 ＿＿16＿＿. He later became the first physically handicapped tennis player to be certified (授予证书) as a teaching professional by the United States Professional Tennis Association. Roger now tours the country, speaking to groups about what it takes to be a winner, ＿＿17＿＿ who you are.

"The only difference __18__ you and me is that you can see my handicap, but I can't see yours. We all have them. When people ask me how I've been able to overcome my physical handicap, I tell them that I haven't overcome __19__. I've simply learnt what I can't do — such as play the piano or eat with chopsticks — but more __20__, I've learnt what I can do. Then I do what I can with all my heart and soul."

1. A. suffered B. closed C. heard D. died
2. A. live up B. care for C. feed up D. stand up
3. A. refuse B. accept C. persuade D. believe
4. A. make B. bring C. take D. get
5. A. hard B. quickly C. slowly D. easily
6. A. asking B. answering C. playing D. looking
7. A. And B. Instead C. Then D. Therefore
8. A. praised B. forced C. encouraged D. criticised
9. A. managed B. meant C. promised D. prepared
10. A. think B. realise C. dream D. hope
11. A. memory B. time C. lesson D. chance
12. A. cheering B. enjoying C. watching D. laughing
13. A. picked B. help C. caught D. kept
14. A. free B. round C. through D. off
15. A. added B. grew C. rose D. raised
16. A. equals B. losing C. failure D. missing
17. A. whatever B. whenever C. no matter D. no wonder
18. A. between B. from C. with D. by
19. A. nothing B. everything C. anything D. something
20. A. regularly B. importantly C. possibly D. successfully

Ⅲ. 阅读理解（共10小题；每小题2分，满分20分）

A

Uganda is a country in East Africa and, as in many such countries, a high percentage of the population, about 80 percent, are village-dwellers living in huts, which are often no bigger than a garage. The walls of the huts are made of mud, which is held together by reeds and sticks, and the roofs of the older ones are thatched with grass, although an increasing number of newer village houses have roofs made from corrugated (波纹形的) iron.

Several generations of the same family live together in the huts, which are usually divided into two sections by a curtain. The inner section, the one furthest from the open door of the hut, is where everyone sleeps and food is prepared and served in the outer part. If the family owns chickens or goats, they are kept in a small room attached to the main house.

Food is usually prepared on open fires although some people prefer to cook inside. However, this is quite dangerous and also means that the walls of the hut are stained by smoke and the atmosphere is acrid. The family sit in a circle on mats while they eat.

Newer village houses are almost always made of corrugated iron and are bigger, with one or two separate bedrooms and the kitchen in a smaller building beside the main house. But, old or new, the houses are not powered by electricity, and all homes are lit by paraffin (石蜡) candles called "tadobba".

Nor is there any running water in the houses. Some villages have their own well, but in many cases, collecting water involves a long and arduous walk to a river or spring, carrying plastic containers or pots made of clay.

Children are the ones who have to fetch water, and they have to do this early in the morning before they go to school, or in the evening when they come home. They often have to climb high hills or walk through valleys with narrow paths through dense vegetation. It is no surprise that they grow up muscular and fit after such daily exercise, walking for several kilometres carrying such heavy weights.

1. Most Ugandans live _____.
   A. with their whole family in large mud houses in the countryside
   B. in towns in small houses made of mud and iron
   C. in villages in small houses made of wet earth, grass and wood
   D. with their parents and children as well as their chickens and goats
2. The underlined word "thatched" in the first paragraph means "_____".
   A. covered   B. built   C. erected   D. buried
3. Where is food usually prepared?
   A. In the kitchen.
   B. On the floor in the middle of the house.
   C. On fires in front of the hut.
   D. In a small room attached to the main house.
4. How are the old and new houses the same?
   A. Both of them have roofs made of corrugated iron.
   B. Neither of them have a garage or kitchen.
   C. Neither of them have electricity, lights or running water.
   D. Both of them have water inside but no electric light.
5. The majority of Ugandan children have to _____.
   A. go to a well or a river and often carry it for a long distance
   B. do a lot of work cooking and carrying water
   C. collect water on the way home from school
   D. get water out of their own well

B

Many people will remember the flight of the space shuttle *Challenger* in June 1983. The achievement of Sally Ride, America's first woman astronaut to fly into space, made this flight especially memorable. Students from two high schools in Camden, New Jersey, however, are likely to remember Norma rather than Sally whenever they think about the flight.

Norma didn't travel alone. She brought about 100 companions along with her. Norma was an ant, a queen ant who, with her <u>subjects,</u> made up the first ant colony (群体) to travel into space. The ants were part of a science experiment designed by the students to test the effects of weightlessness on insects.

The equipment designed by the students for their colony functioned perfectly throughout the long space trip. But the young scientists and their teachers were very sad to find that their insect astronauts had all died at some point before the container was returned to the school and opened. The problem did not occur in space, but on the ground after *Challenger* had landed. The container remained in the desert for nearly a week before the ant colony was removed. The hot, dry desert air dried out the colony's container and the ants died from lack of moisture (水分).

The project was proved a success because it did provide useful information. Students will continue their efforts to find out exactly what went wrong. They will try to prevent the same difficulties from recurring (重现) on future missions. They don't want to be discouraged either by the death of the ants or by the $10,000 shuttle fare they will have to pay to send the next colony of ants into space.

6. The story is mainly about _____.
    A. Sally Ride's first ride   B. space equipment for insects
    C. a space experiment with ants   D. going to school in New Jersey
7. The project wasn't a failure because _____.
    A. some important things were learnt
    B. dead ants are more useful
    C. everything went as expected
    D. students wrote about it
8. The ants died because _____.
    A. weightlessness harmed them   B. space travel caused too much pain
    C. no one fed them in space   D. they were left too long in the desert
9. On the next space trip, ants _____.
    A. will be sent without people
    B. should not be left in the desert too long
    C. will have to pay double fare
    D. will escape the trip completely

10. What does the underlined word "subjects" in the second paragraph refer to?

    A. Things talked about.   B. Lessons you study at school.

    C. Words stated in a sentence.   D. Fellow ants.

IV. 阅读表达（共5小题；每小题3分，满分15分）

    As you ride the bus one day, a foreigner sits down beside you. Finally, here's a perfect opportunity to speak English to a native speaker! But no words come into your head. You're tongue-tied! After 15 minutes, you get off the bus without saying a word. How embarrassing!

    If this experience has happened to you, don't feel bad. You're not alone.

    What you need is a lesson in small talk. Just keep reading and Studio Classroom will show you how to get started talking.

    First, exchange a "hello" with that foreigner on the bus. Observe him to decide whether it is suitable to continue with the talk. Watch his facial expressions and body language for cues (暗示). Does he stare out of the window or keep reading that book in his hand? That's your cue to end the chat. Don't force a conversation on someone who wants to be left alone. But what if he makes eye contact with you or smiles at you? These cues indicate he's probably comfortable chatting with you. Keep talking!

    To strike up a conversation, start with a safe and simple question. Your question should introduce a topic that's easy to discuss. What are the rules for choosing a suitable topic? Don't immediately launch into serious issues like politics or religion. And don't talk about personal matters either. Stick to familiar subjects of a casual nature. Perhaps the most universal topic of conversation is the weather. Everyone has an opinion to share about the weather! Other suitable topics include movies, music, sports, favourite things or likes and dislikes.

    Small talk flows naturally. <u>Ask open-ended questions rather than yes-or-no questions to keep the conversation going.</u> Try to find points of connection between you and the person you are chatting with.

    Try to make short comments on what the other person says, and listen as he does the same. If he says, "That's interesting," or "I agree," or "Me too," then you know you're on the right track.

    You can gain much enjoyment from _____. They will too. Try it! Making small talk can be one of life's simple pleasures.

1. What is the best title for the passage? (Please answer within 10 words.)

    _____

2. Which sentence in the passage can be replaced by the following one?

    Pay close attention to see if he is receptive to chatting with you.

    _____

3. Fill in the blank in the last paragraph with proper words or phrases to complete the sentence. (Please answer within 10 words.)

_____

4. Which of the suggestions do you think is the best for you? Why? (Please answer within 30 words.)

_____

_____

5. Translate the underlined sentence in the sixth paragraph into Chinese.

_____

Ⅴ. 句型转换（共5小题；每空1分，满分15分）

1. His carelessness resulted in the accident.

   The accident _____ _____ his carelessness.

2. It seems that he has seen the film.

   He seems _____ _____ _____ the film.

3. He burst into tears at the bad news.

   He _____ _____ _____ at the bad news.

4. Eleven players make up a football team.

   A football team _____ _____ _____ _____ eleven players.

5. I regretted telling you the secret.

   I regretted to _____ _____ _____ the secret.

Ⅵ. 翻译句子（共5小题；每题3分，满分15分）

1. 当他和他的搭档讲完这个故事，大家哄堂大笑起来。(burst out laughing)

_____

2. 我很遗憾地告诉你，你的宠物狗被车撞了。(knock over)

_____

3. 这对夫妇一句话没说，转身就走开了。(turn round)

_____

4. 他们发自内心地对我们所做的工作表示满意。(from the bottom of one's heart)

_____

5. 正如他在日记中提到的，他毕业后就与女朋友失去了联系。(lose touch with)

_____

第一部分　听力（共两节，满分30分）

第一节 （共5小题；每小题1.5分，满分7.5分）

听下面五段对话。每段对话后有一个小题，从题中所给的三个选项中选出最佳选项。听完每段对话后，你都有10秒钟的时间来回答有关小题和阅读下一小题。每段对话仅读一遍。

1. How long have the speakers been waiting?
   A. Thirty minutes.　　　　B. One hour.　　　　C. One and a half hours.

2. Where does the woman work?
   A. At a restaurant.　　　　B. At a hotel.　　　　C. At a department store.

3. What was the woman probably trying to do?
   A. Play a tape recorder.　　B. Repair a radio.　　C. Start a car.

4. What do we learn from the conversation?
   A. The woman accepted the man's apology.
   B. The man had forgotten the whole thing.
   C. The woman had hurt the man's feelings.

5. What does the man mean?
   A. He didn't get the book he wanted.
   B. He didn't go to the library.
   C. The library is closed on weekends.

第二节 （共15小题；每小题1.5分，满分22.5分）

听下面五段对话或独白。每段对话或独白后有几个小题，从题中所给的三个选项中选出最佳选项。听每段对话或独白前，你将有时间阅读各个小题，每小题5秒钟；听完后，各小题将给出5秒钟的作答时间。每段对话或独白读两遍。

听第6段材料，回答第6至第7小题。

6. Why does the man thank the woman?
   A. She has helped him with his problem.
   B. She has invited him for coffee.
   C. She has agreed to see him on Monday.

7. When does the conversation take place?
   A. Before class.　　　　B. After class.　　　　C. During class.

听第7段材料，回答第8至第10小题。

8. What is the woman going to do?
   A. Have a long drive.　　B. Take a holiday.　　C. Go on a business trip.

9. When does the woman plan to arrive?

    A. Late Friday.   B. Midday Saturday.   C. Saturday night.

10. What is the weather like in the town during the day?

    A. Cold.   B. Wet.   C. Warm.

听第8段材料，回答第11至第13小题。

11. Why does the man make the phone call?

    A. To book some seats for the show.

    B. To get some information about the show.

    C. To know on what day the show will be given.

12. How much does the ticket cost if the man wants to buy one?

    A. Thirty dollars.   B. Thirteen dollars.   C. Thirty-three dollars.

13. When will the show probably end?

    A. At 10:00 pm.   B. At 8:00 pm.   C. At about midnight.

听第9段材料，回答第14至第16小题。

14. What do both of the two speakers want to do in the coming new year?

    A. To save some money.   B. To work harder.   C. To lose weight.

15. What did Henry do last year?

    A. He joined a health club.   B. He stopped smoking.   C. He got a good job.

16. Who wants to have a nice vacation?

    A. Jeff.   B. Alice.   C. Henry.

听第10段材料，回答第17至第20小题。

17. How many laws are discussed in the speech?

    A. Three.   B. Four.   C. Five.

18. Who does the speaker give advice to?

    A. Travellers to the country.

    B. Women who take along children.

    C. Children under 16 years old.

19. What can't you do if you are a boy of 17 here?

    A. Drink alcohol.   B. Smoke.   C. Drive.

20. Which of the following is true according to the passage?

    A. If you need help, please turn to your teachers.

    B. The traffic moves on the left side of the road in this country.

    C. It is against the law for anyone to buy cigarettes or tobacco.

第一节　语法和词汇（共15小题；每小题1分，满分15分）

从A、B、C、D四个选项中，选出可以填入空白处的最佳选项。

21. Animals that live on ＿＿＿＿＿ plain have to survive in ＿＿＿＿＿ hard climate.

    A. /; a   B. the; /   C. a; /   D. the; a

22. I'm afraid that idea won't work ＿＿＿＿＿ when carried out.

    A. in theory   B. in public   C. in practice   D. in secret

23. —What do you think of the TV programme last night?

    —I haven't seen ＿＿＿＿＿ interesting one these years.

    A. the most   B. a most   C. the more   D. a more

24. I have the same opinion as yours ＿＿＿＿＿ the privacy of one's life should be kept secret.

    A. that   B. which   C. whether   D. where

25. When it comes to attending a job interview, your first ＿＿＿＿＿ on the interviewers is often very important.

    A. direction   B. condition   C. impression   D. speech

26. —Did you remember to give Mary the money you owed her?

    —Yes, I gave it to her ＿＿＿＿＿ I saw her.

    A. while   B. the moment   C. until   D. since

27. With many eyes ＿＿＿＿＿ on her, she felt a bit nervous.

    A. depended   B. staring   C. keeping   D. fixed

28. We need one more guitar player to ＿＿＿＿＿ a band to take part in the coming rock music performance.

    A. take up   B. make up   C. work out   D. carry out

29. —Why are you so late, Jimmy? We ＿＿＿＿＿ you for about an hour.

    —Sorry, I'm trapped in a traffic jam.

    A. were expecting   B. expected

    C. have expected   D. have been expecting

30. The Chinese are looking forward to the first ＿＿＿＿＿ to land on the moon after *Shenzhou VI*'s successful launch into space.

    A. measure   B. attempt   C. purpose   D. desire

31. I wonder if you can ＿＿＿＿＿ the report to see if there is anything wrong with it.

    A. look into   B. get through   C. go over   D. work on

32. He had some ＿＿＿＿＿ making himself understood in English although he took the trouble ＿＿＿＿＿ it.

    A. difficulty; to learn   B. difficulties; to learn

    C. trouble; learning   D. troubles; to learn

33. —Are you coming to our get-together party?

—I'm not sure. I _____ go to the concert instead.

    A. must   B. will   C. should   D. might

34. _____ most Englishmen, he enjoys football.

    A. In common with   B. Compared with

    C. Except for   D. Speaking of

35. —Would you mind if I turn down the radio a bit?

    —_____

    A. Yes, do as you please.   B. Not at all, just go ahead.

    C. Never mind. You'll get used to it.   D. Sure, why not?

第二节　完形填空（共20小题；每小题1分，满分20分）

阅读下面的短文，掌握其大意，然后从每题所给的四个选项中选出最佳选项。

One afternoon I toured an art museum while waiting for my husband to finish a business meeting. I was looking forward to a __36__ view of the masterpieces.

A young couple viewing the paintings ahead of me chattered nonstop between __37__. I watched them a moment and __38__ she was doing all the talking. I admired his patience for __39__ with her constant parade (炫耀) of words. Distracted by their noise, I moved on.

I met with them several times __40__ I moved through the various rooms of art. Each time I heard her constant gush of words (滔滔不绝的讲话), I __41__ away quickly.

I was standing at the counter of the museum gift shop making a purchase when the couple __42__ the exit. Before they left, the man __43__ into his pocket and pulled out a white object. He __44__ it into a long cane and then tapped his __45__ into the coatroom to get his wife's jacket.

"He's a __46__ man," the clerk at the counter said. "Most of us would give up if we were blinded at such a young age. During his recovery, he made a promise that his life wouldn't __47__. So, as before, he and his wife come in whenever there's a __48__ art show."

"But __49__ does he get out of the art?" I asked. "He can't see."

"Can't see? You're __50__. He sees a lot. More than you or I do," the clerk said. "His wife __51__ each painting so he can see it in his head."

I learnt something about patience, __52__ and love that day. I saw the patience of a young wife describing paintings to a person without __53__ and the courage of a husband who would not __54__ blindness to change his life. And I saw the love __55__ by two people as I watched this couple walk away with their arms intertwined (缠绕).

36. A. silent   B. noisy   C. unique   D. quiet

37. A. ourselves   B. them   C. themselves   D. us

38. A. declared   B. informed   C. guessed   D. decided

39. A. putting up   B. keeping up   C. making up   D. picking

40. A. before	B. as	C. after	D. if
41. A. smoothed	B. rushed	C. moved	D. drove
42. A. approached	B. left	C. appeared	D. led
43. A. put	B. reached	C. arrived	D. pulled
44. A. developed	B. made	C. extended	D. spread
45. A. direction	B. head	C. way	D. instructions
46. A. wise	B. lazy	C. lucky	D. brave
47. A. stop	B. change	C. shorten	D. lose
48. A. new	B. special	C. love	D. masterpiece
49. A. how	B. when	C. what	D. who
50. A. cruel	B. wrong	C. right	D. clever
51. A. draws	B. changes	C. describes	D. decorates
52. A. kindness	B. care	C. friendship	D. courage
53. A. heart	B. sight	C. hope	D. hearing
54. A. allow	B. forbid	C. help	D. prevent
55. A. robbed	B. controlled	C. shared	D. suffered

第三部分　阅读理解（共20小题；每小题2分，满分40分）

阅读下列短文，从每题所给的四个选项中选出最佳选项。

A

Happy birthday! Do birthdays really make people happy? Of course they do. Birthdays celebrate the day when we were born. Besides, that extra candle on the cake suggests another year of growth and maturity — or so we hope. We all like to imagine that we are getting wiser and not just older. Most of us enjoy seeing the wonder of growth in others as well. For instance, seeing our children develop and learn new things makes us feel proud. For Americans, like people in most cultures, growing up is a wonderful process. But growing old? That is a different story.

Growing old is not exactly for people in youth-oriented (倾向于年轻人的) American culture. Most Americans like to look young, act young and feel young. As the old saying goes, "You're young as you feel." Older people joke about how many years young they are, rather than how many years old. People in some countries value the aged as a source of experience and wisdom. But Americans seem to favour those that are young, or at least "young at heart".

Many older Americans find the "golden years" to be anything but golden. Economically, "senior citizens" often struggle just to get by. Retirement at the age of 65 brings a sharp decrease in personal income. Social security benefits usually cannot make up the difference. Older people may suffer from poor nutrition, medical care, and housing. Some even experience age discrimination. American sociologist Pat Moore once dressed up like an older person and wandered city streets. She was often treated rudely — even cheated and robbed.

However, dressed as a young person, she received much more respect.

Unfortunately, the elderly population in America is increasing fast. Why? People are living longer. Fewer babies are being born. And middle-aged "baby boomers" are rapidly entering the group of the elderly. America may soon be a place where wrinkles are "<u>in</u>".

56. Growing up is a wonderful thing because people _____.

    A. can celebrate their birthdays

    B. can become wiser and more mature

    C. can receive many presents

    D. will feel younger at heart

57. We can infer from the second paragraph that _____.

    A. young people lack experience and wisdom

    B. American older people often joke about their old age

    C. American culture is very young

    D. different countries have different opinions on the old age

58. What does the underlined sentence in the third paragraph mean?

    A. The golden years can make the old earn a lot of money and receive good medical care.

    B. The old in America are leading a hard life without good nutrition, medical care, and housing.

    C. The old in America have to retire at the age of 65.

    D. American social security benefits are not good.

59. What does the underlined word "in" in the last paragraph mean?

    A. Serious.   B. Cool.

    C. Disappearing slowly.   D. Fashionable.

60. According to this passage, which of the following statements is correct?

    A. The young are much more respected than the old in America.

    B. The old are much more respected than the young in America.

    C. Growing old makes people feel proud in America.

    D. The young are often discriminated in America.

B

There are two types of people in the world. Although they have equal degree of health and wealth and other comforts of life, one becomes happy and the other becomes unhappy. This arises from the different ways in which they consider things, persons, events and the resulting effects upon their minds.

People who are to be happy fix their attention on the convenience of things — the pleasant parts of conversation, the well-prepared dishes, the goodness of the wine and the fine weather. They enjoy all the cheerful things. Those who are to be unhappy think and speak only of the opposite things. Therefore, they are continually dissatisfied. By their remarks, they <u>sour the pleasure of society</u>, offend (冒犯) many people, and make themselves disagreeable everywhere. If this turn of mind was founded in nature, such unhappy persons would be the more to be pitied. The intention of criticising (批评) and being disliked is perhaps taken up by imitation (模仿). It grows into a habit, unknown to its possessors. The habit may be strong, but it may be cured when those who have it realise its bad effects on their interests and tastes. I hope this little warning may be of service to them, and help them change this habit.

Although in fact it is chiefly an act of the imagination, it has serious results in life since it brings on deep sorrow and bad luck. Those people offend many others; nobody loves them, and no one treats them with more than the most common politeness and respect. This frequently puts them in bad temper and draws them into arguments. If they aim at getting some advantages in social position or fortune, nobody wishes them success. Nor will anyone start a step or speak a word to favour their hopes. If they bring on themselves public objections, no one will defend or excuse them, and many will join to criticise their wrongdoings. These people should change this bad habit and be pleased with what is pleasing, without worrying needlessly about themselves and others. If they do not, it will be good for others to avoid any contact (接触) with them. Otherwise, it can be disagreeable and sometimes very inconvenient, especially when one becomes mixed up in their quarrels.

61. People who are unhappy _____.
    A. always consider things differently from others
    B. usually are affected by the results of certain things
    C. usually misunderstand what others think or say
    D. always discover the unpleasant side of certain things
62. The underlined phrase "sour the pleasure of society" in the second paragraph most probably means "_____".
    A. have a good taste with social life   B. make others unhappy
    C. tend to scold others openly   D. enjoy the pleasure of life
63. We can conclude from the passage that _____.
    A. we should pity all such unhappy people
    B. such unhappy people are dangerous to social life
    C. people can get rid of the habit of unhappiness
    D. unhappy people cannot understand happy persons
64. If such unhappy people insist on keeping the habit, the author suggests that others should
    _____.
    A. avoid any communication with them
    B. show no respect and politeness to them
    C. persuade them to recognise the bad effects
    D. quarrel with them until they realise the mistakes

65. In this passage, the writer mainly _____.

    A. describes two types of people

    B. laughs at the unhappy people

    C. suggests the unhappy people should get rid of the habits of unhappiness

    D. tells people how to be happy in life

C

Register in person	Register by phone	Register by mail
Use form given	Call 264-8833	1782N Chicago

*Basic Photography

    This is an eight-hour course for beginners who want to learn how to use a 35mm camera. The teacher will cover such areas as kinds of film, light, and lenses. Bring your own 35mm camera to class.

    Course charge: $50.00

    Jan. 10, 12, 17, 19   Tues. & Thurs. 6:00 pm–8:00 pm

    Marianne Adams is a <u>professional</u> photographer whose photographs appear in many magazines.

*Understanding Computers

    This 12-hour course is for people who do not know very much about computers, but who need to learn about them. You will learn what computers are, what they can and can't do, and how to use them.

    Course charge: $75.00

    Equipment charge: $10.00

    Jan. 14, 21, 28   Sat. 8:00 am–12:00 am

    Joseph Saimders is a professor of computer science at New Urban University. He has over 12 years of experience in the computer field.

*Stop Smoking

    Do you want to stop smoking? Have you already tried to stop and failed? Now it is the time to stop smoking using the latest methods. You can stop smoking, and this 12-hour course will help you do it.

    Course charge: $30.00

    Jan. 4, 11, 18, 25   Wed. 4:00 pm–7:00 pm

    Dr John Dodds is a practising psychologist who has helped hundreds of people stop smoking.

*Typing

    This course on weekdays is for typing. You are tested in the first class and practise at one of eight different skill levels. This allows you to learn at your own speed. Each programme lasts 20 hours. Bring your own paper.

    Course charge: $125.00

    Material charge: $25.00

    Two hours each evening for two weeks.

    New classes begin every two weeks.

    This course is taught by a number of business education teachers who have successfully taught typing courses before.

66. The underlined word "professional" in this passage most probably means "_____".

    A. spiritual   B. journalist   C. professor   D. experienced

67. The shortest course is _____.

    A. Basic Photography   B. Understanding Computers

    C. Stop Smoking   D. Typing

68. There are typing courses _____.

    A. on Saturdays and Sundays   B. from Monday to Friday

    C. from Monday to Saturday   D. on each day in the week

69. If you have only $100 and want to take two courses, you should choose _____.

    A. Basic Photography and Stop Smoking

    B. Basic Photography and Typing

    C. Stop Smoking and Understanding Computers

    D. Typing and Stop Smoking

70. What kind of article is the passage?

    A. A novel.   B. A news report.

    C. An advertisement.   D. A detective story.

D

    A white kid sells a bag of cocaine at his high school away from the city. A Latino (美国的拉丁族裔) kid does the same in his inner-city neighborhood. Both get caught. Both are first-time offenders. The white kid walks into juvenile (少年的) court with his parents, his priest, a good lawyer and medical insurance. The Latino kid walks into court with his mom, no legal resources and no insurance. The judge lets the white kid go with his family; he's placed in a private treatment program. The colored kid has no such choice. He's locked up.

    This, in short, is what happens more and more often in the juvenile-court system. Youths of color arrested on serious crimes in California are more than twice as likely as their white fellows to be moved out of the juvenile-justice system and tried as adults, according to a study made last week by the Justice Policy Institute, a research center in San Francisco. Once they are in adult courts, young black offenders are 18 times more likely to be jailed — and Hispanics seven times more likely — than young white offenders. "Discrimination against kids of color increases at every stage of the justice system and skyrockets when juveniles are tried as adults," says Dan Macallair, a co-author of the new study. "California has a double standard: throw kids of colour behind <u>bars</u>, but rehabilitate (改造) white kids who commit comparable crimes."

Even as juvenile crime has declined from its highest point in the early 1990s, more and more serious violence by minors (未成年人) has strengthened a get-tough attitude. Over the past six years, 43 states have passed laws that make it easier to try juveniles as adults. In Texas and Connecticut in 1996, the latest year for which figures are available, all the juveniles in jails were kids of color. Vincent Schiraldi, the Justice Policy Institute's director, admits that "some kids need to be tried as adults. But most can be rehabilitated".

Instead, juveniles tend to be cruelly treated in adult prisons. They are eight times more likely to commit suicide (自杀) and five times more likely to be sexually abused than offenders held in juvenile prisons. "Once they get out, they tend to commit more crimes and more violent crimes," says Jenni Gainsborough, a spokeswoman for the Sentencing Project, a reform group in Washington. The system, fundamentally, is training career criminals. And it's doing its worst work among people of color.

71. From the first paragraph we learn that _____.
    A. the white kid is luckier than the kid of color
    B. the white kid has got a lot of help than the kid of color
    C. the white kid and the colored kid have been treated differently
    D. the colored kid should be set free at once

72. The underlined word "bars" in the second paragraph may refer to places for _____.
    A. keeping prisoners   B. drinking beer
    C. listening to music   D. cocaine sellers

73. It can be inferred from the last paragraph that _____.
    A. something seems to be wrong with the justice system
    B. adult prisons have bad influence on the juveniles
    C. juveniles in adult prison are ill-treated
    D. the career criminals are trained by the system

74. According to the passage, which of the following is TRUE?
    A. Kids should be tried as adults.
    B. Discrimination exists in the justice system.
    C. Kids of color are likely to commit crimes.
    D. Some states shouldn't pass the laws.

75. The passage shows that the author is _____ the present situation.
    A. amazed at   B. puzzled by
    C. disappointed with   D. critical of

第一节 阅读表达（共5小题；每小题3分，满分15分）

阅读下面的短文，并根据短文后的要求答题。

The Olympic Games are seen as the greatest test of an athlete's ability and are supposed to celebrate the spirit of fair play. But in fact, some sportsmen have been using drugs to cheat their way to victory since the Games first began.

In the early years, athletes ate mushrooms and plant seeds to improve their performance. Nowadays, this kind of cheating has a name — doping (服用兴奋剂).

In 2003, the UK's top sprinter (短跑运动员) Dwain Chambers and several American athletes tested positive for the drug THG. Until a coach secretly gave a sample of THG to scientists, no one knew how to test for it.

"We're like policemen chasing criminals — athletes are always adapting and looking for areas we haven't investigated," said Jacques de Ceaurriz, a French anti-doping expert.

Since the first drug test was carried out at the 1968 Olympics in Mexico City, many cheats have been caught out. The most famous case in history is that of Canadian sprinter Ben Johnson.

He broke the 100 metres world record in winning gold at the 1988 Seoul Olympics. But days later, he was tested positive for drug use, lost his gold medal and was banned from the sport. Five years later, he returned to action, only to be found positive again and banned forever.

Experts are worried that doping can _____. It is believed to increase the risk of liver and kidney (肾) diseases, and women may experience reproductive problems.

As long as they can stay ahead of the scientists, it is unlikely that the cheats will stop. But experts say there is a limit to what can be achieved and that athletes will not be able to change their bodies using gene technology.

"For the moment, genetic doping does not exist," said de Ceaurriz. "Even in 10 or 15 years it will not be done easily — the scientific community will not let it happen."

76. What is the best title for the passage? (Please answer within 10 words.)

_____

77. How many countries are mentioned in which there were athletes doping?

_____

78. Fill in the blank in the seventh paragraph with proper words or phrases to complete the sentence. (Please answer within 10 words.)

_____

79. What do you think of doping in the Olympic Games? (Please answer within 30 words.)

_____

_____

80. Translate the underlined sentence in the first paragraph into Chinese.

_____

第二节　写作（满分30分）

你校学生会主办的英语月报正在举办"为建设节约型社会献一计"的活动。你想提的建议是：鼓励毕业的学生把参考书及课本留给下一届学生使用。请向学生会提出你的建议并简单叙述你的理由。

词数要求：120～150词。

_____

_____

_____

_____

_____

Module ④

Music

高考词汇	relative, characteristic, combine, ambition, rhyme, passerby, pedestrian, interval, plug, socket, organ, session, saucer, voluntary, shrink, vacant, lid, handle, tap, mop, popcorn, relay, relief, relax, collection, scene, honour, present, therefore
常用短语	give life to, graduate from, have an influence on, be the same with, be closely connected to, dance to the music, present sth to sb, share feelings and ideas with, give concerts, compose notes / music, depend on, a variety of, respect the traditions, be true of / for, draw upon, push one's way through, all of a sudden
实用句型	1. The same is true of my second instrument, the *guzheng*. 2. Secondly, classical Chinese music is closely connected to Chinese poetry… 3. It's the same with classical Chinese music. 4. In addition to the awards themselves, there are also performances by… 5. On the other hand, the Beatles have won more Grammys than Elvis and the Rolling Stones combined.
交际用语	1. What is your favourite kind of music? 2. I think it's wonderful. 3. It makes me feel very happy. 4. Oh, come on!

◆ 高考词汇

1. respect

n. 1) 尊重，尊敬；2) 考虑，顾及，重视；3) 方面；4) 问候，敬意

v. 尊敬，尊重，敬重

With his successful handling of the incident, he had won the respect of everyone.

Out of respect for the wishes of her family, the affair was not reported in the newspapers.

In many respects the new version is not so good as the old one.

Please give my respects to your parents.

He is not the most popular teacher, but the students respect him.

Molly always told us exactly what she thought, and we respected her for that.

➡ 常用短语：

give one's respects to 向……致敬/问候　　have / show respect for 尊敬，尊重，重视

in respect of 关于，有关　　in no respect 无论在哪个方面都不，完全不

in one / every / all respect(s) 在一个方面/　　with respect to 关于，就……而言
每个方面/所有方面

2. scene

n. 1) 地点，现场；2) 事件，场面；3) (电影、戏剧等的) 一场/幕，片断，镜头；
4) 景象，风景，风光；5) 活动领域

Firefighters were on the scene immediately.

Some of the more violent scenes are very disturbing.

He will appear on Act 1, Scene 2.

They were deeply attracted by the peaceful country scene.

What's new on the film scene?

➡ 常用短语：

behind the scenes 秘密地，在幕后　　be / come on the scene 出现，到来；参与；卷进

on the scene 在场，到场

3. influence

n. 影响力，作用；有影响的人或事物

v. 影响，对……起作用

Literature and art have a great influence upon people's ideology.

What influenced you to behave like that?

➡ 常用短语：

have a good / bad influence on sb / sth 对……有好的/坏的影响

have no real influence over sb / sth 没有左右某人/某事物的力量

under the influence of 在……的影响下

use one's influence with sb 利用对某人的影响

辨 析

influence, affect

influence 意为"影响"，指一个人以其品格或地位获得影响他人的力量，或行为和思想受到某种间接因素影响而发生的变化。这种力量是无形的。

affect 意为"影响"，主要强调能引起感情上强烈反应的力量，而且这种力量是有形的。有时也可暗示不良影响。

It is clear that her painting has been influenced by Picasso.

The sight affected her to tears.

真 题 解 析

Under the _____ of his parents, he made it 20 years later.（2007 重庆一模）

A. reflect   B. cause   C. reason   D. influence

解析：本题考查的是 under the influence of（在……的影响下）这个固定短语的用法。
　　　答案为 D。

4. stand

v. 1) 起立，站立；2) 经受，忍受

He stood at the school gate, waiting for his friend.

She can't stand being kept waiting for such a long time.

注意：stand 作及物动词表示"经受，忍受"时，不用于进行时态，常用于否定句和疑问句，与 can 或 could 连用，其后常接名词或动名词作宾语。

　　　I'm so mad that I can hardly stand the sight of him.

真 题 解 析

I can't stand _____ with Jane in the same office. She just refuses _____ talking while she works.（2006 北京）

A. working; stopping   B. to work; stopping

C. working; to stop   D. to work; to stop

解析：本题考查非谓语动词的用法。stand doing sth 与 refuse to do sth 都是固定搭配。
　　　答案为 C。

◆ 常用短语

1. pick up

pick up 的主要含义有：

1) 拾起，捡起；2) 学会 (尤指无意中学会)；3) (用车) 接

He picked up the book from the floor.

She soon picked up French after she went to live in France.

I have to pick up my daughter every afternoon.

真题解析

1) She _____ Japanese when she was in Japan. Now she can speak it freely. (2006 福建)

   A. picked out   B. made out   C. made up   D. picked up

2) Kathy _____ a lot of Spanish by playing with the native boys and girls. (2005 安徽)

   A. picked up   B. took up   C. made up   D. turned up

解析：这两道高考题考查的内容都是动词短语 pick up 表示"偶然或无意中学会"的含义。两题答案分别为 D 和 A。

2. draw upon / on

draw upon / on 意思是"（为某种目的）利用，动用（钱、经验等）；（时间）临近"。

I'll have to draw upon / on my savings.

The writer drew heavily upon his personal experience.

Winter is drawing on.

> **拓展**
>
> draw a conclusion 得出结论
>
> draw near / close (时间、空间的) 临近，接近
>
> draw sb's attention (to sth) 有意使某人注意 (某事物)
>
> draw the curtains 拉开 (拉上) 窗帘
>
> draw up 起草，草拟，(车辆) 停下

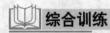

综合训练

考试时间：45分钟　满分：100分

I. 单项选择（共15小题；每小题1分，满分15分）

  1. —I have finished all the three questions, but the teacher still thinks poorly of my homework.

     —I think you _____. We have six questions in the homework.

     A. should be punished   B. had a bad hearing

     C. should come on   D. were missing the point

  2. Now that she is out of a job, Lucy _____ going back to school these days, but she hasn't decided yet.

     A. had considered   B. has been considering

     C. considered   D. is going to consider

3. Don't mention that at the beginning of the story, or it may _____ the shocking ending.

   A. give away   B. give out   C. give up   D. give off

4. He _____ in the company since his graduation from college.

   A. is working   B. works   C. had worked   D. has been working

5. He will have learnt English for eight years by the time he _____ from the university next year.

   A. will graduate   B. will have graduated

   C. graduates   D. is to graduate

6. In order to gain a big share in the international market, many state-owned companies are striving _____ their products more competitive.

   A. to make   B. making   C. to have made   D. having made

7. —Why didn't you tell him about the meeting?

   —He rushed out of the room _____ I could say a word.

   A. before   B. until   C. when   D. after

8. Is this the way you thought of _____ the problem?

   A. solving   B. to solve   C. being solved   D. solve

9. They are now in great need of help. So your support will certainly make a _____.

   A. deal   B. decision   C. point   D. difference

10. The owner of the cinema needed to make a lot of improvements and employ more people to keep it running, _____ meant spending tens of thousands of pounds.

    A. who   B. that   C. as   D. which

11. —What do you prefer to _____, the rock music or the soft music?

    —I'd like rock at first and when we are a bit tired, soft music will be better.

    A. sing to   B. dance to   C. sing with   D. dance with

12. The two small shops have _____ to make a large one.

    A. mixed   B. connected   C. combined   D. linked

13. She is regarded as the best actress here because she sings and dances well, _____ being good at playing the piano.

    A. except for   B. even though   C. as well   D. in addition to

14. He couldn't communicate with the Japanese freely though he _____ quite a lot of Japanese words while living in Japan.

    A. picked out   B. picked up   C. picked at   D. picked on

15. —Betty, could you take a picture of me just at the gate of our school?

    —Of course. But _____?

    —When I return to my country, I want to show it to my friends.

    A. what it   B. what for   C. what about   D. your reason

II. 完形填空（共20小题；每小题1分，满分20分）

Seldom is an invention so great that in 15 seconds most people who experience it realise it could change their everyday life. __1__ the new HyperSonic Sound (HSS) is just that kind of invention.

HSS is a(n) __2__ speaker. __3__ it at a friend standing 100 metres away in a __4__ street, then play a recording of ice __5__ into a glass and your friend will hear the sound as if it was right next to his ear! If he takes two steps to the side, __6__ the sound beam (声波), he hears nothing at all. Step back in, and there it is again.

Sound from an HSS speaker can __7__ nearly 140 metres without being __8__ or losing its volume.

Traditional speakers send out sound waves that quickly spread and __9__. So the further away you stand from __10__, the quieter the sound will get.

HSS is supposed to have many __11__ use. It is being tried in airports. Imagine being able to hear only about your __12__! A beach lifeguard could easily shout to a __13__ who was getting too far out to sea. Over the crashing of __14__, the swimmer would clearly hear the lifeguard's instructions. In hospitals, an HSS TV could allow one patient to watch a show without __15__ others in the room. In restaurants or clubs, music could be __16__ for customers but remain unheard outside the building.

And HSS will be useful in other areas. If you play music from an HSS speaker and point it at a wall, the sound seems to come from the __17__. This could be of great help to police. When they are trying to catch criminals, they could play sounds that __18__ the criminals into thinking the police are coming from __19__ direction and then jump out and take them by __20__.

1. A. And   B. While   C. Though   D. But
2. A. special   B. usual   C. strange   D. excellent
3. A. Put   B. Shout   C. Point   D. Throw
4. A. quiet   B. noisy   C. wide   D. crowded
5. A. putting   B. hiding   C. dropping   D. leaving
6. A. out of   B. within   C. over   D. near to
7. A. stay   B. arrive   C. get   D. travel
8. A. raised   B. interrupted   C. stolen   D. disappeared
9. A. disappear   B. weaken   C. strengthen   D. widen
10. A. it   B. him   C. them   D. /
11. A. scientific   B. future   C. meaningless   D. practical
12. A. flight   B. plane   C. group   D. time
13. A. traveller   B. swimmer   C. visitor   D. stranger
14. A. crowd   B. ships   C. water   D. waves
15. A. hearing   B. seeing   C. disturbing   D. awaking

49

16. A. played   B. placed   C. heard   D. danced

17. A. speaker   B. wall   C. nearby   D. air

18. A. fool   B. make   C. help   D. fall

19. A. the same   B. wrong   C. another   D. back

20. A. mistake   B. the way   C. force   D. surprise

Ⅲ. 阅读理解（共10小题；每小题2分，满分20分）

A

It has been said that all Africans are born with musical talent. Because music is so important in the lives of many Africans and because so much music is performed in Africa, we probably think that all Africans are musicians. The impression is strengthened when we look at ourselves and find that we have become largely a society of musical spectators. Music is important to us, but most of us can be considered consumers rather than producers of music. We have recorders, TVs, and radios to meet many of our musical needs. In most situations where music is performed in our culture it's not difficult to tell the spectators from the performers, but <u>such</u> is often not the case in Africa. Ablan Ayipaga, a musician from northern Ghana, says that when his flute and drum group is performing, "anybody can take part". This is true, but they also recognise that not all people are equally able to take part in the music. Some can sing along with the drummers, but few can drum and even fewer can play the flute with the group. It's fairly common in Africa that a group of expert musicians surrounded by others who join in by clapping, singing, or somehow adding to the totality of musical sound. Performances often take place in an open area (that is, not on a stage) and so the lines between the performing actors and the additional performers, active spectators and passive spectators may be difficult to draw from our point of view.

1. The difference between us and Africans, as far as music is concerned, is that _____.

    A. most of us are performers while most of them are producers of arts

    B. we are musical performers and they are expert musicians

    C. most of them are active spectators while most of us are passive spectators

    D. we are the spectators while they are passive performers

2. The underlined word "such" in the passage refers to the fact that _____.

    A. music is performed with spectators joining in

    B. music is performed without spectators joining in

    C. people try to tell the spectators from the performers

    D. people have recorders, TVs and radios to meet their musical needs

3. The writer writes the passage to tell us that _____.

    A. all Africans are musicians and therefore much music is performed in Africa

    B. not all Africans are born with musical talent though much music is performed in Africa

C. most Africans are able to join in the music by playing musical instruments

D. most Africans perform as well as expert musicians

4. Which of the following is TRUE?

A. All Africans are born musicians.

B. Most Africans don't do very well in taking part in the musical performances.

C. African expert musicians never perform in the open air.

D. It's difficult to tell the musical spectators from the performers in Africa.

5. The best title for the passage is "_____".

A. The Importance of Music to Africans

B. Differences Between African Music and Music of Other Countries

C. The Relationship Between African Music and Music of Other Countries

D. Differences Between African Musical Performances and Ours

B

College graduation brings both the satisfaction of academic achievement and the expectation of a well-paid job. But for 6,000 graduates at San Jose State University this year, there's uncertainty as they enter one of the worst job markets in decades. Ryan Stewart has a freshly-minted (新兴的) degree in religious studies, but no job prospects (前景).

"You look at everybody's parents and neighbours and they're getting laid off and don't have jobs," said Stewart. "Then you look at the young people just coming into the workforce…it's just scary."

When the class of 2003 entered college, the future never looked brighter. But during the four years they've been here, the world outside has changed dramatically.

"Those were the exciting times, lots of <u>dot-com opportunities</u>, exploding offers, students getting top dollar with lots of benefits," said Cheryl Allmen-Vinnidge of the San Jose State Career Centre. "Times have changed. It's a new market."

Cheryl Allmen-Vinnidge ought to know. She runs the San Jose State Career Centre, sort of a crossroad between college and the real world. Allmen-Vinnidge says students who do find jobs after college <u>have done their homework</u>.

"The typical graduates who do have job offers started working on them two years ago. They've postured themselves well during the summer. They've had several internships (实习)," she said. And they've majored in one of the few fields that are still hot, like chemical engineering, accounting, or nursing, where average starting salaries have actually increased over last year. Other popular fields (like information systems management, computer science and political science) have seen big declines in starting salaries.

Ryan Stewart (who had hoped to become a teacher) may just end up going back to school. "I'd like to teach college some day and that requires more schooling, which would be great in a bad economy," he said.

To some students, a degree may not be a ticket to instant wealth. For now, they can only hope its value will increase over time.

6. The expression "dot-com opportunities" in the fourth paragraph probably means _____.

    A. a company making dots   B. jobs related to Internet

    C. teaching on the Internet   D. a well-known website

7. What does Cheryl Allmen-Vinnidge mean when she says students "have done their homework"?

    A. They have spent time preparing themselves to find a job.

    B. They have gone to summer schools for further studies.

    C. They are good students who have finished their homework on time.

    D. They have found full-time jobs as their future career before graduation.

8. The purpose of a college career centre is probably to _____.

    A. help students do their homework

    B. find jobs for students while they are in school

    C. prepare students to find jobs after they graduate

    D. help high school students get accepted to college

9. Ryan Stewart is probably going to _____ after graduation.

    A. get a teaching job   B. become a religious leader

    C. change his major   D. enrich himself more for a better job

10. What can we learn from the last paragraph?

    A. Having a college degree does not provide travel discounts.

    B. A college degree doesn't promise a person a well-paid job.

    C. Most students with degrees will be able to find jobs.

    D. The best way to get rich is to get a college degree.

Ⅳ. 阅读表达（共5小题；每小题3分，满分15分）

Wax apple, also known as Java apple or bell apple, is not only a tasty fruit, but also _____.

The fruit has a waxy appearance and is bell-shaped. Its colour varies from pink-reddish, crimson, greenish-white to cream-coloured. It tastes slightly sweet and sour with a similar fragrance to that of an apple.

The fruit originated from the Malaysian Peninsula and the Andaman Islands. In the 17th century, Dutch colonists introduced wax apples into China's Taiwan from Java.

With breakthroughs in cultivation, the wax apple has become a good choice during the hot summer. The top-quality wax apples in Taiwan are acclaimed as "Black Pearl". Most of them are produced in Pingtung County, where the salty soil is good for wax apple cultivation.

Wax apple has many medical applications. For example, its flowers can be used to treat fever and diarrhea (腹泻). In Taiwan, people make wax apple soup with crystal sugar (冰糖) to treat coughing. The fruit is also served as a cold dish on banquets (宴会) to relieve the effect of alcohol.

The fruit can be sliced and dipped in salty water for a while, then fried with cucumber (黄瓜) and carrot slices. The result is a great dish for summer with pleasant colours and tastes.

The sweetness of the wax apple depends on its ripeness. The sweetest wax apples are dark red at the end.

1. What is the best title for the passage? (Please answer within 10 words.)

_____

2. Which sentence in the passage can be replaced by the following one?
   If the wax apple is ripe enough, it is most sweet.

_____

3. Fill in the blank in the first paragraph with proper words or phrases to complete the sentence. (Please answer within 10 words.)

_____

4. Do you like to eat wax apple after reading the passage? Why or why not? (Please answer within 30 words.)

_____

_____

5. Translate the underlined sentence in the sixth paragraph into Chinese.

_____

Ⅴ. 翻译句子（共10小题；每题3分，满分30分）

1. 我的教学风格和其他多数老师相似。(be similar to)

_____

2. 直到最近，这个边远的部落几乎和外界没有什么联系。(have contact with)

_____

3. 他很聪明，但学习不用功。他哥哥也是这样。(the same)

_____

4. 儿童需要自己经历事情，以便从中学习。(experience)

_____

5. 除了金牌，每一个冠军获得者还能得到十万美元的奖金。(in addition to)

_____

6. 他不能适应那里的炎热天气。(agree with)

_____

7. 拐角处的大楼昨晚着火了，警察正在调查此事。(look into)

_____

8. 我非常乐意明天去机场接你。(more than)

_____

9. 考官们泄露了这次考试的答案。(give away)

_____

10. 最大的挑战就是尊重传统并融入自己的风格，对于我的第二种乐器——古筝，情况也是如此。(be true of)

_____

_____

Module ⑤

Cloning

高考词汇	clone, terrify, wing, murder, refuse, breathe, rush, fear, beneficial, cure, head, acid, bacteria, tissue, transparent, fundamental, component, pea, procedure, insert, controversial, valid, optional, contradictory, vice, virtue, compulsory, regulation, handy, resist, sow, rot, pest, analyse, suspect, spit, fingernail, accompany, absorb, arise, violence
常用短语	shake with fear, burn out, contrast with, throw oneself on, make a sound, again and again, by mistake, treat…as, as follows, discover the secret of, up and down, by the tiny light, be handy to do, open to the public, knock out, be contradictory to, get out of control, as far as sb know(s), break down, bring… back to life
实用句型	1. While studying at university, he discovers the secret of how to create life. 2. It was on a cold November night that I saw my creation for the first time. 3. Now my only thoughts were, "I wish I had not created this creature, I wish I was on the other side of the world, I wish I could disappear!" 4. A fourth reason for cloning is that some scientists and farmers think it would be…
交际用语	1. That's it. 2. Incredible! 3. Nonsense!

知识梳理

◆ **高考词汇**

1. absorb

v. 1) 吸收 (光、热、液体等)；2) 理解，掌握；3) 吸引 (某人)，使专心；4) 并入，吞并

This kind of paper absorbs ink easily.

Black objects absorb more heat than white objects.

I haven't really had time to absorb everything that he said.

Judy lay on the sofa, absorbed in her book.

The video was totally absorbing the children's attention.

The US was able to absorb thousands of new immigrants.

2. handy

adj. 1) 简便的，方便的；2) 手边的，附近的；3) 手巧的

He invented a handy machine for making fruit juice.

Keep an English-Chinese dictionary handy.

She is handy with a pair of scissors.

➡ 常用短语：

be handy for 离……近，在附近

come in handy 派上用场

His flat is handy for the shops.

Put these bottles in the cupboard — they might come in handy some day.

◆ **常用短语**

1. break down

break down 的主要含义有：

1) 毁坏，坏掉，出毛病，失效；

2) (在健康、精神等方面)(使)垮掉，崩溃；

3) (使) 感情上失去控制；

4) 分解

We're sorry to arrive late, but the car broke down.

The elevators in this building are always breaking down.

His health broke down.

She broke down when she heard the news, but quickly recovered.

Chemicals in the body break down our food into useful substance.

拓 展

break away 脱离，改掉 (习惯等)

break in 插话，非法进入

break into 破门而入

break out (突然) 爆发

break through 突破，穿透，取得重大进展

break up 打碎，破裂

To understand the grammar of the sentence, you must break it _____ into parts. (2006 黄冈模拟)

A. down   B. up   C. off   D. out

解析：break down 在此题中是"分解"的引申意义，表示"划分（以便分析）"。其他选项与 break 连用都不符合句意。答案为 A。

2. up to

up to 的主要含义有：

1) 忙于，从事于，正在做；2) 胜任，及得上；3) 多达；4) 由……决定

What's he up to?

He is well up to his work.

The hurricane crossed the southern part of England with winds of up to 160 kph.

You're the manager. It's up to you to decide what to do next.

综合训练

考试时间：45分钟   满分：100分

I. 单项选择（共15小题；每小题1分，满分15分）

1. —You don't like the report about cloning, do you?

   —_____, I can't like it any better.

   A. On the contrary   B. In other words   C. That's it   D. Of course not

2. What a _____ sight of the car accident! The little girl present was so _____ that she almost fainted.

   A. terrifying; terrified   B. terrified; terrifying
   C. terrifying; terrifying   D. terrified; terrified

3. She was quite angry because she was made _____ for over an hour in his office this morning.

   A. waiting   B. wait   C. waited   D. to wait

4. How I wish every family _____ a large house with a beautiful garden!

   A. has   B. had   C. will have   D. had had

5. She thought I was talking about her daughter, _____ in fact, I was talking about my daughter.

   A. whom   B. where   C. which   D. while

6. —There are still 15 minutes before the meeting. I'd like to smoke a cigarette.

   —You'd better not. Look, there's a _____ on smoking on the wall.

   A. permission   B. ban   C. notice   D. warning

7. The disc, digitally _____ in the studio, sounded fantastic at the party that night.

   A. recorded   B. to record   C. to be recorded D. record

8. Because the youth can't _____ the attraction of surfing the Internet, we should take proper measures to help them.

   A. follow   B. affect   C. control   D. resist

9. If my daughter knew as much about music as you do, she _____ much better.

   A. play   B. must play   C. will play   D. would play

10. The teacher _____ to have his daughter in his class for fear of showing favour to her.

   A. agreed   B. refused   C. decided   D. promised

11. —I think my return ticket is _____ for two months.

   —It is, but you have to pay some extra money for the increase of the oil price.

   A. delayed   B. booked   C. valid   D. kept

12. _____ his complete lack of medical experience, he saved several people's lives.

   A. As a result of   B. In place of   C. As though   D. Despite

13. —Mr Zhang was here last night. Did you talk over with him?

   —I wish I _____, but I came back too late.

   A. had   B. should have   C. would have   D. have

14. When he left for the sea, he _____ nothing but some food and water.

   A. took down   B. took along   C. brought on   D. brought away

15. —Will you go to the exhibition tomorrow?

   —Yes, I will go _____ it's windy.

   A. as if   B. as soon as   C. even though   D. as though

Ⅱ. 完形填空（共20小题；每小题1分，满分20分）

    For as long as I can remember, I have been very bad at arguing with people. As soon as someone __1__ with me, I get angry because I feel __2__, like the other person is out to show that I am __3__. And for some reason, I __4__ being wrong! So my __5__ reaction is to get very defensive, I __6__ my voice, and I end up saying something I later __7__. Needless to say, the whole thing ends with me blaming myself, and the other person __8__ alienated (疏远的) from me. This bothers me especially because my mother does the exact same thing and I hate __9__!

    I have noticed this tendency in me for a long time now, but I have never been able to __10__. I did some __11__ management work with a therapist (治疗专家) a while ago, but because I moved and __12__ an advisor at school who cannot see me __13__, I have not been able to continue this important work. They tell you to stop and count to 10, control your __14__, calm yourself down __15__ you talk. But that's the whole problem; I could never __16__ stopping myself until it was too late! The __17__ things had already come out of my mouth, and I was stuck picking up the pieces.

Right now the problem is urgent because my __18__ with a wonderful boyfriend is __19__ because of my being afraid of being wrong. He is closing himself off to me because I have hurt him, and __20__ I am no longer attractive as a woman with no confidence in herself and a bad temper. How can I stop ruining my relationships and hating myself? How can I stop hating being wrong?

1. A. disagrees　　　B. agrees　　　　C. quarrels　　　　D. discusses
2. A. disappointed　B. excited　　　　C. attacked　　　　D. ashamed
3. A. wrong　　　　 B. foolish　　　　C. empty-headed　　D. right
4. A. avoid　　　　　B. enjoy　　　　 C. doubt　　　　　D. hate
5. A. unusual　　　　B. immediate　　　C. following　　　 D. last
6. A. raise　　　　　B. lower　　　　 C. keep　　　　　 D. change
7. A. remember　　　B. regret　　　　 C. forget　　　　　D. realise
8. A. leaving　　　　B. coming　　　　C. running　　　　D. feeling
9. A. it　　　　　　 B. her　　　　　 C. them　　　　　 D. itself
10. A. stop　　　　　B. start　　　　　C. control　　　　D. ignore
11. A. health　　　　B. action　　　　C. calmness　　　　D. anger
12. A. headed to　　　B. asked for　　　C. turned to　　　 D. referred to
13. A. regularly　　　B. carelessly　　 C. immediately　　 D. patiently
14. A. behaviour　　　B. manner　　　　C. talking　　　　D. breathing
15. A. when　　　　　B. while　　　　 C. before　　　　　D. whenever
16. A. prepare for　　B. think of　　　 C. set out　　　　 D. look for
17. A. hurtful　　　　B. surprising　　　C. colourful　　　D. dangerous
18. A. relationship　　B. emotion　　　 C. life　　　　　　D. action
19. A. on the way　　 B. in the end　　　C. in danger　　　 D. in good condition
20. A. no doubt　　　B. no way　　　　C. no problem　　　D. no wonder

Ⅲ．阅读理解（共10小题；每小题2分，满分20分）

A

The right amount of sleep is essential for anyone who wants to do well on a test or play sports without tripping (绊倒) over their feet. Most teens need from 8.5 to more than 9 hours of sleep each night. Unfortunately, many of them don't get enough sleep.

Until recently teens were often blamed for staying up late, oversleeping for school, and falling asleep in class. But recent research shows that adolescent sleep patterns actually differ from those of adults or kids.

The research shows that during the teen years, the body's rhythm is reset, telling a person to fall asleep later and wake up later. Unlike kids and adults, whose bodies tell them to go to sleep and wake up earlier, most teens' bodies tell them to go sleep late at night and sleep into the late morning. Early starting times in some schools play a role in teens' sleep shortage. Teens who fall asleep after midnight may still have to get up early for school, meaning that they may only have 6 or 7 hours of sleep a night. An hour or two of missed sleep a night may not seem like a big deal, but it can create a noticeable sleep shortage over time.

The sleep shortage affects everything from a teen's ability to pay attention in class to his or her mood. The research shows that more than 20 percent of high school students fall asleep in class, and have poorer grades for lack of sleep. In addition, lack of sleep has also been linked to emotional troubles, such as feelings of sadness and depression.

Getting enough sleep helps keep us healthy, physically and mentally, by slowing our bodies' systems enough to re-energise us after everyday activities. The situation of teens' sleep shortage should draw our more attention.

1. The main idea of the passage is _____.
   A. enough sleep is essential for everyone
   B. sleep plays a more important part in teens' life than that of adults
   C. teens' bodies tell them to go to sleep and get up later than kids or adults
   D. the later teens get up, the better grades they will have
2. Why do teens sleep later and wake up later?
   Λ. Because they have too much homework to do at night.
   B. Because their biological clocks have changed during the teen years.
   C. Because they have some serious sleep problems.
   D. Because they have bad sleep habits.
3. According to the passage, the sleep shortage can cause many problems EXCEPT _____.
   A. low grades   B. low spirits   C. weak body   D. serious handicaps
4. What does the underlined phrase "a big deal" in the third paragraph mean?
   A. Something important.   B. An important agreement.
   C. Something cheap.   D. Something easy to finish.
5. The purpose of writing this passage is _____.
   A. to correct teens' bad sleep habits
   B. to warn teens about the bad effects of sleep shortage
   C. to prove that teens' sleep patterns are the same as those of adults
   D. to draw people's attention to teens' lack of sleep

B

With only a small number of pandas left in the world, China is desperately trying to clone the animal and save the endangered species. That's a move similar to what Texas A&M University researchers have been undertaking for the past five years in a project called "Noah's Ark".

Noah's Ark is aimed at collecting eggs, embryos (胚胎), and DNA of endangered animals and storing them in liquid nitrogen (氮). If certain species should die out, Dr Duane Kraemer, a professor in Texas A&M University, says there would be enough of the basic building blocks to reintroduce the species in the future.

This week, Chinese scientists said they had grown an embryo introducing cells from a dead female panda into the egg cells of a Japanese white rabbit. They are now trying to implant the embryo into a host animal. The entire procedure could take from three to five years to complete.

"The nuclear transfer (细胞核移植) of one species to another is not easy, and the lack of available panda eggs could be a major problem," Kraemer believes. "They will probably have to do several hundred transfers to result in one pregnancy. It takes a long time and it's difficult, but this could be groundbreaking science if it works. They are certainly not putting any live pandas at risk, so it is worth the effort," adds Kraemer, who is one of the leaders of the project at Texas A&M, the first-ever attempt at cloning a dog.

"They are trying to do something that's never been done, and this is very similar to our work in Noah's Ark. We're both trying to save animals that face extinction. I certainly appreciate their effort and there's a lot we can learn from what they are attempting to do. It's a research that is very much needed."

6. The aim of "Noah's Ark" project is to _____.
   A. make effort to clone the endangered pandas
   B. save endangered animals from dying out
   C. collect DNA of endangered animals to study
   D. transfer the nucleus of one animal to another

7. If pandas died out in one or two years, what should researchers do now?
   A. To put live pandas under clone experiment immediately.
   B. To store panda eggs, embryos and DNA in liquid nitrogen.
   C. To ask Professor Kraemer for help.
   D. To make more pandas get pregnant.

8. According to Professor Kraemer, the major problem in cloning pandas would be the lack of _____.
   A. available panda eggs   B. live pandas
   C. qualified researchers   D. enough money

9. The underlined word "groundbreaking" in the fourth paragraph probably has the similar meaning to "_____".
   A. creative   B. hardworking   C. destructive   D. surprising

10. The best title for the passage may be _____.
    A. China's Success in Panda Cloning
    B. The First Cloned Panda in the World
    C. Exploring the Possibility of Cloning Pandas
    D. China — the Native Place of Pandas Forever

Leading influenza (流感) experts urged nations not to lower their guard against the deadly and hardy H5N1 virus, saying it now survives longer in higher temperatures and in wet and moist conditions.

Scientists previously found the virus to be most active and transmissible among birds in the cooler months from October to March in the northern hemisphere (半球), and many people were hoping for a halt _____.

But influenza expert Robert Webster warned against underestimating the virus, which made its first recorded jump to humans from birds in 1997 in China's Hong Kong, killing six people.

"When we tested the virus in Hong Kong from 1997, the virus was killed at 37°C in two days. The current H5N1 is still living for six days at 37°C," said Webster, from St Jude Children's Research Hospital in the US city Memphis.

"H5N1 at room temperatures can stay alive for at least a week in wet conditions," Webster said on the eve of a bird flu conference organised by the medical journal, *the Lancet*, in Singapore.

"One of the often overlooked facts about H5N1 virus is that it's more heat stable than people realise, especially under moist, damp conditions," he said.

Webster said heat-stable strains of H5N1 were already circulating (传播) in ducks in Vietnam, Indonesia and China in 2004 and 2005 and experts would have to test if this characteristic was in the variants (变种) now circulating in India, Africa, Europe and parts of the Middle East.

Since re-emerging in Asia in late 2003, the H5N1 virus is known to have infected (感染) 205 people, killing 113 of them. In the past few months, it has spread from Asia to parts of Europe, the Middle East and Africa.

Although it is mainly a bird disease and most of the victims infected the virus directly from poultry (家禽), experts fear it might change into a form that transmits easily among people.

1. What is the best title for the passage? (Please answer within 10 words.)

_____

2. Which sentence in the passage can be replaced by the following one?
It's beyond our expectation that H5N1 virus is very stable in heat environment.

_____

3. Fill in the blank in the second paragraph with proper words or phrases to complete the sentence. (Please answer within 10 words.)

_____

4. Do you think we can ignore the bird flu in the summer months? Why or why not? (Please answer within 30 words.)

_____

_____

5. Translate the underlined sentence in the eighth paragraph into Chinese.

_____

V. 句型转换（共5小题；每空1分，满分15分）

1. Only when the war was over in 1918 did Einstein get back to work.

   Einstein didn't get back to work _____ the war came to _____ _____ in 1918.

2. I often swim in the river when I was a child.

   This is the river _____ _____ I _____ _____ swim in my childhood.

3. I'd like to talk with you after class.

   I _____ _____ _____ a talk with you after class.

4. May all your dreams come true.

   I wish that all your dreams _____ _____ realised.

5. She insisted that I should go shopping with her.

   She insisted _____ _____ _____ some shopping with her.

VI. 翻译句子（共5小题；每题3分，满分15分）

1. 正是由于那个原因，我才不愿意告诉他真相。(强调句)

   _____

2. 录音前我确保录音室内没有其他人。(make sure)

   _____

3. 政府已经明令禁止使用化学武器。(ban)

   _____

4. 新鲜空气有益于健康。(beneficial)

   _____

5. 就在我的蜡烛几乎要燃尽的时候，我听到了我们的飞机发出的巨大响声。(burn out)

   _____

Module ⑥

War and Peace

📖 要点纵览

高考词汇	abandon, operation, last, occupy, beach, troop, commander, eventually, deep, wound, overlook, condemn, memorial, nationality, rescue, afterwards, drop, bomb, campaign, station, chain, view, chaos, courage, sacrifice, company, baggage, bedding, comb, confidential, mess, perfume, razor, scissors, shave, stockings, tractor, yell, barbershop, moustache, wax, sharpener, jar, carrot, cheers, liberation, constitution, vinegar, worthwhile, encourage, helmet, arm, disagreement, personnel, civilian
常用短语	declare war on, land on the beaches, go off the boats, abandon the invasion, make a breakthrough, break the chains, be situated on, be involved in, win the Nobel Peace Prize, war memorial, attempt to do, go down, to one's astonishment, drink to, in return
实用句型	1. If they had reached the beach, they would probably have been killed. 2. The survivors lay on the beach, exhausted and shocked. 3. James Ryan is the fourth brother to be involved in the Second World War. 4. …because we were aware that there might still have been enemy soldiers. 5. …and we all drank to liberation and to the French constitution.
交际用语	1. I often wonder why. 2. If I remember rightly… 3. We weren't supposed to do that. 4. We appreciated the opportunity to talk.

◆ **高考词汇**

1. attempt

n. & v. 企图，试图，尝试

They are beginning a new attempt to solve the problem.

She attempted to get in touch with her son, but failed.

He decided to attempt the difficult task.

2. situated

adj. 坐落在……的，位于……的，处于……境地的

The farmer lived in a house situated at the mouth of the river.

He was very badly situated.

> ···········拓·展··········
> situation *n.* 立场，境遇
> I'm now in a difficult situation.

3. offer

n. 1) 提议，提供；2) 出价，开价，报价

v. 1) 给予；2) 提议；3) 出 (价)，开 (价)，提供，出售

He turned down the offer of a free trip to Milan.

I'm prepared to make you a generous offer for the house.

I offered him a glass of water.

She offered to carry the box for her mother.

We offered him $1,000 for the computer.

真 题 解 析

1) They've _____ us $150,000 for the house. Shall we take it? (2004 湖南)

　　A. provided　　B. supplied　　C. shown　　　　D. offered

解析：通过语境分析，句中的 "they" 是在出价，所以选 offered。答案为 D。

2) —If you like, I can do some shopping for you.

　　—That's a very kind _____. (2006 浙江)

　　A. offer　　　B. service　　　C. point　　　　D. suggestion

解析：这是一个名词辨析题。一方主动提供帮助，接受帮助者对其做出了回应。四个选项中，只有 A 项符合语境。答案为 A。

4. occupy

v. 1) 占领，占用 (空间或时间)；2) 使忙碌

The region was quickly occupied by foreign troops.

Tall bookcases occupy a lot of space in his room.

➡ 常用短语：

be occupied in doing sth (= occupy oneself in doing sth / with sth) 专心于，从事于
I have been occupied in reading books.

◆ 常用短语

1. declare war on

declare war on 意思是"向……宣战"。

Germany declared war on the US on December 11, 1941.

Police have now declared war on drug dealers in the area.

> **拓展**
>
> declare against 声明反对 (某人或某事)
> declare for 声明支持 (某人或某事)
> declare sth open 宣布……开幕

真 题 解 析

The moment the 28th Olympic Games _____ open, the whole world cheered. (2006 福建)
A. declared   B. have been declared   C. have declared   D. were declared

解析：这是一个考查时态的题。根据事件内容及题干后半部分的时态，可以确定用一般过去时。同时，根据动词 declare 的用法，即 declare sth open（宣布……开幕），确定其语态应为被动语态。答案为 D。

2. make a breakthrough

make a breakthrough 意思是"取得突破"。

They have made a new breakthrough in cancer research.

综合训练

考试时间：45分钟   满分：100分

I. 单项选择（共15小题；每小题1分，满分15分）

1. —You were brave enough to raise objections at the meeting.
   —Well, now I regret _____ that.
   A. to do   B. to be doing   C. to have done   D. having done

2. There was such a long queue for coffee at the interval that we _____ had to give up.
   A. eventually   B. unfortunately   C. generously   D. purposefully

3. He _____ to escape from the prison, but he couldn't find anybody to help him.
   A. succeeded   B. attempted   C. advised   D. offered

4. I don't think that John would _____ his friends if they were in trouble.
   A. abandon   B. involve   C. appoint   D. occupy

5. It's always difficult being in a foreign country, _____ if you don't speak the language.

    A. extremely   B. naturally   C. basically   D. especially

6. China has _____ an important breakthrough in the grain storage security technology.

    A. made   B. drawn   C. won   D. set

7. He is my wife's cousin, so we are distantly _____.

    A. linked   B. connected   C. united   D. related

8. News reports say peace talks between the two countries have _____ with no agreement reached.

    A. broken down   B. broken out   C. broken in   D. broken up

9. —Where have you been?

    —I got caught in traffic; _____ I would have been here sooner.

    A. however   B. although   C. anyway   D. otherwise

10. After his journey from abroad, Richard returns home, _____.

    A. exhausting   B. exhausted   C. being exhausted   D. having exhausted

11. I can think of many cases where students _____ knew a lot of English words but couldn't write a good essay.

    A. accidentally   B. comfortably   C. definitely   D. confidently

12. Do let your mother know all the truth. She appears _____ everything.

    A. to tell   B. to be told   C. to be telling   D. to have been told

13. The New Year Evening Party, turning out to be a great success, _____ after midnight.

    A. came to an end   B. came to end

    C. ended up with   D. ended in

14. Police are _____ a reward to anyone with information about the crime.

    A. providing   B. supplying   C. showing   D. offering

15. If he had a bike, he _____ it to you this morning.

    A. would be lending   B. would have lent

    C. would lend   D. could lend

II. 完形填空（共20小题；每小题1分，满分20分）

When I was 6, I went to a local grade school. In grade school, I was __1__ the other children because of my speech and reading __2__. All the children would shout, "You are a dummy; you are a dummy!" and so on. I thought they were __3__ because all my grades showed it. I had no self-confidence.

Through the first five years of grade school, I was small and very clumsy (笨拙的). I would __4__ cups and trays in the café, and sometimes trip myself and fall onto the floor when I __5__. In the sixth grade, I became interested in __6__. The class had its annual field day. Each class would have its own teams to __7__ against each other. I went out for all of the __8__. I was not the best __9__ I was not bad. The thing that I could do was running and I ran fast. This __10__ the other children because I had been so clumsy.

And then __11__ a lot more name-calling from the children. When somebody else won a race, the children told him how __12__ he was. When I __13__, they called me names. I did not know why they were doing this. I think that it was unfair, and it __14__ me.

Between the seventh and eighth grade, I started to __15__. In three months, I grew seven inches. At the start of the eighth grade, I began to play __16__. I was much bigger than everybody else. I was __17__ than most of the backs we played against. They would not run the ball towards me, so I just knocked them __18__. It was the first time in my life that I was really good at something and __19__ it. It was a new feeling of __20__.

1. A. above　　　　B. before　　　　C. behind　　　　D. among
2. A. materials　　B. questions　　　C. skills　　　　D. problems
3. A. right　　　　B. smart　　　　C. clever　　　　D. foolish
4. A. clean　　　　B. drop　　　　C. collect　　　　D. serve
5. A. walk　　　　B. sleep　　　　C. forget　　　　D. move
6. A. studies　　　B. sports　　　　C. books　　　　D. talks
7. A. stand　　　　B. fight　　　　C. quarrel　　　　D. compete
8. A. teams　　　　B. subjects　　　C. tests　　　　D. grades
9. A. because　　　B. if　　　　　　C. but　　　　　D. and
10. A. interested　　B. shocked　　　C. delighted　　　D. disappointed
11. A. happened　　B. continued　　C. made　　　　D. came
12. A. famous　　　B. good　　　　C. happy　　　　D. strange
13. A. won　　　　B. failed　　　　C. told　　　　　D. attended
14. A. frightened　　B. ashamed　　　C. hurt　　　　　D. worried
15. A. progress　　B. change　　　　C. grow　　　　　D. play
16. A. football　　　B. music　　　　C. tricks　　　　D. roles
17. A. faster　　　　B. taller　　　　C. slower　　　　D. harder
18. A. back　　　　B. down　　　　C. off　　　　　　D. away
19. A. judged　　　B. admired　　　C. decided　　　　D. knew
20. A. courage　　　B. sadness　　　C. pride　　　　　D. regret

Ⅲ. 阅读理解（共10小题；每小题2分，满分20分）

A

The name of hurricanes is chosen from a list of first names in alphabetical order. Female and male names are chosen alternatively. For example, the first hurricane of the year will be called "Alexandra", the second "Bernard", the third "Catherine", etc.

When newspapers and radio describe the damage caused by a hurricane named Hazel, girls named Hazel are probably teased by their friends. To keep out of trouble, the Weather Bureau says, "Any resemblance between hurricane names and the names of particular girls is purely accidental."

Some women became angry because hurricanes are given their names, but many other women are proud to see their names make headlines. They don't even care that they are the names of destructive storms. Because more women seem to like it, the Weather Bureau has decided to continue using girls' names for hurricanes.

In some ways a hurricane is like a person. After it is born, it grows and develops, then becomes old and dies. Each hurricane has a character of its own. Each follows its own path through the world, and people remember it long after it's gone. So it is natural to give hurricanes names, and to talk about them almost as if they were alive.

1. The underlined word "resemblance" in the second paragraph means "_____".
    A. sameness   B. difference   C. trouble   D. success

2. What happens to girls named Hazel according to the passage?
    A. They suffer from hurricanes.   B. The Weather Bureau looks for them.
    C. Others often make fun of them.   D. They can't find boyfriend.

3. According to the passage, which is most reasonable?
    A. Some men feel unhappy because hurricanes are given their names.
    B. A lot of women complain of the Weather Bureau.
    C. Many women want to be known.
    D. All the hurricanes are caused by women.

4. Public opinions make the Weather Bureau _____.
    A. consider the disagreement of some women
    B. go on naming hurricanes after women
    C. name hurricanes after men
    D. look for a new method to name hurricanes

5. It is natural to give hurricanes names because _____.
    A. they become old and die
    B. all of them should be remembered
    C. each hurricane has its own day to come
    D. each hurricane has its own character

B

◆ The regular use of text messages and emails can lower the IQ more than twice as much as smoking marijuana (大麻). Psychologists say that sending and receiving messages or looking through the many menu options your mobile phone has, lowers a person's IQ by almost 10 points. British researchers have named this situation "infomania". Instead of being fixed on what they are doing, people's minds are constantly focused on reacting to the technology surrounding them. This means they don't pay full attention to the work they are paid to do. The report also added that the brain cannot do so many things at once. If you try to do so many things, mistakes begin to occur. And while modern technology can have huge benefits, too much use can be damaging not only to a person's mind, but to their social life.

◆ The more televisions four-year-old children watch, the more likely they are to become bullies (欺凌弱小者) later on in school, a newest US study said. At the same time, children whose parents read to them, take them on outings and just generally pay attention to them are less likely to become bullies, said the report from the University of Washington. Researchers also found gaps in learning and understanding such things as social skills early in life make it more difficult for children to relate with other children. Watching violence on television leads to aggressive behaviour.

◆ You could soon be able to add your favourite perfume to your emails. UK net provider Telewest Broadband is testing a system to let people send emails over the Internet with sweet smell. It has developed a kind of hi-tech air freshener that plugs into a PC and sprays a smell linked to the message. Telewest says it could be used by supermarkets to attract people with the smell of fresh bread or by holiday companies seeking to stir up images of sun-kissed beaches.

6. What is the first part of the passage mainly about?
   A. The bad effects of text messages and emails over mobile phones.
   B. How to avoid the bad sides of text messages and emails over mobile phones.
   C. Too much use of text messages and emails over mobile phones can lower a person's IQ.
   D. The relationship between the text messages, emails over mobile phones and a person's IQ .

7. The underlined word "infomania" in the first part refers to a situation in which a person _____.
   A. uses his mobile phone too much
   B. has his IQ lowered using his mobile phone
   C. performs badly at work
   D. lowers his IQ using his mobile phone improperly

8. According to the second part of the text, children whose parents _____ are less likely to become bullies.
   A. care about them   B. give them more freedom
   C. direct them over watching TV   D. stop them watching TV

9. The children who watch TV too much will not _____.
   A. be aggressive
   B. be likely to become bullies
   C. have difficulty communicating with other children
   D. understand social skills as easily as other children

10. The new system provided by Telewest Broadband can _____.
    A. be used as a kind of air freshener
    B. make people have imagination of sun-kissed beaches

C. make people taste fresh bread

D. make emails sweet over the Internet

IV. 阅读表达（共5小题；每小题3分，满分15分）

Can you walk a straight line? The question is much more difficult to answer than you think. Believe it or not, your eyes and ears help you walk!

A recent experiment held in Japan shows that _____ for 60 metres. The Tokyo University of Agriculture and Technology asked 20 healthy men to walk as straight as possible for 60 metres at normal speed. Each man had to wear socks soaked with red ink and walk on white paper fixed flat to the floor. The footprints showed that all walked in a winding rather than a straight line.

Researchers found that people readjust their direction of walking regularly. The amount of meandering (迂回曲折) differed from subject to subject. This suggests that none of us can walk in a strictly straight line. Rather, we meander mainly due to a slight structural or functional imbalance of our limbs. Our body is actually semicircular (半圆的), so steps by the left and right leg of a person are different. As a result, although we may start walking in a straight line, several steps afterwards we have changed direction. Eyesight helps us correct the direction of walking and leads us to the target.

Our ears also help us walk. After turning around a lot with our eyes closed, we can hardly stand still or walk straight. It's all because our ears are still spinning and cannot help us keep our balance. Inside our inner ear there is a structure containing liquids. When we spin, the liquid inside also spins. The difference is that when we stop, the liquid continues to spin for a while. Dizziness is the result. <u>For the moment, although our eyesight tells us to walk in a straight line, our brain listens to our spinning ears, thus we don't walk in a straight line!</u>

1. What is the best title for the passage? (Please answer within 10 words.)

_____

2. Which sentence in the passage can be replaced by the following one?

Without our eyes we never reach where we want to by walking rightly.

_____

3. Fill in the blank in the second paragraph with proper words or phrases to complete the sentence. (Please answer within 10 words.)

_____

4. Do people walk exactly straight for a long distance at normal speed? Why? (Please answer within 30 words.)

_____

_____

5. Translate the underlined sentence in the last paragraph into Chinese.

_____

Ⅴ. 翻译句子（共10小题；每小题3分，满分30分）

1. 他们第一次见面就是在五年前栽种的那棵树下。(meet for the first time)

_____

2. 在大街上徘徊时，他看见两名武装警察卷入了打斗。(get involved in)

_____

3. 他扑倒在地上，因此在这次炸弹爆炸中幸免于难。(escape being killed)

_____

4. 中国科学家在基因研究领域取得了许多重大突破。(make many breakthroughs)

_____

5. 这个小国的国王被迫向邻国宣战。(declare war on)

_____

6. 他工作太努力，结果病倒了。(make oneself ill)

_____

7. 人们发现那辆车被扔在了村子附近。(abandon)

_____

8. 使我吃惊的是，门自动开了。(to one's astonishment)

_____

9. 她给了我们食物和衣服，没有要求任何回报。(in return)

_____

10. 他要求将一切告诉他。(demand)

_____

第一部分 听力（共两节，满分30分）

第一节 （共5小题；每小题1.5分，满分7.5分）

听下面五段对话。每段对话后有一个小题，从题中所给的三个选项中选出最佳选项。听完每段对话后，你都有10秒钟的时间来回答有关小题和阅读下一小题。每段对话仅读一遍。

1. How much will the man pay if he rents the room for three weeks?
    A. $50.   B. $150.   C. $160.

2. What does the man mean?
    A. He is used to wearing no hat.
    B. The weather is going to be fine.
    C. He is used to going out on a cold winter day.

3. How many children are there in the classroom?
    A. Seven.   B. Five.   C. Twelve.

4. From whom did the man get a postcard?
    A. Tim.   B. Sam.   C. The woman.

5. What will the man have to do?
    A. To take his luggage with him.
    B. To paint the room.
    C. To change to a new room.

第二节 （共15小题；每小题1.5分，满分22.5分）

听下面五段对话或独白。每段对话或独白后有几个小题，从题中所给的三个选项中选出最佳选项。听每段对话或独白前，你将有时间阅读各个小题，每小题5秒钟；听完后，各小题将给出5秒钟的作答时间。每段对话或独白读两遍。

听第6段材料，回答第6至第8小题。

6. Where was George yesterday?
    A. At his usual place.   B. In the newspaper office.   C. At home.

7. What did the woman want to do yesterday?
    A. To ask George to a concert.
    B. To go on a holiday with George.
    C. To invite George to dinner at home.

8. Which of the following didn't George do?
    A. Doing some repairing.   B. Going shopping.   C. Doing some washing.

9. What's the weather like?

    A. Cloudy and warm.   B. Lovely and warm.   C. Fine but cloudy.

10. Where are the speakers?

    A. At a station.   B. In a flat.   C. In a park.

11. What is the man doing in England?

    A. Spending his holiday.

    B. Practising his English.

    C. Visiting a Greek family.

12. What are they talking about?

    A. The weather of London.

    B. Travelling in Britain.

    C. The traffic of London.

13. What does the woman think of the London buses?

    A. Rather slow.   B. Very good.   C. Too expensive.

14. In the woman's opinion, what is the best way to travel in London?

    A. By bus.   B. By underground.   C. By taxi.

15. Which of the following positions is the woman interested in?

    A. General manager.   B. Advertising manager.   C. Sales manager.

16. How long has the woman been in the small company?

    A. Eight years.   B. Nine years.   C. Ten years.

17. What does the woman want to do?

    A. To go to different places for holidays.

    B. To get chances of her future development.

    C. To meet more new friends on her trip.

18. What's the cause of the accident?

    A. Too much traffic on the road.

    B. High speed and wet road.

    C. The engine is out of order.

19. Who called the First Aid Centre for help?

    A. A young woman.   B. The writer.   C. A policeman.

20. What did the policeman do?

    A. He took the driver out of his car.

    B. He questioned the writer carefully.

    C. He immediately sent the driver to hospital.

第一节　语法和词汇（共15小题；每小题1分，满分15分）

从A、B、C、D四个选项中，选出可以填入空白处的最佳选项。

21. Don't cheat the customers, or you will damage the _____ of our supermarket.

　　A. view　　　　　　　B. sight　　　　　　　C. opinion　　　　　　D. image

22. Five minutes earlier, _____ we could have caught the train.

　　A. but　　　　　　　　B. so　　　　　　　　C. and　　　　　　　D. or

23. After supper she would sit down by the fire, sometimes for _____ an hour, thinking of her young and happy days.

　　A. as long as　　　　B. as soon as　　　　C. as much as　　　D. as many as

24. —It'll take at least two hours to do this.

　　—_____! I could do it in 30 minutes.

　　A. You are right　　　B. I'm sorry　　　　C. Oh, come on　　　D. Don't mention it

25. We're sorry to arrive late, but the car _____.

　　A. broke down　　　　B. broke out　　　　C. broke in　　　　D. broke up

26. —How _____ feel to cover 60 miles on foot in a single day?

　　—Really tiring. Especially when there is no one in company.

　　A. do you　　　　　　B. does that　　　　C. did you　　　　　D. does it

27. On AIDS Day, the minister of Health Department demanded that the problems _____ paid special attention to.

　　A. referred to being　　B. referred to be　　C. refer to being　　D. refer to be

28. Hopes are high _____ all construction work at the site will be completed within the next two weeks.

　　A. when　　　　　　　B. where　　　　　　C. that　　　　　　　D. what

29. An increasing number of students, year by year, across China _____ hard to realise their dream of studying abroad.

　　A. are trying　　　　B. have tried　　　　C. will try　　　　　D. had tried

30. My watch _____ at nine o'clock, but now it _____.

　　A. went; stopped　　　　　　　　　　　B. was going; stopped

　　C. went; is stopping　　　　　　　　　D. was going; has stopped

31. Mrs White found her husband surrounded by letters and papers and _____ very worried.

　　A. looked　　　　　　B. looks　　　　　　C. looking　　　　　D. to look

32. The senior librarian at the circulation desk promised to get the book for me _____ she could remember who last borrowed it.

　　A. ever since　　　　B. if only　　　　　C. even though　　　D. only if

33. —I think you should have food containing less fat and take more exercise if you want to

keep slim and fit.

— _____.

    A. That's all right   B. It's very nice of you to say so

    C. Thank you for your advice   D. I don't believe so

34. In order to improve our conditions, this new system must be _____.

    A. adopted   B. adapted   C. addicted   D. adored

35. Many people are asking whether traditional research universities in fact have any future _____.

    A. so far   B. at all   C. in all   D. on end

第二节　完形填空（共20小题；每小题1分，满分20分）

阅读下面短文，掌握其大意，然后从每题所给的四个选项中选出最佳选项。

You've probably heard the expression, "What you see is what you get." My grandfather used to say, "If you __36__ a tree long enough, it will move." We see __37__ we want to see. Psychologists tell us that __38__ controls our life more than our self-image. We live like the person we see in the __39__. We are what we think we are. If you don't think you'll be successful, you __40__. You can't be it if you can't see it. Your life is __41__ to your vision. If you want to change your __42__, you must change your vision of life.

Arnold Schwarzenegger was not that famous when he __43__ a newspaper reporter. The reporter asked Schwarzenegger, "__44__ you've retired from body building, what do you plan to do next?" Schwarzenegger answered very calmly and __45__, "I'm going to become the No. 1 movie star in Hollywood." The reporter was __46__ and amused at Schwarzenegger's plan. At that time, it was very hard to __47__ how this muscle-bound body builder, who was not a __48__ actor and who spoke poor English with a strong Austrian accent, could ever __49__ to be Hollywood's No. 1 movie star!

So the reporter asked Schwarzenegger __50__ he planned to make his dream come true. Schwarzenegger said, "I'll do it the same __51__ I became the No. 1 body builder in the world. What I do is creating a vision of who I want to be, then I start living like that person in my __52__ as if it were already true." Sounds almost childishly __53__, doesn't it? But it __54__! Schwarzenegger did become the No. 1 highest-paid movie star in Hollywood! Remember: "If you can see it, you can __55__ it."

36. A. look after   B. live with   C. look at   D. care for

37. A. what   B. where   C. that   D. why

38. A. something   B. everything   C. nothing   D. anything

39. A. water   B. picture   C. novel   D. mirror

40. A. don't   B. won't   C. can't   D. will

41. A. limited   B. contributed   C. devoted   D. offered

42. A. idea   B. image   C. life   D. vision

43. A. turned into   B. met with   C. acted as   D. worked as

44. A. Now that	B. Even if	C. In case	D. Only if
45. A. proudly	B. anxiously	C. confidently	D. happily
46. A. surprised	B. excited	C. disappointed	D. scared
47. A. report	B. imagine	C. find	D. judge
48. A. famous	B. good	C. professional	D. popular
49. A. hope	B. have	C. fail	D. happen
50. A. when	B. why	C. what	D. how
51. A. chance	B. method	C. way	D. effort
52. A. film	B. play	C. family	D. mind
53. A. foolish	B. simple	C. funny	D. clever
54. A. succeeded	B. worked	C. did	D. completed
55. A. move	B. leave	C. get	D. touch

第三部分　阅读理解（共20小题；每小题2分，满分40分）

阅读下列短文，从每题所给的四个选项中选出最佳选项。

A

An elderly woman died and several other passengers were critically injured when a crowded Virgin Express train crashed in Cumbria last night.

A huge rescue operation involving RAF helicopters and dozens of ambulances arrived after passengers were trapped in the train for more than four hours because fallen power line poles made access for emergency workers difficult.

Authorities reported up to 80 injuries. Thirteen people were taken to hospital in a "critical or serious condition".

Between 180 and 200 passengers were on the 5:15 pm Virgin service from London Euston to Glasgow Central when all nine carriages left the rails between Oxenholme and Tebay. Witnesses said that the train shook violently before toppling (倒下) over into an embankment (路堤) with at least four carriages overturning. Early this morning, authorities confirmed an elderly woman had died and some other passengers had suffered injuries including back strains, head wounds and broken bones.

Ruth Colton, a passenger on the train, said she was reading a book when the journey became uncomfortable. It seemed that the train was being beaten by heavy winds, "as if we were on a plane".

The accident brought concerns that Britain's busiest rail route would be crippled (瘫痪) for some time. The line between Preston and Carlisle was postponed as Virgin Trains promised a rapid investigation into the "serious incident" — the company's first big crash.

It is understood that the investigation will examine whether there was an obstacle on the track and the possibility of speeding or mechanical breakdown. The driver, who was injured, will be interviewed and a black-box recorder installed in the train will be examined.

56. What made the rescue come so late?

 A. It was difficult to reach the accident spot.

 B. No enough helicopters and ambulances could be found at that time.

 C. It was too far from hospital to Cumbria.

 D. No one called the emergency centre.

57. The underlined word "critical" in the third paragraph probably means _____.

 A. important   B. careless   C. dangerous   D. surprising

58. According to the passage, the busiest rail route in Britain is _____.

 A. from Preston to Carlisle   B. between Euston and Glasgow

 C. from Oxenholme to Tebay   D. between Virgin and Pendolino

59. Which of the following is the possible cause of the accident?

 A. Careless driving.   B. Heavy wind.

 C. Overloading.   D. Obstacle on the track.

60. We can learn from the passage that Virgin Trains _____.

 A. made no quick reaction to this accident

 B. seldom had so serious an accident before

 C. had made full preparations for the accident

 D. didn't mind how many passengers the train can hold

B

The Beijing government has set out to recruit thousands of university graduates to work as junior officials in rural areas to both improve rural administration and ease the city's employment problems.

The government plans to recruit 3,000 university graduates this year, 1,000 more than last year, to work as assistants to village heads or Party secretaries in suburban areas.

People interested in jobs in Beijing's rural villages and townships can submit applications to Beijing Municipal Bureau of Personnel or online at www.bjbys.com from February 1 through March 15.

"We hope university graduates will seize this opportunity to use their knowledge in rural villages and to start their careers," said Sun Zhenyu, deputy director of Beijing Municipal Bureau of Personnel.

The government has promised successful candidates a monthly salary of 2,000 *yuan* in the first year, 2,500 *yuan* the second year and 3,000 *yuan* the third year, provided their performance is up to the required standards, Sun said.

Wang Lina, who graduated from Beijing Union University last year, was one of the first graduates to find work in the city's countryside. After majoring in industrial and commercial administration, Wang served as the assistant to the village head of Ertiaojie Village in suburban Beijing's Pinggu District. For one project, Wang contacted people at the Chinese Academy of Agricultural Sciences and arranged for the local farmers to receive training in strawberry planting. Her efforts paid off. The village had a plentiful harvest of organic strawberries earlier this year.

Nationwide, about 150,000 university graduates found employment in rural areas last year, according to figures provided by the Ministry of Education.

The ministry predicts that 4.95 million students will graduate from universities across the country this year, 820,000 more than last year. About 1.4 million of them are unlikely to find jobs when they graduate.

In Beijing, a record of 200,000 people are expected to graduate from university this year. Less than half of them are expected to be offered jobs, according to Beijing Municipal Bureau of personnel.

61. The underlined word "recruit" in the first paragraph probably means "_____".
   A. employ   B. force   C. encourage   D. train
62. We can see from the passage that _____.
   A. once you are hired as a junior official, you can get an endlessly rising salary
   B. the government guarantees a relatively high salary for the successful candidates
   C. working as junior officials is easy and very meaningful
   D. the competition for the job as junior officials is very fierce
63. From the story of Wang Lina we can learn that _____.
   A. the sooner you go to the countryside, the sooner you will be successful
   B. local farmers can get big harvests if they learn more knowledge
   C. university graduates can also realise their value in rural areas
   D. Wang had great difficulty in helping villagers plant organic strawberries
64. The last two paragraphs aim to tell us that _____.
   A. more and more graduates will work as junior officials
   B. the universities should not have so many students
   C. there are more and more graduates in recent years
   D. it is not easy for graduates to find jobs nowadays
65. Which of the following can be the best title for this passage?
   A. Go to the Countryside
   B. Job Hunting for University Graduates
   C. What Is the Best Career?
   D. A Good Choice for University Graduates

C

Psychiatrists (精神病专家) who work with older parents say that maturity can be a valuable thing in raising child — older parents are more thoughtful, use less physical discipline and spend more time with their children. But raising kids takes money and energy. Many older parents find themselves balancing their limited financial resources, declining energy and failing health against the growing demands of an active child. Dying and leaving young children is probably the older parents' biggest, and often unspoken, fear. Having late-life children, says an economics professor, often means parents, particularly fathers, "end up retiring much later". For many, retirement becomes an unobtainable dream.

Henry Metcalf, a 54-year-old journalist, knows it takes money to raise kids. But he's also worried that his energy will give out first. Sure, he can still ride bikes with his athletic fifth grader, but he's learnt that young at heart doesn't mean young. Lately he's been taking afternoon naps to keep up his energy. "My body is aging," says Metcalf. "You can't get away from that."

Often, older parents hear the ticking of another kind of biological clock. Therapists who work with middle-aged and older parents say fears about aging are nothing to laugh at. "They worry they'll be mistaken for grandparents, or that they'll need help getting up out of those little chairs in nursery school," says Joann Galst, a New York psychologist. But at the core of those little fears there is often a much bigger one, "that they won't be alive long enough to support and protect their child," she says.

Many late-life parents, though, say their children came at just the right time. After marrying late and undergoing years of fertility (受孕) treatment, Marilyn and her husband, Randy, had twins. "We both wanted children," says Marilyn, who was 55 when she gave birth. The twins have given the couple what they desired for years, "a sense of family".

Kids of older dads are often smarter, happier and more sociable because their fathers are more involved in their lives. "The dads are older, more mature," says Dr Silber, "and more ready to focus on parenting."

66. Why do psychiatrists regard maturity as a useful thing in raising child?

A. Because older parents can better balance their resources against children's demands.

B. Because older parents are usually more experienced in bringing up their children.

C. Because older parents are often better prepared financially.

D. Because older parents can take better care of their children.

67. What does the author mean by saying "For many, retirement becomes an unobtainable dream" in the first paragraph?

A. They can't make up their mind to retire when they reach their retirement age.

B. They can't obtain the retirement benefits they have dreamed of.

C. They can't get full pension unless they work some extra years.

D. They have to go on working beyond their retirement age to support the family.

68. The author gives the example of Henry Metcalf to show that _____.

A. many people are young in spirit despite their advanced age

B. taking afternoon naps is a good way to maintain energy

C. older parents tend to be concerned about their aging bodies

D. older parents should exercise more to keep up with their athletic children

69. What's the biggest fear of older parents according to New York psychologist Joann Galst?

    A. Being laughed at by other people.

    B. Slowing down of their pace of life.

    C. Being mistaken for grandparents.

    D. Approaching of death.

70. What do we learn about Marilyn and Randy?

    A. They thought they were an example of successful fertility treatment.

    B. Not until they had the twins did they feel they had formed a family.

    C. They believed that children born of older parents would be smarter.

    D. Not until they reached middle age did they think of having children.

D

There are many theories about the beginning of drama in ancient Greece. The one most widely accepted today is based on the assumption that drama evolved (演化) from ceremony. The argument for this view goes as follows.

In the beginning, human beings viewed the natural forces of the world — even the seasonal changes — as unpredictable, and they sought through various means to control these unknown and feared powers. Those measures which appeared to bring the desired results were then kept and repeated until they hardened into fixed ceremonies. Eventually stories arose which explained the mysteries of the ceremonies. As time passed some ceremonies were abandoned, but the stories, later called myths, remained and provided material for art and drama.

Those who believe that drama evolved out of ceremony also argue that those ceremonies contained the seed of theatre because music, dance, masks, and costumes were almost always used. Furthermore, a suitable site had to be provided for performances and when the entire community did not participate, a clear division was usually made between the "acting area" and the "auditorium". In addition, there were performers, and, since considerable importance was attached to avoiding mistakes in the performing of ceremonies, religious leaders usually took that task. Wearing masks and costumes, they often acted other people, animals, or supernatural beings, and imitated the desired effect — success in hunt or battle, the coming rain, etc — as an actor might. Eventually such dramatic representations were separated from religious activities.

Another theory traces (追溯) the theatre's origin from the human interest in storytelling. According to this view, tales (about the hunt, war, etc) are gradually developed, at first through the use of action and dialogue, and then through the assumption of each of the roles by a different person. A closely related theory traces theatre to those dances that are primarily rhythmical and gymnastic or that are imitations of animal movements and sounds.

71. Which is the best title for the passage?

    A. Religious Activities in Ancient Greece

    B. The Ceremonies in Ancient Greece

    C. Drama Theories

    D. The Origin of Greek Drama

72. According to the most widely accepted theory, drama _____.

    A. was played in memory of ancient Greek ceremonies

    B. was a form of ceremony played by ancient Greeks to control unknown powers

    C. evolved out of ancient Greek ceremonies

    D. was one of the measures Ancient Greeks took to view natural forces

73. What do drama and ancient ceremonies have in common according to the passage?

    A. Both of them were performed in theatres.

    B. Music, dance, masks, costumes and so on were contained in both of them.

    C. Religious leaders were in charge of both of them.

    D. Both of them were concerned about natural power.

74. In tracing the beginning of drama, which of the following is not mentioned?

    A. Planting.   B. Religious ceremonies.

    C. Gymnastics.   D. Storytelling.

75. It can be inferred from the passage that _____.

    A. human beings loved to tell stories

    B. people could do nothing about nature

    C. religious leaders tried to develop the effective form of drama

    D. religious activities played a very important role in the evolvement of drama

第四部分　书面表达（共两节，满分45分）

第一节　阅读表达（共5小题；每小题3分，满分15分）

阅读下面的短文，并根据短文后的要求答题。

    Help your child keep what he reads — an essential skill, especially as he gets older and needs to gain important information from textbooks.

    1. **Have him read aloud**. This forces him to go slower, which gives him more time to process what he reads. Plus, he's not only seeing the words, he's hearing them too.

    2. _____. Make sure your child gets lots of practice reading books that aren't too hard. He should recognise at least 90 percent of the words without any help. Stopping any more often than that to figure out a word makes it tough for him to focus on the overall meaning of the story.

    3. **Read to build fluency**. To gain meaning from text, your child needs to read quickly and smoothly — a skill known as fluency. Rereading familiar, simple books gives your child practice at decoding words quickly, so he'll become more fluent.

4. **Talk to the teacher**. If your child is struggling awfully with comprehension, he may need more help with his reading — for example, building his vocabulary or practising phonics skill.

5. **Supplement class reading**. If his class is studying a particular theme, look for easy-to-read books or magazines on the topic. Some prior knowledge will help him get prepared and make his way through tougher classroom texts.

6. **Talk about what he's reading**. This "verbal processing" helps him remember and think through the themes of the book. Ask questions before, during, and after a reading session.

For example:

Before reading: "What interests you in this book? What doesn't?"

During reading: "What's going on in the book? Is it turning out the way you thought it would?"

After reading: "Can you summarise the book? What did you like about it?"

76. What is the best title for this passage? (Please answer within 10 words.)

_____

77. Which sentence in the passage can be replaced by the following one?

It will benefit him a lot to get some knowledge about the topic before class.

_____

78. Fill in the blank in the third paragraph with proper words or phrases to complete the sentence. (Please answer within 10 words.)

_____

79. If your classmate has difficulty in reading English materials, what advice will you give him? (Please answer within 30 words.)

_____

_____

80. Translate the underlined sentence in the third paragraph into Chinese.

_____

第二节 写作（满分30分）

现在，在各种节日到来时，越来越多的人喜欢给亲朋好友发送电子贺卡（electronic card）。请你根据自己对电子贺卡的了解，用英语给某英文报纸写一篇阐述电子贺卡优越性的稿件。

词数要求：120～150词。

_____

_____

_____

_____

_____

_____

高考英语总复习点击与突破

顺序选修7

Module ① Basketball

📖 要点纵览

高考词汇	star, court, association, league, hold, title, centre, attend, average, per, steak, alongside, awesome, various, entire, deserve, outstanding, generation, live, half, coach, rely, selfish, nature, instant, hit, nationwide, boxing, upwards, angle, parallel, sock, absorb, bound, vest, abrupt, accelerate, bounce, appoint, typical, slim, stout, belly, obtain, circuit, aside, dip, commit, howl, bleed, cheek, pulse, confirm, dizzy, bandage, blanket, ambulance, apologise, sniff, weep, teamwork, scar, oval, pole, basis, version
常用短语	grow up, hold a record, be used to, name sb sth, find success as an actor, take possession of
实用句型	1. They have fantastic stories to tell about Michael Jordan, such as the time when he rescued the Bulls from ending a game in a tie. 2. But there is no doubt that he deserves the title "outstanding player of his generation".
交际用语	1. I'm really looking forward to it. 2. The Rockets and the Bulls are really hot at the moment. 3. Both teams showed a lot of character. 4. The period of overtime was fast and furious.

◆ **高考词汇**

1. attend

v. 1) 参加，出席，到场；2) 上 (学)，去 (教堂)

Only seven people attended the meeting.

All children between the ages of 5 and 16 must attend school.

辨 析

attend, go in for, join, join in, take part in

attend 指参加会议、仪式；上课、上学或听报告等。

go in for 着重指参加某项比赛或考试；从事；爱好等。

join 通常指参加或加入（某个团体或组织等），后面直接跟名词作宾语。

join in 后跟表示"活动"的名词，意为"参加（某活动）"，多指参加正在进行的活动。也可用 join sb in sth / doing sth，表示加入到某人的行列中一起做某事。

take part in 常指参加会议或群众性活动，强调参与其中并发挥作用。

They didn't attend the wedding.

She went in for a singing competition.

He joined the party in 1978.

Why didn't you join in the talk last night?

We often take part in physical labour.

2. absorb

v. 消减，缓冲

The solid walls absorbed much of the impact of the explosion.

3. apologise

v. 道歉，谢罪

You should apologise to your mother for your rudeness.

4. deserve

v. 应得，应受到 (奖赏或惩罚)

You've been working all morning — I think you deserve a rest.

I hit him but he deserved it.

> 拓 展
>
> apology *n.* 道歉
>
> He made a public apology for his remarks.

5. obtain

v. (尤指凭借自身努力、技能或工作等) 获得，得到

They've extended the growing season to obtain a larger crop.

Further information can be obtained from head office.

6. point

v. 指，指向

I could see her pointing at me and telling the other guests what I had said.

辨 析

point to / at, point out

point to / at 意思是"指着，指向"。

point out 意为"指出"。

He shook his head and pointed to a gate at the bottom of the field.

I wish you'd stop pointing that gun at men.

He pointed out the dangers of setting out without proper equipment.

7. doubt

n. 怀疑，不确信

➡ 常用短语：

be in doubt (对……的将来或成功) 不太有把握

beyond doubt 毫无疑问地

without (a) doubt 无疑地，确实地

doubt 的用法还有：

1) 与 about 或 as to 连用

  I have some doubt about his words.

  There can be no possible doubt as to their intention.

2) doubt 后还可接 whether / if 或 that 引导的从句。

  There is some doubt whether he is the best man for the job.

  I have no doubt that he will pass the examination.

v. 怀疑，不确信

主要用法有：

1) doubt + 名词

  I doubt the truth of the news.

2) doubt + whether / if 从句

  I doubt whether / if he will keep his word.

3) doubt + that 从句

  I don't doubt that our team will win.

◆ 常用短语

1. be / get / become used to (doing) sth

be / get / become used to (doing) sth 意思是"习惯于（做）某事"。

He is used to getting up early.

I'm sure I'll get used to the hard work.

辨析

be used to do sth, be / get / become used to doing sth 与 used to do sth 的区别

be used to do sth 意为 "被用来做某事"。

be / get / become used to (doing) sth 指 "习惯于（做）某事"。

used to do sth 意为 "过去常常做某事"。

Nylon is used to make stockings.

I shall probably oversleep as I am not used to getting up so early.

I used to like jazz when I was young.

2. hold a record

hold a record 意思是 "保持纪录"。

By the time he retired, Wilt held many NBA records.

3. grow up

grow up 意思是 "成长，成熟；兴起，发展"。

He never saw his father while he was growing up.

It was not until my marriage ended that I really grew up.

Many small toy factories have grown up and flourished in this area.

> ·········· 拓·展 ··········
>
> keep a record of 做记录
> break a record 打破纪录
> set a record 创造纪录
> Keep a record of any money you pay out.
> He broke the world record for the high jump.
> The Americans set a new world record in the sprint relay.

辨析

grow up, bring up

grow up 指的是主体长大。

bring up 指主体带大客体。

What do you want to be when you grow up?

She brought up three sons on her own.

◆ **实用结构**

with 结构

"with + *n.* / *pron.* + *adj.* / *adv.* / *prep.* / doing / done / to do" 是一种很常见的结构，在句子中可以作伴随状语或定语。

In summer, the students often have class with the door and windows open.

How can you lock the door with your guests in?

The girl, with a heavy bag on her back, walked slowly towards the top of the mountain.

She fell asleep with the light burning.

With different techniques used, different results can be obtained.

I can't go out with all these dishes to wash.

考试时间：45分钟　满分：100分

Ⅰ. 单项选择（共15小题；每小题1分，满分15分）

1. With summer coming on, the weather gets hot _____.
   A. little and little　　B. little by little　　C. bit and bit　　D. by and by

2. —Have you finished all of the exercises?
   —Yes, completely. _____ is left.
   A. Nothing　　B. No one　　C. Neither　　D. None

3. With the guide _____ the way, I think you will find the place soon.
   A. to lead　　B. led　　C. leading to　　D. leads

4. I think you have dropped _____ "r" in spelling "merry".
   A. an　　B. a　　C. the　　D. /

5. —Where is _____ guide?
   —He's standing in line to buy _____ tickets for us.
   A. a; the　　B. an; the　　C. the; /　　D. /; /

6. —Stay a bit longer. It's been such fun having you.
   —_____, but I've got an early start tomorrow morning.
   A. No Problem　　B. Thanks anyway　　C. All right　　D. Never mind

7. We'd better prepare a news bulletin about changes that _____ taken place in our hometown.
   A. has　　B. has been　　C. have　　D. have been

8. If I have made some mistakes, please point them _____ for me.
   A. at　　B. to　　C. out　　D. for

9. _____ invited, he won't attend such get-togethers.
   A. Until　　B. Unless　　C. Till　　D. Before

10. Knives are _____ cutting things.
    A. used to　　B. used by　　C. being used　　D. used for

11. This is the village where the hero was born and _____.
    A. brought up　　B. raising　　C. grown up　　D. growing up

12. The president spoke at the business meeting for nearly an hour without _____ his notes.
    A. bringing up　　B. referring to　　C. looking for　　D. trying on

13. I always wear a hat _____ I work in the garden.
    A. but　　B. since　　C. whether　　D. when

14. We wanted a new table for dinner, so Father bought _____ from a furniture department yesterday.
    A. it　　B. one　　C. them　　D. another

15. She said that the building would be finished by October, _____ I doubt very much.

　　A. that　　　　　　B. this　　　　　　C. when　　　　　D. which

II. 完形填空（共20小题；每小题1分，满分20分）

One evening after dinner Mr and Mrs Bond called a family meeting. "We've had to make a __1__ decision," Mr Bond announced. "You see, your mother has been offered a post as co-director of a TV station. __2__, the station is not here but in Chicago. After __3__ long and hard about it, we've __4__ that the right decision is to move to Chicago."

Marc looked __5__, while his sister Rachel breathlessly started asking when they'd be moving. "It's surprising but exciting!" she said. Marc simply said, "I can't leave my __6__. I'd rather stay here and live with Tommy Lyons!"

The Bonds hoped that by the time they moved to Chicago in August, Marc would grow more __7__ the idea of leaving. However, he showed no __8__ of accepting the decision, refusing to __9__ his belongings.

__10__ the morning of their move, Marc was nowhere to be found. His parents called Tommy Lyons' house, but Mrs Lyons said she hadn't seen Marc. Mrs Bond became increasingly __11__ while her husband felt angry with their son for behaving so __12__.

What they didn't know was that Marc had started to walk over to Tommy's house with a faint idea of __13__ in Lyons' attic (阁楼) for a few days. But as he walked along, all the __14__ landscape of his neighbourhood __15__ him of the things he and his family had done together: the green fence he and his mother had painted; the trees he and his sister used to __16__ while playing hide-and-seek; the park __17__ he and his father often took walks together. How much would these __18__ without his family, who made them special in the first place? Marc didn't take the __19__ to answer that question but instead, he hurried back to his house, __20__ if there were any boxes having the right size to hold his record collection.

1. A. different　　　B. quick　　　　　C. wise　　　　　D. final

2. A. Besides　　　　B. However　　　　C. Therefore　　　D. Even though

3. A. thinking　　　 B. quarrelling　　 C. complaining　　D. guessing

4. A. known　　　　 B. understood　　　C. concluded　　　D. insisted

5. A. shocked　　　　B. puzzled　　　　 C. happy　　　　　D. excited

6. A. classmates　　 B. friends　　　　 C. neighbours　　 D. parents

7. A. delighted at　　B. pleased with　　C. used to　　　　D. worried about

8. A. ways　　　　　 B. signs　　　　　 C. interests　　　D. hopes

9. A. pack　　　　　 B. collect　　　　 C. tie　　　　　　D. pile

10. A. Before　　　　B. In　　　　　　 C. On　　　　　　D. During

11. A. anxious　　　　B. angry　　　　　C. frightened　　 D. miserable

12. A. rudely　　　　 B. wildly　　　　　C. irresponsibly　D. naughtily

92

13. A. hiding   B. staying   C. sleeping   D. playing

14. A. beautiful   B. familiar   C. splendid   D. modern

15. A. recalled   B. remembered   C. warned   D. reminded

16. A. plant   B. water   C. climb   D. walk

17. A. which   B. where   C. that   D. what

18. A. cost   B. value   C. mean   D. measure

19. A. time   B. courage   C. strength   D. patience

20. A. looking   B. wondering   C. asking   D. expecting

III. 阅读理解（共10小题；每小题2分，满分20分）

A

In the United States the most popular form of folk dancing since the earliest days has been square-dancing. In those days, men and women worked in groups to build a house or harvest crops. When the work was done, they usually danced merrily and happily in a store or in a farm kitchen.

A square is formed by four couples who stand facing the centre of the square. Each couple stands on one side of the square with the boy on the left and the girl on the right.

Large or small numbers of people can dance at one time. Sometimes 800 or 1,000 people may be dancing all the same time. Or there may be one square of eight people.

<u>Costumes</u> are worn by those who do the square-dance. This makes the dancing more colourful to watch. Women often wear full skirts of different colours with a pretty blouse. Men may have coloured shirts and Western trousers they wear only when they are square-dancing. In some country areas, everyone wears his best clothes.

Today in all parts of the US you will find some schools, clubs, or other groups that are square-dancing for fun.

1. In the early time people did square-dance _____.

   A. before they did something important

   B. when they were getting in crops

   C. after they finished their work

   D. when they were building a house

2. If 1,000 people dance at the same time, how many squares can be formed?

   A. Just 100 big squares.   B. Less than 100 small squares.

   C. 250 squares.   D. As many as 125.

3. The underlined word "costumes" in the fourth paragraph means _____.

   A. special clothes people wear on particular days

   B. clothes people wear when working

   C. something people wear round the neck

   D. something expensive and beautiful

4. Which of the following is TRUE according to the passage?

   A. One can join in square-dancing in a hotel every evening.

   B. Some squares are made up of young girls.

   C. Square-dancing party is usually held in the morning.

   D. People, old or young, women or men enjoy square-dancing.

5. Square-dancing _____.

   A. used to be a sport in the club   B. is now popular all over the US

   C. has disappeared long   D. can only be seen in the country

B

   Most recent British graduates do not have an independent financial advisor. Most enter their first job already in debt. The average student debt in Britain has risen by more than 50 percent in the past four years and is now between 10,000 and 12,000 pounds.

   The priority (需优先考虑的事) for most is to get into credit — few have the cash to spare for investing (投资) in their future. The charity Age Concern says that 43 percent of 25- to 34-year-olds are not saving towards a pension and those that are, are not saving enough.

   Some students, however, can afford to start looking ahead while still at university. These students can get maximum amount of cash from their banks' interest-free overdraft (透支) (about 1,500 pounds) allowance, or take out low-interest student loans and put the money into a high-interest savings account. They can leave university with 10,000 pounds in credit, rather than in debt.

   We hope this is one lesson that secondary school children will be learning before they go to university.

6. The passage mainly tells _____.

   A. that most recent British graduates leave university in debt

   B. that the writer criticises the British young for not thinking about their future life

   C. how some students think of a good idea to get through their higher education

   D. what secondary school children can learn from their seniors

7. The word "credit" in the following sentences "The priority for most is to get into credit…" and "They can leave university with 10,000 pounds in credit, rather than in debt." means "_____" and "_____".

   A. payment at a later date for buying things; money received in payment

   B. good or positive things; very favourable reputation

   C. the source of honour; influence based on the good opinion or confidence of others

   D. money lent by a bank to a customer; money one has in a bank account

8. The underlined phrase "looking ahead" in the third paragraph means _____.

   A. directing one's eyes forward

B. considering and making plans for the future

C. turning one's head over the shoulder

D. worrying about studies

9. How do some of the university students get out of financial difficulty?

A. They borrow money from banks.

B. They borrow money from banks, and delay the payment or don't pay back the money.

C. They try to obtain low-interest loans and put the money in a high-interest account.

D. They are working while studying.

10. What can be inferred from the passage?

A. Most British university students can't afford their schooling and other expenses.

B. British parents aren't willing to support their children through their higher education.

C. It is not easy for students to finish their studies.

D. British government doesn't spend enough funds on education.

IV. 阅读表达（共5小题；每小题3分，满分15分）

Everybody's blood is red, but it's not all the same. There are eight blood types, described by the letters A, B, and O. Those letters stand for certain proteins (蛋白质) found in the red blood cells. Not everyone has the same proteins.

In addition to getting a letter or two, a person's blood is either "positive" or "negative". That doesn't mean one person's blood is good and another person's blood is bad. It's a way of keeping track of whether someone's blood has a certain protein called Rh protein. This protein is called "Rh" because scientists found it while studying Rhesus monkeys. If your blood is positive, you have this protein. _____, you don't. Either way is totally fine.

People have one of these eight different blood types:

A negative, A positive, B negative, B positive, O negative, O positive, AB negative, AB positive.

Blood types are important if a person wants to donate blood or needs a blood transfusion. Getting blood of the wrong type can make a person sick. That's why hospitals and blood banks are very careful with donated blood and make sure the person gets the right type.

Someone might need a blood transfusion when they're sick or if they lose blood. Without enough healthy blood, the body won't get the oxygen and energy it needs. Healthy blood also protects you from germs and other invaders.

Now that you know how important blood is, what will you do? Kids generally aren't allowed to donate blood, but when you're older, consider giving the gift of life!

1. What is the best title for the passage? (Please answer within 10 words.)

_____

2. Which sentence in the passage can be replaced by the following one?

   If your blood is not healthy enough, your body won't get the necessary oxygen and energy.

_____

3. Fill in the blank in the second paragraph with proper words or phrases to complete the sentence. (Please answer within 10 words.)

_____

4. Why are hospitals and blood banks very careful about blood transfusion? (Please answer within 30 words.)

_____

_____

5. Translate the underlined sentence in the second paragraph into Chinese.

_____

Ⅴ．写作（满分30分）

假设你是陈卫，从第一中学毕业一年了。你准备召集一次同学聚会，请你根据下面的提示给你的同学李强写一封邀请信。

提示：1. 时间：7月20日上午10点；

      2. 地点：中山路20号，乘22路公共汽车可直达；

      3. 联系电话：94673413；

      4. 请他出席。大家都希望他来，如果不能来，请他务必在7月10日前写信或打电话告知。

词数要求：120～150词。

_____

_____

_____

_____

Module ②

Highlights of My Senior Year

要点纵览

高考词汇	forever, settle, elect, suit, rent, attract, consider, develop, activity, ability, tradition, recite, alphabet, institution, sew, woollen, suitcase, luggage, innocent, pillow, quilt, worn, armchair, shabby, cushion, kettle, decoration, curtain, washroom, basin, bathtub, sob, arithmetic, multiply, algebra, geometry, concept, cubic, acre, gram, microscope, regulation, punctual, T-shirt, weekday, upset, polish, zipper, button, mailbox, airmail, fortnight, scholarship, cheer, course
常用短语	look back at, work as, a real success, go on a trip, quite a few times, be pleased about, have one's hair specially done, as far as I'm concerned, in other words, to one's disappointment, once a fortnight
实用句型	1. I feel too excited to think clearly! 2. It seems strange to think that in a few days' time I'll be walking out of the school gate forever. 3. It took two hours but it was worth it, as everyone told me I looked very elegant! 4. It's a great pity that it's probably the last time this will happen. 5. This was so unexpected, and I can't tell you how good this made me feel! 6. It was not until the 1920s that pompoms began to play an important part in cheerleading.
交际用语	1. Let's get going. 2. It's up to you. 3. She's really got something. 4. We're through. 5. I'm with you on that.

◆ **高考词汇**

1. settle

v. 1) 解决；2) 定居，使定居

We settled the dispute among ourselves.

My son has settled in America.

We are settled in our new home.

真 题 解 析

With a lot of difficult problems _____, the newly elected president is having a hard time. (2002 上海)

A. settled　　　　　B. settling　　　　　C. to settle　　　　　D. being settled

解析：A、C、D 都可以用在这个 with 结构中作宾补，settled 表示"已经解决"，being settled 表示"正在被解决"，而 to settle 表示"有待解决"。根据句意，答案为 C。

2. competitive

adj. 1) 充满竞争的；2) 好强的，好竞争的

He quit playing competitive football at the age of 24.

She has a reputation for being a fiercely competitive player.

3. consider

v. 1) 考虑，细想；2) 认为，料想；3) 体贴，关心

I am considering going abroad.

We considered him to have broken the window.

We must consider his physical condition.

4. develop

v. 1) 发展；2) 生长；3) 提高，改善；4) 冲洗 (底片)

Several industries are developing in this area.

> **拓 展**
>
> compete *v.* 竞争，竞赛
>
> competitively *adv.* 竞争地，好竞争地
>
> competitor *n.* 竞争者
>
> competition *n.* 竞争，竞赛
>
> You'll be competing against the best athletes in the world.
>
> If the value of the pound falls, our exports will be more competitively priced.
>
> All our major competitors are also bidding for the contract.
>
> They are faced with fierce competition.

> **拓 展**
>
> consideration *n.* 考虑
>
> considering *prep.* 考虑到
>
> One of the possibilities under consideration is closing the street to motor vehicles.
>
> They've made remarkable progress, considering they only started last week.

Plants develop from seeds.

Some children develop more slowly than others.

He is trying to develop his skill.

I had the photos developed yesterday.

拓 展

development *n.* 发展；培养

We encourage our staff in their development of new skills.

辨 析

a developing country 发展中国家

a developed country 发达国家

5. upset

v. 使心烦意乱

adj. 心烦的；不适的，不舒服的

I'm sorry. I didn't mean to upset you.

James was upset because he had lost his ticket.

They felt too upset to talk about the incident.

I went to see the doctor this afternoon because I had an upset stomach.

6. outdoor

adj. 室外的，户外的，野外的

It was outdoor work.

拓 展

outdoors *adv.* (在) 户外，(在) 野外

n. 野外

The cat lives mainly outdoors.

We enjoyed the great outdoors last weekend.

辨 析

indoor *adj.* 室内的

indoors *adv.* 在户内

There is an indoor swimming pool in our school.

Don't stay indoors since the weather is so fine.

7. worn

adj. 1) 用旧的；2) 疲倦的

a pair of worn blue jeans

His face looked worn and sad.

8. suit

v. 1) 适合，对……方便；2) 使显得漂亮；适合于；3) 使感到满意

—Does Sunday suit you?

—Yes, it suits me fine.

The new dress suited her very well.

The climate here suits me very well.

He suited his speech to his audience.

suit, fit, match

suit 多指合乎需要、口味、性格、条件或地位等。

fit 多指大小、尺寸合适，有时可引申为"吻合"。

match 多指大小、色调、形状或性质等方面的搭配。

Does the time suit you?

No dish suits all tastes.

This coat fits me well.

Try the new key and see if it fits the keyhole.

These shoes do not match; one is large and the other is small.

His deeds don't match his words.

◆ 常用短语

1. quite a few

quite a few 意思是"很多"，修饰可数名词。

His encouragement inspired quite a few people to take up skiing.

➡ 近义短语：

quite a lot / bit 许多，大量

With a penny you could buy quite a lot of sweets in those days.

There's still quite a bit of snow on the ground.

2. have fun

have fun 意思是"玩得开心"，fun 是不可数名词。

We had great fun racing each other down the ski slopes.

We haven't had such fun for years.

辨 析

for fun 意思是"闹着玩儿地，为了好玩儿"。

make fun of 意思是"嘲笑、取笑"。

I made those small toys just for fun.

The other children made fun of her because she was always so serious.

真 题 解 析

This is not a match. We're playing chess just for _____. (2001 上海)

A. habit   B. hobby   C. fun   D. game

解析：这句话的意思是：这不是比赛，我们下棋是为了好玩儿。答案为 C。

3. as far as I'm concerned

as far as I'm concerned 意思是"据我所知，就我而言"。

As far as I'm concerned, the issue is over.

➡ 同义短语：

as far as I know

As far as I know, the whole thing will cost £500.

 综合训练

考试时间：45分钟　满分：100分

I. 单项选择（共15小题；每小题1分，满分15分）

1. _____ a train was attacked by terrorists on March 11 is true.
   A. When   B. Where   C. That   D. /

2. _____ caused the accident is still a complete mystery.
   A. What   B. That   C. How   D. Where

3. _____ is a fact that English people and American people share a lot of customs.
   A. There   B. This   C. That   D. It

4. _____ a pity that I didn't see you last week.
   A. That's   B. What's   C. It's   D. There's

5. _____ we do must be in the interests of the people.
   A. How   B. Which   C. Whatever   D. That

6. What _____ it is to travel in _____ spaceship!
   A. a fun; a   B. fun; a   C. the fun; a   D. a fun; the

7. It's already 9 o'clock and mother _____ come here any moment.
   A. likely   B. possible   C. is likely to   D. is possible to

8. When first _____ to the market, these products enjoyed great success.
   A. introducing   B. introduced   C. introduce   D. being introduced

9. A cook will be immediately fired if he is found _____ in the kitchen.
   A. smoke   B. smoking   C. to smoke   D. smoked

10. The manager is considering _____ another secretary.
    A. to hire   B. hiring   C. to take   D. to employ

11. The flu is believed _____ by viruses that like to reproduce in the cells inside the human nose and throat.
    A. causing   B. being caused   C. to be caused   D. to have caused

12. Don't forget _____ the book to the library when you finish _____ it.
    A. to return; reading   B. to return; to read
    C. returning; reading   D. returning; to read

13. —You forgot your purse when you went out.
    —Good heavens, _____.
    A. so did I   B. so I did   C. I did so   D. I so did

101

14. —Peter has grown taller than before recently.

    —_____, and _____.

    A. So he has; so have you   B. So he has; so you have

    C. So has he; so have you   D. So has he; so you have

15. The English Evening was _____ last night.

    A. succeed   B. a success   C. successfully   D. success

II. 完形填空（共20小题；每小题1分，满分20分）

    Every kid wishes to be an adult. But now as grown-ups, some adults find they cannot __1__. They become "kidults (kid + adult) ". Being a kidult has become a __2__ choice among __3__ people across Asia.

    Some kidults collect __4__ they once played with. Hello Kitty, Garfield, and Snoopy have many adult __5__ around the world. It is not __6__ to see a 20-something woman with a big, Garfield-shaped cushion on her sofa or a Hello Kitty mobile phone accessory.

    Other kidults still __7__ children's stories and fairy tales. __8__, Bloomsbury even released an adult __9__ of the Harry Potter novels with an adult cover. __10__, no one else on the subway will __11__ that an adult is actually reading a children's book!

    "Kidults can be like __12__ to society. Adults who __13__ their childhood and hold on to pure, childlike emotion may be needed in such a __14__ and dry society," said Lee So-jung, professor at Hankuk University of Foreign Studies (韩国外国语大学). He added that kidult culture may __15__ the generation gap between adults and kids. It could give children and their parents books, movies, and cartoon shows to enjoy __16__. He may be right.

    Tim Greenhalgh, a professor in London explained that some kidults just __17__ grow up. They cling to (放不下) childhood because life in a busy and stressful (压力大的) city __18__ them. Kidults would like to forget their __19__ and __20__ show their fear of society and adulthood.

1. A. face the fact   B. leave childhood behind

   C. live independently   D. stand the stress

2. A. lifestyle   B. professional   C. smart   D. first

3. A. young   B. serious   C. female   D. older

4. A. memories   B. characters   C. games   D. toys

5. A. readers   B. sections   C. friends   D. fans

6. A. strange   B. natural   C. common   D. unusual

7. A. find   B. buy   C. keep   D. enjoy

8. A. For example   B. No wonder   C. Such as   D. Even though

9. A. edition   B. copy   C. type   D. series

10. A. Indeed   B. As a result   C. So that   D. That way

11. A. believe   B. watch   C. think   D. know

12. A. time   B. dreams   C. vitamins   D. water

13. A. cherish   B. escape   C. hate   D. seek

14. A. fast   B. changeable   C. developed   D. rough

15. A. fill   B. replace   C. enlarge   D. affect

16. A. freely   B. frequently   C. sometimes   D. together

17. A. wait to   B. expect to   C. stop to   D. refuse to

18. A. tires   B. frightens   C. changes   D. controls

19. A. situation   B. puzzles   C. age   D. future

20. A. openly   B. somehow   C. just   D. hardly

III. 阅读理解（共10小题；每小题2分，满分20分）

A

Deep inside a mountain near Sweetwater in East Tennessee is a body of water known as the Lost Sea. It is listed by *Guinness World Records* as the world's second largest underground lake. The Lost Sea is part of an extensive and historic cave system called Craighead Caverns.

The caverns have been known and used since the days of the Cherokee Indian nation. The cave expands into a series of huge rooms from a small opening on the side of the mountain. Approximately one mile from the entrance, in a room called "The Council Room", many Indian artifacts have been found. Some of the items discovered include pottery, arrowheads, weapons and jewellery.

For many years there were persistent rumors of a large underground lake somewhere in a cave, but it was not discovered until 1905. In that year, a 13-year-old boy named Ben Sands crawled through a small opening 300 feet underground. He found himself in a large cave half filled with water.

Today tourists visit the Lost Sea and ride far out onto it in glass-bottomed boats powered by electric motors. More than 13 acres of water have been mapped out so far and still no end of the lake has been found. Even though teams of divers have tried to explore the Lost Sea, the full extent of it is still unknown.

1. According to the passage, the Craighead Caverns have been known _____.

  A. throughout history

  B. since the time of the Indian nations

  C. since 1905

  D. since divers explored them

2. What was found in "The Council Room"?

  A. A small natural opening.

  B. A large cave.

C. Another series of rooms.

D. Many old Indian objects.

3. Who located the Lost Sea in recent times?

    A. The Cherokee Indians.   B. Tourists.

    C. Ben Sands.   D. Scientists.

4. According to the passage, how can the caverns be entered?

    A. From an opening in a mountainside.

    B. By diving into the water.

    C. By riding far out onto the lake.

    D. From "The Council Room".

5. It can be inferred from the passage that the Craighead Caverns presently serve as

_____.

    A. an underground testing site

    B. an Indian meeting ground

    C. a tourist attraction

    D. a motorboat race course

B

"Bang! Bang!" Setting off firecrackers is the happiest part of Spring Festival for most Chinese kids. But these firecrackers can also be dangerous. Therefore, many big Chinese cities began to ban them in the 1990s.

Good news arrived for teens in Beijing in 2005. The ban on firecrackers was <u>lifted</u> on September 9. It has added much fun to Spring Festival in the capital.

According to Chinese custom, lighting firecrackers is a must on the Chinese Lunar New Year, because people believe they can drive away demons and ill luck for the coming year. Their beautiful colours and big sound also bring much joy and jubilation (欢乐) during this most important Chinese festival. But since the ban in 1993, people in Beijing complained that Spring Festival was too quiet and not traditional enough. Some even worried that if the ban continued, the next generation would only know through books the custom of lighting firecrackers. This would be a great loss for tradition. Everybody knows that we can't give up eating for the slight risk of choking (噎住). So in recent years, many cities have resumed the old customs at the request of local residents.

However, every year there are kids injured by setting off firecrackers in a dangerous way. So while enjoying yourself, please bear safety in mind. No matter how much fun firecrackers are, the most important thing is to keep away from danger.

6. The ban on firecrackers has been questioned for the following reasons EXCEPT

_____.

    A. firecrackers are traditionally believed to be a symbol of happiness

B. the beautiful colours and big sound of firecrackers bring great joy to the children

C. it was unacceptable to change folk tradition handed down from our forefathers

D. the ban has played an active role in keeping public security and normal social order

7. The underlined word "lifted" in the second paragraph refers to "_____".

A. something is raised to a high level or position

B. something is taken from its resting place

C. the restrictions are removed

D. rise

8. What's the author's attitude towards lifting the ban on firecrackers?

A. He is firmly against it because firecrackers make great noise.

B. He is in favour of the idea but reminds people of safety.

C. He is neither against nor for it.

D. He is afraid that firecrackers can cause danger.

9. What is implied but not stated in the passage?

A. For security and environmental protection, the ban on firecrackers should continue.

B. People must bear safety in mind while lighting firecrackers.

C. Beijingers would enjoy a different Spring Festival accompanied by firecrackers in 2006.

D. Firecrackers would add much fun to the coming Spring Festival in the capital.

10. The passage may be best entitled "_____".

A. Keep Away from Firecrackers

B. Beijing's Lifting Twelve-year Ban on Firecrackers

C. To Ban or Not to Ban

D. Bear Safety in Mind

Ⅳ. 阅读表达（共5小题；每小题3分，满分15分）

The percentage of students who go into further education is seen as a key factor in the development of a country's social and economic infrastructure. In the UK, about 33 percent of 18-years-olds opt to go into further education, whereas in the USA, the figure is near half.

A new survey suggests that a lot of students who apply to university may not be taking the best option. In Britain, the university acceptance ratio is anything from one in two applications to one in 12, which means there is serious competition for the best university places. Not getting into the university of their choice can have a serious effect on students' self-esteem (自尊), and some students do so badly at interview that they become traumatised (受伤的) by the process.

The survey quotes examples of the experiences of different students. Five years ago, for example, Alan Hill _____ after just one term and started his own business.

"I felt instinctively that a history degree wasn't the best use of my time, despite the warnings of my tutors and the protest of my parents, I dropped out and set up my own company. It's been an unqualified success. In fact, I've just taken on two extremely clever people who also dropped out after their first year at university, both of whom could have sailed through a degree. Instead, they're doing useful work and earning money." Elaine Lawrence has a different opinion, but knows from her own experience that people can make mistakes when they choose what to study.

"Somewhat reluctantly, I took the advice of my maths teacher and studies applied mathematics. I loved it but now I'm working in a bank, which I don't really like very much. My brother, on the other hand, started a business course and hated every minute of it. After the first year, he realised that what he really wanted was to be a nurse, so he dropped out and did a nursing diploma. Now he works in a hospital and is really happy. It just goes to show that it can take time before you know if you've made the right decision."

1. What is the passage mainly about? (Please answer within 10 words.)

_____

2. Fill in the blank in the third paragraph with proper words or phrases to complete the sentence. (Please answer within 10 words.)

_____

3. What does Alan Hill's experience imply? (Please answer within 10 words.)

_____

4. What does Elaine Lawrence and her brother's experience prove? (Please answer within 20 words.)

_____

5. Translate the underlined sentence in the second paragraph into Chinese.

_____

Ⅴ. 写作（满分30分）

假设你是李平，现在在朝阳中学学习。你得知你的朋友刘英今年考入了北京大学，请你按照下面的提示给她写一封信。可适当增加细节，以使行文连贯。信的开头和结尾已经给出，不计入总词数。

提示：1. 向刘英表示祝贺；

2. 说明她能考上北京大学的原因：她一向学习努力，各门功课都很出色，功夫不负有心人；

3. 你的决心和打算。

词数要求：80～100词。

Dear Liu Ying,

_____

_____

_____

_____

Wish you greater achievements in your college years.

Yours,
Li Ping

Module ③

Literature

高考词汇	novelist, eager, appetite, desperate, seize, rough, drag, escape, prison, wedding, intend, cast, distribute, chapter, sparrow, seagull, pipe, smog, choke, swallow, rag, dustbin, attain, nutrition, starvation, welfare, concern, taxpayer, compass, anchor, inn, carrier, accumulate, corporation, navy, pile, paperwork, trial, pump, fountain, pub, maid, bunch, accomplish, ambassador, pedestrian, lantern, mourn
常用短语	ask for, become wild with hunger, next to, be desperate with, rise from the table, in astonishment / excitement, in a weak voice, hit sb on the head, disagree with, put up a notice, be sure of, suffer from, put sb in prison, pay bills, in one's early thirties, bring sth to the attention of sb, a large number of, as a result of
实用句型	1. It was Oliver Twist who was chosen. 2. Frightened by his own courage, he said, "Please sir, I want some more." 3. Never have I heard anything like it!
交际用语	1. Thank goodness. 2. What's going on? 3. It will do him good. 4. You rascal!

◆ **高考词汇**

1. serve

v. 1) 为……服务；服役；2) 接待 (顾客)；端上 (饭菜等)，送上 (食物或饮料等)；3) 提供 (货物或服务)

He served more than 20 years in the army.

The school board members serve a two-year term.

There was no one in the shop to serve me.

What kind of wine should we serve?

We are well served with gas in this town.

2. whisper

n. & v. 低语；耳语

"They're coming," he said in an excited whisper.

He whispered to me that he failed in the maths exam.

➡ 常用短语：

in a whisper / whispers 低声地

He answered in a whisper.

They were talking in whispers.

3. seize

v. 1) 抓住，捉住；2) 掌握，理解；3) 夺取，攻占；4) (常用被动) (疾病) 侵袭

Did you see the cat seize the mouse?

She seized him by the arm. (= She seized his arm.)

He immediately seized her idea.

The enemy army seized the city.

The child was seized with a slight fever.

4. intend

v. 1) 打算，想要，计划；2) 意指，意思是

intend 的常用表达有：

1) intend + *n.* / doing / to do / that 从句

　　We intended no harm.

　　I intended coming / to come back soon.

　　They intend that this reform shall be carried through this year.

2) be intended for

　　This book is intended for you.

5. concern

n. 关心；担心

v. 关系到，对……有影响

The main cocern is that the health of the employees will be at risk.

The energy problem concerns us all.

➡ 常用短语：

be concerned about sb / sth 担心，操心

Please don't be concerned about me.

We are all concerned about her safety.

6. eager

adj. 渴望的，热切的

He was eager for success.

They listened to his story with eager attention.

辨 析

eager, anxious

eager 强调对成功的期望或进取的热情，含有积极向上的意思。

anxious 强调担心或焦急，表达对结果感到不安的意思。

I am eager to do that interesting work.

I am anxious to know the news from the battlefield.

◆ **常用短语**

1. 与 feed 有关的短语

1) feed...on 意思是 "用……喂养"。

The little girl feeds the cat on fish.

2) feed...to 意思是 "把……喂给"。

I wouldn't feed that stinking meat to my dog.

3) feed on 意思是 "以……为主食"。

Cattle feed chiefly on grass.

2. suffer from

suffer from 意思是 "受……之苦，患有"。

She often suffers from headaches.

◆ **实用结构**

1. 强调句型：It is / was + 被强调部分 + that / who + 句子的其他部分

1) 强调主语

It was a lady that / who replied.

2) 强调宾语

It was a bag that Oliver was holding.

3) 强调时间状语

It was yesterday that the accident took place.

4) 强调地点状语

It was in the street that I met Li Ming.

5) 强调原因状语

It was because he got up late that he didn't get to school on time.

注意：

1) 当强调人时，可用 who 代替 that。如：

It was Oliver who was locked in a room.

2) 当强调 not...until 句型时，强调句型有如下变化：

He didn't go to bed until his father came back.

→ It was not until his father came back that he went to bed.

真 题 解 析

— _____ that he managed to get the information?

— Oh, a friend of his helped him. (2005 山东)

A. Where was it   B. What was it   C. How was it   D. Why was it

解析：此题为特殊疑问句变强调句型，其结构为"特殊疑问词 + is it + that...?"。根据答语，此题应选择由 how 引导的语句。答案为 C。

2. 倒装句常见的几种情况

1) 在以 here，there，now，then，out，in，into，up，down，away 或 off 等副词开头的句子里，用完全倒装语序表示强调。

Here comes the bus.

There goes the bell.

Into the hall came three women.

Down came the rain.

注意：当主语是代词时，不倒装。

—Look! Here comes the teacher.

—Oh, here he comes.

2) only 所修饰的副词、介词短语或状语从句放在句首时，主句用半倒装形式。

Only in this way can you succeed.

注意：当 only 修饰主语时，不倒装。

Only he can work out the problem.

3) hardly, never, not only, little, seldom, scarcely, rarely, nowhere, no sooner...than, not until, at no time, by no means, hardly / scarcely...when... 等副词或连词放在句首时，

句子用半倒装形式。

No sooner had I walked into the room than the phone rang.

4) 地点状语放在句首，表示强调，句子用完全倒装形式。

By the window stood an old man; he seemed very sad.

In a lecture hall of a university in England sits a professor.

5) "so + 助动词/系动词/情态动词 + 主语"表示前面所陈述的情况也适用于后者。

"neither / nor + 助动词/系动词/情态动词 + 主语"表示前一否定的情况也适用于后者。

I love sports, so does my father.

You don't care much for sweets, neither / nor do I.

真 题 解 析

1) Never before _____ in greater need of modern public transport than it is today. (2005 上海)

　 A. has this city been 　 B. this city has been 　　 C. was this city 　　 D. this city was

解析：否定副词 never 放在句首，应用倒装语序。由 never before 判断，该句时态应该是现在完成时。答案为 A。

2) Only after my friend came _____. (2005 福建)

　 A. did the computer repair 　　　　　　　 B. he repaired the computer

　 C. was the computer repaired 　　　　　　 D. the computer was repaired

解析：only 加状语从句放在句首，句子要用倒装语序。computer 与 repair 之间应为被动关系，所以应该使用被动语态。答案为 C。

综合训练

考试时间：45分钟 　满分：100分

I. 单项选择（共15小题；每小题1分，满分15分）

1. _____ can you expect to get a pay rise.

　 A. With hard work 　　　　　　　　　　 B. Although work hard

　 C. Only with hard work 　　　　　　　　 D. Now that he works hard

2. It was for this reason _____ her uncle moved out of New York and settled down in a small village.

　 A. which 　　　　 B. why 　　　　　　 C. that 　　　　　 D. how

3. _____ was in 1979 _____ I graduated from the university.

　 A. That; that 　　 B. It; that 　　　　 C. That; when 　　 D. It; when

4. It was not _____ she took off her glasses _____ I realised she was a famous film star.

　 A. when; that 　　 B. until; that 　　　 C. until; when 　　 D. when; then

5. It was in the park _____ I met his uncle the day before yesterday.

    A. that   B. where   C. when   D. in which

6. Who is it _____ is waiting outside the room?

    A. who   B. whom   C. which   D. that

7. Just as the soil is a part of the earth, _____ is the atmosphere.

    A. that   B. such   C. so   D. it

8. Hardly _____ when it began to rain.

    A. had he got home   B. he had got home   C. did he go home   D. he went home

9. Only in this way _____.

    A. we can well do it   B. can we well do it

    C. we can do it well   D. can we do it well

10. Not only _____ but also she likes singing.

    A. she likes painting   B. does she like painting

    C. she liked painting   D. she did like painting

11. She's been _____ to work every day.

    A. used to driving   B. used to drive   C. used for driving   D. used driving

12. My brother got married _____.

    A. in his early twenties   B. in his early twenty

    C. on his early twenties   D. on his early twenty

13. It _____ child poverty _____ the attention of the public, and for this reason alone it is a very important novel.

    A. brought; to   B. caught; to   C. paid; to   D. got; on

14. He stared at me _____ astonishment.

    A. for   B. in   C. on   D. of

15. Millions of people became homeless _____ the big earthquake.

    A. with the result of   B. with the result   C. as a result   D. as a result of

Ⅱ. 完形填空（共20小题；每小题1分，满分20分）

    I watch her and her mother decorate her college dormitory room. Everything is in place, organised and arranged. Her room nicely accommodates not only her clothes and bric-a-brac (小饰品), but her __1__ as well. I begin to accept that her room at home is no longer hers. It is now ours, our room for her when she __2__.

    I __3__ myself thinking of when I cradled her in my arms, in the chair alongside my wife's hospital bed. One day old. So __4__, so beautiful, so perfect, so __5__ dependent on her new, __6__ parents. How time flies!

    Now she looks up, catching me __7__ at her, causing her to say to her mother, "Mum, Dad's looking at me __8__."

    These days, I touch her arm, her face — anything — __9__ that when my wife and I return home, she will not be with us, and there will be nothing to __10__. I have so much to say, but no __11__ with which to say it.

My __12__ changed from the day I drove this child home from the hospital. I saw myself __13__ that day, and it has led to a lot of places that I would never have found on my own.

She says, "It'll be all right, Dad. I'll be home from school __14__." I tell her she will have a great year but I say little else. I am afraid somehow to speak and I only hold on to our goodbye hug a little longer, a little __15__.

I gaze into her eyes and __16__ to go. My wife's eyes follow her as she leaves us. __17__ do not. Maybe if I don't look, I can imagine that she really hasn't __18__; I know that what she is embarking upon (开始) is exciting and wonderful. I remember what the world looked like to me __19__ everything was new.

As I walk to the car with my wife at my side, my eyes are wet, my heart is sore, and I realise that my life is __20__.

1. A. sister's   B. teacher's   C. mother's   D. roommate's
2. A. lives   B. visits   C. separates   D. graduates
3. A. force   B. leave   C. find   D. has
4. A. small   B. big   C. funny   D. strong
5. A. severely   B. totally   C. slightly   D. strictly
6. A. untested   B. experienced   C. qualified   D. casual
7. A. laughing   B. staring   C. glaring   D. looking
8. A. funny   B. frightening   C. kind   D. sad
9. A. expecting   B. imagining   C. knowing   D. doubting
10. A. see   B. touch   C. kiss   D. hug
11. A. sentence   B. quotes   C. saying   D. words
12. A. day   B. career   C. life   D. age
13. A. easily   B. carefully   C. differently   D. seriously
14. A. quick   B. soon   C. fast   D. rapidly
15. A. gentler   B. softer   C. tighter   D. warmer
16. A. start   B. turn   C. run   D. wonder
17. A. Hers   B. My wife's   C. Mine   D. Ours
18. A. gone   B. grown   C. born   D. found
19. A. although   B. so long as   C. when   D. every time
20. A. destroying   B. beginning   C. ending   D. changing

III. 阅读理解（共10小题；每小题2分，满分20分）

A

I entered high school having read hundreds of books. But I was not a good reader. Merely bookish, I lacked a point of view when I read. Rather, I read in order to get a point of view. I searched books for good expressions and sayings, pieces of information, ideas, themes — anything to enrich my thought and make me feel educated. When one of my teachers suggested to his sleepy 10th-grade English class that a person could not have a "complicated idea" until he had read at least 2,000 books, I heard the words without recognising either its irony (讽刺) or its very complicated truth. I merely determined to make a list of all the books I had ever read. Strict with myself, I included only once a title I might have read several times. (How, after all, could one read a book more than once?) And I included only those books over 100 pages in length. (Could anything shorter be a book?)

There was yet another high school list I made. One day I came across a newspaper article about an English professor at a nearby state college. The article had a list of the "hundred most important books of Western Civilisation". "More than anything else in my life," the professor told the reporter <u>with finality</u>, "these books have made me all that I am." That was the kind of words I couldn't ignore. I kept the list for the several months it took me to read all of the titles. Most books, of course, I hardly understood. While reading Plato's *The Republic*, for example, I needed to keep looking at the introduction of the book to remind myself what the text was about. However, with the special patience and superstition (迷信) of a schoolboy, I looked at every word of the text. And by the time I reached the last word, pleased, I persuaded myself that I had read *The Republic*, and seriously crossed Plato off my list.

1. On hearing the teacher's suggestion of reading, the writer thought _____.

   A. one must read as many books as possible

   B. a student should not have a complicated idea

   C. it was impossible for one to read 2,000 books

   D. students ought to make a list of the books they had read

2. While at high school, the writer _____.

   A. had plans for reading   B. learnt to educate himself

   C. only read books over 100 pages   D. read only one book several times

3. The underlined phrase "with finality" in the second paragraph probably means "_____".

   A. clearly   B. proudly   C. pleasantly   D. firmly

4. The writer's purpose in mentioning *The Republic* is to _____.

   A. show that he read the books blindly when he couldn't understand them

   B. explain why it was included in the list

   C. describe why he seriously crossed it off the list

   D. prove that he understood most of it because he had looked at every word

5. The writer provides two book lists to _____.

   A. show how he developed his point of view

   B. introduce the two persons' reading methods

C. tell his reading experience at high school

D. explain that he read many books at high school

B

Thanks to the huge success of *Harry Potter*, many teenagers dream about living in an ancient castle. These dreams may include beautiful silk dresses, delicious food, servants and of course, magic. However, real life in an English castle was not easy. With thick stone walls and high towers, castles were built for defence. So they were not good places to live in. In medieval times, castles must have been noisy and smelly places. Horses, cattle, chickens and sheep walked free; blacksmiths (铁匠) did ironwork; soldiers practised sword (剑) fights, and children of all ages played around them. Castles did not have central heating; the only heat came from the fireplace. Even in summer the castle was cool. People living in the castles had to use blankets to keep warm while at work.

Life during the Middle Ages began at sunrise. Servants lit the fire, swept the floor and cooked the morning meal. The mid-morning meal was the main meal of the day and often included three or four courses (一道菜). After dinner, everyone continued his or her work. The owner of the castle, the lord, sometimes took his guests hunting or shooting. His wife, the lady, spent much of the day watching the maids (女仆) work, as well as people working in the kitchen. She also kept an eye on the weavers and embroiderers who made clothes for the family. Supper was simple and eaten late, just before bedtime.

You may find some old magic books in a castle as Harry Potter once did. Read them before you go to bed, because when you fall asleep the magic of castle life may appear before your eyes.

6. For what purpose were the castles built in England?

A. To raise poultry (家禽) and livestock (家畜).

B. To provide a working place for blacksmiths.

C. To defend the city or country against enemies.

D. To provide a place for teenagers to learn magic.

7. Why were the ancient castles noisy?

A. Because soldiers practised sword fights there.

B. Because blacksmiths did ironwork there.

C. Because children of all ages played around them.

D. All of the above.

8. Which of the following about family life in castles is TRUE according to the passage?

A. The servants in castles lived an easy life.

B. Supper was eaten before sunset.

C. The wife spent much of the day at home.

D. Dinner was eaten in the middle of the day.

9. We can infer that the writer _____.

   A. wants teenagers to drop the dream of living in a castle

   B. wants to change our unrealistic ideas about castles

   C. blames *Harry Potter* for misleading people about life in a castle

   D. doesn't like the life in ancient castles

10. The main idea of this passage is _____.

   A. castles were not good places to live in

   B. castles in novels are different from those in history

   C. Harry Potter's story in a castle affected people

   D. what real life was like in an ancient castle

IV. 阅读表达（共5小题，每小题3分；满分15分）

An old man was childless and got sick frequently. Tired of loneliness, he decided to live in a nursing home. So he announced that his splendid house would be sold at 80,000 pounds by auction. So many buyers took part in the auction that the price of the house was soon increased by 20,000 pounds and it was still rising.

Sitting deep in a sofa, the old man looked justifiably heavy-hearted. If he had been in good health, he wouldn't have thought of selling the house where he had lived for the greater part of his life. A plainly-dressed young man approached him, bent forward and whispered, "Sir, I am eager to buy your house but I only have 10,000 pounds."

"You know the base price is 80,000 pounds," the old man said gently. "And now it has been raised to 100,000 pounds." Not depressed, the young man honestly said, "If you sell me the house, I promise you will _____ and enjoy your happy life, drinking tea, reading newspaper and taking a walk with me every day. Please believe me I shall care for you with all my heart!" The old man nodded with a smile. He stood up, motioned to silence everyone present. "Ladies and gentlemen," he said, patting the young man on his shoulder. "I announce the result of the auction. The young man is the new owner of the house!"

1. What is the best title for the passage? (Please answer within 10 words.)

_____

2. Which sentence in the passage can be replaced by the following one?

   So many people came swarming (云集) to the auction that the price of his house was soon jacked up from 80,000 pounds to 100,000 pounds and it was still rising.

_____

3. Fill in the blank in the last paragraph with proper words or phrases to complete the sentence. (Please answer within 10 words.)

_____

4. Why did the old man sell the house to the young man? (Please answer within 30 words.)

_____

_____

5. Translate the underlined sentence in the second paragraph into Chinese.

_____

Ⅴ．写作（满分30分）

假设你是李华，希望通过你的外籍教师 Peter 找一个英语笔友。请写一封短信，描述一下你理想中笔友的条件，并说明为什么选这样的笔友。描述中须包括笔友的年龄、性别、爱好（旅游、运动、宠物等）。可以适当增加细节，以使行文连贯。信的开头已经给出，不计入总词数。

词数要求：120词左右。

Dear Peter,

　　I am writing to ask whether you are able to do me a favour.

_____

_____

_____

　　Best regards,

　　　　　　　　　　　　　　　　　　　　　　　　Yours,

　　　　　　　　　　　　　　　　　　　　　　　　Li Hua

第一部分　听力（共两节，满分30分）

第一节　（共5小题；每小题1.5分，满分7.5分）

听下面五段对话。每段对话后有一个小题，从题中所给的三个选项中选出最佳选项。听完每段对话后，你都有10秒钟的时间来回答有关小题和阅读下一小题。每段对话仅读一遍。

1. How does the woman feel about the TV programmes?

   A. She thinks they are too bad.

   B. She thinks they are good on the whole.

   C. She doesn't like watching TV at all.

2. What is the woman's opinion about the man?

   A. She thinks he can pass the exam.

   B. She thinks he should use a month to prepare for the exam.

   C. She thinks he will fail in the exam.

3. What does the woman imply?

   A. They have to wait for 11 hours.

   B. The boat trip will take 11 hours.

   C. The man is mistaken about the arrival time.

4. What can we learn from the conversation?

   A. The man persuades the woman to give it up.

   B. The man thinks the problem is easy.

   C. The man tells the woman to stop working for it at the moment.

5. Why does Professor White think the second paragraph should be crossed out?

   A. Because there are too many spelling mistakes in it.

   B. Because the man's handwriting is poor.

   C. Because it has nothing to do with the article.

第二节　（共15小题；每小题1.5分，满分22.5分）

听下面五段对话或独白。每段对话或独白后有几个小题，从题中所给的三个选项中选出最佳选项。听每段对话或独白前，你将有时间阅读各个小题，每小题5秒钟；听完后，各小题将给出5秒钟的作答时间。每段对话或独白读两遍。

听第6段材料，回答第6至第8小题。

6. What might the relationship between the girl and her parents be?

   A. Good.　　　　　B. Bad.　　　　　C. Hard to tell.

7. How old might the girl be?

    A. Fifteen.   B. Seventeen.   C. Eighteen.

8. Which of the following is true?

    A. The girl has no pocket money.

    B. The girl has much freedom.

    C. The girl wants to go on holiday with her parents.

听第7段材料，回答第9至第11小题。

9. What is the woman planning to do?

    A. To move to a warmer place.

    B. To study at a different school.

    C. To start a new programme at State College.

10. How long has the woman been studying at the State College?

    A. Since mid-spring.

    B. Since summer.

    C. For a year and a half.

11. What concern does the woman have about West University?

    A. It's not that famous.

    B. She can't get a good recommendation there.

    C. She may not get accepted there.

听第8段材料，回答第12至第14小题。

12. What do the two speakers have in common?

    A. They take the same maths course.

    B. They are going on a camping trip together.

    C. They both enjoy painting.

13. What was the woman doing on Friday?

    A. Packing for her vacation.

    B. Taking part in a special class activity.

    C. Preparing for the exam.

14. What did the man think of Death Valley?

    A. It was too far away to visit.

    B. It would be too hot for camping.

    C. It would be a nice place to go camping.

听第9段材料，回答第15至第17小题。

15. Where does this conversation take place?

    A. At a restaurant.   B. At the woman's office.   C. In the street.

16. What present does the man give to the woman?

    A. Some candies.   B. A handicraft.   C. A small toy.

17. What is it made of?

    A. Wool.   B. Wood.   C. Bamboo.

听第10段材料，回答第18至第20小题。

18. How many cameras were lost in the park that week?

    A. Three.   B. Four.   C. Five.

19. How did Harry know the camera was his?

    A. It was an old black one like his.

    B. It looked like his.

    C. It had the same number as his.

20. Who was the man that came to Harry's house with cameras on Sunday?

    A. A thief.·   B. The owner of the cameras.   C. A man selling cameras.

第二部分　英语知识运用（共两节，满分35分）

第一节 语法和词汇（共15小题；每小题1分，满分15分）

从 A、B、C、D 四个选项中，选出可以填入空白处的最佳选项。

21. He said he would _____ me to Professor Michael as his postgraduate student.

    A. comment   B. suggest   C. command   D. recommend

22. —She decided to _____ a kidney (肾) to her dying son.

    —She is a great mother.

    A. contribute   B. donate   C. subscribe   D. sell

23. —What took you so long?

    —I got lost. I have no _____ of direction.

    A. sense   B. idea   C. feeling   D. ability

24. China opened its door to the outside world in 1978. _____ that had far-reaching effects.

    A. Did a new development come then

    B. Came then a new development

    C. Then came a new development

    D. Then did a new development come

25. _____ and we'll get everything ready for the taking off.

    A. Have one more hour   B. One more hour

    C. Given one more hour   D. If I have one more hour

26. Doctors are concerned that the children _____ too much time in front of TV don't get enough exercise.

    A. those spend   B. who spend   C. to spend   D. spend

27. The next moment, _____ she had time to realise what was happening, she was hit over the head.

    A. since   B. when   C. before   D. after

28. —I let my secretary call you several times. Do you know that?

—I _____ in a meeting. I'm sorry.

A. had been   B. was   C. am   D. have been

29. How many expressways _____ by the end of next year?

A. has been completed   B. has completed

C. will have been completed   D. will have completed

30. —This is for you.

—You _____ have! I don't know how to thank you.

A. mustn't   B. couldn't   C. needn't   D. shouldn't

31. —Do you think _____ worthwhile to go all the way to Los Angeles to buy that computer?

—Well, I'm going to visit some relatives too.

A. it   B. /   C. this   D. that

32. _____ parents may have a stronger desire to see their children step into the world of _____.

A. Poor; rich   B. The poor; rich   C. Poor; the rich   D. The poor; the rich

33. He was disappointed to find his suggestions _____.

A. to turn down   B. turned down   C. to be turned down   D. been turned down

34. —How often do you eat out?

—_____, but usually once a week.

A. Have no idea   B. It depends   C. As usual   D. Generally speaking

35. —Here. Your new computer is ready.

—Thank you.

—_____ to call this number if you have any problems or questions.

A. You're free   B. It is free   C. Feel free   D. Don't forget

第二节 完形填空（共20小题；每小题1分，满分20分）

阅读下面的短文，掌握其大意，然后从每题所给的四个选项中选出最佳选项。

Sometimes, I doubted that there was any love between my parents. Every day they were __36__ earning money. They didn't __37__ in the romantic __38__ that I read in books. For them, "I love you" was too luxurious (奢侈的). When he was __39__ working, my father had a bad temper.

One day, my mother was __40__ a quilt. I sat beside her and looked at her. "Mum, I have a question to ask you," I said.

"__41__ is it?" she replied.

"Is there any love between you and Dad?" I asked __42__. My mother stopped her work and raised her head with __43__ in her eyes. She didn't answer immediately. __44__ she continued her work.

I was very __45__ because I thought I had __46__ her. But at last, my mother said __47__, "Susan, look at this thread. Sometimes it is __48__, but most of it disappears into the quilt. The thread really makes the quilt strong. If life is a __49__, then love should be a thread. It can hardly be __50__ anywhere, but it's really there. Love is inside." I listened carefully but I didn't __51__ her until the next spring, when my father became seriously ill. My mother had to stay with him in the hospital for a month.

After they were back, every day in the morning, my mother __52__ my father walk slowly along the country road. My father had never been so gentle. The doctor had said my father would __53__ in two months. But after two months he still couldn't walk by himself.

"Dad, how are you feeling now?" I asked him one day.

"Susan, don't worry about me," he said gently. "To tell you the truth, I just like __54__ with your mum." Reading his eyes, I knew he __55__ my mother a lot.

36. A. interested in   B. busy in   C. devoted to   D. used to
37. A. act   B. work   C. live   D. speak
38. A. times   B. spaces   C. ways   D. thoughts
39. A. back from   B. late for   C. kept from   D. tired from
40. A. washing   B. sewing   C. spreading   D. folding up
41. A. How   B. Why   C. Where   D. What
42. A. immediately   B. carefully   C. in a low voice   D. in a romantic tune
43. A. sorrow   B. fear   C. excitement   D. surprise
44. A. But   B. Then   C. Therefore   D. Thus
45. A. sorry   B. anxious   C. sad   D. terrified
46. A. interested   B. embarrassed   C. puzzled   D. troubled
47. A. clearly   B. sadly   C. attentively   D. thoughtfully
48. A. inside   B. visible   C. short   D. long
49. A. thread   B. quilt   C. family   D. home
50. A. seen   B. felt   C. kept   D. got
51. A. misunderstand   B. understand   C. complain to   D. agree with
52. A. asked   B. sent   C. helped   D. supported
53. A. recover   B. walk   C. work   D. satisfy
54. A. living   B. staying   C. working   D. walking
55. A. loved   B. understood   C. admired   D. depended on

第三部分　阅读理解（共20小题；每小题2分，满分40分）

阅读下列短文，从每题所给的四个选项中选出最佳选项。

A

Dear Susan,

Losing a best friend is never easy.

Your problem, Susan, is not just that you miss your best friend. It is that you feel empty and lost without her friendship.

It takes time to get over a loss, and during that time, your mind is getting used to <u>a new way of being</u>. This is usually a good thing, even if it feels like a bad thing.

Now that you are on your own, you are being forced to learn to be by yourself and to rely upon your own inner voice for guidance. I am sure that this feels strange for you, but if you can hang on for a bit, it may work to your advantage.

Best friends are cool, but it is important to know the difference between missing someone and being too dependent upon them.

At your age, girls do tend to stick together and having a boyfriend may not yet be the better choice. <u>Your friend is a little ahead of herself</u> in leaving you, her best friend, for a boyfriend. Boyfriends are completely different from best friends; the distinction being that boyfriends come and go, while girlfriends often stay in your life throughout high school, and even afterwards. It is a completely different sort of bond.

I suggest that you take advantage of this period in your life to expand your horizons. Enjoy the freedom of having no best friend for a while, and hang with the group. By the time your former best friend breaks up with her boyfriend, you will be in a completely different place, a far better place; in your head that is.

And, by the way, next time that you feel empty and lost, try to write about it in a diary or just simply on paper. In several months, you will look back and read it with curiosity about yourself, "Who was I then, and what could I have been thinking?"

56. Judging from the letter, Susan's problem was that she didn't know _____.
    A. whether to give up her best friend   B. what to do without her best friend
    C. who to choose between two friends   D. how to stop missing her former friend
57. By "a new way of being" in the third paragraph, the writer referred to the situation in which Susan had to _____.
    A. find a new friendship   B. live with a best friend
    C. learn to give up   D. be independent
58. When the writer said "Your friend is a little ahead of herself" in the sixth paragraph, he / she meant Susan's friend was _____.
    A. acting without thinking   B. doing something she might regret later
    C. too young to fall in love   D. unwise to leave Susan so soon
59. The writer believed Susan would _____ by the time her former best friend lost her boyfriend.
    A. grow physically stronger   B. do better at school
    C. feel more independent and confident   D. win her best friend back
60. The last paragraph seems to suggest that _____.
    A. keeping a diary helps correct oneself
    B. Susan will get over her problem soon
    C. unhappy experiences are easy to forget
    D. one shouldn't forget the past experiences

B

Many children first learn the value of money by receiving an allowance. The purpose is to let children learn from experience at an age when financial mistakes are not very costly.

The amount of money that parents give to their children to spend as they wish differs from family to family. Timing is another consideration. Some children get a weekly allowance. Others get a monthly allowance.

In any case, parents should make clear what, if anything, the child is expected to pay for with the money.

At first, young children may spend all of their allowance soon after they receive it. If they do this, they will learn the hard way that spending must be done within a budget. Parents are usually advised not to offer more money until the next allowance. The object is to show young people that a budget demands choices between spending and saving. Older children may be responsible enough to save money for larger costs, like clothing or electronics.

Many people who have written on the subject of allowances say it is not a good idea to pay your child for work around the home. These jobs are a normal part of family life. Paying children to do extra work around the house, however, can be useful. It can even provide an understanding of how a business works.

Allowances give children a chance to experience the three things they can do with money. They can share it in the form of gifts or giving it to a good cause. They can spend it by buying things they want. Or they can save it.

61. What is special about children's learning financial management by experience?
    A. They learn more quickly.　　　　B. They are not likely to make mistakes.
    C. Their mistakes won't matter so much.　　D. They have plans made by their parents.
62. When the writer says some young children "will learn the hard way that spending must be done within a budget" in the fourth paragraph, he means _____.
    A. they will know a budget is hard to carry out
    B. they will have a hard time learning the lesson
    C. what they will learn is absolutely true
    D. their parents will teach them a hard lesson
63. Judging from the article, it is all right if a couple gives their son an allowance _____.
    A. regularly twice every month
    B. whenever he has run out of money
    C. telling him to ask for permission before spending
    D. without telling him what to spend on
64. The writer would agree to encourage the kids to _____ to deal with a tight budget.
    A. borrow money from others　　　　B. ask their parents for more money
    C. get paid for their household routines　　D. earn money by extra work

65. When a kid donates some of his allowance to wild animal protection, he is _____.

    A. sharing it with others   B. giving it to a good cause

    C. buying things for himself   D. saving for his future spending

C

Psychologists take opposing views of how external rewards, from warm praise to cold cash, affect motivation and creativity. Behaviourists, who study the relation between actions and their consequences, argue that rewards can improve performance at work and school. Cognitive (认知学派的) researchers, who study various aspects of mental life, maintain that rewards often destroy creativity by encouraging dependence on approval and gifts from others.

The latter view has gained many supporters, especially among educators. But the careful use of small monetary (金钱的) rewards sparks creativity in grade-school children, suggesting that properly presented inducements (刺激) indeed aid inventiveness, according to a study in the June Journal of *Personality and Social Psychology*.

"If kids know they're working for a reward and can focus on a relatively challenging task, they show the most creativity," says Robert Eisenberger of the University of Delaware in Newark. "But it's easy to kill creativity by giving rewards for poor performance or creating too much anticipation for rewards." A teacher who continually draws attention to rewards or who hands out high grades for ordinary achievement ends up with uninspired students, Eisenberger holds. As an example of the latter point, he notes growing efforts at major universities to tighten grading standards and restore failing grades.

In earlier grades, the use of so-called token economies, in which students handle challenging problems and receive performance-based points towards valued rewards, shows promise in raising effort and creativity, the Delaware psychologist claims.

66. Psychologists are divided with regard to their attitudes towards _____.

    A. the choice between spiritual encouragement and monetary rewards

    B. the amount of monetary rewards for students' creativity

    C. the study of relationship between actions and their consequences

    D. the effects of external rewards on students' performance

67. What is the response of many educators to external rewards for their students?

    A. They have no doubts about them.

    B. They have doubts about them.

    C. They approve them.

    D. They avoid talking about them.

68. Which of the following can best raise students' creativity according to Robert Eisenberger?

    A. Assigning them tasks they have not dealt with before.

B. Assigning them tasks which require inventiveness.

C. Giving them rewards they really deserve.

D. Giving them rewards they anticipate.

69. It can be inferred from the passage that major universities are trying to tighten their grading standards because they believe _____.

A. rewarding poor performance may kill the creativity of students

B. punishment is more effective than rewarding

C. failing uninspired students help improve their overall academic standards

D. discouraging the students' anticipation for easy rewards is a matter of urgency

70. The underlined phrase "token economies" in the last paragraph probably refers to _____.

A. ways to develop economy   B. systems of rewarding students

C. approaches to solving problems   D. methods of improving performance

D

Crocodiles are amongst the largest reptiles (爬行动物) in the world. They have long, low bodies, short legs and long powerful tails. Their hides are tough and they have very sharp teeth. They live in tropical countries throughout the world and prefer a large area of shallow water, being especially happy in open swamps. Their feet are designed to allow them to walk on soft ground.

One unusual feature of the crocodile is that its eyes and nostrils are higher than the rest of its head. This is extremely useful, as they like nothing better than to float menacingly in the water, with only their eyes and nose above the surface. It is often extremely difficult to see if a particular stretch of water contains any crocodiles.

Crocodiles are much more aggressive than American or Chinese alligators (短吻鳄). Thanks to their powerful jaws, they can eat a variety of small fishes and other animals, such as birds and turtles. Occasionally they attack larger animals and sometimes people. Even large water buffalos (水牛) have no chance of surviving an encounter with a crocodile.

The crocodile's method of catching water buffalos is terrifying and very successful. Lying just below the surface of the water, it moves slowly towards its prey, leaving the surface of the water almost undisturbed.

Suddenly the crocodile explodes out of the water and closes its jaws upon the nearest part of the water buffalo, usually one of its legs. The water buffalo stumbles and falls. With the help of its powerful tail, the crocodile then rolls over and over, causing the water to become disorientated (分不清方向的). The victim is then dragged into deeper water, where it drowns and ceases to struggle.

Despite their immense power and savagery, there are some species of crocodiles which are endangered species, almost entirely because they are hunted for hides, which manufacturers make into leather for shoes and handbags. There are laws forbidding crocodile hunting in many parts of the world, and conservationists have begun programmes to collect crocodile eggs and hatch them in incubators (孵化器). The baby crocodiles are then released into the wild.

71. Which of these statements about crocodiles is true?

   A. Crocodiles are not as aggressive as American and Chinese alligators.

   B. Crocodiles are dangerous because they live in the water.

   C. Crocodiles are endangered species all around the world because they are hunted for their skins.

   D. Crocodiles cannot be seen easily in the water even though their eyes and nose are above water.

72. The underlined expression "like nothing better than to float menacingly" in the second paragraph means crocodiles _____.

   A. enjoy lying dangerously still on the surface of the water

   B. like nothing more than swimming dangerously at the surface of the water

   C. like to swim dangerously at the surface of the water

   D. dislike lying still in the water because it's dangerous

73. The underlined word "prey" in the fourth paragraph means _____.

   A. other crocodiles   B. animals that hunt

   C. buffalos' feet   D. animals that are hunted

74. Why are water buffalos in danger from crocodiles?

   A. Because crocodiles don't worry them.

   B. Because when crocodiles bites their legs, they fall and drown.

   C. Because crocodiles swim faster than water buffalos.

   D. Because crocodiles swim quickly up to them and surprise them.

75. Why are some species of crocodiles endangered?

   A. They were hunted and made into leather for shoes and handbags.

   B. They are aggressive.

   C. They trace the buffalos.

   D. Their eggs were collected and the baby crocodiles were released into the wild.

第四部分 书面表达（共两节，满分45分）

第一节 阅读表达（共5小题；每小题3分，满分15分）

阅读下面的短文，并根据短文后的要求答题。

You are about to become a college freshman. You enter college expecting to leave with a degree. The following are tips on how to get the most out of your college education.

Time management

"Man is first a social animal, then a rational (理性的) one." So you may find it hard to say "No!" each time your roommate wants to see a movie when you need to read *Paradise Lost*.

Think about what you want from college and from friends. Study after breakfast, between classes, whatever works best for you. Don't cut off all social contacts, which are as vital to surviving in college as reading. Study Hegel first, then catch a late movie.

Study method

Would you take a trip by _____ instead of reading a map? Of course not. Studying in college demands more independence than in high school. Survey the material first to get a sense of it; ask some questions; write down key ideas; tell yourself the essence (本质) of what you've read and review it.

Keeping up

Professors may not notice whether you attend a large lecture, but you could notice later on. <u>Some professors use lectures to discuss material not found in the reading on which they will base an exam.</u> Others stress key points. Skip at your own risk. If you must miss a lecture, get the notes in time. If too much time elapses (逝去), the notes will make no sense. Never fall more than a week behind in reading the notes. If you don't do the reading, you won't understand the lecture.

76. What is the best title for the passage? (Please answer within 10 words.)

   _____

77. Which sentence in the passage can be replaced by the following one?
   As a college student, getting yourself involved in social activities is as important as studying.

   _____
   _____

78. Fill in the blank in the fourth paragraph with proper words or phrases to complete the sentence. (Please answer within 10 words.)

   _____

79. Which of the suggestions do you think is the best for you? Why? (Please answer within 30 words.)

   _____
   _____

80. Translate the underlined sentence in the last paragraph into Chinese.

   _____

第二节 写作（满分30分）
随着经济的发展，许多人为城市未来的交通状况而担忧。你对此有何想法？请以 "Traffic in the City" 为题写一篇短文，谈谈自己的见解和设想。
词数要求：100～120词。

Traffic in the City

Module ④

Music Born in America

要点纵览

高考词汇	movement, technique, approach, decline, touch, arise, offshore, boom, friction, conventional, fancy, blouse, neat, mom, consensus, budget, cheque, consultant, vain, bonus, DVD, VCD, pace, tight, schedule, spokesman, deadline, otherwise, allowance, part-time, devote, swap, super, yell, beg, pension, quit, pioneer, humorous
常用短语	be / become known as, in my case, side by side, be made up of, turn on, in order, try out, come out, be devoted to, beg for, make an impression on sb, dance to, spread to
实用句型	1. Shouting DJs became known as MCs. 2. Later, they experimented with different vocal and rhythmic approaches, using rhyming words, often words from African-American culture.
交际用语	1. Can you turn that music down a bit? 2. It isn't my cup of tea. 3. We didn't play music as loudly as you do these days. 4. Why are you inside listening to music? 5. It's her turn to call me.

◆ **高考词汇**

1. spread

n. 扩展，蔓延

v. 1) 伸开，展开；2) 流传，传播；3) 扩展，蔓延

There were concerns about the spread of fighting to other regions.

We spread the blanket on the grass and sat down on it.

Soldiers returning from the war soon spread the disease through most of the region.

UN leaders hope to prevent the fighting from spreading.

A desert spreads for hundreds of miles.

2. bore

v. (使) 厌烦

I hope I'm not boring you.

➡ 常用短语：

bore sb with 使某人厌烦

bore sb to death / tears 使某人烦得要命

My brother's always boring us with his stories about the war.

The child has bored his mother to tears.

> ········ 拓展 ········
>
> bored *adj.* 厌烦的，不感兴趣的
>
> boring *adj.* 令人厌烦的
>
> I felt bored to lie in the sofa to watch TV.
>
> It's boring to listen to such a long speech.

3. approach

n. 1) (处理问题的) 方式，方法；2) 靠近，接近

v. (距离、时间等的) 接近

His method presents a new approach to studying a language.

Our approach drove away the wild animals.

We approached the birds quietly and watched them carefully.

The time of his graduation is approaching.

4. otherwise

adv. 1) 否则，要不然；2) 除此之外，在其他方面；3) 另外，别样

conj. (并列连词，同 or else) 否则，不然

adj. 别的，不同的

He reminded me of what I should do otherwise I have forgotten.

He is a little stubborn, but he is otherwise quite suitable for the job.

I think it will snow this afternoon, but my sister thinks otherwise.

You should go now, otherwise you'll miss the bus.

I thought I would be welcomed by the family, but it was otherwise.

5. devote

v. 为……付出时间/努力/金钱等

He's devoted most of his time to his painting.

Mother Teresa has devoted herself to caring for the poor.

6. beg

v. 1) 请求，恳求；2) 乞讨

He begged me for some money.

He begged me to stay.

They were reduced to begging food in the streets.

7. quit

v. 1) 离开，离去；2) 停止；3) 辞去（工作）

adj. 摆脱的，免除的

I quit him in disgust.

Quit work when the siren sounds.

She quit her job because of ill health.

He was glad to be quit of the troublesome person.

◆ 常用短语

1. be / become known as

be / become known as 意思是 "作为……而被人所知"。

Samuel Clemens, known as Mark Twain, was a famous American writer.

辨·析

be / become known as, be / become known to 与 be / become known for

be / become known as 指的是 "作为……而被人所知"。

be / become known for 指的是 "因……而被人所知"。

be / become known to 指的是 "为……所熟知"。

John is known as a singer for his beautiful songs, and he is well known to the younger generation.

2. in my case

in my case 意思是 "就我个人情况而言"。

In my case, when I'm trying to concentrate and get an essay written or do some revision, I listen to some music.

in no case 决不

Traffic is bad, but in any case we'll be there in time for dinner.

Take an umbrella in case it rains.

In case of bad weather, the wedding will be held indoors.

In no case should you give it up.

3. side by side

side by side 意思是"肩并肩"。

We rode side by side through the forest.

hand in hand 手拉手

shoulder to shoulder 肩并肩

face to face 面对面

They walked along the cliff top hand in hand.

She stood shoulder to shoulder with her husband throughout his trial.

I've never met her face to face. We've only talked on the phone.

4. be made up of

be made up of 意思是"由……组成",与 be composed of 和 consist of 意义相近,但 consist of 要用主动语态。

The committee is made up of representatives from every state.

Life is made up of little things.

5. 与 turn 有关的短语:

turn about 转身

turn against 背叛,对……不利

turn away 走开,离开;转过脸去

turn back 折回,往回走,返回到

turn down 向下翻;调低 (声音);拒绝

turn in 转身进入;上床睡觉;交出,上缴

turn into 进入;使成为;翻译成

turn off 关上 (电源等)

turn on 打开 (电源等)

turn out 证明是,结果是

turn over 打翻,倾倒;反复考虑

turn up 向上翻，调大 (声音)；出现

turn upside down 把……完全颠倒

◆ 实用结构

引导时间状语的特殊词语和结构

as soon as / the moment / the minute / the instant / immediately / directly / instantly
一……就

No sooner + had + 主语 + 动词的过去分词形式 + than + 主语 + 动词过去式 一……就

Hardly / Scarcely + had + 主语 + 动词的过去分词形式 + when + 主语 + 动词过去式 一……
就

every time 每次　the first time 第一次　the last time 最后一次

I gave the money to her the moment I saw her.

You see the lightning the instant it happens, but you hear the thunder later.

Make sure the property you are buying is insured immediately you exchange contracts.

No sooner had we reached the top of the hill than we all sat down to rest.

Scarcely had I opened the door when the dog came running in.

真 题 解 析

—Did Linda see the traffic accident?

—No, no sooner _____ than it happened. (2006 天津)

A. had she gone　　　B. she had gone　　　C. has she gone　　　D. she has gone

解析：no sooner…than 表示"一……就"，no sooner 后用过去完成时，than 后用一般
过去时，no sooner 放在句首，后面的部分用倒装句式。答案为 A。

综合训练

考试时间：45分钟　满分：100分

I. 单项选择（共15小题；每小题1分，满分15分）

1. I don't understand how you got a ticket. I always _____ you _____ a careful driver.

A. think; are　　　B. am thinking; are　　　C. thought; were　　　D. think; were

2. I hope that the little _____ I have been able to do does good to them all.

A. which　　　B. what　　　C. that　　　D. when

3. Have you got a free evening next week? _____, let's have dinner together.

A. While so　　　B. Since so　　　C. When so　　　D. If so

4. —How can I wake up so early?

—Set the alarm at 5 o'clock, _____ you'll make it.

   A. but   B. or   C. and   D. so

5. She wasn't very polite but _____ I helped her.

   A. any way   B. anyway   C. at any way   D. in a way

6. Kate is _____ than Bob. Bob has a billion dollars while Kate has a million.

   A. less rich   B. richer   C. no rich   D. less poor

7. —Did you lose the match?

   —Yes, we lost the match _____ one goal.

   A. by   B. at   C. with   D. only

8. _____ nice weather it is! Let's go out for a walk, shall we?

   A. How   B. How a   C. What a   D. What

9. Babies sleep 16 to 18 hours in every 24 hours, and they sleep less _____ they grow older.

   A. while   B. as   C. when   D. after

10. I have been keeping the portrait _____ I can see it every day, as it always reminds me of my childhood in Paris.

   A. since   B. where   C. as   D. if

11. With a lot of difficult problems _____, the manager felt worried all the time.

   A. settled   B. to be settled   C. settling   D. to settle

12. —_____ you be happy!

   —The same to you!

   A. Wish   B. Hope   C. May   D. Should

13. —How do you find the talk given by Mr Smith?

   —_____.

   A. Very well   B. Excited   C. Boring   D. Not at all

14. —_____ the car seat. It's wet.

   —Thank you for telling me.

   A. Touch   B. Feel   C. Hand   D. Sense

15. The driver began to speed up to _____ for the hour he lost in the traffic jam.

   A. keep up   B. take up   C. catch up   D. make up

Ⅱ. 完形填空（共20小题；每小题1分，满分20分）

   George Pickens had been making a wish daily as a worker at Central Bank.

   All over the country banks were being __1__, George thought. __2__ this bank? Didn't robbers hear of its four-million-dollar __3__? Were they afraid of Mr Ackerman, the old __4__ guard, who hadn't __5__ his gun in 22 years?

   Of course George had a(n) __6__ for wanting the bank to be robbed. __7__, he couldn't simply take bills that were under his __8__ all day long. So he had thought of another __9__ to get them. His plan was __10__. It went like this:

If Bank Robber A holds up Bank Teller B…

And if Bank Teller B gives Bank Robber A a certain sum of money…

What is to prevent Bank Teller B from __11__ all the money left and __12__ that it was taken away by Bank Robber A?

There was only one __13__. Where was Bank Robber A?

One morning George entered the bank feeling something was about to happen. "Good morning, Mr Burrows," he said __14__. The bank president said something in a __15__ voice to George and went into his office.

At two o'clock Bank Robber A walked in. George __16__ he was a bank robber. For one thing, he stole in. For another thing, he wore a mask (面罩). "This is a holdup," the man said __17__. He took a gun from his pocket. The __18__ made a small sound. "You!" the bank robber said, "Lie down on the floor!" Mr Ackerman lay down. The robber stepped __19__ to George's cage.

"All right," he said. "Hand it over."

"Yes, sir," George reached into his drawer and took all the bills from the top part, close to 6,000 dollars. He passed them through the window. The robber took them, put them into his pocket, and __20__ to leave.

Then, while everyone watched Bank Robber A, Bank Teller B calmly lifted off the top part of the drawer and got the bills from the bottom part into his pockets.

1. A. repaired	B. broken	C. robbed	D. built
2. A. Why not	B. What about	C. How about	D. How is
3. A. money	B. capital	C. note	D. bill
4. A. door	B. body	C. money	D. bank
5. A. pulled out	B. got	C. carried out	D. kept
6. A. chance	B. reason	C. excuse	D. time
7. A. Of all	B. In all	C. Above all	D. After all
8. A. hands	B. desks	C. drawers	D. eyes
9. A. man	B. day	C. way	D. robber
10. A. perfect	B. complete	C. complicated	D. simple
11. A. robbing	B. stealing	C. keeping	D. holding
12. A. telling	B. thinking	C. insisting	D. imagining
13. A. secret	B. problem	C. thing	D. puzzle
14. A. cheerfully	B. calmly	C. anxiously	D. eagerly
15. A. aloud	B. low	C. big	D. worrying
16. A. trusted	B. recognised	C. supposed	D. knew
17. A. angrily	B. roughly	C. firmly	D. politely
18. A. robber	B. manager	C. guard	D. customer
19. A. on	B. above	C. through	D. over
20. A. turned	B. decided	C. signed	D. drew

137

A

Besides the question of the time given to pronunciation, there are two other requirements for the teacher: the first, knowledge; the second, technique.

It is important that the teacher should be in possession of the necessary information. This can generally be got from books. It is possible to get from books some idea of the speech, and of what we call general phonetic rules. It is also possible in this way to get a clear mental picture of the relationship between the sounds of different languages, between the speech habits of English people and those, say, of your students. Unless the teacher has such a picture, explanations he makes on his students' pronunciation are unlikely to be of much use, and lesson time spent on pronunciation may well be wasted.

But it does not follow that you can teach pronunciation successfully as soon as you have read the necessary books. It depends, after that, what use you make of your knowledge; and this is a matter of technique.

Now the first and most important part of a language teacher's technique is his own performance, his ability to show off the spoken language, in every detail of sound as well as in fluent speaking, so that the students' ability for imitation (模仿) is given the fullest space and encouragement. The teacher, then, should be as perfect a model in this field as he can make himself. And to make his own performance better, however satisfactory this may be, the modern teacher has in his hand recordings and a radio, to supply the real voices of native speakers, or, if the teacher happens to be a native speaker himself, or speaks just like one, then to change the method of presenting the language material.

However, the process of showing pronunciation, whether by personal example or with the help of machines, is only the beginning of teaching pronunciation. The technique of teaching each sound also needs to be considered.

1. How might the teacher find himself wasting lesson time?

   A. By spending lesson time on pronunciation.

   B. By making explanations upon pronunciation.

   C. By not using books on phonetics in the classroom.

   D. By not having a clear mental picture of the difference between sounds of different languages.

2. Students have the ability for imitation which is _____.

   A. plain and obvious   B. well developed

   C. not yet developed   D. too weak to be useful

3. What is the main point the author makes about students' imitation of the teacher?

   A. It is a matter of secondary importance.

   B. Students should be given every chance for it.

   C. It depends on the students' ability.

   D. Teachers are perfect models for students to imitate.

4. To a language teacher mechanical aids (技术手段) can _____.
   A. improve his own performance   B. replace his own performance
   C. provide examples of native speech D. make his voice louder
5. Showing pronunciation is regarded as _____.
   A. a part of teaching pronunciation
   B. an exercise of value in itself
   C. an example of the use of mechanical aids
   D. a technique for teaching separate sounds

B

Listening to music while you drive can improve your speed and ability to get away from accidents, according to Australian psychologists. But turning your car radio up to full volume could probably make you end up in an accident. The performance of difficult tasks can be affected if people are subjected to loud noise. The experience of <u>pulling up</u> at traffic lights alongside care with loud music made some psychologists in the University of Sydney look into whether loud music has something to do with driving.

The psychologists invited 60 men and women aged between 20 and 28 as subjects and tested them on almost the same driving tasks under three noise conditions: silence, rock music played at a gentle 55 decibels (分贝), and the same music at 85 decibels.

For l0 minutes the subjects sat in front of a screen operating a simple machine like a car. They had to track a moving disk on screen, respond to traffic signals changing colour, and brake (刹车) in response to arrows that appeared without warning.

On the tracking task, there was no difference in performance under the three noise conditions. But under both the loud and quiet music conditions, the performers "braked" at a red light about 50 milliseconds sooner than they did when there was no rock music at all. That could mean a reduction in braking distance of a couple of metres actually, the difference between life and death for a pedestrian.

When it came to the arrows that appeared across the visual field, the psychologists found that when the music was quiet, people responded faster to objects in their central field of sight by about 50 milliseconds. For the people listening at 85 decibels, response times dropped by a further 50 milliseconds — a whole 10th of second faster than those "driving" with no music.

"But there's a trade-off," the psychologists told the European Congress of Psychology. "They lose the ability to look around the whole situation effectively." In responding to objects that suddenly appeared, people subjected to 85-decibel rock music were around 100 milliseconds slower than both the other groups. Since some accidents — such as children running into the road — take place without any notice, drivers listening to loud music must be less safe as a result.

6. Which of the following is the best to make driving safer?

   A. Loud music.
   B. Quiet music.

   C. Silence.
   D. Heavy metal music.

7. The underlined phrase "pulling up" in the first paragraph probably means "_____".

   A. stopping
   B. giving somebody a lift

   C. putting up with
   D. driving

8. Where did the researchers do the experiment?

   A. At crossroads.
   B. At a police traffic station.

   C. In a crowded street.
   D. Under similar conditions as those of the streets.

9. Which of the following didn't help the performers "brake" sooner at red lights?

   A. Silence.   B. Loud music.   C. Quiet music.   D. Rock music.

10. Which of the following is TRUE of loud music?

    A. It made the performers brake slower at red lights.

    B. It made the performers be less careful.

    C. It helped the performers respond faster to objects suddenly stepping in the way.

    D. It can do more harm than good to drivers.

IV. 阅读表达（共5小题，每小题3分，满分15分）

Many high schools and colleges with a football team in the United States usually have a homecoming day. This can be the most important event of the year next to graduation. Students plan homecoming day for many weeks. When the day arrives, they begin before dawn to decorate the schools. There are signs to wish luck to the team and many other signs to welcome all the graduates. Many people still come to homecoming 20 or 30 years after their graduation. The members of school clubs build booths and sell lemonade, apples or sandwiches. Some clubs help welcome visitors. During the day people like to look for teachers that they remember from long ago. Often they see old friends and they talk together about those happy years in school. Everyone soon comes to watch the football game. When the game is half over, the band comes onto the field and plays school songs. Another important moment is when the homecoming queen or king appears. All the students vote a most popular student _____. It is a great honour to be chosen. Homecoming is a happy day. Even if the team loses, the students still enjoy homecoming. Some stay at the school to dance, and others go to a party. For everyone it is a day to remember for a long, long time.

1. What is the best title for the passage? (Please answer within 10 words.)

_____

2. Of all the events, what are the two things that all the students do on homecoming day? (Please answer within 15 words.)

_____

3. Fill in the blank with the proper words or phrases to complete the sentence. (Please

answer within 10 words.)

_____

4. Why do the students still enjoy homecoming even if the team loses? (Please answer within 30 words.)

_____

_____

5. Translate the underlined sentence into Chinese.

_____

Ⅴ. 写作（满分30分）

请以"How to Protect Your Eyesight"为题写一篇短文，说明保护视力的重要性及主要措施。

提示：1. 越来越多的学生近视；

2. 应该注意用眼时间不宜太长；

3. 读书时眼睛应该与书保持一定的距离；

4. 不要在昏暗的角落里看书，也不要在车上或躺在床上看书；

5. 坚持每天做眼保健操。

词数要求：120～150词。

How to Protect Your Eyesight

_____

_____

_____

_____

_____

Module ⑤

Ethnic Culture

高考词汇	minority, diverse, native, bright-coloured, belt, run, custom, hatch, pineapple, apparently, crop, opera, farm, fish, hammer, foolish, lame, tyre, firm, jungle, soul, ox, spear, garment, sleeve, necklace, jewellery, arch, rigid, framework, fasten, loose, fibre, corn, spade, tool, chick, rooster, fold, adjust, mat, teapot, bare, waist, widow, nephew, garage, awkward, rainbow, gatherer
常用短语	come across, make up, put up, go on about sth, fall for, think over, too much, pick up, have a population of, in the distance, set off
实用句型	They sit in small circles in the square, with their babies on their backs, completely uninterested in the tourists.
交际用语	1. What are the local people like? 2. Tell me more. 3. This is fascinating! I'm fascinated. 4. How come? 5. I'm green with envy. 6. What do you reckon?

◆ **高考词汇**

1. adjust

v. 1) 调整，调节；2) 适应，使适合

Please do not adjust the setting of this machine.

The body adjusts itself to changes in temperature.

You should adjust your expenditure to your income.

2. bare

adj. 1) 赤裸的；2) 空的，无装饰的；3) 仅有的，勉强的

Mary's bare feet made no sound in the soft sand.

The room was cold and bare.

He earned a bare living.

> **拓·展**
> barely *adv.* 贫乏地；几乎没有
> barely furnished rooms
> He can barely read and write.

3. jewellery

n. 珠宝，首饰

Her jewellery was insured for one million dollars.

a piece of jewellery

4. loose

adj. 1) 自由的，无约束的；2) 不紧的，宽松的；3) 不严谨的，不确定的

v. 释放，放开

The dog is too dangerous to be left loose.

She wears a loose garment.

This is a loose translation of the letter.

He loosed the animal from the cage.

5. fold

n. 褶痕

v. 1) 折叠，对折；2) 折起，叠好；3) 可折叠；4) 交叉 (双臂、双腿等)

Bend back the card and cut along the fold.

Fold the paper along the dotted line.

I wish you kids would fold up your clothes!

This is a useful little bed that can fold away when you don't need it.

George stood silently with his arms folded.

◆ 常用短语

1. come across

come across 的主要含义有：

1) 偶然发现或遇见某人/某物 (= meet with / run into)；2) 被理解

I came across this old brooch in a curio shop.

Your point really came across at the meeting.

2. put up

put up 的含义有：

1) 举起，抬起；2) 建起，树立；3) 公布，公告；4) 提高，增加；5) 包装；6) 提供 (一笔钱或一事业等)；7) 供以食宿

We put up a flag when we got there.

He put up a tent in the open air.

The president put up a notice in the meeting.

The landlord put up the rent by five pounds a week.

He put his lunch up in a paper bag.

I will supply the skill and knowledge if you put up the ￡2,000 capital.

We can put you up for the weekend.

3. fall for

fall for 意思是"为……倾倒，被……迷住"。

Dick fell for basketball when he was a little boy.

4. think over

think over 意思是"仔细想，作进一步考虑，谨慎思考"。

I'd like more time to think things over.

5. too much 和 much too

too much 用在不可数名词前，也可用作代词或副词。

much too 用在形容词前，much 用在 too 前来加强语气。

too much beer / water

Too much was happening all at once.

You work too much.

You are much too kind to me.

6. pick, pick out 和 pick up

pick 意为"挑选，选择；采摘 (花朵等)；剔，扒"等。

pick out 意为"选出来，拣出来"。

pick up 意为"拿起，捡起；(用车) 接送；偶然获得，偶然学会；接收，收听"等。

They spent the summer picking strawberries.

144

We picked some strawberries to eat on the way.

She sits and picks the loose skin on her feet.

Have you picked out a dress for the party?

He picked the phone up and dialled.

Will you pick me up after the party?

In that city, there is a small market where you can pick up some amazing bargains.

She picked up a few German phrases while staying in Berlin.

I don't think this thing can pick up foreign stations.

综合训练

考试时间：45分钟　满分：100分

I. 单项选择（共15小题；每小题1分，满分15分）

1. _____ beauty of _____ picture does not depend only on its subject but on its style.

   A. The; a   B. /; the   C. The; the   D. /; a

2. Wang Li, I don't think you _____ Feng Yang, a newcomer to our class.

   A. having met   B. to have met   C. have met   D. had met

3. —Have you brought my book?

   —Oh no! I _____ again. That was stupid of me.

   A. forgot   B. have forgotten   C. had forgotten   D. forget

4. Some children are mad over video games. They just can't tear themselves away from them _____ they start.

   A. since   B. once   C. even if   D. as

5. —What did you think of the food?

   —Well, it _____ worse.

   A. couldn't have been   B. couldn't be

   C. might not have been   D. might not be

6. Sir, I wouldn't ask for a day off if I didn't feel I _____. You know, my son is running a high fever.

   A. used to   B. happened to   C. failed to   D. had to

7. In the north, summer is short and cool at night, _____ winter is not so bad with heating.

   A. while   B. though   C. if   D. for

8. —Why did he write to the mayor's office?

   —_____ about the poor taxi service of the city.

   A. He complains   B. To complain   C. Complaining   D. For complaining

9. —Travelling is usually expensive.

—You _____ be right but I should say it depends on how you do it.

    A. can   B. must   C. will   D. may

10. The policeman questioned the _____ workers on the scene about the _____ thief.

    A. retiring; escaping   B. retired; escaping

    C. retired; escaped   D. retiring; escaped

11. In darkness he ran into a huge vase, which fell, _____ to pieces.

    A. broke   B. broken   C. breaking   D. having broken

12. I wonder _____ we shall have to walk _____ catch the last bus.

    A. whether; or else   B. either; or   C. that; or that   D. whether; or

13. _____ many quality problems with the goods, they decided to put off the meeting.

    A. Having found   B. Finding   C. Found   D. Being found

14. When _____ why he left without permission, he just dropped his head and _____ nothing.

    A. asking; saying   B. asked; said   C. asking; said   D. asked; saying

15. He was so shy that he _____ strangers the way to his home.

    A. not dare ask   B. dare not ask   C. dared not to ask   D. not dared to ask

Ⅱ. 完形填空（共20小题；每小题1分，满分20分）

    Like most July days, it was hot. I __1__ into a tiny ice cream shop to cool off with a chocolate ice cream. It was a very __2__ store with little round tables and chairs.

    As I entered, I found a very old woman bent __3__ a table near the door. Her __4__ was so badly bent that her face nearly __5__ the table top. I sat down facing her a couple of __6__ away.

    "Poor woman," I thought. "What does she get __7__ life? Why does God let people live so long past their youth? "As I thought, another __8__ lady entered the shop and sat down with her. Soon the two of them were __9__ childhood days. They talked of how little the shop had __10__ in 70 years… In minutes, the two of them were shaking with laughter.

    I looked again at the first woman, then in the __11__ on a nearby wall, catching the picture of myself. I was __12__ a dirty shirt. She was well dressed in white, her hands shining with gold rings. I was __13__. She was laughing, smiling. I was putting the __14__ of my life together. She had millions of wonderful memories to recall. I sat alone. She was __15__ them with a good friend. I was __16__ worried about getting old. She was old, but it wasn't __17__ her.

    As I left the shop, I __18__ my foolish question about God letting people live past their youth. Why, that woman was more alive, more sensitive to __19__ than I was. Age has not bent her __20__.

  1. A. looked   B. knocked   C. stepped   D. came

2. A. old   B. modern   C. pretty   D. ugly

3. A. under   B. below   C. over   D. above

4. A. head   B. chest   C. neck   D. back

5. A. connected   B. touched   C. hit   D. joined

6. A. tables   B. miles   C. kilometres   D. inches

7. A. for   B. off   C. away from   D. out of

8. A. young   B. beautiful   C. aged   D. middle-aged

9. A. speaking of   B. talking about   C. discussing   D. remembering

10. A. changed   B. become   C. increased   D. reduced

11. A. newspaper   B. window   C. mirror   D. TV

12. A. dressing   B. wearing   C. putting on   D. having on

13. A. happy   B. surprised   C. poor   D. sad

14. A. periods   B. pieces   C. points   D. masses

15. A. sharing   B. spending   C. killing   D. sparing

16. A. really   B. mostly   C. publicly   D. secretly

17. A. pleasing   B. hurting   C. leaving   D. punishing

18. A. realised   B. wondered   C. gave up   D. thought of

19. A. life   B. work   C. pleasure   D. friendship

20. A. courage   B. spirit   C. beauty   D. fortune

Ⅲ. 阅读理解（共10小题；每小题2分，满分20分）

A

Every human being, no matter what he is doing, gives off body heat. The usual problem is how to get rid of it. But the designers of the University of Pittsburgh set themselves the opposite problem — how to collect body heat, and the heat given off by such objects as electric lights and refrigerators as well. The system works so well that no fuel is needed to make the university's six buildings warm and comfortable.

Some parts of most modern buildings — theatres and offices as well as classrooms — are heated by people and lights far more than necessary, and sometimes they must be aired, even in winter. The skill of saving heat and sharing it out again in a different way is called "heat recovery". A few modern buildings recover heat, but the university's system is the first to recover heat from some buildings and reuse it in others.

Along the way, the University of Pittsburgh has learnt a great deal about some of its heat producers. The harder a student studies, the more heat his body gives off. Boy students send out more heat than girl students, and the larger a student is, the more heat he produces. It sounds rather reasonable to draw the following conclusion that the <u>hottest prospect</u> for the University of Pittsburgh would be a hardworking, overweight boy student who is very clever in the university.

1. According to this passage, the heat system of the University of Pittsburgh is supplied by _____.

    A. human bodies

    B. human bodies and electrical equipment

    C. human bodies and fuel

    D. human bodies, electrical equipment and fuel

2. The skill of heat recovery is used to _____.

    A. find out the source of heat

    B. produce a special form of air conditioning

    C. provide heat for the hot water system

    D. collect and reuse heat

3. Which of the following persons would produce the least amount of heat?

    A. A fat boy student who is clever and studies hard

    B. A thin girl student who is not clever and does not study hard

    C. A thin boy student who is clever and studies hard.

    D. A fat girl student who is both clever and hard-working.

4. In the last sentence, the underlined phrase "hottest prospect" refers to the person who _____.

    A. produces the most heat

    B. suffers most from heat

    C. takes in the most heat

    D. bears the most heat

5. The best title for this passage is _____.

    A. Modern Building's Heat System

    B. A New Heat Recovery System in the University of Pittsburgh

    C. Recovery of Body's Heat in the University of Pittsburgh

    D. The Best Way to Save Fuel or Electricity

B

San Francisco is now an Asian city.

When Jeannie Gant left China in 1993 to move to the US, she chose San Francisco because she knew she could find her favourite dishes there.

"And also because San Franciscans better know the fact that the Asian community is not one," she added. "Tell them that you are Korean or Chinese, and they will know the difference."

This year San Francisco will become the only city in the US besides Honolulu with more Asians than whites. "For the Chinese population particularly, this is a historic event," says David Lee, executive director of the Chinese-American Voter Education Committee.

Lee says that Chinese make up about 65 percent of San Francisco's Asian population. But he says it is important to remember that they were not always welcomed here. "The founding fathers of San Francisco, who were Irish and Italian, did all they could to prevent the Chinese and Asians in general from growing as a community," Lee says. "Now 100 to 150 years later, the Asian community has developed in ways that were unimagined just 50 years ago, when almost all of San Francisco's Chinese lived in a 5- or 6-block area known as Chinatown," he says.

"<u>Travel anywhere in Asia, ask which American cities people have heard of, and San Francisco will be at the top of the list.</u>" The immigration trend started in 1965. "Through the 1970s and 1980s there were many Asians coming, that continues today."

"African-American families are being taken the place of from low-income neighbourhoods in the south of the city by Asian immigrants who have more capital," Lee says. Asians have begun to have their influence politically by becoming American citizens and registering to vote.

6. How many cities are there in America, where there are more Asians than whites?
    A. One.   B. Two.   C. Three.   D. Four.
7. Suppose there are 1 million Chinese in San Francisco, there are _____ Asians in all.
    A. 65 million   B. 6.5 million   C. about 3.5 million   D.1.54 million or so
8. The founding fathers of San Francisco were from _____.
    A. Asia   B. America   C. Europe   D. Africa
9. The underlined sentence in the sixth paragraph means that _____.
    A. people in Asia have heard of San Francisco
    B. Asians like to travel in San Francisco
    C. San Francisco is the only place that is known to Asians
    D. San Francisco is better known to Asians than any other American city.
10. Which of the following is TRUE according to the passage?
    A. Jeannie Gant left China for San Francisco in order to make more money.
    B. Chinese began to immigrate to America in 1965.
    C. Asians stopped immigrating to the US at present.
    D. Asians in San Francisco have more rights than before.

IV. 阅读表达（共5小题；每小题3分，满分15分）

I want you to have fun reading this book. I'll do my best to make it enjoyable. You'll find that I'm much like you — I want to bring up the gifts inside my children. <u>With this book, my goal is to provide some practical tools for your toolbox as you attempt to develop the leadership qualities already inside of your children.</u> I will furnish leadership principles for them, and lots of ideas for how you can invest in them and develop them. I'll tell stories to illustrate how the principles work and help you evaluate how you and your child are developing them. I hope to give you a plan to develop a young leader.

By the way, this book _____. It might be helpful for a coach, teacher, pastor (牧师) , or university staff member. I'm writing to anyone who wants to bring out the leader inside a young person. With that said, let me paint you a broad picture of what I've laid out in this book.

The first section of this book provides insights on what you need to know about connecting with kids in this culture. You need to understand their world. I will unpack the colourful culture in which this generation lives. I'll try to give you tools to reach them.

1. What is the passage mainly about? (Please answer within 10 words.)

_____

2. To whom is this passage written? (Please answer within 15 words.)

_____

3. Fill in the blank in the second paragraph with proper words or phrases to complete the sentence. (Please answer within 10 words.)

_____

4. Guess what will be presented in the following paragraph right after this passage. (Please answer within 15 words.)

_____

5. Translate the underlined sentence in the first paragraph into Chinese.

_____

V. 写作（满分30分）

在现代生活中，人人都感到压力大。你的三个朋友 Mary Yan, Jack Park 和 Paul Wilson 对减压有不同看法。Mary Yan 认为最好的方法是每天早晨做一小时瑜珈；Jack Park 认为大笑能减轻压力；而 Paul Wilson 却认为睡觉是减压的最好办法。请你写一篇文章阐述他们三人的观点。

词数要求：120～150词。

_____

_____

_____

_____

_____

_____

Module ⑥

The World's Cultural Heritage

要点纵览

高考词汇	preserve, agreement, invest, primitive, existence, relation, beast, sharpen, list, evolution, weed, contribute, maintain, recommend, awareness, propose, assistance, precious, estimate, length, request, mankind, directory, bid, enlarge, discrimination, advocate, status, virus, compromise, seminar, mercy, absence, thorough, federal, guidance, ignore, honour
常用短语	agree on, go through, consist of, at the mercy of, in return, be honoured for, remind sb of sth
实用句型	1. They have recommended that the site be closed and repaired. 2. They have suggested that the general public be encouraged to help with the problem.
交际用语	1. Not to worry. 2. No matter what happens, you'll have a good time. 3. You'll have a day to remember. 4. No one knows for certain. 5. We'd better get back into the bus now.

◆ 高考词汇

1. absence

n. 1) 不在，外出；2) 缺席；3) 缺少

Please look after my house during my absence.

I soon noticed his absence from the lecture.

Absence of rain caused the plants to die.

➡ 常用短语：

absence of mind 心不在焉

in the absence of 由于缺乏

leave of absence 准假

2. bid

n. 1) 投标；2) 出价

v. 1) 投标 (on)；2) (在拍卖场所) 出价；3) 祝，表示

We want to make a bid for this project.

Is there no bid for this very fine painting?

I have no idea whether the firm will succeed in bidding on the construction of the bridge.

To everybody's surprise, a fellow bid as much as 5,000 dollars for this vase.

He bid me good morning as he passed.

3. contribute

v. 1) 捐献；2) 贡献，提供

The kind-hearted person has contributed a large sum of money to the charity.

This warm-hearted TV viewer contributed a lot of good proposals to the TV station.

4. recommend

v. 1) 劝告，建议；2) 推荐，建议

Sam's father strongly recommended sending the boy to school in New York.

Can you recommend a good lawyer?

➡ 常用结构：

recommend + doing / that 从句 劝告做某事

recommend sb for 推荐某人做

recommend sth to sb / recommend sb sth 向某人推荐某物

I recommend travelling by subway in Beijing because it is very convenient and cheap.

We recommend him for the post.

Can you recommend a good book to me?

5. undertake

v. 1) 承担，承办；2) 着手，进行；3) 保证，担保

In spite of danger, he undertook the difficult task without any hesitation.

It is three years since he undertook a new experiment.

I can't undertake that you will make a profit.

6. remains

n. 1) 剩余物，残余；2) 遗迹；3) 遗体

She feeds the remains of meals to the dog.

The sports meeting was held in Rome where you can see some remains of ancient Rome.

His remains were buried in the churchyard.

7. damage

n. 损害

v. 损伤，损害

Frost caused heavy damage to the crops.

Smoking can damage your health.

辨 析

damage, destroy, harm, hurt, injure, wound

damage 主要指对于物的损害，强调对于价值、用途、外观等所造成的破坏。

destroy 一般指毁灭性的摧毁。

harm 指对身心健康的损害、伤害或对抽象事物的伤害。

hurt 常指因不小心而引起的痛苦或意外地受到伤害，也常指精神上、情感上的伤害。
　　此外，作不及物动词时，表示"疼痛"。

injure 意为"受伤，伤害"，一般指由于意外或事故而造成伤害，可用于无生命物体的
　　损坏，更多用于对人的某个部位的损坏。

wound 指枪伤或刀伤，是出血的、严重的伤，特指在战场上受伤。

The car was badly damaged when it hit the wall.

The building was destroyed in the earthquake.

Don't harm your eyes by reading in dim light.

She felt hurt at your words.

In the traffic accident ten were killed and eight were injured.

The bullet wounded him in the shoulder.

◆ 常用短语

1. agree on

agree on 意思是"就……达成一致意见"。

After a week's negotiations, the two companies agreed on the contract eventually.

辨析

agree on, agree to, agree with

agree on 意思是"就……达成一致意见"。

agree to 意思是"同意(办法、提议、计划等)"。

agree with 意思是"同意(某人的话或观点);适合,与……一致"。

They finally agreed on the plan.

We all agree to the plan.

I agree with you / your words.

The climate here agrees with me.

2. at the mercy of

at the mercy of 意思是"在……支配下,任凭……的摆布"。

The boat was at the mercy of the rapid river.

3. in return

in return 意思是"作为回报"。

If you give me your photo, I'll give you mine in return.

He didn't expect anything in return for his help.

4. be honoured for

be honoured for 意思是"因……而受到尊敬"。

She will be honoured for her work in promoting friendship between the two countries.

5. remind sb of sth

remind sb of sth 意思是"使某人想起某事"。

He reminded me of my dentist's appointment the next day.

拓 展

have mercy on / upon (= show mercy to sb / show sb mercy) 对……表示怜悯/宽恕

We should learn to have mercy on others.

They showed little mercy to the prisoners.

拓 展

remind sb to do sth 提醒某人去做某事

remind sb about sth 提醒某人某事

Please remind Jenny to bring her laptop when she comes.

Will you remind me about that appointment?

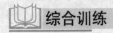

考试时间：45分钟　满分：100分

I. 单项选择（共15小题；每小题1分，满分15分）

1. You will succeed in the end _____ you give up halfway.
   A. even if　　　　B. as though　　　　C. as long as　　　　D. unless

2. The team _____ only 10 people won the game finally.
   A. consists of　　B. consisting of　　C. consist of　　　D. consisted of

3. I wonder if your wife will go to the ball. If she _____, so _____ I.
   A. does; will　　B. will; do　　　C. does; do　　　D. would; will

4. Five _____ three is eight.
   A. adding to　　B. added to　　C. added up to　　D. added up

5. He insisted that he _____ really very tired and that he _____ to have a rest.
   A. was; be allowed
   B. was; must be allowed
   C. should be; must be allowed
   D. should be; be allowed

6. Musical traditions around the world form part of the intangible heritage of mankind in the same way _____ monuments and natural sites.
   A. with　　　　B. like　　　C. as　　　　D. that

7. They were lost at sea, _____ the mercy of wind and weather.
   A. with　　　　B. on　　　C. at　　　　D. in

8. _____, he couldn't persuade his mother to agree with him.
   A. No matter he tried how hard
   B. No matter tried how hard he
   C. No matter how hard he tried
   D. No matter how he tried hard

9. —Do you know her address?
   —I'm sorry. I don't know it _____.
   A. as certain　　B. certainly　　C. for certain　　D. sure

10. The band played a lot of songs, _____ some of my favourites.
    A. included　　B. including　　C. includes　　D. to include

11. His doctor suggested that he _____ a short trip abroad.
    A. will take　　B. would take　　C. take　　　D. took

12. He ordered that the work _____ right away.
    A. should finish　　B. finished　　C. would be finished　　D. be finished

13. When you read the book, you'd better make a mark _____ you have questions.
    A. at which　　B. at where　　C. the place where　　D. where

14. —I've got your invitation.
    —Oh, good. _____
    A. Can you come?
    B. Thanks a lot.
    C. I'll take it.
    D. May I help you?

15. I won't forgive her unless she _____.

    A. will apologise   B. apologised

    C. would apologise   D. apologises

II. 完形填空（共20小题；每小题1分，满分20分）

    It was raining. I went into an Internet café and asked for a coffee. __1__ I was waiting for my drink, I realised there were other people in the place, but I sensed __2__. I saw their bodies, but I couldn't feel their souls, __3__ their souls belonged to the __4__.

    I stood up and walked between the tables. When I came to the biggest computer, I saw a thin, small man __5__ in front of it. "I'm Steve," he finally answered after I asked him a couple of times what his name was. "I can't talk with you. I'm __6__," he said. He was chatting online and __7__, he was playing a computer game — war game. I was __8__.

    Why didn't Steve want to talk with me? I tried __9__ to speak to that computer geek (怪人), __10__ not a word came out of his mouth. I touched his shoulder, but no reaction. I was __11__. I put my hand in front of the monitor, and he started to shout, "__12__!"

    I took a few steps back, wondering if all those people in the café were looking at me. I __13__, and saw nobody show any interest.

    __14__, I realised that the people there were having a nice conversation with their machines, not with people. They were more __15__ having a relationship with the __16__, particularly Steve. I wouldn't want to __17__ the future of human beings if they preferred sharing their lives with machines __18__ with people.

    I was worried and sank in my thoughts. I didn't even __19__ that the coffee was bad, __20__ Steve didn't notice there was a person next to him.

1. A. Before   B. Since   C. Although   D. While
2. A. pain   B. loneliness   C. sadness   D. fear
3. A. because   B. when   C. until   D. unless
4. A. home   B. world   C. Internet   D. café
5. A. sleeping   B. laughing   C. sitting   D. learning
6. A. busy   B. thirsty   C. tired   D. sick
7. A. first of all   B. just then   C. at the same time   D. by that time
8. A. surprised   B. delighted   C. moved   D. frightened
9. A. once   B. again   C. first   D. even
10. A. but   B. so   C. if   D. or
11. A. excited   B. respected   C. afraid   D. unhappy
12. A. Shut up   B. Enjoy yourself C. Leave me alone   D. Help me out
13. A. walked about B. walked out   C. raised my hand   D. raised my head
14. A. From then on B. At that moment C. In all   D. Above all

15. A. interested in	B. tired of	C. careful about	D. troubled by
16. A. computer	B. soul	C. shop	D. guy
17. A. tell	B. plan	C. imagine	D. design
18. A. other than	B. instead of	C. except for	D. as well as
19. A. pretend	B. understand	C. insist	D. realise
20. A. as if	B. just as	C. just after	D. even though

III. 阅读理解（共10小题；每小题2分，满分20分）

A

George Daniels lives in London. He is a watchmaker. His work continues the tradition of the English watchmakers of the 18th and 19th centuries. Today this tradition is almost dead. Daniels is the only man in the world who designs his own watches, makes all the parts himself, and then puts them together.

A Daniels watch is the product of his hands alone. One of his watches, which is now in an American museum, took 3,500 hours to complete. He usually makes one watch a year. Each one is written "Daniels London", and costs about 10,000 pounds. Of course, these are not ordinary watches — they are very beautiful and will last three centuries.

George Daniels has always been fascinated by clocks and watches. When he was 5, he used to take his father's clock to pieces, and put it back together again. At school he used to repair the teachers' watches. When he was in the army, he repaired watches in his spare time. After he had left the army, he became a professional (职业的) watch repairer. Then from 1958 to 1968, he restored antique (古董) watches, and finally began making his own watches.

He is now internationally famous and many people would like him to make watches for them. Most of them will be disappointed. He chooses his customers very carefully indeed. "It must be someone who understands the subject," he says, "not someone who will leave the watch in the drawer and only show it to dinner guests."

1. George Daniels is _____.

   A. one of the few remaining watchmakers in the world

   B. the last of the great watchmakers who makes his watches by his hands alone

   C. one of the few who can restore antique watches

   D. the greatest watchmaker who repairs watches

2. His interest in watches _____.

   A. is strong because his family were all watchmakers

   B. grew because he had to repair watches in the army

   C. started when he studied at school

   D. is lifelong

3. Which of the following statements is TRUE?

   A. All Daniels watches are kept in museums.

B. There are not many Daniels watches in the world.

C. His family was very poor and he had to make a living by repairing watches.

D. He has made hundreds of watches and become very rich.

4. George Daniels makes watches for _____.

   A. anyone who wants to show them off to his friends

   B. anyone who asks him to make one

   C. someone who is very rich and wants to buy one

   D. someone who appreciates his watches

5. From the article we can learn that _____.

   A. no one can afford to buy a Daniels watch because it is too expensive

   B. as it takes too much time to complete a watch, the tradition of the English watchmakers of the 18th and 19th centuries is almost dead

   C. the watches made in the 18th and 19th centuries are now kept in American museums

   D. few people can understand the subjects of Daniels watches

B

Fred and Bonnie Cappuccino have 21 children. First they had two of their own and then they adopted 19 others from countries around the world. They adopted children from many countries, like Japan, India and Vietnam. Each time they made sure they had music, food, pictures, and books of the children's native country so they would feel good about themselves.

Fred and Bonnie had pre-school children running around the house for 26 years without a break! The washer was always going and clothes hung from one end of the room to the other. Everyone helped out with the housework. The family drank 10 litres of milk a day!

The Cappuccinos enjoyed their children. They took care of small problems right away so they wouldn't become big problems. Fred says, "If you have trouble with one of your children, don't worry. Worry doesn't help, and in time your child will be all right."

The family lives in a log cabin they bought for $8,000 thirty years ago. After Bonnie got permission from the Canadian government to sponsor 100 Vietnamese, Fred asked some neighbours to build an extra room for the boat people.

When the children were older, Bonnie began travelling to India. She opened with them homes for 170 homeless children. She travels there four times a year to bring vitamins, medicine, and used clothing to the needy children.

Back home, Bonnie cooks vegetarian meals for her seven children still living with them. The other children keep in touch. When Tran got married, 18 brothers and sisters danced at his wedding.

The Cappuccinos hope their children will find their own way to help others. They want them to be happy, healthy and independent.

Fred says, "<u>Let me light my lamp and never wonder if it will take away the darkness.</u>"

6. What did the Cappuccinos do to make sure that the children felt good about themselves?

A. To offer them things from their own country.

B. To feed them well.

C. To make sure they could play well.

D. To handle small problems right away.

7. What does the underlined phrase "the boat people" in the fourth paragraph mean?

A. People who live on fishing.

B. People who escape in small boats.

C. People who you pay for the use of a boat.

D. People who make boats.

8. Why does Bonnie often travel to India?

A. She likes travelling.　　　　　B. She loves India.

C. To care for the homeless children.　　D. To find more Indian children to adopt.

9. What does Fred mean by saying "Let me light my lamp and never wonder if it will take away the darkness"?

A. He will light his lamp to take away the darkness.

B. Though he lights his lamp, he can't take away the darkness.

C. No matter how much it weighs, he will offer his help with no doubt.

D. Although what he does is helpless, he will still go on offering his help.

10. Why would the couple want such a life in the first place?

A. To get extra money from the government.

B. To be allowed to build more rooms.

C. To have more chances to travel abroad.

D. To offer help and show their love.

IV. 阅读表达（共5小题；每小题3分，满分15分）

Every country has many good people who help take care of others. For example, some high school and college students in the United States often spend many hours as volunteers in hospitals, orphanages or homes for the aged. They read books to the people in these places. Or they just visit them and play games with them or listen to their problems.

Other young people volunteer to collect food or money, or they work in the homes of people who are sick or old. They paint, clean up or repair their houses, do their shopping or mow their lawns. For boys who no longer have fathers there is an organisation called Big Brothers. College students and other men take these boys to baseball games or on fishing trips and help them know about things that boys usually learn from their fathers.

Every city has a number of clubs where boys and girls can go to play games or learn crafts. Some of these clubs show films or organise short trips to the mountains, the beaches, the museums or other places of interest. Most of these clubs use many high school and college students as volunteers because they still remember the problems of younger boys and girls. Volunteers believe that some of the happiest people in the world are those _____.

1. What is the passage mainly about? (Please answer within 10 words.)

_____

2. What do volunteers usually do in the homes for the aged? (Please answer within 30 words.)

_____

_____

3. Fill in the blank in the third paragraph with proper words or phrases to complete the sentence. (Please answer within 10 words.)

_____

_____

4. What else would you do if you got a chance to be such a volunteer? (Please answer within 30 words.)

_____

_____

5. Translate the underlined sentence in the third paragraph into Chinese.

_____

Ⅴ. 写作（满分30分）

你们班的班会就高三学生是否应开设计算机课展开讨论。请你根据下列提示，用英语写一篇短文，阐明你的观点。

提示：1. 你赞同开设计算机课；

2. 可以使用计算机练习英语听力；

3. 可以用计算机上网冲浪，放松自己；

4. 要学会自控，沉迷于计算机对学习当然会有影响。

注意：不能逐条翻译上述要点。

参考词汇：上网冲浪 surf the Internet

词数要求：120～150词。

_____

_____

_____

_____

_____

_____

第一部分　听力（共两节，满分30分）

第一节　（共5小题；每小题1.5分，满分7.5分）

听下面五段对话。每段对话后有一个小题，从题中所给的三个选项中选出最佳选项。听完每段对话后，你都有10秒钟的时间来回答有关小题和阅读下一小题。每段对话仅读一遍。

1. What can we learn from the conversation?
   A. The woman is wearing a hairpiece.
   B. The woman has a new hairstyle.
   C. The woman's hair is combed nicely.

2. Where does this dialogue most probably take place?
   A. In a hospital.　　　　B. In a hotel.　　　　C. In a company.

3. What will the woman do?
   A. She will go to the store with the man.
   B. She will meet the man at the store.
   C. She won't go to the store.

4. Where does this dialogue most probably take place?
   A. In a theatre.　　　　B. At home.　　　　C. In an office.

5. What does the woman mean?
   A. All the things in America are cheap.
   B. All the things in America are expensive.
   C. Not all the things in America are cheap.

第二节　（共15小题；每小题1.5分，满分22.5分）

听下面五段对话或独白。每段对话或独白后有几个小题，从题中所给的三个选项中选出最佳选项。听每段对话或独白前，你将有时间阅读各个小题，每小题5秒钟；听完后，各小题将给出5秒钟的作答时间。每段对话或独白读两遍。

听第6段材料，回答第6至第8小题。

6. Why did the man call the woman?
   A. He wanted to invite her to the football game.
   B. He lost his ticket to the football game.
   C. He wanted directions to the stadium.

7. What advice did the woman give the man?
   A. To go early.　　　B. To buy his ticket early.　　　C. To listen to the radio.

8. How did the woman know there would be many people at the stadium?

    A. She heard it from a friend.

    B. Peter told her.

    C. The radio said that the tickets had been sold out.

听第7段材料，回答第9至第11小题。

9. Who do you think Jack probably is?

    A. A tourist.   B. A Londoner.   C. A guide.

10. Why won't they be able to see *Swan Lake* together?

    A. They haven't booked seats yet.

    B. Jack will have to leave London.

    C. They will have to leave for the airport.

11. What can we learn from this conversation?

    A. The man goes to the Grand Theatre every week.

    B. The man has booked a seat for the woman.

    C. The woman has interest in seeing plays.

听第8段材料，回答第12至第14小题。

12. In the man's opinion, what are usually broadcast on the radio nowadays?

    A. Music, talk shows and news.   B. Talk shows only.   C. Talk shows and news.

13. What does the woman think of some talk show hosts' being rude to the listeners against their ideas?

    A. It's acceptable.   B. It's terrible.   C. It's exciting.

14. When does the woman usually listen to the radio?

    A. While working at home.   B. While driving a car.   C. Before going to sleep.

听第9段材料，回答第15至第17小题。

15. Why does the man decide to give up eating meat?

    A. Because he realises meat is bad for his health.

    B. Because he loves to eat vegetables.

    C. Because he wants to lose weight.

16. Why did the man stop jogging to work according to himself?

    A. Because he was always late for work.

    B. Because he felt too tired to keep doing so.

    C. Because he hurt himself in the leg.

17. What is the probable relationship between the speakers?

    A. Workmates.   B. Husband and wife.   C. Doctor and patient.

听第10段材料，回答第18至第20小题。

18. Why couldn't Tom buy any food?

    A. Because he had no money.

    B. Because he didn't want to eat.

C. Because he didn't do anything.

19. What was Tom's great dream?

A. To be a scientist.

B. To be a singer.

C. To be a great man in the world of films.

20. What happened to Tom many years later?

A. He was famous.

B. He was still a poor man.

C. He was not liked by others.

第二部分　英语知识运用（共两节，满分35分）

第一节　语法和词汇（共15小题；每小题1分，满分15分）

从 A、B、C、D 四个选项中，选出可以填入空白处的最佳选项。

21. _____ he's 24 now, he's still like a little child.

A. When　　　　B. Even though　　C. If　　　　　D. Whether

22. He really _____ the name of the most valued player in the league.

A. fits　　　　B. matches　　　C. deserves　　　D. suits

23. His head soon appeared out of the second-storey windows, _____ he could see nothing but trees.

A. there　　　　B. which　　　C. from it　　　D. from where

24. —Why do you look so worried?

—I got _____, and I don't have any money _____.

A. fired; saved　B. firing; saving　C. fired; to save　D. firing; save

25. It's quite obvious that the aging population in China will cause _____ heavy pressure on _____ whole society in the future.

A. a; /　　　　B. /; /　　　　C. the; a　　　D. a; the

26. —We want to go to the seashore.

—A summer at the seashore _____ the entire family.

A. benefits　　B. gains　　　C. profits　　　D. cures

27. —What do you want to be like when you grow up?

—I take Bill Gates _____ my role model.

A. for　　　　B. to　　　　C. with　　　D. as

28. —Did you hear that Jane went to Vietnam?

—That's funny… _____.

A. I think she hates to travel　　　　B. I thought she hated to travel

C. I think she hated to travel　　　　D. I thought she hates to travel

29. Excuse me for breaking in, _____ I have some news for you.

A. but　　　　B. so　　　　C. yet　　　D. and

30. I work in a business _____ almost everyone is waiting for a great chance.

    A. how   B. which   C. where   D. that

31. Everybody knows _____ that makes the teacher so proud.

    A. why it does   B. what he does   C. how it is   D. what it is

32. Tony, _____ to the teachers' office; everybody else, stay where you are.

    A. go   B. goes   C. is going   D. went

33. The Swiss football team lost today's match against Ukraine. They _____ enter the next round.

    A. can't   B. mustn't   C. needn't   D. shouldn't

34. —I was wondering if you'd like to go out this weekend.

    —_____ And I'll be free then.

    A. Mm, let me think.   B. Sure, I'd love to.

    C. What do you mean?   D. You're welcome.

35. —Nowhere in the world _____ a man who loves you so much.

    A. you may find   B. may you find   C. you can find   D. can you find

第二节　完形填空（共20小题；每小题1分，满分20分）

阅读下面的短文，掌握其大意，然后从每题所给的四个选项中选出最佳选项。

In America, Father's Day does not fall in August. And it wasn't __36__ by a proud parent either. While Mother's Day in the US was started by a __37__, Father's Day was __38__ started by a daughter, Sonora Dodd.

Dodd's mother __39__ while giving birth to her sixth child. Dodd's __40__, William Smart, a Civil War veteran, __41__ Sonora and the five other __42__ by himself on a farm in Eastern Washington State.

__43__ Dodd became an adult, she __44__ the sacrifices her father had made to raise the family. His birthday was in __45__, so she wanted to make a holiday to honour him that __46__. She held the first Father's Day __47__ in Spokane, Washington on June 19, 1910. The celebration soon caught on around the __48__.

In 1924 President Calvin Coolidge supported the idea of a __49__ Father's Day, but it didn't become __50__ until 1966 when President Lyndon Johnson declared the third Sunday of June as Father's Day.

These days, when children can't __51__ their fathers or take them out to dinner, they send a greeting __52__. Ties, flowers and cookies are also __53__ gifts. And while such companies may be grateful for the extra __54__, fathers everywhere are real __55__.

36. A. named   B. designed   C. created   D. caused

37. A. father   B. mother   C. daughter   D. son

38. A. actually   B. already   C. usually   D. exactly

39. A. went away   B. was sick   C. was divorced   D. died

40. A. grandfather   B. father   C. brother   D. neighbour

41. A. fed	B. cared for	C. educated	D. raised
42. A. kids	B. orphans	C. neighbours	D. friends
43. A. Before	B. As	C. After	D. Since
44. A. saw	B. realised	C. was told	D. understood
45. A. May	B. June	C. July	D. August
46. A. day	B. week	C. month	D. year
47. A. celebration	B. party	C. holiday	D. congratulation
48. A. farm	B. town	C. city	D. country
49. A. civil	B. national	C. worldwide	D. global
50. A. official	B. true	C. reality	D. effect
51. A. see	B. visit	C. call	D. understand
52. A. call	B. gift	C. hug	D. card
53. A. common	B. popular	C. valuable	D. usual
54. A. gifts	B. greetings	C. business	D. cards
55. A. winners	B. losers	C. fathers	D. supporters

第三部分　阅读理解（共20小题；每小题2分，满分40分）

阅读下列短文，从每题所给的四个选项中选出最佳选项。

A

Premier Wen Jiabao has a dream.

"I have a dream that one day every Chinese man, woman and child will be able to drink 500 grams of milk every day." He said this when visiting a farm in Chongqing. He expects milk to become more widely available and affordable. More than that, he also seeks to encourage people to change lifelong eating habits and enjoy the nutrition-rich and healthy drink.

For many Chinese people, a breakfast including milk is part of a Western diet. But it now appears on more and more Chinese tables. More people are beginning to realise how important drinking milk is for their health.

Today, a variety of milk is available on the market. Many claim to be fresh and some say they have added nutritional value. But what's the reality? How fresh should milk be? Is a certain type of milk better for your health? What are your options?

According to national standards, fresh milk refers to raw milk and milk that has been sterilised (消毒) by 80℃. Most of fresh milk's nutritional value is well preserved in this process but it can only be stored in a refrigerator for a maximum of seven days.

Another kind of milk can be stored safely for more than a month. It doesn't even have to be stored in a refrigerator. It does, however, need to have been sterilised by temperatures of as high as 137℃. But it is not as nutritionally rich as fresh milk, according to nutritionists. Vitamins A and D are sometimes added to milk, for nutritional purposes.

Different people actually need different things from milk. Therefore, a variety of milk is produced. The following are four different types of milk.

Different types of milk
Low fat milk (低脂奶) contains 1.0–1.5 percent of milk fat. (Milk usually contains about 3.0 percent of milk fat.)
Fat-free milk (脱脂奶) contains less than 0.5 percent of milk fat.
Flavoured milk (调味奶) is a kind of milk that has had things like chocolate, strawberry, vanilla or peanut flavouring added. It is mainly targeted at children and consumers who dislike the taste of milk. Some flavoured milk is coloured and extra sugar is added to make it taste sweeter.
Powdered milk (奶粉) is a mixture of milk powder and water. The nutritional value of powdered milk is less than fresh milk.

56. Why is it now still a dream for every Chinese to drink milk every day?

    A. Because milk is not easy to preserve and easily goes bad.

    B. Because many people are not used to drinking milk.

    C. Because many people have still not realised the importance of drinking milk.

    D. Because it is not easy to get milk in some places and the price is still high for many people.

57. Which of the following is "fresh milk"?

    A. Milk that needn't to be stored in a fridge.

    B. Milk sterilised by 80 ℃.

    C. Milk sterilised by 137 ℃.

    D. Milk stored for more than a month.

58. Which type of milk is more nutritious?

    A. Fresh milk.   B. Milk with additional Vitamins A and D.

    C. Milk sterilised by 100 ℃.   D. Powdered milk.

59. What type of milk contains less than 0.5 percent of milk fat?

    A. Low fat milk.   B. Fat-free milk.   C. Flavoured milk.   D. Powdered milk.

60. The purpose of this story is to _____.

    A. analyse the nutritional value of milk   B. tell you milk might not be suitable for you

    C. tell you new findings about milk   D. help you learn more about milk

B

The new mayor of Hillsdale, Michigan, is a man of the people, ready to listen to their every concern, but only until 6 pm. Then he has to do his homework.

The local elections on Tuesday may have been dismal for George Bush's Republican

Party, but they were a victory for Michael Sessions, an independent who emerged as the country's youngest mayor at the age of 18.

Mr Sessions, who is too young to drink in his own town, won by just two votes after a recount. By 670 votes to 668, he beat the <u>sitting mayor</u>, who is 51.

He was too young to stand by the spring deadline for registration (登记), so after he turned 18 he entered as a <u>write-in candidate</u> — meaning voters had to remember his name and add it to the ballot (选票) by hand in order to support him.

He started by winning the support of a powerful interest group, the Hillsdale firefighters' union, who had fallen out with the town council.

The union has a membership of three, but in post-September 11 America wields symbolic clout (力量). Before supporting Mr Sessions, its president, Kevin Pauken, called his teachers to check on his credentials (证明信).

"The guys were a little leery (不信任的) at first because of his age, but he really impressed us with his openness and his energy," Mr Pauken told reporters.

To help get his name known, Mr Sessions raised $700 selling toffee apples over the summer and spent it on posters and placards (广告牌) which were sprinkled around Hillsdale's lawns by election day.

His month-long campaign involved going door to door, explaining his vision of the town's future in the kitchens of his initially doubtful neighbours.

"They'd look at me, and say 'How old are you again? How much experience do you have?' And I say 'I'm still in high school'," he recalled.

61. What might be the proper title for this story?

    A. The Youngest Mayor in the USA   B. Running for Mayor

    C. Voting for the Young   D. A Fair Election

62. The strongest support for Mr Sessions comes from _____.

    A. the whole city   B. the firefighters' union

    C. the housewives   D. the schoolmates

63. What does the underlined phrase "sitting mayor" in the third paragraph mean?

    A. A mayor who is used to sitting in the office.

    B. A person who is the mayor at present time.

    C. A disabled mayor who is unable to stand up.

    D. A mayor who doesn't like sports much.

64. What does the underlined phrase "write-in candidate" in the fourth paragraph mean?

    A. A candidate who is not so qualified.

    B. A candidate who is not old enough for the election.

    C. The candidate's name is not on the ballot and has to be written on it by hand.

    D. A candidate that a voter can recommend by himself on the ballot.

65. Which of the following is TRUE according to the story?

    A. The election in the USA is totally free and fair.

    B. The drinking age allowed by law in Hillsdale is 18 years old.

    C. The former mayor is 33 years older than the newly-elected mayor.

    D. Mr Sessions is the very top student in his school.

C

The 32 teams at the World Cup are kicking a state-of-the-art ball, designed by Adidas. And at a museum in Hamburg, not far from the stadium, fans can examine a football centuries old.

The Museum of Volkerkunde is displaying some of football's most famous historical objects. What is thought to be the world's oldest football forms the centrepiece. The ancient football is usually on display in the Museum of Stirling Castle, in Scotland. It once belonged to the royal house at the time of Mary, Queen of Scots, who was born in 1542. The ball is made from a pig's bladder (膀胱) covered with pieces of leather, then tightly laced together. Museum director Dr Wulf Kopke said scientific tests proved the ball dates back to the reign (统治时期) of Mary.

Dr Wulf Kopke said, "It's a ball from the private collection of Queen Mary. It was found a few years ago in the private rooms of her castle. It's a well-known fact that she was a football fan, and scientific analysis has proved the ball was made in those days."

The exhibition, called "fascination football", takes the visitor through the history of the most popular sport on the planet. It features another interesting piece, a precise copy of the Jules Rimet World Cup trophy (奖杯). The original trophy went missing briefly at the 1966 World Cup. It was recovered, and given to Brazil in 1970, after they completed a hat trick of World Cup victories.

The exhibition holds 2,000 objects, from more than 70 countries. In contrast to Scotland's centuries-old ball, which is laced with heavy stitching (针脚), innovations have led to a football with no outside stitching at all.

Adidas unveiled the 2006 World Cup ball, named "Teamspirit", at the FIFA draft, in December 2005. The company says thermal bonding (热粘合) technology makes the new ball virtually waterproof, so it will play the same in wet or dry conditions. Hans Peter Nuernberg, Developer of Adidas Teamspirit Ball said, "Due to the introduction of the thermal bonding technology, no more stitching on the outer shell is needed." The company has also changed the surface arrangement, reducing the number of panels from 32 to 14. Fewer intersections make a smoother contact area for the foot.

66. When was the oldest football made in Scotland?

    A. About 400 years ago.   B. Less than 400 years ago.

    C. More than 400 years ago.   D. Not known yet.

67. The oldest football in Scotland formerly belonged to _____.

    A. Museum of Volkerkunde   B. Queen Mary

C. Stirling Castle   D. Brazil

68. In what ways is the oldest football different from the modern ones?

    A. It is made from a pig's bladder.   B. It is made of real leather.

    C. It is made of artificial leather.   D. It is made without stitching.

69. What makes the newest football special?

    A. It is named "Teamspirit" for the first time.

    B. It is not waterproof.

    C. The number of panels reduces to 32.

    D. Thermal bonding technology is applied.

70. What would be the best title for this passage?

    A. The FIFA   B. The Museum of Footballs

    C. The Oldest Football   D. The Development of Football

D

Throughout the history of the arts, the nature of creativity has remained constant to artists. No matter what objects they select, artists are to bring forth new forces and forms that cause change — to find poetry where no one has ever seen or experienced it before.

Landscape (风景) is another unchanging element of art. It can be found from ancient times through the 17th-century Dutch painters to the 19th-century romanticists and impressionists. In the 1970s Alfred Leslie, one of the new American realists, continued this practice. Leslie sought out the same place where Thomas Cole, a romanticist, had produced paintings of the same scene a century and a half before. Unlike Cole who insists on a feeling of loneliness and the idea of finding peace in nature, Leslie paints what he actually sees. In his paintings, there is no particular change in emotion, and he includes ordinary things like the highway in the background. He also takes advantage of the latest developments of colour photography to help both the eye and the memory when he improves his painting back in his workroom.

Besides, all art begs the age-old question: What is real? Each generation of artists has shown their understanding of reality in one form or another. The impressionists saw reality in brief emotional effects, the realists in everyday subjects and in forest scenes, and the Cro-Magnon people in their naturalistic drawings of the animals in the ancient forests. To sum up, understanding reality is a necessary struggle for artists of all periods.

Over thousands of years the function of the arts has remained relatively constant. Past or present, Eastern or Western, the arts are a basic part of our immediate experience. Many and different are the faces of art, and together they express the basic need and hope of human beings.

71. The underlined word "poetry" in the first paragraph most probably means "_____".

    A. an unusual quality   B. an object for artistic creation

C. a collection of poems   D. a natural scene

72. Leslie's paintings are extraordinary because they _____.

    A. are close in style to works in ancient times

    B. draw attention to common things in life

    C. look like works by 19th-century painters

    D. depend heavily on colour photography

73. What is the author's opinion of artistic reality?

    A. It will not be found in future works of art.

    B. It does not have a long-lasting standard.

    C. It is expressed in a fixed artistic form.

    D. It is lacking in modern works of art.

74. What does the author suggest about the arts in the last paragraph?

    A. They are regarded as a mirror of the human situation.

    B. They express people's curiosity about the past.

    C. They make people interested in everyday experience.

    D. They are considered important for variety in form.

75. Which of the following is the main idea of the passage?

    A. History of the arts.   B. Use of modern technology in the arts.

    C. New developments in the arts.   D. Basic elements of the arts.

第四部分　书面表达（共两节，满分45分）

第一节　阅读表达（共5小题；每小题3分，满分15分）

阅读下面的短文，并根据短文后的要求答题。

Members of China's latest South Pole exploration became the first humans to reach Antarctica's highest point, the Dome-A inland icecap, on Tuesday.

A 13 strong team set out from the Zhongshan Station on the southeast coast of the Antarctica on December 12, 2004 for a freezing, high-altitude journey covering about 1,200 kilometres. Machinist Gai Junxian had to turn back due to severe altitude sickness, but the 12 others made it to the summit in fairly good condition.

The explorers set up the Chinese flag on the spot and held a solemn ceremony as it was first raised.

Preliminary measurement by global positioning system showed the peak at Dome-A is 4,093 metres above sea level. Its cruel climate has earned it a reputation as one of the world's most underlined inaccessible places.

"Dome-A is a crucial point on the South Pole. No systematic scientific research has been done by any country at Dome-A before," Wei Wenliang, an official with China's Arctic and Antarctic Administration, said to *China Daily*. "To climb up the peak of Dome-A and do scientific research there will bring a breakthrough in humanity's polar ventures."

The area could hide valuable clues about the history of human evolution, according to information from the administration. The Dome-A plateau has relatively simple dynamic processes, making it a good place for icecap research. It is also one of the coldest places on Antarctica, so it is an important vantage point (有利位置) for collecting meteorological data (气象资料).

In keeping with the unwritten rule of Antarctic exploration that the first group to reach a place is responsible for leading scientific work there, the Arctic and Antarctic Administration has decided China will complete the exploration of Dome-A even at the sacrifice of some other polar programmes.

76. What is the passage mainly about? (Please answer within 10 words.)

_____

77. Did all the team members reach the destination? Why or why not? (Please answer within 15 words.)

_____

78. What does the underlined word "inaccessible" in the fourth paragraph mean? (Please answer within 5 words.)

_____

79. What do you know about the unwritten rule of Antarctic exploration according to the last paragraph? (Please answer within 15 words.)

_____

80. Translate the underlined sentence in the fifth paragraph into Chinese.

_____

第二节　写作（满分30分）

你在美国生活的姑姑邀请你去美国学习，对此你的父母有些犹豫。请你给姑姑写封电子邮件谈谈你的看法与理由。邮件的开头和结尾已经给出，不计入总词数。

词数要求：120词左右。

Dear Aunt,

First of all, I'd like to thank you for your hearty invitation.

_____

_____

_____

What do you think of my idea? I'm looking forward to your opinion.

Yours,
Li Hua

高考英语总复习点击与突破

顺序选修8

Module ①

Deep South

高考词汇	explorer, Antarctica, annual, rainfall, state, depth, gravity, extreme, flower, adapt, trap, mass, balance, exploration, treaty, commercial, nuclear, test, radioactive, promote, via, lifeboat, crew, voyage, glare, intense, sunglasses, suncream, eyesight, sunburnt, minus, numb, frost, clothing, portable, pure, millimetre, abnormal, sunrise, sunset, absence, daylight, tiresome, aircraft, platform, powder, minimum, modest, cosy, dormitory, canteen, stock, laundry, discourage, emergency, conventional, drill, tricky, fragile, battery, ecology, delicate, privilege, trader, jewel, befriend, tale, reliability, inspiration
常用短语	close to, set foot on, in case of, cut sth in two, in a state of, on average, a depth of, adapt to, lack of, be made up of, as a result, in the form of, stand out against, in particular, aim to do, the symbol of, leave for, come into sight, be trapped in, give up, set up, come up with, keep one's promise, according to, in the open air, become numb with, except for, be situated on, a well-stocked library of, discourage sb from doing sth, be well-known for, in great detail, leave behind, be fond of, keep one's spirits up
实用句型	1. it took sb some time to do sth 2. there is no truth to sth
交际用语	1. I suppose it runs in the family. 2. Welcome to the South Pole. 3. Is there anything good about the weather?

175

◆ **高考词汇**

1. explore

v. 1) 勘探，探测，考察；2) 检查，研究，探讨

Columbus discovered America but did not explore the new continent.

As soon as they arrived in the town they went out to explore.

We must explore all the possibilities for the solution of the problem.

> **拓 展**
>
> explorer *n.* 勘探者，探测者，探险者
>
> exploration *n.* 勘察，考察
>
> This famous explorer finally died in loneliness.
>
> The Elizabethan Age was a time of exploration and discovery.

2. state

n. 1) 国家；政府；州；2) 状态，状况；情况；情形

v. 陈述，说明

adj. 政府的；国家的；正式的

Should industry be controlled by the state?

His general state of health is fairly satisfactory.

Please state your name and address.

The late president, Mr Yeltsin, was given a state funeral.

> **辨 析**

state, condition, situation

state 指人或物存在或所处的状态，尤指物质和精神状态。

condition 指由于一定的原因、条件或环境所产生的特定情况，作"状态"讲时多作不可数名词，在有形容词修饰时可以用不定冠词，意思同 state；作"情况"讲时，多用复数 conditions；作"条件"讲时是可数名词。

situation 指多种具体情况造成的综合状态，常作政局、情景、形式等讲。

He is in a good state.

Hard work is a condition of success.

They went on strike for better working conditions.

We are in a difficult situation.

3. adapt

v. 1) (使)适应，(使)适合；2) 改编，改写；

3) 改建，改造

He tried hard to adapt himself to the new conditions.

> **拓 展**
>
> adaptable *adj.* 能适应的；可改编的
>
> adaptation *n.* 适应；改编
>
> He is not very adaptable.
>
> The novel's most adaptable parts for theatre were performed.
>
> He made a quick adaptation to the new environment.
>
> This play is an adaptation of a novel.

The author is going to adapt his play for television.

The boys adapted the old barn for use by the club.

4. trap

n. 1) 陷阱，罗网；2) (陷害人的) 圈套，诡计，阴谋

v. 1) 设陷阱；2) 使陷入圈套，使陷于困境；3) 阻止，抑制

The hunter set traps to catch foxes.

I knew perfectly well it was a trap.

He lives by trapping animals and selling their fur.

The lift broke down and we were trapped inside it.

A filter traps dust from the air.

➡ 常用短语：

be trapped in 被困在   trap sb into doing sth 用计谋诱使某人做某事

trap water 储水

be caught in a trap 落入陷阱   set / lay a trap for 设下圈套

5. mass

n. 1) 团，块，堆；2) 众多，大量，大宗；3) 大众，民众

adj. 1) 大众的，民众的；2) 大量的，大规模的，大批的

The vegetables had turned into a sticky mass at the bottom of the pan.

There was a mass of children in the yard.

I wonder if they are truly concerned with the interests of the masses.

Mass education is essential in promoting democracy.

We want to promote literacy on a mass scale.

➡ 常用短语：

a mass of (= masses of) 大量的   be a mass of sth 遍布着

in the mass 总体上，整个地

6. balance

n. 1) 天平，秤；2) 平衡，均衡；3) 结存，差额

v. 1) (使) 平衡，保持平衡；2) 抵消，补偿；3) 权衡，比较；4) 结算，使收支平衡

Do the firm's accounts balance?

His wife's sudden death upset the balance of his mind.

I must check my bank balance.

How long can you balance on one foot?

His lack of experience was balanced by his willingness to learn.

She balanced the attractions of a high salary against the prospect of working long hours.

➡ 常用短语：

be / hang in the balance 悬而未决   keep one's balance 保持平衡

lose one's balance 失去平衡   on balance 总的说来

7. promote

v. 1) 晋升，升级；2) 促进，发扬，提倡；
   3) 发起，创立；4) 宣传，推销(商品等)

She worked hard and was soon promoted.

The Prime Minister's visit will promote the cooperation between the two countries.

Several bankers promoted the new company.

They launched a publicity campaign to promote her new book.

辨 析

promote, advance, proceed, progress

以上四个词都含有"前进"的意思。

promote 作"提升"解时可与 advance 通用，它强调促使某种事业向前发展以达到预期的结果，并侧重于对人或事物（尤指公开性质）的赞助和鼓励。

advance 指向某一目标或方向前进的运动或效果。

proceed 多指继续前进。

progress 则指稳定、经常的进步，这种进步可能有间隔，常用于抽象事物。

A sound forest economy promotes the prosperity of agriculture and rural life.

Our soldiers advanced bravely against the enemy.

This being done, let's proceed to the next.

Our research work is progressing steadily.

8. privilege

n. 1) 特权，优惠；2) 优待，荣幸

v. 1) 给予……特权 (或优待)；2) 特免，免除

He enjoys diplomatic privileges.

It is a great privilege to know you.

Use of the library is a privilege, not a right.

This pass will privilege you to attend the closed hearings.

In some countries, the president can privilege somebody from capital punishment.

◆ 常用短语

1. close to

close to 意思是：1) 在近处；2) 接近于

Close to, these eyes were inspecting me.

178

She was close to tears.

The assessment is pretty close to the truth.

.辨 析

close, closely

close 表示具体的行为和动作，说明的动作或状况有可测量性和可见性。

closely 所表达的常常是抽象性的行为和状况。

类似的词还有 high 与 highly，wide 与 widely，deep 与 deeply，low 与 lowly 等。

He stood close against the wall.

He was watched closely.

Do you see that butterfly flying high above the street?

The distinguished guests were highly praised.

They had to dig deep to reach water.

You have offended him deeply.

2. in case

in case 含义有：1) 假使；2) 以防万一；3) 也许，说不定

In case she comes back, let me know immediately.

Take the raincoat in case it rains.

Wait outside in case you can be useful.

真 题 解 析

1) I always take something to read when I go to the doctor's _____ I have to wait. (2005 全国)

  A. in case   B. so that   C. in order   D. as if

解析：这句话的意思是：我去看病的时候总是带一些东西去读，以备必须等候时打发时间。in case 指"以防万一"，符合句子的意思。答案为 A。

2) —I'm afraid Mr Wood can't see you until 4 o'clock.

  —Oh, _____ I won't wait. (2005 浙江)

  A. no doubt   B. after all   C. in that case   D. in this way

解析：根据这个对话的语境，第二个人的回答应是"如果是那样的话我就不等了"。no doubt 的意思是"无疑地"，after all 的意思是"毕竟，终究"，in this way 的意思是"这样"，均不符合题意。答案为 C。

3. on average

on average 意思是"平均"，还可以写成on an / the average。

On average we receive five letters each day.

On an average I work 10 hours a day.

On the average, there are 300 tourists a week.

4. lack of

lack of 意思是"缺乏，不足"。

He can't buy it because of his lack of money.

Will training make up for lack of experience?

5. except for

except for 意思是"除了，除……之外"。

The museum is open, except for Monday.

The meal was excellent except for the first course.

辨析

besides, except, except for, but

besides 意思是"除……外还有"。

What have you done besides reading the newspaper?

except 意思是"除……之外，若不是，除非"。

1) 跟名词或代词

　　They all went to sleep except the young Englishman.

2) 跟介词短语

　　I can take my vacation at any time except in April.

3) 跟动词不定式

　　It had no effect except to make him angry.

4) 跟从句

　　I would go with you, except that I have to work that day.

except for 意思是"除了（某些方面或特征等）之外"。

Your composition is good except for a few spelling mistakes.

but 多与 no，not，every，any 等连用，或用于 nobody，all，who 等词的后面，表示"除去，除开"。通常可译成"只……"。

I haven't told anybody but you.

Put it anywhere but on the floor.

Nobody but Jenny surprised me.

They did nothing but complain.

拓展

average n. 1) 平均，平均数；2) 平均标准，一般水平

adj. 1) 平均的；2) 一般的，普通的

v. 平均，平均为

above / below the average 在平均水平之上/下

be up to the average 达到一般水平

average sth out 算出某事物的平均数

拓展

lack n. 1) [U] 欠缺，不足，没有；

2) [C] 缺少的东西，需要的东西

v. 缺少，没有

The teacher was dismayed at the students' lack of response.

Water is a lack of this region.

He is good at his job but he seems to lack confidence.

We had no choice but to arrive late.

如果 but 后面跟的是形容词，常译作"恰恰不，才不"。

She's anything but considerate.

6. stand out (from / against sth)

stand out (from / against sth) 的主要含义有：1) 突出，显眼；2) 坚持抵抗

Nancy stands out from the rest of the singers.

His height makes him stand out in the crowd.

We managed to stand out against all attempts to close the company down.

◆ **实用结构**

with + 宾语 + 宾补

在这个结构中，宾补可以由不同的词或短语来充当，如形容词、副词、介词短语、分词、动词不定式等，有时 with 可省略。

He fell asleep with the door open.

He left the classroom with the lights still on.

The woman with a baby in her arms is Beckham's wife.

The Changjiang River is very busy with so many ships and boats coming and going every day.

I stayed in my room with the door locked all day long.

I cannot go out with so much homework to do.

综合训练

考试时间：45分钟　满分：100分

I. 单项选择（共15小题，每小题1分，满分15分）

1. The newspaper decided to _____ and publish the story.

　A. wait　　　　B. come along　　C. keep up　　　D. go ahead

2. With two children _____ a middle school in the nearby town, the man has to work very hard.

　A. to attend　　B. attending　　C. attend　　　D. having attended

3. —What _____ is it on the desk?

　—It is a blue ball.

　A. on earth　　B. on the earth　　C. in earth　　D. in the earth

4. People should _____ their children _____ being addicted to computer games but _____ them to study scientific knowledge.

A. encourage; to; discourage   B. discourage; to; encourage

C. encourage; from; discourage   D. discourage; from; encourage

5. The exchange of high-level vists will contribute to _____ the mutual (相互的) understanding of the two nations.

     A. increasing   B. improving   C. promoting   D. advancing

6. I left him after the quarrel, determining never to _____ that house again.

     A. set in   B. set back   C. set foot in   D. set on

7. When I give up work, I shall make a long sea _____.

     A. travel   B. trip   C. voyage   D. journey

8. The estimated investment for the project is $6.59 million, with $2.57 million of that coming in the _____ of bank loans.

     A. form   B. shape   C. style   D. appearance

9. The young dancers looked so charming in their beautiful clothes that we took _____ of pictures of them.

     A. many   B. masses   C. the number   D. the amount

10. He was _____ being killed by a passing car when he was walking in the street.

     A. almost   B. nearly   C. closely   D. close to

11. This movie is _____ boring; it is, in fact, rather exciting and interesting.

     A. anything but   B. nothing but   C. no more   D. all but

12. The region has _____ some of the fiercest fighting in the war.

     A. seen   B. watched   C. come   D. taken

13. He was so tired that he fell asleep _____ reading the newspaper.

     A. until   B. before   C. while   D. after

14. When they went into the shop and asked to look at the engagement rings, the girl brought out the cheaper ones, _____ she had arranged with James.

     A. the which was what   B. what was that

     C. which was what   D. that was what

15. He lay on the operating table, his teeth _____, and his eyes _____ straight upward.

     A. setting; looking   B. set; looked

     C. set; looking   D. setting; looked

II. 完形填空（共20小题；每小题1分，满分20分）

I never thought that I would have taken such an airplane. It is 2:30 am and I'm stuck in a __1__, uncomfortable seat. The entire plane is __2__, except for this fat, disgusting man sitting next to me who is snoring (打鼾) __3__ than the plane's engines.

Now he has started drooling (流口水) on me. I try to move in order to __4__ the spit dripping from the corner of his mouth. Every bone in my body cracks as I try to move; I have been in the __5__ position ever since my seatmate got back from his fourth __6__ to the bathroom in the first hour of the flight. I try to wake him by throwing all of my __7__ strength at his shoulder, but __8__. Just then the seatbelt light comes on, and __9__ I think I've been __10__, because we are about to land. But that dream is quickly __11__ as I look at my watch and realise that there are still three hours left in my __12__ nightmare. The plane begins to shake violently, which __13__ why the seatbelt light came on. Now the sound of two babies crying at the top of their voices __14__ the man's snoring. The plane shakes suddenly to the side, and this thing sitting next to me, which I don't believe is __15__ human, rolls its head in my direction just enough to __16__ its breath.

Maybe it's a __17__ of the turbulence (气流), the snoring and crying and the __18__ of this fat man, or maybe it's just the French fries and fish that I ate for dinner, but I feel sick and am starting to __19__ what is nothing left in my stomach. All I can do now is sit here. Only three hours more. All I can think about is the time in the not-so-distant future when I can __20__ being off this plane and waiting in the airport for six hours to catch my connecting flight.

1. A. broad   B. tiny   C. soft   D. long
2. A. noisy   B. crowded   C. advanced   D. silent
3. A. louder   B. more pleasantly C. faster   D. harder
4. A. stop   B. prevent   C. avoid   D. receive
5. A. right   B. comfortable   C. same   D. dangerous
6. A. trip   B. try   C. escape   D. appearance
7. A. increasing   B. surprising   C. encouraging   D. remaining
8. A. without luck   B. with no result C. without permission D. with difficulty
9. A. for a moment   B. in a moment   C. after a moment D. for no moment
10. A. fooled   B. returned   C. killed   D. saved
11. A. realised   B. continued   C. destroyed   D. expected
12. A. waking   B. exciting   C. interesting   D. moving
13. A. suggests   B. explains   C. puzzles   D. announces
14. A. joins in   B. competes   C. gets on   D. changes
15. A. generally   B. specially   C. completely   D. perfectly
16. A. stop   B. spread   C. offer   D. share
17. A. mixture   B. change   C. relay   D. competition
18. A. sight   B. performance   C. remark   D. fun
19. A. give up   B. call up   C. throw up   D. turn up
20. A. escape   B. enjoy   C. forget   D. remember

Ⅲ. 阅读理解（共10小题；每小题2分，满分20分）

A

Tens of thousands of baby penguins (企鹅) face starvation after two giant icebergs broke off the Antarctic ice sheet and blocked their parents' way to feeding areas.

Adélie and emperor penguins nesting on the Ross Island are now forced to walk long distances over the icebergs to obtain food for their chicks, born during the November–December breeding season.

"The penguins are having to walk 50km farther than usual to reach the sea," said Dean Peterson, a US scientist. The flightless birds travel on land at just one to two kilometres per hour.

The problem could halve the chick survival rate among the estimated 130,000 breeding pairs at the three Adélie penguin colonies on Ross Island. In all Antarctica, there is an estimated 3 million Adélie penguin breeding pairs. Around 12,000 breeding pairs of emperor penguins, the largest penguin species up to four feet tall, are also affected.

The icebergs broke from the vast Ross Ice Shelf, south of New Zealand, in March 2000 and are now sandwiched between Ross Island and Franklin Island, 93 miles to the north.

Peterson, estimated that penguins were taking days to make the round trip to the sea to fish, and then back to their nests to regurgitate (反刍) food for their chicks. "At that point they are quite tired and probably don't have much to regurgitate," he said. Penguins already <u>have long odds on</u> reaching adulthood, with only 10 percent surviving beyond adolescence (青春期).

"We are probably looking at halving that again — we are sitting down at maybe the five percent rate," Peterson said, adding some penguins already appeared to be leaving the Ross Island to breed elsewhere.

Penguins come ashore to breed and then take it in turns to leave the nest to fetch fish and other seafood to feed their young.

Researchers say large blocks of the Antarctic ice sheet are breaking off for several reasons, including global warming.

Emperor and Adélie penguins are limited to Antarctica. The emperor penguins weigh up to 66 pounds while the Adélie penguins are much smaller, weighing around 11 pounds.

1. What happened to the baby penguins?

A. Their parents left the Antarctic.

B. The ice covers the Antarctic.

C. They can't fetch fish.

D. Two giant icebergs blocked their parents' way to feeding areas.

2. After the long trip, penguin parents _____.

A. have already ate up all the food

B. are too tired to feed their young

C. can't bring up much to feed their young

D. are too hungry themselves

3. The underlined phrase "have long odds on" in the sixth paragraph probably means "_____".

A. have great hope of   B. have little chance of

C. have no difficulty in   D. spend long time in

4. From what Peterson said, we can infer that _____.

   A. penguins usually have a high survival rate

   B. the survival rate of penguins is dropping

   C. there are few penguins left on Ross Island

   D. the present situation can cause the penguins to die out

5. Which of the following best summarises the main idea of the passage?

   A. Broken icebergs endanger penguin chicks.

   B. Global warming caused the icebergs to break off.

   C. The long trip made penguin parents too tired to feed their young.

   D. The change of weather affects penguins.

B

Hungry prehistoric hunters, not climate change, drove elephants and woolly mammoths (猛犸) to extinction during the Pleistocene era, new research suggests.

At least 12 kinds of elephants and mammoths used to roam the African, Eurasian, and American continents. Today, only two species of elephants arc lcft in South Asia and sub-Saharan Africa. One theory for this dramatic demise holds that rapid climate shifts at the end of the most recent major ice age, some 10,000 years ago, altered vegetation and broke up habitats, causing the death of those that were unable to adapt to the new conditions. Another hypothesis (假设) blames prehistoric humans, whose improved weapons and hunting techniques allowed them to wipe out whole herds of elephants and mammoths.

To help resolve the debate, archaeologist Todd Surovell of the University of Wyoming and his colleagues tested the two assumptions. If humans caused the elephant and mammoth extinction, Surovell reasoned, the timing of the die-offs in specific regions should match human expansion into those regions. On the contrary, if the extinction of these mammals were due to climate change, elephants and mammoths should remain in regions already colonised by humans and would only begin to die off once climate change occurred.

The team tested both theories by analysing where and when elephants and mammoths were killed. In all, the study included 41 archaeological sites on five continents. The researchers found that, as humans migrated out of Africa, they left a trail of dead elephants and mammoths in their wake (紧随……之后). The creatures disappear from the fossil record of a region once it became colonised by humans. "Modern elephants survived in refuges uninviting to humans, such as tropical forests," said Surovell, whose team reports its findings online this week in *The Proceedings of the National Academy of Sciences*.

6. How many species of elephants and mammoths died out in history?

    A. More than twelve.   B. At least two.

    C. At least ten.   D. More than forty-one.

7. Which of the following has the similar meaning to the underlined word "demise" in the second paragraph?

    A. Death.   B. Disappearance.   C. Absence.   D. Change.

8. Which kind of view would archaeologist Todd Surovell probably agree to?

    A. Climate shifts caused the extinction of some elephants.

    B. The change in temperature brought some elephants to death.

    C. The prehistoric hunters were to blame for the extinction of some elephants.

    D. Human weapons led to the extinction of some prehistoric elephants.

9. Why do modern elephants survive according to the passage?

    A. Because human beings protect them from being harmed.

    B. Because the climate at present is suitable for modern elephants.

    C. Because modern elephants live where human beings rarely go.

    D. Because modern elephants are kept in the zoo.

10. What is the best title for this passage?

    A. Humans and Elephants   B. Debate on Elephants

    C. Development of Elephants   D. Who Killed the Elephants?

IV. 阅读表达（共5小题；每小题3分，满分15分）

If a beaver (海狸) needed dental work, where would it go? In this case, a beaver who lost her four front teeth in an accident with a car has been checked into Washington State University's Veterinary (兽医的) Teaching Hospital to recover.

The 41-pound animal, nicknamed Bailey, lost her chewing teeth when struck by a car last week near Lewiston, Idaho. A retired Idaho Fish and Game agent brought the injured beaver to the WSU's College of Veterinary Medicine.

Nickol Finch, the veterinarian who heads the veterinary hospital's Exotics and Wildlife Department, said the beaver's prognosis (预期治疗效果) is good, and treatment will be to let nature take its course as her teeth grow back.

"Her four front teeth _____ in about three months," Finch said.

A beaver's front teeth grow continually throughout its life and require constant biting to keep them at a healthy length. Beavers in the wild usually eat the bark of poplar, willow, birch and maple trees, using the wood for their homes.

"Since she doesn't have her front teeth, we've been feeding her salad greens, apple sauce and vegetable-based baby foods," Finch said by email Wednesday. "She's not eating much on her own, doesn't recognise what we have as a food source, so we've been syringe-feeding (用注射器喂养) her."

Once the bumps and bruises she suffered from the accident are healed in a few weeks, Bailey will be taken to a wildlife recovering centre for long-term care and eventual release near where she was found, Finch said.

1. What's the best title for this passage? (Please answer within 10 words.)

_____

2. Which sentence in the passage can be replaced by the following one?

The front teeth of a beaver keep growing during its whole life, and it needs to grind its teeth constantly to avoid their becoming too long.

_____

_____

3. Fill in the blank in the fourth paragraph with proper words or phrases to complete the sentence. (Please answer within 10 words.)

_____

4. Summarise the passage within 50 words.

_____

_____

_____

5. Translate the underlined sentence in the first paragraph into Chinese.

_____

V. 写作（满分30分）

根据下面这幅图写一篇短文，发表一下自己的看法。

企鹅宝宝：妈妈，这几年天气怎么这么热啊？我都快受不了了。您看那冰山都快融化光了。

企鹅妈妈：孩子！这都是全球气候变暖导致的。你看，这是咱们的"新家"！

词数要求：120～150词。

_____

_____

_____

_____

_____

Module ②

The Renaissance

要点纵览

高考词汇	disturbing, subject, dull, basically, work, effect, shade, frontier, motivate, skilled, tank, ferry, tax, anecdote, authentic, spokesman, burglar, antique, basement, courtyard, passerby, moustache, parcel, dash, crossing, crossroads, flee, sideroad, appeal, suspect, loss, circulate, seek, tentative, behalf, fundamental, drawback, superb, substitute, confidential, debt, merely, outcome, blame, liberty, gifted, movable, press, squeeze, passion, official, inspire, profession
常用短语	the combination of, more than, even if, hear of, begin with, trade with, afford to do, put together, contrast with, hand in hand, of little value, compared with, as well as, in short, describe…as, be shaped like, or so, end up, be different from, be made of, at the end of, depend on, instead of, in history, leave for, leave behind, appeal to, a gang of, make an attempt to do, on behalf of, get tired of, turn up, get the blame for, at liberty, a number of, be thirsty for, up to, set up, lead to, take up
实用句型	1. It is believed that… 2. It doesn't matter whether… 3. What's more… 4. Printing made it possible to do… 5. So did the demand for the Greek and…
交际用语	1. It's a typical satisfied smile of a mother-to-be. 2. I've read a fair bit about Mona Lisa. 3. Most of the theories about…are complete rubbish. 4. It looks as if she has the whole world on her shoulders. 5. It was only a short ride.

188

◆ 高考词汇

1. disturb

v. 1) 妨碍，打扰；2) 扰乱，搞乱；3) 使 (某人) 烦恼或不安

They were charged with disturbing the public peace.

Don't disturb the papers on my desk.

She was disturbed to hear you had been injured in the accident.

辨析

disturb, bother, trouble, upset

disturb 语气最强，常指较为强烈、持久的干扰，甚至可以指精神失常。

bother 常表示较小的烦扰，常与 about 或 with 连用。

trouble 语气强于 bother，弱于 disturb，指被某事搞得心神不宁。

upset 指心理突然暂时失去平衡，过一段时间即可恢复正常。

Heavy truck traffic disturbed the neighbourhood.

She didn't bother me with the details.

His failing grades troubled his parents deeply.

Losing the necklace upsets her.

拓展

disturbing *adj.* 令人不安的，使人震惊的

disturbance *n.* 1) 搅乱，打扰；

2) 骚乱，引起骚动的事物；

3) 烦恼，忧虑

The news from the front is very disturbing.

We can work here without disturbance.

There were disturbances in the crowd as fans left the stadium.

He is now in a period of painful disturbance.

2. effect

n. 结果；效力；影响

Did the medicine have any effect?

This had a great effect upon the future of both mother and son.

I tried to persuade him, but with little effect.

➡ 常用短语：

bring / put sth into effect 实施计划；落实想法

cause and effect 因果

come into effect (法律、规划或制度) 生效

have an effect on / upon 对……有影响或起作用

in effect 实际上，事实上

take effect 生效　　　to the effect that 大意是

拓展

effective *adj.* 1) 有效的；2) 实际的，现有的

effectively *adv.* 1) 有效地；2) 事实上，实际上

The ads were simple, but remarkably effective.

The rebels are in effective control of the city.

Children have to learn to communicate effectively.

Effectively, it has become impossible for us to help.

effect, consequence, result, outcome

effect 表示结果和原因的关系是立刻性的，即马上可以看到的。与 cause 相对，意为"效果，效力；作用，影响"。

consequence 表示结果和原因的关系没有那么紧密，并非马上可以看到。一般表示一种不好的结果，译为"后果"。

result 这个词较为常用，用途最广，指很多效果和后果的综合，带有"最后的结果"的意味。

outcome 通常译为"结果，结局"，常指某项活动、比赛或悬而未决的事情最后的结果。

Tax reform will have the effect of improving the distribution of income.

Do you know what the consequences of your action will be?

When the first radio messages have been received, the results of the trip will be announced immediately.

There were not many people who could predict the outcome of the general election.

3. motivate

v. 1) 刺激，激发；2) 为……的动机

A good teacher should be able to motivate the students to seek more knowledge.

Do you think he was motivated only by a desire for power?

motivation *n.* 动力；兴趣

motive *n.* 动机，目的

They lack the motivation to study.

In case of murder, the police question everyone who might have a motive.

4. suspect

n. 嫌疑犯，可疑分子

v. 1) 怀疑，不信任；2) 猜想

adj. 可疑的，受到怀疑的，不可信的

He's a prime suspect in the murder case.

What made you suspect her of having stolen the money?

I suspect the truth of her statement.

She has more intelligence than we suspected her to possess.

His statements are suspect.

5. loss

n. 1) 失去，丧失；2) 损失；3) 减少，减低；4) 输，失败

He suffered a temporary loss of memory.

His death means a great loss to science.

When heavy atoms are split in this way, some loss of mass occurs.

The loss of the first game did not discourage them.

→ 常用短语：

at a loss 亏本地；茫然，困惑　　　　　　dead loss 净亏，毫无价值的人或物
without (any) loss of time 立即，马上

6. seek

v. 1) 寻找；探索；追求；2) 在……中搜索，搜查；3) 企图，试图；4) 征求，请求
They were seeking employment.
We sought long and hard but found nothing.
The explanation is not far to seek.
Something suspicious was found after the room was sought through.
I have never sought to hide my views.
You should seek advice from your lawyer on this matter.

→ 常用短语：

be not far to seek 不难找到，显而易见的　be (much) to seek 还需要探求，还远未找到
much sought after 供不应求，极受欢迎　　seek after / for 寻求，探索，追求，寻找
seek one's fortune 寻找致富及成功之道　seek out 找出，搜出，挑出
seek through 搜遍

7. blame

n. 过失，责备
v. 1) 责备，指责；2) 把……归咎于，归因于
I am ready to take the blame for the mistake.
He blamed you for the neglect of your duty.
She was in no way to blame.
She blamed him for the failure of their marriage. / She blamed the failure of their marriage
on him.

→ 常用短语：

be to blame 应受指责　　　　　　　　　blame sb for sth 因某事而责备某人
blame sth on sb 把某事归咎于某人　　　lay / put the blame on sb 把责任推到某人身上
take the blame 承担责任

辨　析

blame, condemn, scold
这三个词都有"责怪"的意思。
blame 意思是"责怪，把……归咎于"。
condemn 意思是"谴责"，一般用于比较正式的、严肃的场合。
scold 意思是"责骂，训斥"，指由于某人的错误或对某人不满而暴躁地表示气愤，其
理由可能是充分的，但通常是不充分的。
You can't blame other people for your failure in the exam.

They strongly condemned the bombing.

His father scolded him for staying out late.

真 题 解 析

_____ for the breakdown of the school computer network, Alice was in low spirits. (2006 福建)

A. Blaming　　B. Blamed　　C. To blame　　D. To be blamed

解析：此题考查分词作状语。blame 是及物动词，意为"责备"，与主语之间是被动 关系，所以用过去分词 blamed。答案为 B。

8. inspire

v. 1) 鼓舞，激励；2) 赋予……灵感，给…… 以启示；3) 激起，唤起 (感情、思想等)

His noble example inspired the rest of us to greater efforts.

The beautiful scenery inspired the composer.

His encouraging remarks inspired confidence in me.

拓 展

inspiration *n.* 1) 灵感；2) 鼓舞人心 的人 (或事物)

I cannot write without inspiration.

His wife was a constant inspiration to him.

辨 析

inspire, encourage, excite, motivate, stimulate

这几个动词都有"鼓励、刺激"的意思。

inspire 常常带有"启迪，启发"的意思。

encourage 含有"使增强勇气或给予希望"的意思。

excite 指"使人感到激动、兴奋"。

motivate 强调激发去做某事的动机。

stimulate 强调刺激反应的结果。

My mother inspires us with stories of her difficult childhood.

He encouraged his son to go to a good college.

The band played louder and excited the audience.

A desire to go to medical school motivates her to study hard every day.

The cold air stimulates me.

◆ 常用短语

1. more than

这个词组的用法很多，主要含义有：

1) "more than＋名词"表示"多于，不仅仅是"。

　　Modern science is more than a large amount of information.

2) "more than＋数词"含"以上"或"不止"之意。

I have known David for more than 20 years.

3) "more than＋形容词"指"很，非常"。

In doing scientific experiments, one must be more than careful with the instruments.

I assure you I am more than glad to help you.

4) 在"more...than"结构中，肯定 more 后面的部分而否定 than 后面的部分，这种用法的意义近似于"是……而不是"。

Hearing the loud noise, the boy was more surprised than frightened.

5) "more than / more...than ＋ 含 can 的分句"结构表示否定的意味。

Don't bite off more than you can chew.

In delivering his lecture, Jason makes sure not to include more things than the students can understand.

6) "no more...than"表示"同……一样不"。

I can no more do that than anyone else.

A learner can no more obtain knowledge without reading than a farmer can get good harvest without ploughing.

Dr Hu is no more a poet than Dr Wu is a philosopher. (= Dr Hu is not a poet any more than Dr Wu is a philosopher.)

> **拓 展**
>
> more...than 也在一些惯用语中出现。
>
> More often than not, people tend to pay attention to what they can take rather than what they can give.
>
> If you tell your father what you have done, he'll be more than a little angry.

2. in short

in short 意思是"总之，简言之"。

In short, he is one of the most promising students I've ever known.

In short, there is a slight change in emphasis away from education and toward outright competition.

3. depend on

depend on 的主要含义有：1) 依靠，依赖；2) 相信；3) 取决于

All living things depend on the sun for their growth.

Children shouldn't depend on their parents too much.

He is a man to be depended on.

A lot will depend on how she responds to the challenge.

How much can be produced depends on how hard we work.

真 题 解 析

—Will you go skiing with me this winter vacation?

—It _____. (2002 上海)

A. all depend   B. all depends   C. is all depended   D. is all depending

解析：本题考查的是"It (all) depends."（那要看情况而定），也可说成"That (all) depends."。答案为 B。

4. leave behind

leave behind 意思是：1) 遗留，忘带；2) 超过

Take care not to leave anything behind.

He left behind an immortal example to all posterity.

If you ask the fast runner to set the pace, then most of them will be left behind.

She soon left the other runners behind.

> **拓展**
>
> 和 leave 有关的短语还有：
> leave for 出发去……
> leave out 漏掉
> leave sth to others 把某物留给他人
> leave sb / sth alone 不打扰某人/某事

5. on behalf of sb (= on sb's behalf)

on behalf of sb (= on sb's behalf) 意思是"做某人的代表或代言人，为了某人的利益"。

On behalf of my colleagues and myself, I thank you.

Ken is not present, so I shall accept the prize on his behalf.

The legal guardian must act on behalf of the child.

6. turn up

turn up 主要含义有：1) 开大，调高；2) 露面，出现；3) 突然发生

I can't hear the radio very well; could you turn it up a bit?

We arranged to meet at the cinema at 7:30, but he failed to turn up.

He's still hoping something will turn up.

> **拓展**
>
> 和 turn 有关的短语还有：
> turn sth inside out 把……翻过来
> turn to 转向，求助于
> by turns 轮流，交替
> in turn 依次，反过来，转而
> take turns 轮流，依次

真 题 解 析

1) A clean environment can help the city bid for the Olympics, which _____ will promote its economic development. (2006 山东)

　　A. in nature 　　　　　B. in return

　　C. in turn 　　　　　　D. in fact

解析：in turn 在这里的意思是"反过来"。答案为 C。

2) With no one to _____ in such a frightening situation, she felt very helpless. (2006 陕西)

　　A. turn on 　　　B. turn off 　　　C. turn over 　　　D. turn to

解析：根据全句的意思，这里说的是"求助于别人"，turn to sb for help 意为"向某人求助"。答案为 D。

7. at liberty (to do sth)

at liberty (to do sth) 意思是：1)(指人)自由的，不受限制或支配的；2)获许可的

You're at liberty to say what you like.

The prisoners were all set at liberty. (= The prisoners were all set free.)

He is at liberty to act on their behalf.

综合训练

考试时间：45分钟　满分：100分

Ⅰ. 单项选择（共15小题；每小题1分，满分15分）

1. The dictionary is _____ must for the students of _____ English.

   A. the; the   B. a; a   C. a; /   D. the; /

2. The new research team was led by the _____ engineer.

   A. main   B. major   C. chief   D. primary

3. I believe he is on duty, _____ he is in plain clothes.

   A. because   B. even though   C. as if   D. unless

4. The local government decided to _____ the two firms into a big one.

   A. motivate   B. combine   C. compact   D. nominate

5. You can _____ Jane — she always keeps her promises.

   A. depend   B. believe   C. depend on   D. believe in

6. Finally, they found a new material _____ the old one.

   A. instead   B. take place of   C. in place of   D. in place

7. The winter of 2002 was extremely bad. _____, most people say it was the worst winter of their lives.

   A. At last   B. In fact   C. In a word   D. As a result

8. The blue sky of the holiday brochure was such a _____ this rainy March day.

   A. compare to   B. compare with   C. contrast to   D. contrast as

9. Please follow your supervisor's instructions, or you'll _____ him.

   A. discourage   B. offend   C. disturb   D. bother

10. He hid himself behind the door, _____ he still could see what would happen to his classmates.

    A. there   B. which   C. from which   D. from where

11. _____, many of the men have gone off to cities _____ higher pay, _____ women in the village.

    A. Making things worse; in search for; to leave

    B. To make things worse; in search of; leaving

C. Making things worse; in search of; to leave

D. To make things worse; in search for; leaving

12. The new appointment of our president _____ from the very beginning of next semester.

    A. takes effect   B. takes part   C. takes place   D. takes turns

13. Some parents can't _____ their children, which often sets off the conflicts between two generations.

    A. relate to   B. find out   C. turn to   D. take in

14. —What do you enjoy most _____ in the summer holiday?

    —Playing table tennis.

    A. killing time   B. to kill time   C. spending the time   D. to spend the time

15. Happy birthday, Alice! So you have _____ 21 already.

    A. become   B. turned   C. grown   D. passed

II. 完形填空（共20小题；每小题1分，满分20分）

Both Albert Einstein and Charles Dickens had mental illness. The artist Van Gogh cut off his ear after years of depression. It seems that great artists and scientists often __1__ mental problems. Now __2__ have started to look at whether mental illness and genius (天才) are __3__.

Dr Adele Juda studied 5,000 __4__ people in Germany. She found there were more people with mental illness in this group than in the __5__ population. __6__ had the highest rate of mental illness (50 percent), __7__ by musicians (38 percent), with lower numbers for painters and architects (17–20 percent). The __8__ rate of mental illness in the population is 6 percent.

Other scientists did research which also __9__ a strong link between mental problems and creativity. But, it did nothing to __10__ it.

Dr Ruth Richards of Harvard University made a breakthrough. __11__ studying creative people, she took a group of psychiatric (精神病的) patients and __12__ them for creativity. The patients got much __13__ scores than a normal group.

Also, the study showed the patients' close relatives were __14__ creative. This __15__ that the key to the link between creativity and mental illness is in our genes.

But this is a problem. As mental illness is __16__, why should its genes survive in at least 6 percent of the population? Some scientists believe that evolution has created a balance, where the madness of a few people __17__ the development of the whole human race.

Geniuses may be mad, bad or just difficult to __18__, but their discoveries have __19__ the world we live in. It seems that a little creative madness is __20__ for us all.

1. A. prevent from   B. suffer from   C. prefer to   D. tend to

2. A. teachers   B. students   C. scientists   D. patients

3. A. mixed   B. separated   C. divided   D. linked

4. A. creative   B. mad   C. clever   D. famous

5. A. large   B. other   C. special   D. general

6. A. Peasants   B. Poets   C. Teachers   D. Workers

7. A. followed   B. compared   C. found   D. inspired

8. A. usual   B. lowest   C. average   D. former

9. A. founded   B. picked   C. showed   D. proved

10. A. break   B. connect   C. protect   D. explain

11. A. Without   B. Instead of   C. Together with   D. Soon after

12. A. searched   B. asked   C. required   D. tested

13. A. lower   B. fewer   C. higher   D. more

14. A. less   B. not   C. /   D. more

15. A. suggests   B. tells   C. says   D. infers

16. A. helpful   B. harmful   C. useless   D. dangerous

17. A. leads to   B. stops for   C. starts with   D. slows down

18. A. get   B. control   C. understand   D. learn

19. A. influenced   B. puzzled   C. decided   D. improved

20. A. good   B. harmful   C. unavoidable   D. favourite

Ⅲ. 阅读理解（共10小题；每小题2分，满分20分）

A

Five years ago, David Smith wore an expensive suit to work every day. "I was a clothes addict," he jokes. "I used to carry a fresh suit to work with me so I could change if my clothes got wrinkled." Today David wears casual clothes — khaki (卡其布) pants and sports shirt — to the office. He hardly ever wears a necktie. "I'm working harder than ever," David says, "and I need to feel comfortable."

More and more companies are allowing their office workers to wear casual clothes to work. In the United States, the change from formal to casual office wear has been gradual. In the early 1990s, many companies allowed their employees to wear casual clothes on Friday (but only on Friday). This became known as "dress-down Friday" or "casual Friday." "What started out as an extra one-day-a-week benefit for employees has really become an everyday thing," said business consultant Maisly Jones.

Why have so many companies started allowing their employees to wear casual clothes? One reason is that it's easier for a company to attract new employees if it has a casual dress code. "A lot of young people don't want to dress up for work," says the owner of a software company, "so it's hard to hire people if you have a conservative dress code." Another reason is that people seem happier and more productive when they are wearing comfortable clothes. In a study conducted by Levi Strauss & Company, 85 percent of employers said that they believe casual dress improves employees' morale

(精神面貌). Only 4 percent of employers said that casual dress has a negative impact on productivity. Supporters of casual office wear also argue that a casual dress code helps them save money. "Suits are expensive, if you have to wear one every day," one person said. "For the same amount of money, you can buy a lot more casual clothes."

1. David Smith refers to himself as having been "a clothes addict", because _____.
   A. he often wore khaki pants and a sports shirt
   B. he couldn't stand a clean appearance
   C. he wanted his clothes to look neat all the time
   D. he didn't want to spend much money on clothes

2. David Smith wears casual clothes now, because _____.
   A. they make him feel at ease when working
   B. he cannot afford to buy expensive clothes
   C. he looks handsome in casual clothes
   D. he no longer works for any company

3. According to this passage, which of the following statements is FALSE?
   A. Many employees don't like a conservative dress code.
   B. Most employers believe that comfortable clothes make employees more productive.
   C. A casual dress code is welcomed by young employees.
   D. All the employers in the US are for casual office wear.

4. According to this passage, which of the following statements is TRUE?
   A. Company workers started to dress down about 20 years ago.
   B. Dressing casually has become an everyday phenomenon since the early 1990s.
   C. "Dress-down Friday" was first given as a favour from employers.
   D. Many workers want to wear casual clothes to impress people.

5. In this passage, the following advantages of casual office wear are mentioned EXCEPT _____.
   A. saving employees' money
   B. making employees more attractive
   C. improving employees' motivation
   D. making employees happier

B

About 2,000 years ago, nearly 20,000 Roman soldiers under the commander of Aulus Plautius invaded Britain. The Roman Emperor Claudius arrived later with reinforcements (including elephants) and personally accepted the surrender of 11 tribal kings. He then appointed Aulus Plautius as the first Governor of Britain and returned to Rome. The Roman occupation of Britain lasted for 400 years before a combination of warriors from Britain and other nations managed to oust (驱逐) them.

Although there is no doubt that the Romans were always unwelcome masters as far as the original British inhabitants were concerned, the fact is that the Romans improved life for the inhabitants of the island nation in many ways.

Before the Romans came, the people of Britain lived in different tribes. With no central government structure, the island was ruled by kings, each controlling a different region of the country. The kings were in a constant state of war with each other, there were frequent invasions of each other's territories, and people were in a permanent state of tension.

The Romans brought a new style of very efficient central leadership. They built towns, which were connected by a system of well-constructed roads and their superior engineering technology meant that the roads were straight, had good drainage (排水系统) and only flooded in the severest weather. They also built drains and bathhouses in towns, which improved public hygiene (卫生) considerably and they even introduced a way of centrally heating houses.

The Romans also radically altered the way illnesses were treated, which led to increased life expectancy, which in turn led to a rapid growth in the population. And they were the first people to work out a way of counting this newly-increased population. "Census", the word we still use for counting the population, is one of the many words we borrowed from Latin which was the language spoken by the invaders. More Latin words came into the language when the Romans introduced a justice system and even more to explain aspects of trade and commerce. The language we now call English was radically changed by these borrowed Latin words.

So, although the Romans were unwelcome visitors, they improved daily life for ordinary people and turned Britain into one of the wealthiest and most valuable provinces in the Roman Empire.

6. After Aulus Plautius invaded Britain, _____.

   A. he returned to Rome

   B. British warriors managed to oust him

   C. the Roman Emperor became the first Governor of Britain

   D. Claudius arrived and the British kings surrendered to him

7. Roman engineering ensured that the _____.

   A. roads they built flooded regularly

   B. roads they built only flooded when the weather was really bad

   C. roads had drains but still flooded regularly

   D. towns were connected by flooded roads

8. The population of Britain _____.

   A. grew fast because people lived longer

   B. fell rapidly because of the way illnesses were treated

   C. grew because the Romans had a census

   D. didn't really change very much

9. Why did the number of Latin words in English increase?

A. Because there weren't enough words in English.

B. Because the Romans couldn't speak English.

C. Because the Romans wanted to radically change English.

D. Because they were needed for the systems of justice and trade that the Romans introduced.

10. Life in Britain changed a lot _____.

A. despite the fact that the Romans were unwelcome visitors

B. because the Romans were unwelcome visitors

C. because it had always been a wealthy province

D. because the Romans were very wealthy

IV. 阅读表达（共5小题；每小题3分，满分15分）

Sports are all about change. A team gets better. A kid practises more and swims a personal best or learns a new move on the basketball court.

In 2006, two things happened that got me thinking about change — in sports and in life.

One of them is tennis champion Andre Agassi, who retired in 2006. Agassi was a terrific player who won 60 titles, including 8 major championships. But his greatest achievement might have been how much he changed during his career.

When he was young, Agassi was a show-off who seemed to care only about himself. He didn't train very hard, but he won matches because of his tremendous talent. Eventually, though, injuries and his bad attitude caught up with him. He fell from No. 1 in the world rankings to No. 141.

So Agassi changed as a player. He trained harder and became a world-class player again. More importantly, he changed as a person. He was nicer to fans and opponents. He stopped thinking just about himself and started _____. Through his efforts, he raised more than $60 million to help disadvantaged kids around his hometown of Las Vegas, Nevada. He even started a school for at-risk kids.

At the start of a new year, lots of people promise themselves they will change. They might vow to get in good physical shape, do better in school or be nicer to others.

Changes such as those can be difficult. But they do happen. Just remember Andre Agassi: It wasn't easy, but he changed, and changed for the better.

1. What is the best title for the passage? (Please answer within 10 words.)

_____

2. Which sentence in the passage can be replaced by the following one?

   However, he received punishment out of his injuries and his bad attitude in the end.

_____

_____

3. Fill in the blank in the fifth paragraph with proper words or phrases to complete the sentence. (Please answer within 10 words.)

_____

4. What do you plan to do in order to improve yourself? (Please answer within 30 words.)

_____

_____

5. Translate the underlined sentence in the third paragraph into Chinese.

_____

Ⅴ. 写作（满分30分）

请以 "The Celebration of Western Festivals" 为题，根据下面的提示写一篇短文，可适当发挥。

提示：1. 现在国内有不少人更喜欢过西方的一些节日；

   2. 产生这种现象的原因；

   3. 这种现象可能带来的影响。

词数要求：120～150词。

The Celebration of Western Festivals

_____

_____

_____

_____

_____

Module ③

Foreign Food

要点纵览

高考词汇	owe, poison, taste, dish, greedily, chopstick, dessert, tongue, chew, delicacy, infamous, appetising, manner, requirement, fixed, mushroom, filling, unrecognisable, guest, fork, entertain, menu, remark, casually, punctuation, porridge, bacon, lamb, roast, consume, butcher, cattle, outnumber, mutton, consequence, gradual, trend, cuisine, recipe, raw, eggplant, lemon, loaf, artificial, grocery, customer, cocoa, cookie, maple, honey, fragrant, abundant, ripe, peach, melon, stove, fry, microwave, reheat, barbecue, grill, slice, breast, buffet, pint, brewery, altogether, ample, pattern, fence, foreground, overhead, transform
常用短语	owe to, be obsessed with, a bit of, to one's surprise, no wonder, end up, be amazed at, make out, go against, have…in common, on close terms with, save…from, in short, by nature, before long, follow one's example, in a… manner, at the end of, huge amounts of, refer to…as, name after, be based on, fall in love with, dress up, set fire to
实用句型	1. No wonder my fellow guests had had only a few bites of each dish. 2. But I was already so full that I could only watch as the banquet continued. 3. It seemed to be just a bowl of grey liquid and it was only after I had tasted it that I knew it was actually cooked with mushrooms. 4. As he grew up, he found…
交际用语	1. go without saying 2. on the dot 3. as a rule 4. make a beeline for 5. do the done thing

◆ **高考词汇**

1. owe

v. 1) 欠；应给予；2) (应) 感激；3) 应该把……归功于

I owe the landlord 100 dollars. / I owe 100 dollars to the landlord.

She owes it to herself for a long while to do some serious reading.

We owe a great deal to our parents.

We owe to Newton the principle of gravitation.

He owes his success more to luck than to ability.

2. taste

n. 1) 味道；2) 味觉；3) 品尝；4) 感受，体验；5) 趣味，情趣，审美力；6) 爱好，兴趣

v. 1) 尝，辨 (味)；2) 尝到，感到，体验；3) 吃起来，有……的味道

I've got a cold and so I have no taste / have lost my sense of taste.

Please have a taste of this pudding.

He will never forget his first taste of life in a big city.

Pop music is not to everyone's taste.

She has a taste for music.

He tasted both cakes and decided neither was good.

He has never tasted defeat.

The meat tastes delicious.

This sauce tastes of tomato.

➡ **常用短语：**

be in bad / poor taste (言谈举止) 不得当的，粗俗的   have a taste for 喜欢

have excellent taste in 在……上有极高的鉴赏力   to one's taste 合某人的口味

3. manner

n. 1) 方式，方法；2) 态度，举止；3) [plural] 礼貌，规矩，习惯

We walked in a leisurely manner, looking in all the windows.

I don't object to what she says, but I strongly disapprove of her manner of saying it.

It is bad manners to interrupt.

辨 析

manner, means, method, way

这四个名词均可表示"方法，方式"。

manner 指规范、独特的方式，manner 前常与介词 in 连用。需要注意的是，manner 表

203

示"方式，方法"时是可数名词，常用作单数形式；表示"态度，举止"时，只用作单数形式。

means 指为达到某一目的而采用的方法，前面常与介词 by 连用。means 是可数名词，单数与复数形式相同。表示单数意义时，谓语动词用单数形式；表示复数意义时，谓语动词用复数形式；单复数意义不明确时，谓语动词用单数或复数形式皆可。

method 着重强调系统的、科学的方法。

way 多指思想、行动、办事的方法，前面常与介词 in 连用。用 way 表示做某事的方法时，定语可用 of doing sth 或 to do sth，不可用 for doing sth。

I love duck cooked in the Chinese manner.

He has a very rude manner.

He succeeded by means of perseverance.

One means has not been tried.

All possible means have been adopted.

Is / Are there any means of getting there before dark?

Do you know any new method of teaching a language?

I have a new method of doing the experiment.

You shouldn't go on living in this way!

They are trying to find ways to prevent the disease.

He doesn't like American way of living.

4. altogether

adv. 1) 完全，全然；2) 全部，合计；3) 总之，总而言之

I am altogether on your side in this matter.

He bought altogether 500 hectares of land.

Altogether, exports are looking up.

辨 析

altogether, all together, together

altogether 是副词，意思是"完全地，全部，总共"，语气比 together 强。

all together 是副词短语，意思是"一道，同时"，强调一个群体中的每一个。

together 是副词，意思是"一起，一道，共同地"。

He had 10 guns altogether.

They arrived all together.

They lived together in the same house.

5. transform

v. 1) 使改变，使改观，将……改成；2) 改造，改革，改善；3) 使变换

> 拓 展
>
> transformation n. 改变，改观，转变
> transformer n. 变压器
> His character seems to have undergone a complete transformation since his marriage.
> Transformer is a piece of equipment that can change electricity from one voltage to another.

The Greggs have transformed their garage into a guest house.

Success and wealth transformed his character.

A generator transforms mechanical energy into electricity.

6. require

v. 1) 需要；2) 要求，命令

We require extra help.

The situation requires that I should be there.

You must satisfy the required conditions to get your voucher.

He only did what was required (of him).

·········拓·展·········

requirement *n.* 1) 需要，必需品；
2) 要求，必要条件，规定
Food is a requirement of life.
He has filled all requirements for promotion.

◆ 常用短语

1. be obsessed with / by

be obsessed with / by 的意思是：1) 对……着迷；2) 被……困扰

Don't be too obsessed with computers.

She is obsessed with / by fear of unemployment.

表示"对……着迷"的短语还有：be crazy about，be absorbed in，be addicted to，be fascinated by 等。

2. no wonder

no wonder 意思是"难怪"。

No wonder the firm makes a loss — the office is terribly overstaffed.

No wonder you can't sleep when you eat so much.

真 题 解 析

1) He hasn't slept at all for three days. _____ he is tired out. (2005 湖北)

    A. There is no point   B. There is no need

    C. It is no wonder   D. It is no way

解析：此题对考生来说有一定的干扰力。这里考查的是 it is no wonder 这一固定句型，意为"难怪"。答案为 C。

2) —Brad was Jane's brother!

   —_____ he reminded me so much of Jane. (2004 浙江)

    A. No doubt   B. Above all

    C. No wonder   D. Of course

解析：no wonder 是固定搭配。这句话的意思是：难怪我一看到 Brad 就想起 Jane。答案为 C。

wonder 的其他常见用法有：

n. 1) [U] 惊奇，惊异，惊叹；2) [C] 奇迹，奇观，奇事

v. 1) 纳闷，想知道；2) 觉得奇怪，感到惊讶

a look of wonder 惊异的表情

do / work wonders 创造奇迹

wonder at 感到惊奇，惊讶

be filled with wonder 感到十分惊异

it is a wonder that 奇怪的是

wonder + that / wh- 从句 想知道

wonderful *adj.* 令人惊奇的，意想不到的，绝妙的

It's wonderful that they managed to escape.

The weather is wonderful.

3. end up

end up 意思是"结束，告终"。

How does the story end up?

"These affairs always end up the same way," he complained.

The class ended up with an English song.

If you continue to steal, you'll end up in prison.

At first he refused to accept any responsibility but he ended up apologising.

If he carries on driving like that, he'll end up dead.

和 end 有关的短语还有：

at the end of the street / the year 在街道尽头/年末

bring sth to an end (使某事物) 结束，终止

gain / win / achieve one's ends 达到目的

make (both) ends meet 使收支相抵

no end of sth 无数，大量

on end 竖着，连续地

put an end to sth 终止或废止某事物

end in sth 以某物作为末端或结尾

辨 析

at the end, in the end

at the end 不单独使用，通常要跟 of 和名词，如：at the end of the story。

in the end 之后不接 of，意思同 finally。

4. make out

make out 主要含义有：

1) 设法应付；活下来，过活；2) 理解，了解；3) 辨认出某人/某物；4) 写出，填写

How did he make out while his wife was away?

What a strange person she is! I can't

和 make 有关的短语还有：

make against 和……相对，不利于，有害于

make away 离去，逃走

make into 制成，做成，使转变为

make...into 使……变成

make off 匆忙离去，逃走

make over 转让，移交

make up 虚构，组成，和解，化妆

make up for 弥补

make use of 利用

make her out at all.

I could just make out a figure in the darkness.

Mary made out a cheque for $100.

make out that..., make oneself / sb / sth out to be... 声称，断言，坚持

He made out that he had been robbed.

He makes himself out to be cleverer than he really is.

真题解析

1) Someone who lacks staying power and perseverance is unlikely to _____ a good researcher. (2006 山东)

    A. make   B. turn   C. get   D. grow

解析：make 在这里的意思是"成为，变成"。turn 作系动词时，后面接形容词或抽象名词作表语；get 作系动词时，后面接形容词；grow 作系动词时，表示"变得"，后面接形容词。答案为 A。

2) Everybody in the village likes Jack because he is good at telling and _____ jokes. （2005 江苏）

    A. turning up   B. putting up   C. making up   D. showing up

解析：make up 在这里是"编造，虚构"之意。答案为 C。

5. have...in common

have...in common 意思是"有……共同之处"。

have much / little / nothing / something in common 意思是"有很多/有很少/没有/有某个共同之处"。

Their methods have much in common.

辨析

common, general, ordinary, usual

这几个词都含有"普通的"意思。

common 意为"常见的，不足为奇的"。

general 意为"普遍的，一般的"。

ordinary 强调"平常的，平淡无奇的"。

usual 指"与往常没有两样"，强调"一贯如此"。

Colds are common in winter.

This book is intended for the general readers, not for the specialists.

His ordinary breakfast consists of bread and milk only.

He sat on his usual chair.

Letterboxes are much more _____ in the UK than in the US, where most people have a mailbox instead. (2006 浙江)

A. common　　B. normal　　C. ordinary　　D. usual

解析：这句话的意思是：（装在门上的）信箱在英国比在美国更常见，大多数美国人都有一个（在房子外的）邮箱。在这里要表达的是"常见的"意思，所以选择 common。答案为 A。

6. on...terms with

on...terms with 意思是"有着……的关系"。

We are on good terms with each other.

I haven't been on speaking terms with her after that quarrel.

> **拓 展**
>
> 与 term 有关的短语还有：
> be on equal terms 关系平等
> bring sb to terms 迫使某人接受条件
> come to terms 达成协议
> in terms of 就……而论；在……方面
> in the long / short term 就长期/短期而言
> on one's term 依照某人的条件

_____ achievement, last week's ministerial meeting of the WTO here earned a low, though not failing, grade. (2006 湖南)

A. In terms of　　B. In case of　　C. As a result of　　D. In face of

解析：这句话的意思是：就成果而言，上周在这里举行的 WTO 部长会议虽然没有失败，但成效甚微。答案为 A。

7. set fire to

set fire to 意思是"放火烧"，相当于 set sth on fire。

I believe the house was deliberately set fire to.

The sparks set fire to the oily rags.

> **拓 展**
>
> 与 fire 有关的短语还有：
> be on fire 着火（强调状态）
> catch fire 着火（强调动作）
> escape from the fire 逃离大火
> fight a fire 扑火，灭火
> make / start / light a fire 点火
> play with fire 玩火
> put out a fire 灭火

8. the first time

the first time 意思是"第一次……时"。

The camera just came apart the first time he used it.

The first time I saw him, he was busy working on a new novel.

辨 析

the first time, for the first time

the first time 意思是"第一次……时"。相当于从属连词，引导状语从句。the first time 常构成 It + be + that 从句的句型，that 从句的时态由 be 来决定，若 be 是 is，那么 that 从句的时态用现在完成时；若 be 是 was，则 that 从句的时态用过去完成时。

for the first time 意思是"第一次"。只用作句子的状语，不能引导状语从句。

The first time I flew in a plane, I was really nervous.

It is the first time that he has been in China.

For the first time luck hooked onto me.

综合训练

考试时间：45分钟　满分：100分

I. 单项选择（共15小题；每小题1分，满分15分）

1. —Do you think the Stars will beat the Bulls?

　　—Yes. They have better players, so I _____ them to win.

　　A. expect　　　　　B. hope　　　　　　C. prefer　　　　　　D. demand

2. _____ this cake and tell me whether you like it.

　　A. Tasting　　　　B. To taste　　　　　C. Taste　　　　　　D. To have tasted

3. Your performance in the driving test didn't reach the required standard. _____, you failed.

　　A. In the end　　　B. After all　　　　C. In other words　　D. At the same time

4. Christmas is _____ special holiday when _____ whole family are supposed to get together.

　　A. the; the　　　　B. a; the　　　　　　C. a; an　　　　　　D. the; an

5. Is the painting in the Louvre the _____ work by Leonardo da Vinci, or just a copy?

　　A. abundant　　　B. ambiguous　　　　C. authentic　　　　D. academic

6. —You look so upset, Jane. _____?

　　—I have been told that my father has got lung cancer.

　　A. What's up　　　B. What's for　　　　C. So what　　　　　D. Guess what

7. —It cost me 30 *yuan* to get here.

　　—Well, it was crazy of you to take a taxi _____ you could come by bus as well.

　　A. and　　　　　　B. if　　　　　　　　C. but　　　　　　　D. when

8. _____ in her best clothes, the girl tried to make herself _____ at the party.

　　A. Dressed; noticed　　　　　　　　　　B. Dressing; to be noticed

　　C. Get dressed; noticed　　　　　　　　D. Dressing; noticing

9. This _____ girl is Linda's cousin.

　　A. pretty little Spanish　　　　　　　　B. Spanish little pretty

　　C. Spanish pretty little　　　　　　　　D. little pretty Spanish

10. _____ appeared to be a war between his heart and his mind.

　　A. It　　　　　　　B. There　　　　　　C. Where　　　　　D. What

11. —Are you satisfied with the work?

　　—Not in the least. I wonder if anyone could have done it _____.

　　A. worse　　　　　B. as well　　　　　C. the worst　　　　D. better

209

12. There is an increasing _____ to make movies describing violence.

    A. strength   B. direction   C. tradition   D. trend

13. They are trying to discover a land abundant _____ minerals, that is, a land having minerals _____ abundance.

    A. in; in   B. to; in   C. in; to   D. to; to

14. The soldiers soon reached _____ was once an old temple _____ the villagers used as a school.

    A. which; where   B. what; which   C. where; which   D. what; where

15. According to the art dealer, the painting _____ to go for at least a million dollars.

    A. is expected   B. expects   C. expected   D. is expecting

II. 完形填空（共20小题；每小题1分，满分20分）

When I was a college student, I did a lot of travelling abroad. That was because a professor __1__ me to do so. She said, "Now's the time for you to travel around the world, __2__ your knowledge through actual experiences and have fun!" I __3__ her.

Since I started to work for a __4__ company, however, I have done most of my travelling through the Internet. By using the Internet, I have seen the __5__ of many cities on my computer screen. And I have really made business __6__ too. With the help of the Internet, I have also got __7__ about food in different countries.

Therefore, I was beginning to feel that actual trips were __8__ necessary when I happened to read a famous chef's comment on the Internet. He said, "It is very difficult to have real Italian food in a foreign country, because we enjoy food and the __9__ around us at the same time. So why don't you fly over to Italy and enjoy real Italian __10__?" Those words reminded me of my __11__ advice. As information technology __12__, you might be able to do without making some real trips. But this also means that you will miss the various __13__ you can get from travelling.

Today there are people who __14__ direct contact with others and spend much of their time on the Internet. It is not surprising to see a group of people __15__ not with each other but into their mobile phones. It seems as if such people are __16__ by an invisible wall. They seem to be losing out on a good chance to __17__ and talk with other people. I don't think that they are taking good advantage of information technology. We should use information technology as a tool to make our daily __18__ more fruitful. However, we should never let it __19__ our time for face-to-face communication. Let's make use of information technology more __20__, and have great fun in experiencing the actual world.

    1. A. promised   B. allowed   C. hurried   D. encouraged

    2. A. expand   B. use   C. practise   D. exchange

    3. A. agreed with   B. learnt from   C. followed up   D. listened to

    4. A. computer   B. food   C. clothing   D. machine

    5. A. life   B. rivers   C. sights   D. houses

6. A. plans   B. bargain   C. progress   D. trips

7. A. information   B. taste   C. cooks   D. feelings

8. A. even more   B. no longer   C. much   D. actually

9. A. people   B. drink   C. atmosphere   D. environment

10. A. shoes   B. dishes   C. customers   D. situations

11. A. friend's   B. parent's   C. professor's   D. boss's

12. A. produces   B. advertises   C. forms   D. advances

13. A. news   B. pleasures   C. troubles   D. places

14. A. avoid   B. keep   C. lose   D. enjoy

15. A. meeting   B. talking   C. communicating   D. travelling

16. A. stopped   B. met   C. surrounded   D. hurt

17. A. look at   B. employ   C. travel   D. meet

18. A. communication   B. study   C. work   D. action

19. A. spare   B. increase   C. reduce   D. use

20. A. wisely   B. correctly   C. closely   D. slowly

Ⅲ. 阅读理解（共10小题；每小题2分，满分20分）

A

Balanced nutrition is the cornerstone of physical health. People of all ages should watch out for their diet for the sake of health and disease prevention.

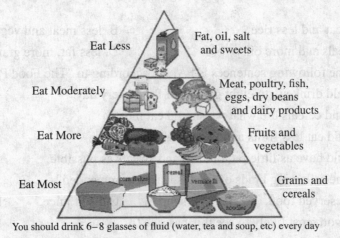

Eat Less — Fat, oil, salt and sweets

Eat Moderately — Meat, poultry, fish, eggs, dry beans and dairy products

Eat More — Fruits and vegetables

Eat Most — Grains and cereals

You should drink 6-8 glasses of fluid (water, tea and soup, etc) every day

The Food Pyramid

Physical fitness cannot do without a balanced diet. Follow the "Food Pyramid" guide as you pick your food. Cereals should be taken as the major dietary source. Keep the consumption of meat, eggs, bean and dairy products and calcium food to an appropriate level. Reduce salt, oil and sugar. Trim fat from meat before cooking. Choose cooking methods which use small amount of oil such as steaming, stewing, simmering and boiling. Cooking with non-stick frying pans is recommended. The core principle of cooking is to avoid frying and deep-frying. These are the keys to a balanced diet and physical fitness.

Principles of Healthy Eating

Follow the principles of healthy eating to attain good health:

- Choose a variety of food and eat cereals as the largest portion of food in every meal.
- Eat a lot of vegetables and fruits.
- Reduce the consumption of foodstuffs with high salt, fat and sugar content as well as those that are preserved.
- A daily fluid intake of six to eight glasses (including clear soup, fruit juice and tea).
- Take meals regularly and in adequate amounts.

Deep-fried food and food that is very sweet or salty are popular because they taste fabulous. But things that delight your taste may not be good for your body. High consumption of these foods may cause overweight, high blood pressure, high blood cholesterol (胆固醇) level etc, which may threaten your health.

1. According to the first paragraph, if you don't want to threaten your health, you should _____.
   A. do more physical exercise   B. watch your age
   C. have a balanced diet   D. sleep more

2. According to the paragraph with the subheading "The Food Pyramid", we should eat _____.
   A. more meat and less rice   B. less meat and vegetables
   C. less cereals and more oil   D. less fat, more grains and cereals

3. Which of the following sentences is FALSE according to "The Food Pyramid" part?
   A. We should drink six to eight glasses of fluid every day.
   B. Grains and cereals are what we should eat most.
   C. We should eat less fruits and vegetables.
   D. We should have as little fat, oil, salt and sweets as possible.

4. Which of the following kinds of food is least recommended?
   A. Salty preserved food.   B. Clear soup.   C. Fruit juice.   D. Bread.

5. Where are you most likely to see this passage?
   A. In a letter.   B. On an Internet webpage.
   C. On the front page of a newspaper.   D. In a book of short stories.

B

If you're confused by all the news about the health effects of eating fish, you're not alone. On one hand, the omega-3 fatty acids (脂肪酸) in fish are known to reduce the risk of heart disease, as the American Heart Association reminded us two weeks ago when it restated its recommendation that everybody eat at least two fish servings a week. On the other hand, fish that feed in polluted waterways contain high levels of mercury (汞), which can lead to cognitive problems in developing brains. That's why pregnant women and nursing mothers arc advised to limit their consumption.

As if that wasn't confusing enough, two new studies published last week in *New England Journal of Medicine* investigated the possible effects of mercury on the heart, and they seem to have reached contradictory conclusions. One found no clear link between mercury levels and heart disease; the other found that men with high levels of mercury in their toenails were more likely to suffer a heart attack than those with low levels. What are we to make of this? The first thing to remember is that this is how science proceeds, <u>by fits and starts</u> and seemingly contradictory results that get resolved only by further study. The second is that not all fish are created equal.

Compared with all the other things you might eat, fish are an excellent source of protein. They tend to eat algae (藻类) as part of their natural life cycle, converting it into omega-3 fatty acids that can improve your cholesterol profile. But it's also true that our waterways have become increasingly contaminated (被污染的) with all sorts of pollutants, including mercury, and that these pollutants tend to accumulate at different levels in different species. The fish most at risk are predators high in the pelagic (远洋的) food chain, such as swordfish and sharks.

It was to test the effects of mercury on the heart that the two new studies compared the mercury levels in clippings from toenails, where heavy metals tend to be deposited. In one study, researchers led by Dr Eliseo Guallar at Johns Hopkins University found that European and Israeli men with the highest mercury levels were nearly 2.2 times as likely to have a heart attack as those with the lowest levels. The other study, led by Dr Walter Willett at the Harvard School of Public Health, looked at a selection of American men and found no connection between mercury exposure and risk of heart disease, although Willett said a "weak association" cannot be ruled out.

For most of us, eating two servings of fish a week should not pose any problems.

6. In the first paragraph, the author introduces his topic by _____.
   A. making a comparison   B. justifying an assumption
   C. posing a contrast   D. explaining a phenomenon
7. The underlined phrase "by fits and starts" in the second paragraph most probably means something _____.
   A. happens smoothly   B. keeps starting and then stopping again
   C. deserves a lot of effort   D. is troublesome
8. Clippings from toenails were chosen for the research most probably because they
   _____.
   A. are more likely to contain mercury
   B. influence a person's heart

C. can be easily obtained

D. are connected with the heart

9. The views of Dr Eliseo Guallar and Dr Walter Willett are _____.

    A. identical   B. similar   C. opposite   D. complementary

10. What can we infer from the last paragraph?

    A. Fish is no threat to man.

    B. Do not be frightened to eat some fish.

    C. Eat fish oil supplements instead of fish.

    D. Taste is more important than the safety of the food.

IV. 阅读表达（共5小题；每小题3分，满分15分）

Overweight children may be more inclined (倾向于) to get outside and get moving when their TV time depends on it, a new study shows. Researchers found that when parents made TV and video games a reward for exercise, their overweight children increased their physical activity by 65 percent. The plan also cut children's TV time by nearly two hours a day, and reduced their snacking.

Experts believe that the growing problem of childhood obesity has much to do with the increasing amount of time kids are spending in front of TV and computer screens — often with high-calorie snacks in hand. Goldfield and his colleagues were interested in what would happen if children's TV time was contingent (依条件而定的) upon exercise time.

The researchers randomly assigned 30 overweight 8- to 12-year-olds to one of two groups: an "intervention" group where the children won TV and video game time by exercising; or a "control" group in which children were encouraged to exercise but could watch TV when they wanted. After eight weeks, children in the first group had raised up their overall activity levels by nearly two-thirds. In contrast, children in the control group showed only a small change in overall exercise levels.

The change in the intervention group's TV viewing was even greater, the researchers found. On average, these children were spending about 45 minutes a day in front of the TV, versus nearly three hours at the beginning of the study. Along with that reduction came a decline in snacking, which lowered the children's overall intake of calories and fat. Making TV contingent upon exercise, they conclude, could help overweight children

_____.

1. What is the best title for the passage? (Please answer within 10 words.)

_____

2. Which sentence in the passage can be replaced by the following one?

    If overweight children's TV time is contingent upon exercise, they may be more active to take exercise.

_____

3. Fill in the blank in the last paragraph with proper words or phrases to complete the sentence. (Please answer within 10 words.)

_____

4. Why can we say too much TV time can cause weight gain? (Please answer within 30 words.)

_____

5. Translate the underlined sentence in the second paragraph into Chinese.

_____

Ⅴ. 写作（满分30分）

健康一直是人们关注的问题。请以"Health"为题写一篇短文，谈谈你对这个问题的看法。请注意在你的叙述中包含以下要点：
1. 健康的重要性；
2. 保持健康的方法：
 1) 摒弃不良生活习惯；
 2) 多锻炼，强身健体；
 3) 保持饮食平衡，多吃水果、蔬菜，避免食用糖和脂肪含量过高的食物。
3. 结论。
请适当增加细节，不可逐条翻译。
词数要求：120～150词。

Health

_____

_____

_____

_____

_____

_____

_____

复习检测题（一）

第一部分 听力（共两节，满分30分）

第一节 （共5小题；每小题1.5分，满分7.5分）

听下面五段对话。每段对话后有一个小题，从题中所给的三个选项中选出最佳选项。听完每段对话后，你都有10秒钟的时间来回答有关小题和阅读下一小题。每段对话仅读一遍。

1. Where are the two speakers now?
   A. At a shop.　　　　　B. At a table.　　　　　C. At a school.

2. What will the speakers most probably do?
   A. Look for a more expensive hotel.
   B. Go to another hotel by bus.
   C. Walk to look for another hotel.

3. What will the woman probably do?
   A. Sit down.　　　　　B. Stand there.　　　　　C. Wait for someone coming.

4. What are the two speakers talking about?
   A. A radio.　　　　　B. A dinner.　　　　　C. The weather.

5. What will the woman do this evening?
   A. Meet her mum at the airport.
   B. Say goodbye to her mum at the airport.
   C. Fly to another city together with her mum.

第二节 （共15小题；每小题1.5分，满分22.5分）

听下面五段对话或独白。每段对话或独白后有几个小题，从题中所给的三个选项中选出最佳选项。听每段对话或独白前，你将有时间阅读各个小题，每小题5秒钟；听完后，各小题将给出5秒钟的作答时间。每段对话或独白读两遍。

听第6段材料，回答第6至第8小题。

6. Where does this conversation take place?
   A. In London.
   B. At a railway station.
   C. At a bus station.

7. What time does the bus leave?
   A. At 1:45.　　　　　B. At 2:00.　　　　　C. At 2:15.

8. How many suitcases does the man want to check?
   A. One.　　　　　B. Two.　　　　　C. Three.

9. Who are the two speakers?

    A. A man and his wife.   B. A man and his sister.   C. A man and his girlfriend.

10. Why is the man unhappy about their weekend?

    A. They seldom invite friends over.

    B. They seldom go out for a picnic.

    C. They seldom do anything together.

11. In which aspect of the picnic do the man and woman differ?

    A. Who should get the car ready.

    B. How many friends they should invite.

    C. What food and drink they should prepare.

12. What is the man?

    A. A clerk.   B. A student.   C. A teacher.

13. What do we know about the man?

    A. He loves the children.   B. He is very worried.   C. He doesn't like his job.

14. What can we learn from the conversation?

    A. The children are not friendly.

    B. The children are very shy.

    C. The man is going to leave the school.

15. Where does the woman live?

    A. In a hotel.   B. In her friend's house.   C. In a flat.

16. What is the advantage of keeping a cat?

    A. It's clean and easy to take care of.

    B. It needs no room.

    C. It's beautiful.

17. Which of the following is TRUE?

    A. The woman hates animals.

    B. The woman insists on getting a dog instead of a cat.

    C. Older cats can't agree with the new home.

18. Which of the following is considered rude in Britain when you are eating?

    A. Using a bowl to have liquid food.

    B. Lifting the bowl for more food.

    C. Drinking directly from the bowl.

19. According to the speaker, in which country is it all right to make a noise while eating?

    A. Britain.   B. Japan.   C. Mexico.

20. What advice does the speaker give to people visiting a foreign country?

A. Follow the example of the people there.

B. Ask people for advice before you go to a meal.

C. Do as you do at home.

第二部分　英语知识运用（共两节，满分35分）

第一节　语法和词汇（共15小题；每小题1分，满分15分）

从 A、B、C、D 四个选项中，选出可以填入空白处的最佳选项。

21. In _____ city of Paris, stands _____ famous Eiffel Tower.

A. / ; the   B. the ; /   C. the ; a   D. the ; the

22. —Did you remember to pay the telephone bill?

—The telephone bill? _____

A. That isn't due yet.   B. Are you sure?

C. My telephone is out of order.   D. Please remember the amount.

23. It was reported that the forest fire _____ last Sunday and that it _____ itself and wasn't _____.

A. went out; broke out; put out   B. broke out; went out; put out

C. broke out; put out; went out   D. put out; broke out; went out

24. These two problems are _____ linked, and it makes sense to consider them together.

A. closely   B. close   C. wide   D. widely

25. —Did you enjoy yourself at the party?

—Sorry to say I didn't. It was _____ a meeting than a party.

A. more of   B. rather like   C. less of   D. more or less

26. Though small, the ant is as much a creature as _____ all other animals on earth.

A. are   B. is   C. do   D. have

27. When he realised the police had seen him, the thief _____ the exit as quickly as possible.

A. made off   B. made for   C. made out   D. made up

28. —How wide is the Yellow River?

—That _____ from where to where.

A. depends   B. changes   C. refers   D. lies

29. _____, he talks a lot about his favourite singers after class.

A. A quiet student as he may be   B. Quiet student as he may be

C. Be a quiet student as he may   D. Quiet as he may be a student

30. —Mum, what did your doctor say?

—He advised me to live _____ the air is fresher.

A. in where   B. in which   C. the place where   D. where

31. Your uncle seems to be a good driver; _____ I wouldn't dare to travel in his car.

A. even so   B. even though   C. therefore   D. so

32. How can you find a job _____ you are not suited?

    A. which   B. in which   C. at which   D. to which

33. He lay on his back, his right hand _____ on his breast, and his glaring eyes looking straight upward.

    A. clenching   B. clenched   C. clench   D. to clench

34. I _____ pay Tracy a visit, but I am not sure whether I have time this Sunday.

    A. should   B. might   C. would   D. could

35. How can they finish the work in the _____ of any other help?

    A. shortage   B. absence   C. lack   D. hunger

第二节　完形填空（共20题；每小题1分，满分20分）

阅读下面的短文，掌握其大意，然后从每题所给的四个选项中选出最佳选项。

Learning Chinese

"Huixin Dongjie, qing?", "Huixin Dongjie?", "Ting bu dong?"

The __36__ was scratching (抓) his head as I tried, once again, to make myself __37__. I moved my lips, clicked my tongue, and opened my eyes wide, but no __38__.

I had failed yet __39__ and was going to have to turn to my trusty, tourist-friendly __40__. "Ahhh, Huixin Dongjie", said my driver when I pointed the __41__ out, __42__ I had been trying to trick him all along.

As we sped off, I __43__ that although I thought I had said the __44__ correctly, I was obviously doing something wrong. The intonations (声调) I needed to speak Chinese properly were still __45__, even though I __46__ trying now for the best part of two months.

__47__ I went, the noodle shop, the dry cleaners, the bank, I carefully studied the phrases I might need, saying them out loud to __48__. "Liang wan lamian, xiexie, xiexie", "Duoshao qian?" "Zai lai yi ping pijiu!"

Sometimes I was __49__. Most of the time I __50__ to sign language and pointing. It is so frustrating!

I think the main problem is that Chinese is so different from the __51__ I learnt in school.

Learning to speak Chinese is a __52__. Words have many different meanings and are __53__ with phrases that have no English equivalent. On top of this is the thick Beijing __54__. It seems I am going to have my work cut out. Hopefully one day, that taxi driver and I will be able to __55__.

36. A. teacher	B. passer-by	C. taxi driver	D. policeman
37. A. understood	B. heard	C. interested	D. known
38. A. answer	B. reply	C. use	D. sound
39. A. once	B. even	C. then	D. again
40. A. book	B. neighbour	C. map	D. translator
41. A. name	B. way	C. road	D. direction
42. A. as if	B. just as	C. even if	D. in case

43. A. reflected   B. remembered   C. wondered   D. noticed
44. A. words   B. questions   C. sentences   D. intonations
45. A. lacking   B. missing   C. difficult   D. low
46. A. have been   B. had been   C. am   D. was
47. A. Every day   B. Every time   C. Everywhere   D. Somewhere
48. A. use   B. communicate   C. exercise   D. practise
49. A. happy   B. misunderstood   C. understood   D. worried
50. A. refer   B. devote   C. change   D. turn
51. A. dialogues   B. words   C. courses   D. language
52. A. choice   B. challenge   C. chance   D. trouble
53. A. filled   B. full   C. mixed   D. ended
54. A. slang   B. tradition   C. flavour   D. accent
55. A. meet   B. try   C. understand   D. communicate

第三部分　阅读理解（共20小题；每小题2分，满分40分）

A

阅读下列短文，从每题所给的四个选项中选出最佳选项。

Moving in with a boyfriend causes women to eat more unhealthily and put on weight. But the opposite is true for men, whose long-term health benefits when they move in with a female partner. Dieticians (饮食学家) at Newcastle University said both partners try to please one another, and so change their dietary habits to suit their other half.

It leads men to eat more <u>light</u> meals, such as salads, fruit and vegetables, while women choose to make creamier, heavier dishes like curry or rich pasta sauces, which may please their partner.

Women still have the strongest long-term influence over the couple's diet and lifestyle, as they still have the traditional role of shopper and cook in most households.

The report, by Newcastle University's Human Nutrition Research Centre, reviewed the findings of a variety of research projects from the UK, North America and Australia, which looked at the eating and lifestyle habits of cohabiting couples and married couples.

The research shows that women are more likely to put on weight and increase their consumption of foods high in fat and sugar when they move in with their partner.

Women also use food as a comfort when dealing with emotional stress and have been found to gain weight when a relationship ends, while the same finding has not been observed in men.

Many couples reported food as being central to their partnership, and eating together in the evening was particularly important to many.

Report author and registered dietician Dr Amelia Lake said, "The research has shown that your partner is a strong influence on lifestyle and people who are trying to live healthier lives should take this factor into consideration."

56. According to the passage, moving in with a girlfriend, men _____.

    A. have new changes of their dietary habits

    B. have to eat more unhealthy food

    C. don't like foods high in fat and sugar at all

    D. try to eat foods that their girlfriends like

57. The underlined word "light" in the second paragraph probably means "_____".

    A. not very heavy in weight   B. less in fat and sugar

    C. gentle and soft   D. not serious or important

58. According to the report by Newcastle University's Human Nutrition Research Centre, _____.

    A. women put on weight only because they want to suit their other half

    B. when men are faced with emotional stress, they will change their dietary habits

    C. eating together in the evening is a good way to communicate for a couple

    D. it is wrong to change your dietary habits to suit your partner

59. From the passage, we can infer that _____.

    A. women should pay more attention to their partner's influence on them

    B. more men will play roles of shopper and cook in most households

    C. couples will not change their dietary habits and lifestyle to please their partners

    D. men haven't benefited from their female partners

60. What is the best title for the passage?

    A. Don't Be Silly Anymore, Women!   B. Which Are Better Dietary Habits?

    C. Boyfriends Make You Fat   D. Dr Amelia Lake and Her Research

B

    Harvard University named historian Drew Gilpin Faust as its first female president on Sunday, ending a lengthy and secretive search to find a successor to Lawrence Summers.

    The seven-member Harvard Corporation elected Faust, a noted scholar on History of the American South and dean of Harvard's Radcliffe Institute for Advanced Study, as the university's 28th president.

    "This is a great day, and a historic day, for Harvard," James R. Houghton, chairman of the presidential search committee, said in a statement. "Drew Faust is an inspiring and accomplished leader, a superb scholar, a dedicated teacher and a wonderful human being."

    Her selection is noteworthy given the heated debates over Summers' comments that genetic differences between the sexes might help explain the lack of women in top science jobs.

    Faust has been dean of Radcliffe since 2001, two years after the former women's college was combined into the university as a research centre with a mission to study gender issues.

    Some professors have quietly groused that the 371-year-old university is appointing a fifth president who is not a scientist. No scientist has had the top job since James Bryant Conant retired in 1953; its last four have come from the fields of classics, law, literature and economics.

Faust is the first Harvard president who did not receive a degree from the university since Charles Chauncey, a graduate of Cambridge University, who died in office in 1672. She attended the University of Pennsylvania.

"Teaching staff turned to her constantly," said Sheldon Hackney, a former president of the University of Pennsylvania and historian who worked closely with Faust. "She's very clear. She has a sense of humour, but she's very strong-minded. You come to trust in her because she's so solid."

61. Lawrence Summers held the view that _____.

　　A. women cannot achieve as much as men in management

　　B. women cannot hold important positions in society

　　C. women can match men in science jobs

　　D. few women make top scientists owing to genes

62. The underlined word "groused" in the sixth paragraph means "_____".

　　A. approved　　　B. commented　　　C. complained　　　D. indicated

63. Which is NOT true about Drew Gilpin Faust?

　　A. She is the 28th president of Harvard University.

　　B. She is a famous scholar from the American South.

　　C. She isn't a graduate from Harvard University.

　　D. She was head of Radcliffe Institute for Advanced Study.

64. Which might be the best title for the passage?

　　A. Harvard Named Its First Female President

　　B. History of Harvard University Changed

　　C. Debates on Female Equality Ended

　　D. Drew Gilpin Faust, A Famous Woman Historian

65. This passage probably appears in a _____.

　　A. biography　　　B. letter　　　　C. research paper　　　D. newspaper report

C

Room for Revolution: George Washington and His Philadelphia Friends
March 16–August 30

Charles Wilson Peale's *George Washington at Princeton* is on view at the Museum which was lent from a private collection. This visually striking and finely made life-size portrait records Washington's 6-foot-2-inch figure in a pose highlighting strength, composure, and elegance. It is put up in a room neighbouring to the Powel House parlor, a period room from one of Philadelphia's greatest 18th-century private homes, where Washington was frequently entertained by his friends, Samuel and Elizabeth Powel. Both spaces contain important examples of furniture by Philadelphia's finest craftsmen, such as Thomas Affleck and John Aitken. Among these is a side chair specially ordered by the Washingtons when living in Philadelphia.

Painted in Philadelphia in 1779, Peale's painting was immediately sent to Europe to promote Washington's reputation as a leader and the cause of the American Revolution, then in progress. Later, during Europe's Napoleonic Wars, a Spanish duke with strong sympathies with American Revolution owned the picture. At that time he added the complicated carved caption to it, which describes Washington as "a liberator of his country who abandoned absolute power".

Curators

American Art Department Staff, website commentary by Carol Soltis

Location

Galleries 286 and 287, second floor

66. This passage is mainly about _____.

A. the cause of the American Revolution

B. the information of a portrait on view

C. the description of life of George Washington

D. the friendship between Washington and his friends

67. What is the name of the portrait?

A. *Room for Revolution*.

B. *Charles Wilson Peale*.

C. *George Washington at Princeton*.

D. *George Washington and His Philadelphia Friends*.

68. What happened in the Powel House parlor?

A. Washington entertained his friends.

B. Washington made a chair on his own.

C. Charles Wilson Peale finished the portrait.

D. Samuel and Elizabeth Powel met Washington a lot.

69. According to the passage, Washington _____.

A. lived between 1741 and 1827

B. ordered the portrait painted in 1779

C. was sympathised by a Spanish duke

D. was a great man not greedy for power

70. The passage tells us that _____.

A. when the portrait was finished, America was at war

B. the portrait was originally hanging in Samuel's room

C. the portrait was sent to Europe to gain support from Napoleon

D. the caption of the portrait was carved by Philadelphia's finest craftsmen

D

How do you decide what you are going to buy in a supermarket? Do you look in your refrigerator and kitchen cupboards and make a list of the things you need? Do you think about what you want to cook and then buy the food you need for each meal? Even if you do these things, marketing specialists at the supermarket make some of your buying decisions for you.

Specialists in marketing have studied how to make people buy more food in a supermarket. They work for things that you do not even notice. For example, the simple, ordinary food that everybody must buy, like bread, milk, flour and oil, is spread all over the store. Bread might be in Aisle 2 and milk in Aisle 10. You have to walk by all the more interesting and more expensive items to find what you need.

The more expensive food is in packages with bright colours and pictures. This food is placed at eye level so you see it right away and want to buy it. The things you have to buy are usually located on a higher or lower shelf. However, candy and other things that children like are on lower shelves so that children can see them easily and ask their parents to buy them. This method of marketing really works. One study showed that when a supermarket moved four products from a low shelf to a shelf at eye level, it sold 78 percent more of those products.

Another study showed that for every minute a person spends in a supermarket after the first half hour she or he will spend $1.00. If someone stays for 40 minutes, the supermarket makes an additional $10.00. A store usually has a comfortable temperature in summer and winter, and it plays soft music. It is a pleasant place for people to stay — and spend more money.

Supermarkets also sell some things at lower, or special prices every week. The prices on some of these "specials" are not really cheaper than their regular prices. For example, an item that is usually $0.50 might be a special at 2/$1.00 (that's two for one dollar). Or if something is not selling very fast at $0.69, it is put on special at 2/$1.40. People think the product is cheaper than usual and buy it.

Some stores have red or pink lights over the meat so the meat looks redder and fresher. They put light green paper around lettuce and put apples in red plastic bags.

So be careful in the supermarket. You may go home with a bag of food you were not planning to buy.

71. According to the passage marketing specialists study _____.

    A. the ownership of supermarkets

    B. how to build cupboards

    C. methods of buying and selling products

    D. the price of food

72. Where can you find the food that is more expensive?

    A. On high shelves.   B. In bright coloured packages.

    C. Usually on special shelves.   D. Near the front.

73. Why does the writer say that you should be careful in the supermarket?

    A. There are some thieves in the supermarket.

    B. The food in the supermarket is of bad quality.

    C. Maybe you will buy a lot of unnecessary food.

    D. Some people often persuade you to buy more food.

74. In the author's opinion, "special" is _____ than that item usually is.

    A. sometimes more expensive   B. always cheaper

    C. never more expensive   D. more delicious

75. It can be inferred from the passage that _____.

    A. it is marketing specialists who decide what you should buy or not

    B. marketing specialists try every way to make people spend as much money in the supermarket as possible

    C. the sweet music and comfortable temperature in the store can attract people to buy more things than they planned

    D. the red or pink lights over the products and the pleasing colour persuade people to buy more products

第四部分　书面表达（共两节，满分45分）

第一节　阅读表达（共5小题；每小题3分，满分15分）

阅读下面的短文，并根据短文后的要求答题。

Courage is admitting that you're afraid and facing that fear directly. It's being strong enough to ask for help and humble enough to accept it.

Courage is standing up for what you believe in without worrying about the opinions of others. It's following your own heart, living your own life, and settling for nothing less than the best for yourself.

Courage is daring to take a first step, a big leap, or a different path. It's attempting to do something that no one has done before, and all others thought impossible.

<u>Courage is keeping heart in the face of disappointment, and looking at defeat not as an end but as a new beginning.</u> It's believing that things will ultimately getting better even as they get worse.

Courage is _____ your own actions, and admitting your mistakes without placing blame on others. It's relying not on others for your success, but on your own skills and efforts.

Courage is refusing to quit even when you're threatened by impossibility. It's choosing a goal, sticking to it, and finding solutions to the problems.

Courage is thinking big, aiming high, and shooting far. It's taking a dream and doing anything, risking everything, and stopping at nothing to make it a reality.

76. What is the best title for the passage? (Please answer within 5 words.)

_____

77. Which sentence in the passage can be replaced by the following one?
Courage is supporting what you trust without being influenced by others.

_____

78. Fill in the blank in the fifth paragraph with proper words or phrases to complete the sentence. (Please answer within 10 words.)

_____

79. What definition of courage do you most agree? Why? (Please answer within 30 words.)

_____

_____

80. Translate the underlined sentence in the fourth paragraph into Chinese.

_____

_____

第二节　写作（满分30分）

随着中国经济的发展和国际地位的提高，汉语也受到了越来越多的关注。世界许多国家都开设了汉语课程，来华学习汉语和中国文化的留学生也逐年增多，并且有越来越多的外国人参加汉语水平考试（HSK）。"汉语热"（Chinese Craze）正在持续升温。请你用英语写一篇短文，简要介绍这一现象及其背景、原因和你的感想（感想不得少于两条）。

词数要求：120～150词。

_____

_____

_____

_____

Module ④

Which English?

要点纵览

高考词汇	instantly, recognisable, matter, count, trace, unique, author, ancestor, link, rhythm, debate, complain, media, revolution, investigate, acquire, convinced, telecommunication, furthermore, splendid, straightforward, association, ambiguous, dilemma, explicit, relevant, absurd, convey, thus, clarify, tendency, disorganised, vague, clumsy, select, significance, withdraw, reject, potential, abuse, offence, statesman, betray, overcome, prayer, oppose, prejudice, resist, conflict, moral, superior, status, classify, sex, approval, curiosity, initially, candidate, spin-off
常用短语	tell…apart, as long as, in conclusion, a huge number of, get down to sth, let sb down, for that matter, or rather, be unique to, lie in, in case, end with, in particular, hold up, ever since, in…form, look the same to, find one's way into, combine…and…, be relevant to, trade with, be meant for, regard as
实用句型	1. It's communication that counts. 2. This is not the case. 3. It is estimated that 1.3 billion people will use English as… 4. Experts are convinced that this will happen in the future… 5. The demand for Chinese as a foreign language is growing fast... 6. I remember the first time I heard a native of Beijing speaking, it was so clear.
交际用语	1. Sorry, I've got no idea. 2. The bus got held up in traffic. 3. It doesn't matter. 4. Long time no see.

◆ 高考词汇

1. instantly

adv. 立刻，马上

I recognised him instantly.

Her voice was instantly recognisable.

2. count

n. 1) 计数，计算；2) 总计，总数

v. 1) 数，计数；2) 把 (某人/某物) 计算在内

The count showed that 20,000 votes had been cast.

What's the exact count?

He can't count yet.

Don't forget to count your change.

There are 50 people, not counting the children.

➡ 常用短语：

count as 认可，认为　　　　　count for 有价值，有重要性

count on sb / sth 依靠，依赖，指望　　count sb / sth in 把某人/某事物计算在内

Locally produced sales by American firms in Japan do not count as exports.

Knowledge without common sense counts for little.

Don't count on a salary increase this year.

If you're all going to the party, you can count me in.

拓 展

instant *adj.* 1) 立即的，立刻的；2) 速成的；3) 紧迫的，迫切的，迫在眉睫的

n. 顷刻，刹那，瞬间，片刻

The new book is an instant success.

He often eats out at an instant Chinese restaurant.

The flood victims were in instant need of help.

Come here this instant!

I shall be back in an instant.

Just for an instant I thought he was going to refuse.

the instant (that) 一……(就……)

I recognised her the instant I saw her.

表示"一……(就……)"之意的短语还有：

the moment, as soon as, hardly…when…, no sooner…than…

辨 析

count, calculate

count 意为"计算，数"，表示最基本的计算，指逐个数过而得出总数。

calculate 意为"计算，核算"，指较复杂的计算过程，如算术中的加、减、乘、除运算或数学上的精密运算等。

He counted the children before they started the game.

Have you calculated what a holiday in China would cost?

3. trace

n. 1) 痕迹，踪迹；2) 极少量，微量

v. 1) 描绘；2) 跟踪；3) 追溯

The police have been unable to find any trace of the gang.

He spoke without a trace of emotion.

The book traces the decline of the Roman Empire.

The police traced the criminal.

The book traces the development of philosophy.

➡ 常用短语：

trace (sth) back to 追溯到

trace sth out 画出或描绘出某物的轮廓

Her fear of water can be traced back to a childhood accident.

We traced out our route on the map.

4. debate

n. 辩论，讨论

v. 争论，辩论，讨论

After a long debate, the House of Commons approved the bill.

We have been debating about current affairs.

➡ 常用短语：

heated debate 热烈的讨论   beyond debate 无可争辩地

have / hold a debate on sth 针对某事进行讨论

debate with sb about sth 与某人争论某事   debate with oneself 独自考虑，心中盘算

辨 析

debate, argue, discuss

debate 强调辩论的目的在于说服对方。

argue 指条理清晰地陈述赞成或反对的理由。

discuss 指从不同的角度出发与某人讨论某事。

We debated for several hours before taking a vote.

Woolf's report argued for an improvement in prison conditions.

We have to discuss what we can do to prevent crime.

5. complain

v. 1) 抱怨，诉苦，发牢骚；2) 控诉，投诉

She complained to me about his rudeness.

He complained (to the waiter) that his meal was cold.

He complained to the police of the boys' stealing his apples.

拓 展

complaint *n.* 1) 抱怨，埋怨，不满；2) 申诉，投诉，诉苦

The roadworks caused much complaint among local residents.

You have no cause for complaint.

I have a number of complaints about the hotel room you've given me.

We've received a lot of complaints of bad workmanship.

6. furthermore

adv. 而且，此外，再者

Furthermore, he felt that he wasn't really an authority on preventive medicine.

He is inefficient, and furthermore, he is innocent of any sense of responsibility.

与 furthermore 意义相近的词或短语还有：moreover, in addition, besides, similarly, what's more, also。

7. acquire

v. 1) 取得，获得；2) 学到，养成

The museum has just acquired a famous painting by Pablo Picasso.

Gradually we acquired experience in how to do the work.

She has mastered English grammar and acquired a large vocabulary without the help of the teacher.

辨 析

acquire, get, obtain

这三个词都有"获得"的意思。

acquire 意为"取得，获得"，强调通过努力或经过某一过程得到某物。

get 意为"获得，得到"，是常用词，指用某种手段或方式得到某种东西，这种东西可能是某人需要的或希望获得的，也可能是他不需要的。因此，得到这种东西不一定需要主动性或经过很大的努力。

obtain 意为"取得，得到"，指通过努力工作或奋斗得到想要的东西或达到某种目的。

You must work hard to acquire a good command of English.

We must get a ladder to pick the apples.

They realised that only through struggle could they obtain their rights.

8. convince

v. 1) 使确信，使明白；2) 说服

How can I convince you (of her honesty)?

He tried to convince them of the safety of travelling by airplane.

What she said convinced me that I was mistaken.

What convinced you to vote for them?

拓 展

convinced *adj.* 坚信不疑的，有坚定信仰的

She didn't look convinced, but said nothing.

9. convey

v. 1) 运送，搬运；2) 传播 (声音等)；3) 传达，传递；4) 转让 (财产等)

Passengers are conveyed by bus to the air terminal.

A wire conveys an electric current.

I found it hard to convey my feelings in words.

The old farmer conveyed his farm to the young man.

10. clarify

v. 1) 澄清，阐明；2) 净化

clarify a remark / statement 澄清一个意见/声明

He clarified his stand on the issue.

His explanation clarified the mystery.

It requires of us great efforts to clarify sewage in cities.

11. select

v. 挑选，选拔

Mr Reed has been selected to represent us on the committee.

He selected a team for the special task.

拓 展

selector *n.* 挑选人，选择者

selection *n.* 挑选，选择，选拔

the Olympic selectors 奥运会代表队选拔委员会委员

Her selection of a hat took a long time.

辨 析

select, choose, elect, opt, pick

select 是书面用语，具有庄严、正式的感情色彩，强调"精选"。

choose 是普通用语，侧重根据个人意愿和判断从众多的对象中进行选择，着重强调被选者的优点。

elect 是指按照一定的规章或法律，用投票等方式进行认真慎重的选择。

opt 多指在几种可能性之间进行选择，且具有权衡利弊之意。

pick 是口语用词，多指从个人角度仔细挑选，也含任意挑选之意。

Our shops select only the very best quality products.

She chose the red sweater rather than the pink one.

He was elected president.

Most people opt for buying their own homes rather than renting them.

You can pick whichever one you like.

真 题 解 析

This picture was taken a long time ago. I wonder if you can _____ my father. (2005 湖北)

A. find out   B. pick out   C. look out   D. speak out

解析：find out 指"查明（真相等），认识到"，look out 意为"照料"，speak out 指"大声说"，只有 pick out 意为"辨别出，看出"，符合句子的意思。答案为 B。

12. reject

n. 被抛弃的东西，废品

v. 1) 拒绝接受；2) 抛弃，摈弃，剔除

The rejects were stacked in a corner.

She rejected his offer of marriage.

After the transplant his body rejected the new heart.

Children feel abandoned or rejected if they don't see their parents regularly.

辨 析

reject, decline, refuse

reject 指以否定或敌对的态度当面拒绝。

decline 指较正式地、有礼貌地谢绝。

refuse 指坚决、果断或坦率地拒绝。

The board rejected all our ideas.

She declined to have lunch with her friend, saying that she wasn't feeling well.

He refused to take the money.

13. oppose

v. 1) 反对，反抗，妨碍；2) 使相对，使对抗

I am opposed to going shopping with others.

He is strongly opposed to the plan.

Do not oppose your will against mine.

She is opposed by three other candidates.

➡ 常用短语：

as opposed to 与……对照之下，而不是

be opposed to / against 反对

14. resist

v. 1) 抵抗，对抗；2) 抗 (酸)，耐 (热等)；

　　3) (常用于否定句) 忍耐，忍住

resist an enemy / attack 抵抗敌人/进攻

can't resist sth / doing sth 忍不住

The nation was unable to resist the invasion.

This special coating is designed to resist rust.

She can never resist buying new shoes.

辨 析

oppose, object, protest, resist

oppose 为常用词，指对某人、某事采取积极行动来反对，着重强调动作，尤指反对某

种观念、思想、计划等。

object 常指用言论或论据等表示反对，着重强调个人嫌厌和（由于与个人有关的原因）提出反对意见，常与 to 连用。

protest 一般指通过语言、文字或行为表示出强烈抗议或反对。

resist 指奋力抗争或抵抗某些行动、效果和力量，用武力阻止……的前进。

Congress is continuing to oppose the president's health care budget.

They objected that the policy would prevent the patients from receiving the best treatment.

Crowds of people protested against the war.

If the enemy continues to resist, wipe them out.

15. approval

n. 赞成，认可，满意，同意

Do the plans meet with her approval?

The plan had the approval of the school authorities.

➡ 常用短语：

general approval 一致同意

with the approval of 经……的批准

> **拓 展**
>
> approve *v.* 赞成，批准
>
> approve of sth 赞成某事
>
> The minister approved the building plan.
>
> I'm afraid your parents won't approve of your going there.

◆ 常用短语

1. tell…apart

tell…apart 意思是"区分开"。

I just can't tell the twins apart.

与这个短语意义相近的短语还有：tell…from，tell the difference between，differentiate between，separate…from 等。

Can you tell Tom from his twin brother?

Can you tell the difference between an ape and a monkey?

It is wrong to differentiate between people according to their family background.

It is not difficult to separate a butterfly from a moth.

2. as long as

as long as 含义有：1) 和……一样长；2) 只要 (可以和 so long as 换用)

This line is four times as long as that one.

You can keep my book as long as you like.

As long as there is life, there is hope.

As / So long as you clear your desk by this evening, you can have tomorrow's leave.

3. get down to

get down to 意思是"开始认真做"。

He got down to his work after the holidays.

Let's get down to business.

4. hold…up

hold…up 的主要含义有：1) 阻碍；2) 拦截；抢劫；3) 举出

They were held up by fog.

The criminals held up the train.

Don't hold me up as a model husband.

5. or rather

or rather 的意思是"更确切地说"。

I worked as a secretary, or rather, a typist.

The American, or rather, the Afro-American, are good at Jazz music.

6. be relevant to

be relevant to 意思是"与……有关的，切题的，恰当的"。

His nationality isn't relevant to whether he is a good lawyer.

The essay isn't even remotely relevant to the topic.

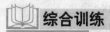

考试时间：45分钟　　　满分：100分

I．单项选择（共15小题；每小题1分，满分15分）

1. The cakes are delicious. He'd like to have _____ third one because _____ second one is too small.
   A. a; a　　　　　　　B. the; the　　　　　　C. a; the　　　　　　D. the; a

2. He made an attempt to _____ the misunderstanding about the origin of the language.
   A. clarify　　　　　B. check　　　　　　C. claim　　　　　　D. clap

3. I like black coffee so much; the stronger it is, _____.
   A. I like it better　　　　　　　　B. the more I like
   C. the better I like it　　　　　　D. I like it more

4. _____ he heard the news, he telephoned his mother.
   A. Immediate　　　B. The instant　　　C. If　　　　　　　　D. Although

5. I have read the material several times but it doesn't make any _____ to me.
   A. meaning　　　　B. importance　　　C. sense　　　　　　D. significance

6. What they said _____ nothing.
   A. counts on　　　B. counts for　　　C. counts off　　　D. counts down

7. Jerry did research in that field for a long time. He _____ to invent something useful.
   A. got down　　　B. hoped himself　　C. set out　　　　　D. devoted himself

8. He accidentally _____ he had quarrelled with his wife and then he hadn't been home for a couple of weeks.
   A. let out　　　　B. took care　　　　C. made sure　　　　D. made out

9. Beethoven is my favourite musician. I regard him _____ other musicians.
   A. more superior to　　　　　　B. more superior than
   C. superior to　　　　　　　　　D. superior than

10. Allow children the space to voice their opinions, _____ they are different from your own.
    A. until　　　　　B. even if　　　　　C. unless　　　　　D. as though

11. "You can't catch me!" Janet shouted _____ away.
    A. run　　　　　　B. running　　　　　C. to run　　　　　D. ran

12. During the conference the speaker tried to _____ his feelings concerning the urgency of a favourable decision.
    A. comment　　　B. announce　　　　C. imply　　　　　D. convey

13. This magazine is very _____ with young people, who like its content and style.
    A. familiar　　　　　　　　　　　　B. popular
    C. similar　　　　　　　　　　　　D. particular

235

14. We can work wonders so long as we try our best, that is, we can make _____.

    A. impossible possible   B. the impossible possible

    C. possible impossible   D. the possible impossible

15. —He would go to see you.

    —_____ he did not come?

    A. What if   B. Where if   C. What come   D. Why whether

II. 完形填空（共20小题；每小题1分，满分20分）

    Health implies more than physical fitness. It also implies mental and emotional well-being. An angry, frustrated, emotionally __1__ person in good physical condition is not __2__ healthy. Mental health, therefore, has much to do __3__ how a person copes with the world as she or he exists. Many of the factors that __4__ physical health also affect mental and emotional well-being.

    Having a good self-image means that people have positive __5__ pictures and good, positive feelings about themselves, about what they are capable __6__, and about the roles they play. People with good self-images like themselves, and they are __7__ like others. Having a good self-image is based __8__ a realistic __9__ of one's own worth, value and capabilities.

    Stress is an unavoidable, necessary, and potentially healthful __10__ of our society. People of all ages __11__ stress. Children begin to __12__ stress during antenatal (胎儿期的) development and during childbirth. Examples of stress inducing __13__ in the life of a young person are death of a pet, pressure to __14__ academically, the divorce of parents, or joining a new youth group. The different ways in which individuals __15__ to stress may bring healthful or unhealthy results. One person experiencing a great deal of stress may function exceptionally well __16__ another may be unable to function at all. If stressful situations are continually encountered, the individual's physical, social, and mental health are eventually affected.

    Satisfying social relations are vital to __17__ mental and emotional health. It is believed that in order to __18__, develop, and maintain effective and fulfilling social relationships people must __19__ the ability to know and trust, understand, influence, and help each other. They must also be capable of __20__ conflicts in a constructive way.

    1. A. unstable   B. unsure   C. imprecise   D. impractical

    2. A. normally   B. generally   C. virtually   D. necessarily

    3. A. on   B. at   C. to   D. with

    4. A. signify   B. influence   C. predict   D. mark

    5. A. intellectual   B. sensual   C. spiritual   D. mental

    6. A. to be doing   B. with doing   C. to do   D. of doing

    7. A. able better to   B. able to better   C. better to able   D. better able to

    8. A. on   B. from   C. at   D. about

9. A. assessment   B. decision   C. determination   D. assistance
10. A. ideality   B. realisation   C. realism   D. reality
11. A. occur   B. engage   C. confront   D. encounter
12. A. tolerate   B. sustain   C. experience   D. undertake
13. A. evidence   B. accidents   C. adventures   D. events
14. A. acquire   B. achieve   C. obtain   D. fulfill
15. A. respond   B. return   C. require   D. reply
16. A. why   B. when   C. while   D. where
17. A. sound   B. all-round   C. entire   D. whole
18. A. keep   B. end   C. finish   D. start
19. A. access   B. assess   C. process   D. possess
20. A. resolving   B. saluting   C. dissolving   D. solving

III. 阅读理解（共10小题；每小题2分，满分20分）

A

So long as teachers fail to distinguish between teaching and learning, they will continue to undertake to do for children what only children can do for themselves. Teaching children to read is not passing reading on to them. It is certainly not endless hours spent in activities about reading. Douglas insists that "reading cannot be taught directly and schools should stop trying to do the impossible".

Teaching and learning are two entirely different processes. They differ in kind and function. The function of teaching is to create the conditions and the climate that will make it possible for children to devise the most efficient system for teaching themselves to read. Teaching is also a public activity. It can be seen and observed.

Learning to read involves all that each individual does to make sense of the words of printed language. Almost all of it is private, for learning is an occupation of the mind, and that process is not open to public scrutiny.

If teacher's and learner's roles are not interchangeable, what then can be done through teaching that will aid the child in the quest (探索) for knowledge? Smith has one principal rule for all teaching instructions, "Make learning to read easy, which means making reading a meaningful, enjoyable and frequent experience for children."

When the roles of teacher and learner are seen for what they are, and when both teacher and learner fulfill them appropriately, then much of the pressure and feeling of failure for both is eliminated. Learning to read is made easier when teachers create an environment where children are given the opportunity to solve the problem of learning to read by reading.

1. The problem with the reading course as mentioned in the first paragraph is that _____.

    A. it is one of the most difficult school courses

B. students spend endless hours in reading

C. reading tasks are assigned with little guidance

D. too much time is spent in teaching about reading

2. The teaching of reading will be successful if teachers can _____.

    A. improve conditions at school for the students

    B. enable students to develop their own way of reading

    C. devise the most efficient system for reading

    D. make their teaching activities observable

3. The underlined word "scrutiny" in the third paragraph most probably means "_____".

    A. inquiry   B. observation   C. control   D. suspicion

4. According to the passage, learning to read will no longer be a difficult task when _____.

    A. children become highly motivated

    B. teacher's and learner's roles are interchangeable

    C. teaching helps children in the search for knowledge

    D. reading enriches children's experience

5. The main idea of the passage is that _____.

    A. teachers should do as little as possible in helping students learn to read

    B. teachers should encourage students to read as widely as possible

    C. reading ability is something acquired rather than taught

    D. reading is more complicated that generally believed

B

"Tear them apart!" "Kill the fool!" "Murder the referee!"

These are common remarks one may hear at various sporting events. At the time they are made, they seem innocent enough. But let's not kid ourselves. They have been known to influence behaviour in such a way as to lead to real bloodshed. Volumes have been written about the way words affect us. It has been shown that words having certain connotations (内涵意义) may cause us to react in ways quite foreign to what we consider to be our usual humanistic behaviour. I see the term "opponent" as one of those words. Perhaps the time has come to delete it from sports terms.

The dictionary meaning of the term "opponent" is "adversary; enemy; one who opposes your interests". Thus, when a player meets an opponent, he or she may tend to treat that opponent as an enemy. At such times, winning may dominate one's intellect, and every action, no matter how gross, may be considered justifiable. I recall an incident in a handball game when a referee refused a player's request for a time out for a glove change because he did not consider them wet enough. The player proceeded to rub his gloves across his wet T-shirt and then exclaimed, "Are they wet enough now?"

In the heat of battle, players have been observed to throw themselves across the court without considering the consequences that such a move might have on anyone in their way. I have also witnessed a player reacting to his opponent's intentional and illegal blocking by deliberately hitting him with the ball as hard as he could during the course of play. Off the court, they are good friends. Does that make any sense? It certainly gives proof of a court attitude which departs from normal behaviour.

Therefore, I believe it is time we elevated (提升) the game to the level where it belongs, thereby setting an example to the rest of the sporting world. Replacing the term "opponent" with "associate" could be an ideal way to start.

The dictionary meaning of the term "associate" is "colleague; friend; companion". Reflect a moment! You may soon see and possibly feel the difference in your reaction to the term "associate" rather than "opponent".

6. Which of the following statements best expresses the author's view?

A. Aggressive behaviour in sports can have serious consequences.

B. The words people use can influence their behaviour.

C. Unpleasant words in sports are often used by foreign athletes.

D. Unfair judgments by referees will lead to violence on the sports field.

7. Harsh words are spoken during games because the players _____.

A. are too eager to win

B. are usually short-tempered and easily offended

C. cannot afford to be polite in fierce competitions

D. treat their rivals as enemies

8. What did the handball player do when he was not allowed a time out to change his gloves?

A. He refused to continue the game.

B. He angrily hit the referee with a ball.

C. He claimed that the referee was unfair.

D. He wet his gloves by rubbing them across his T-shirt.

9. According to the passage, players, in a game, may _____.

A. deliberately throw the ball at anyone illegally blocking their way

B. keep on screaming and shouting throughout the game

C. lie down on the ground as an act of protest

D. kick the ball across the court with force

10. The author hopes to have the current situation in sports improved by _____.

A. calling on players to use clean language on the court

B. raising the referees' sense of responsibility

C. changing the attitude of players on the sports field

D. regulating the relationship between players and referees

Chat rooms and messaging can be great fun, but remember, you never really know who you are talking to online. It could be someone trying to trick you, some kind of weirdo (古怪的人), or someone really dangerous. Here are some tips to help you keep safe:

● Never use your real name in chat rooms — pick a special online nickname.

● Never tell anyone personal things about yourself or your family — like your address or telephone number, or the school or clubs you go to. That goes for sending them photos as well (that way if you don't want to hear from them again, you only have to log off). Remember, even if somebody tells you about themselves, never tell them things about you.

● If you arrange to meet up with someone you've only spoken to once, remember that they might not be who they said they were, so only meet people in public places and take along an adult — they should do this too, because they don't know who you really are either!

● Never respond to nasty (污秽的) or rude messages, and never send any either! If you feel suspicious or uncomfortable about the way a conversation is going, or if it's getting really personal, save a record of it and stop the conversation. That way you can show someone and ask what they think.

● Be careful with any email attachments or links that people send you, they might contain nasty images, or computer "viruses" that could ruin your PC. So if _____, don't open it.

1. What is the best title for the passage? (Please answer within 10 words.)

_____

2. Which sentence in the passage can be replaced by the following one?
   The person you are talking to online may mean to do harm to you.

_____

_____

3. Fill in the blank in the last paragraph with proper words or phrases to complete the sentence. (Please answer within 10 words.)

_____

4. Which of the suggestions do you think is the best for you? Why? (Please answer within 30 words.)

_____

_____

5. Translate the underlined sentence into Chinese.

_____

_____

V. 写作（满分30分）

三班的同学进行了一场有关英语学习的讨论，讨论的主题是：学习英语要不要从儿童时期开始？请你根据下表的提示写一篇短文，介绍讨论的情况。文章的开头已经给出，不计入总词数。

提示：

一些同学认为	另一些同学认为
应从儿童时期开始学习英语： 1. 儿童时期记忆力好，可以记住很多单词； 2. 能为以后的英语学习打下坚实的基础。	不应从儿童时期开始学习英语： 1. 儿童时期既要学汉语又要学英语，易混淆； 2. 基础打不好，会影响汉语学习和以后的英语学习。
讨论未取得一致意见	

参考词汇：基础 foundation，汉语拼音 Chinese pinyin

词数要求：120~150词。

The students of Class 3 had a discussion about whether it is necessary to start learning English from childhood.

_____

_____

_____

_____

_____

_____

Module ⑤

The Conquest of the Universe

 要点纵览

高考词汇	leap, joint, probe, accustomed, shuttle, historic, tune, witness, assume, patience, advanced, burst, depend, planet, view, decade, acknowledge, random, backwards, deed, tension, autonomous, defeat, authority, accuse, swear, sorrow, latter, grasp, relief, glory, division, airspace, motherland, abstract, foresee, destiny, aid, broad, sympathy, commitment, ought, consistent, faith, dignity, devotion, pray, stable, supreme, scholar, consult, arguably, impact, inescapable, assumption, underway, mounting, deliberately
常用短语	describe…as, set foot on, take off, slow down, head for, ever since, become accustomed to, be aware of, be enthusiastic about, tune in to, in shock, in a state of, in spite of, a series of, result in, accuse sb of, put aside, rather than, be consistent with, as opposed to, be similar to, set out, at the beginning of, to one's relief, set in motion, in panic, or so, be contrary to, consist of, lead to, make a treaty, make peace with, needless to say
实用句型	1. This was the start of a new age of space travel. 2. It is well-known / believed / acknowledged that… 3. The fact that…is…
交际用语	1. How about you? 2. That's food for thought. 3. Maybe we will be able to take short cuts.

◆ **高考词汇**

1. accustom

v. 使习惯于

accustom oneself to 使自己习惯于

He quickly accustomed himself to this new way of life.

拓展

accustomed *adj.* 通常的，惯常的；习惯的

He took his accustomed seat by the fire.

These people are accustomed to hard work.

My eyes slowly grew accustomed to the gloom.

He quickly became accustomed to the local food.

辨 析

be accustomed to doing, be used to doing

be accustomed to doing 的意思是"习惯于做某事"，尤指适应陌生环境的过程，为书面用语，较正式。

be used to doing 的意思是"习惯于做某事"，相当于 be accustomed to doing，为口头用语。

注意：get accustomed / used to doing 指的是从不习惯到习惯的转变，强调动作，不可延续。

Conditions here are not what she is accustomed to.

He soon gets accustomed / used to dormitory life and makes two or three friends.

2. witness

n. 1) (= eyewitness) 目击者，证人；2) (主要用于 give witness, bear witness 中) 证据，证明，证词

v. 1) (为……) 作证；2) 目击

I was a witness to the argument.

These facts are a witness to his carelessness.

She gave witness on behalf of the accused person.

Several people witnessed against the accused.

Police were appealing to any driver who might have witnessed the traffic accident.

3. assume

v. 1) 假定，假设；2) 装出，假装；3) 开始从事，承担；4) 呈现出

I am assuming that the present situation is going to continue.

We must assume him to be innocent until he is proved guilty.

The look of innocence she assumed had us all fooled.

拓展

assumed *adj.* 假定的，假装的，假的

assumption *n.* 假定，假装

He lives under an assumed name.

His air of assumption made him unpopular.

He assumes his new responsibilities next month.

The problem is beginning to assume massive proportions.

4. patience

n. 耐性；忍耐力；耐心

I'm beginning to lose (my) patience (with you).

After three hours of waiting for the train, our patience was finally exhausted.

Patience is a virtue.

辨 析

patience, endurance

patience 指的是容忍一般性痛苦、困难等的能力。

endurance 指忍受较长期、较严重的痛苦、困难等的能力。

Her patience with children was exhausted.

Running the marathon tests a person's endurance.

拓 展

patient *adj.* 忍耐的，耐心的

n. 病人

You'll have to be patient with my mother, for she's going rather deaf.

She's a patient worker.

The doctor visited his patients in hospital.

真 题 解 析

—You know, Bob is a little slow _____ understanding, so…

—So I have to be patient _____ him. (2005 重庆)

A. in; with　　B. on; with　　C. in; to　　D. at; for

解析：in 表示"在某一方面"；be patient with 是固定搭配，意为"对……有耐心"。

　　　答案为 A。

5. burst

n. 1) 爆炸，破裂，缺口，裂口；2) 爆发，突发

v. 1) (使) 爆炸，(使) 破裂；2) 冲，闯；3) 爆发，胀破

We saw a burst in the water pipe.

A burst of hand-clapping followed the ending of the song.

The tyre burst.

The sun burst through the cloud.

I am bursting with pride.

➡ 常用短语：

burst away 急速四散　　　　　　　burst forth 突然爆发，喷出

burst in 突然进入　　　　　　　　burst out doing 突然……起来

a burst of anger 发怒　　　　　　a burst of gunfire 一阵炮火

6. acknowledge

v. 承认，公认

I acknowledge that her criticism is just.

He is widely acknowledged as the world's greatest living authority on impressionist painting.

辨 析

acknowledge, admit, confess

acknowledge 意思是"承认"，指公开承认事情的真实性，常用于指过去隐瞒或否认之事。

admit 意思是"承认"，指在外界压力、证据下不得不承认，含有"不情愿"之意。

confess 意思是"坦白，供认，忏悔"，指严肃、正式地承认过错或罪恶。

I have to acknowledge the force of his arguments.

You must admit the task to be difficult.

He confessed himself to be unfaithful to his friends.

7. accuse

v. 1) 指控，控告 (+ of)；2) 指责，把……归咎于

She accused him of stealing her watch.

He accused his boss of having broken his word.

He was accused of murder.

Man often accuses nature for his own misfortunes.

辨 析

accuse, blame, charge, scold

accuse 意思是"指控，指责"，指的是当面指控或指责，不一定诉诸法律。固定用法为 accuse sb of doing sth。

blame 意思是"责备，指责，责怪"，固定用法为 blame sb for sth，blame sth on sb。

charge 意思是"控告，控诉"，指因较大错误或重大罪行而进行法律控诉。固定用法为 charge sb with sth。

scold 意思是"（愤怒地）责骂，训斥，谩骂"，固定用法为 scold sb for sth。

Are you accusing me of lying?

Mum blamed herself for David's problems.

The police have charged him with murder.

My father scolded me for cheating on the test.

真 题 解 析

Mr Green stood up in defense of the 16-year-old boy, saying that he was not the one _____. (2006 安徽)

A. blamed　　　B. blaming　　　C. to blame　　　D. to be blamed

解析：be to blame 是固定搭配，意为"该受责备"。答案为 C。

8. defeat

n. 失败，战败，挫折

v. 1) 战胜，击败；2) 使困惑，使落空

The government has suffered a serious defeat.

The French defeated the English troops.

I've tried to solve the problem, but it defeats me!

Our hopes were defeated.

The aggressors were doomed to defeat.

辨 析

defeat, conquer, overcome

defeat 指赢得胜利，尤其指军事上的胜利，如：defeat the enemy。

conquer 意思是"征服，战胜"，尤其指取得对人、物或感情的控制，如：conquer the nature。

overcome 意思是"战胜，压倒，克服"，尤其侧重强调战胜或克服非物质的东西，如：overcome difficulties。

9. consult

v. 1) 与……商量；2) 请教，（向专业人员）咨询；
　　3) 当顾问(+for)

I consulted with a friend on the matter.

I consulted a doctor about my pains.

The retired executive consults for several large companies.

拓 展

consultant *n.* 顾问

consulting *adj.* 咨询的，顾问的

consultation *n.* 商量，建议，咨询，

a management consultant 经营管理顾问

consulting service 咨询服务

in consultation with 和……协商

◆ 常用短语

1. in spite of

in spite of 意思是"尽管"。意思相近的词和短语还有：despite，regardless of，although 等。

I went shopping in spite of the rain.

In spite of my efforts at persuasion, he wouldn't agree.

We held on for two days in spite of the violent attacks of the enemy.

辨 析

although / though, despite, regardless of

although / though 都是连词，后面跟一个完整的句子。

despite 意为"尽管，虽然，不顾"，与 in spite of 的含义近似，但程度有所不同。in spite of 的语气较强，使用范围也较广；despite 的语气较弱，多用于诗歌或正式的文体中。两者后面都跟名词、代词或动名词。

regardless of 意为"不管，不顾"，强调不受任何外界影响。

Although / Though it was so cold, he went out without an overcoat.

Despite the drought, we expect a good crop.

He continues speaking, regardless of my feelings on the matter.

2. take off

take off 的含义有：1) 脱下，移去；2) 起飞；3) 休假

He took off his raincoat and took out the key.

The plane will take off soon.

He took two weeks off in August.

真 题 解 析

1) Ladies and gentlemen, please fasten your seat belts. The plane _____. (2006 福建)

A. takes off   B. is taking off

C. has taken off   D. took off

解析：本题考查时态的运用。这句话的意思是飞机即将起飞，因此要用一般将来时。A 项是一般现在时，用来表示习惯性、常识性的事；B 项是现在进行时，可表示按计划、安排将要发生的事情；C 项是现在完成时，表示已发生或完成了的事情；D 项是一般过去时，表示发生在过去某个时间的事情。答案为 B。

> **拓 展**
>
> 与 take 有关的短语还有：
>
> take after sb 长得像某人
>
> take action 开始行动，采取行动
>
> take over 接收，接管，接替
>
> take root 生根，扎根
>
> take sth back 退货，撤回，使想起
>
> take up 拿起；占据；从事；继续

2) Look at the timetable. Hurry up! Flight 4026 _____ off at 18:20. (2006 四川)

A. takes   B. took   C. will be taken   D. has taken

解析：凡是根据时间表或事先安排好的计划来讲述将来要做或要发生的事情时，常用一般现在时。答案为 A。

3) After he retired from office, Rogers _____ painting for a while, but soon lost interest. (2006 山东)

A. took up   B. saved up   C. kept up   D. drew up

解析：take up 意为"从事"；save up 意为"储蓄"；keep up 意为"维持，继续"；draw up 意为"写出，草拟；逼近"。答案为 A。

3. be aware of / that...

aware 意思是"意识到的，觉察到的"，主要用法有：

1) aware 后面跟 of 短语或 that 引导的从句。

He has been aware of having done something wrong.

He was not aware that he was in danger.

2) 在 how, what, when 等词前，aware 后面的 of 可有可无。

She was not aware (of) how much her husband earned.

3) aware 是表语形容词，前面不能用 very 修饰，习惯上通常用 well, quite 等词修饰。

I am quite / well aware how you must feel.

4. rather than

rather than 意思是"宁可……也不愿，与其……倒不如，而不是"。

I think I'll have a cold drink rather than coffee.

Rather than risk breaking up his marriage he told his wife everything.

The sweater she bought was beautiful rather than cheap.

I prefer to tell him the truth rather than keep it from him.

5. at the beginning of

at the beginning of 意思是"在……之初"，与其意义相反的短语是 at the end of。

A war broke out at the beginning of the century.

You will find the word at the beginning of the passage.

> **拓 展**
>
> 与 beginning 有关的其他短语有：
> from beginning to end 从头至尾
> in the beginning 当初，开始时
> make a good beginning 良好的开端

6. set out

set out 主要含义有：1) 出发；2) 安排，摆放；3) 陈述，阐明；4) 开始做某事

She set out at dawn.

We'll need to set out chairs for the meeting.

You haven't set out your ideas very clearly in this essay.

She set out the reasons for her resignation in a long letter.

He set out to break the world record.

> **拓 展**
>
> 与 set 有关的其他短语有：
> set a new record 创造新纪录
> set about doing sth 开始做某事
> set an example 树立榜样
> set aside 把……放在一边，存储
> set back 使受挫折，倒退
> set free 释放
> set in motion 使开始
> set off 出发，引爆
> set right 改正，使恢复到良好状态
> set up 竖立，建起

7. be likely to

be likely to 意思是"可能"。

Noticing that there was likely to be trouble, they sneaked away.

辨 析

likely, possible, probable

likely 是常用词，指"从表面迹象来看很有可能"。

possible 指"由于有适当的条件和方法，某事可能发生或某人可能做到某事"，强调

"客观上有可能"，但常含有"实际上希望很小"的意思。

probable 语气比 possible 强，指"有根据、合情理、值得相信的事物"，带有"大概、很可能"的意思。

The likely outcome of the contest varies from moment to moment.

It is possible to go to the moon now.

I don't think the story is probable.

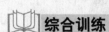

综合训练

考试时间：45分钟　　满分：100分

Ⅰ. 单项选择（共15小题；每小题1分，满分15分）

1. It is quite obvious that the aging population in China will cause _____ heavy pressure on _____ whole society in the future.
   A. a; a　　　　　　B. the; /　　　　　　C. a; the　　　　　　D. /; the

2. Mum is coming back. What present _____ for your birthday?
   A. expect she has got　　　　　　B. you expect has she got
   C. do you expect she has got　　　　D. do you expect has she got

3. I can think of many cases _____ students obviously knew a lot of English words and expressions but couldn't write a good essay.
   A. why　　　　B. which　　　　C. as　　　　D. where

4. As the economy develops, the national income goes up with a _____.
   A. beep　　　　B. peep　　　　C. leap　　　　D. heap

5. Somebody was _____ firecrackers down the street.
   A. setting off　　B. setting out　　C. setting on　　D. giving off

6. It has been reported that the Galileo Space Project is a satellite positioning and navigation system _____ for civilian use.
   A. intending　　B. intended　　C. to intend　　D. to be intended

7. Native Americans from the southeastern part of _____ is now the United States believed that the universe in which they lived was made up of three worlds.
   A. that　　　　B. why　　　　C. where　　　　D. what

8. _____ the beautiful island, we will reach it in two hours.
   A. Headed for　　　　　　B. Heading to
   C. Heading for　　　　　　D. We head for

9. Maybe it is time for the rest of society to get used to the fact _____ I may not be

able to walk, there are many other great things I can do.

    A. that   B. whether   C. although   D. that while

10. Most smokers are perfectly _____ of the dangers of smoking.

    A. known   B. famous   C. aware   D. upset

11. His breakfast _____ of dry bread and a cup of tea.

    A. takes   B. has   C. makes   D. consists

12. Rolando was _____ to win the 110-metre hurdle race, but he fell to the ground and missed the chance.

    A. possible   B. probably   C. likely   D. maybe

13. He remained kind to me _____ my wrong deeds to his family.

    A. in spite of   B. instead of   C. whether   D. because of

14. —What did she _____ so much money _____?

    —Nothing but a necklace made of glass.

    A. spend; on   B. pay; for   C. buy; for   D. sell; for

15. Honey, why not bring along some skin cream for the trip? To my knowledge, _____ to sunlight in Hainan will surely burn your skin.

    A. having been exposed   B. being exposed

    C. exposed   D. having exposed

Ⅱ. 完形填空（共20小题；每小题1分，满分20分）

    China's astronaut Yang Liwei __1__ out of the re-entry capsule of the *Shenzhou V* spaceship, smiling and __2__ to the recovery team on the grassland of the Gobi Desert, Inner Mongolia.

    Yang had __3__ about 21 hours in outer space, __4__ more than 600,000 kilometres in the earth's orbit before *Shenzhou V* __5__ him back at 6:23 at Beijing time October 16, 2003. Yang said he felt __6__ after the long journey, the first by a(n) __7__ astronaut.

    Chinese Premier Wen Jiabao said in a __8__ message on Thursday morning that China's first manned space mission has been "a complete success" which shall be __9__ into the history of China's space programme development.

    At about 6:00 am, guided by the Beijing Aerospace Command and Control Centre, the __10__ capsule of *Shenzhou V* entered China's air space. Several minutes __11__ the capsule landed safely in Northwest China's Inner Mongolia Autonomous Region, and Yang reported "condition good".

    Five __12__ helicopters raced towards the capsule and found it at 6:33 am. They said Yang felt good and the __13__ within the capsule also seemed __14__.

    At 6:51 am, Yang Liwei came out of the capsule by himself, waving and smiling to rescuers and __15__.

    After Yang came out of the capsule, __16__ immediately conducted a physical checkup, __17__ found him in good condition. At around 7:40 am, Yang was __18__ by a military helicopter to Beijing, where a gala celebration party was __19__.

All this __20__ the complete success of the manned flight.

1. A. walked   B. ran   C. moved   D. crawled
2. A. waving   B. said   C. spoke   D. signing
3. A. cost   B. spent   C. used   D. taken
4. A. going   B. working   C. travelling   D. observing
5. A. gave   B. brought   C. took   D. sent
6. A. excellent   B. so-so   C. nervous   D. tired
7. A. American   B. Russian   C. Chinese   D. German
8. A. celebration B. congratulation C. consolation   D. invitation
9. A. put   B. written   C. taken   D. made
10. A. returned   B. turned   C. turn   D. return
11. A. later   B. late   C. after   D. early
12. A. help   B. emergency   C. rescue   D. advice
13. A. situations B. conditions   C. cases   D. circumstances
14. A. usual   B. unusual   C. abnormal   D. normal
15. A. reporters   B. foreigners   C. students   D. teachers
16. A. nurses   B. rescuers   C. physicians   D. reporters
17. A. that   B. which   C. on which   D. on that
18. A. made   B. picked   C. ferried   D. landed
19. A. hold   B. holding   C. held   D. holds
20. A. signed   B. marked   C. suggested   D. said

III. 阅读理解（共10小题；每小题2分，满分20分）

A

One of America's most important exports is her modern music. American popular music is played all over the world. It is enjoyed by people of all ages in all countries. Though the lyrics are English, nevertheless people not speaking English enjoy it. The reasons for its popularity are its fast pace and rhythmic beat.

The music has many origins in the United States. Country music, coming from the rural areas in the Southern United States, is one source. Country music features simple themes and melodies describing day-to-day situations and the feelings of country people. Many people appreciate this music because of the emotions expressed by country music songs.

A second origin of American popular music is the blues. It depicts mostly sad feelings reflecting the difficult lives of American blacks. It is usually played and sung by black musicians, but it is popular with all Americans.

Rock music is a newer form of music. This music style, featuring fast and <u>repetitious</u> rhythms, was influenced by the blues and country music. It was first known as rock-and-roll in the 1950s. Since then there have been many forms of rock music — hard rock, soft rock, punk rock, disco music and others. Many performers of popular rock music are young musicians.

American popular music is marketed to a demanding audience. Now popular songs are heard on the radio several times a day. People hear these songs sung in their original English or sometimes translated to other languages. The words may differ but the enjoyment of the music is universal.

1. What is mainly discussed in the passage?
   A. Country music.   B. The blues.
   C. Rock music.   D. American popular music.

2. Why is American modern music so popular?
   A. Because of its fast pace and rhythmic beat.
   B. Because it is usually played by black musicians.
   C. Because of the emotions expressed by the songs.
   D. Because it describes the feelings of country people.

3. Which of the following is TRUE about the blues?
   A. It comes from the rural areas in the Southern United States.
   B. It reflects the difficult lives of American blacks.
   C. It features fast and repetitious rhythms.
   D. It features simple themes and melodies.

4. The meaning of the underlined word "repetitious" is close to "_____".
   A. loudly   B. sad   C. active   D. repeating

5. Which of the following has similar meaning to the underlined sentence in the last paragraph?
   A. More and more people like American popular music, which makes it popular.
   B. The American people make a lot of money out of the popular music.
   C. People can buy American popular music CDs in the market all over the world.
   D. Many American popular songs have been translated into other languages.

B

Doctors and medical groups around the world last weekend reacted with strong opposition to the news that an Italian specialist is on the brink of cloning the first human baby.

Dr Severino Antinori, who is the head of a hospital in Rome, has been referred to in an Arab newspaper as claiming that one of his patients is eight weeks pregnant (怀孕) with a cloned baby. Antinori refused to comment on the reports, but in March 2001 he said he hoped to produce a cloned embryo (胚胎) for implantation within two years. So far several kinds of mammals have already been successfully cloned, including sheep, cats, rabbits and so on.

Doctors showed their doubt and were strongly opposed although they admitted that human cloning would finally come true unless there was a worldwide <u>ban</u> on the practice. Professor Rudolf Jaenisch of the Whitehead Institute for Biomedical Research at the Massachusetts Institute of Technology said, "I find it astonishing that people do this where the result can be foretold that it will not be a normal baby. It is using humans as guinea pigs. It makes people feel sick."

But Ronald Green, director of the Ethics Institute at Dartmouth College in the US, said it is unlikely that an eight-week-old pregnancy would lead to a birth.

So far all cloned animals have suffered from some different serious disorders, many of them died soon after their births.

Doctors are opposed to human cloning because they are worried about the welfare of the cloned child if there is one. "There are no benefits of cloned human beings, just harm," said Dr Michael Wilks of the UK.

6. The underlined phrase "on the brink of" in the first paragraph most probably means "_____".

   A. on the side of   B. on the point of   C. in search of   D. in favour of

7. What is the doctors' general attitude towards human cloning according to the passage?

   A. They are against it.   B. They support it.

   C. They welcome it.   D. They pay no attention to it.

8. What does the underlined word "ban" in the third paragraph most probably mean?

   A. Order that forbids cloning.   B. Suggestion to carry on cloning.

   C. Anger at cloning.   D. Cheer for cloning.

9. Which of the following statements is TRUE according to the passage?

   A. Doctor Severino Antinori is strongly opposed to cloning human beings.

   B. Up to now, no animal has been successfully cloned.

   C. Professor Rudolf Jaenisch is carrying on an experiment on cloning an eight-week-old embryo.

   D. Ronald Green doubts about the successful birth of the so-called cloned embryo.

10. Which is the best title for the passage?

   A. The Success of Cloning Humans   B. The Anger at Cloning Humans

   C. The Failure of Cloning Humans   D. The First Cloned Human?

IV. 阅读表达（共5小题；每小题3分，满分15分）

For the next seven days, sit down each evening and write down ten things you are grateful for each day. Better still, do this with your partner or a friend. <u>Before we practise gratitude (感恩), we are in the dark and there appears to be very little to be grateful for.</u> Once we begin, a new light dawns.

To whom are you grateful in your life? Do these people know the full extent of your gratitude? Do you realise how grateful they will be when you tell them? Gratitude is more than an attitude; gratitude is a philosophy. The philosophy of gratitude begins as a hope, grows into a belief, and finally becomes an absolute knowing. It is a knowing that within any given situation — peaceful or painful, beautiful or ugly — there is always a gift waiting for you to see.

If it appears you have nothing to be grateful for, it is because you are not allowing yourself to receive. Just because you do not receive does not mean there is nothing to receive. On the contrary, there is always _____, and so there is always a reason to be grateful. Gratitude is good medicine. One single serving of gratitude is often enough to open the heart, energise the body, warm the bones, put a spring in your step, start you humming, and make you smile like a baby!

1. What is the best title for the passage? (Please answer within 5 words.)

   _____

2. Which sentence in the passage can be replaced by the following one?
   Showing even a bit gratitude can make everything look fine, and it will be of great benefit to you.

   _____

3. Fill in the blank in the last paragraph with proper words or phrases to complete the sentence. (Please answer within 5 words.)

   _____

4. Do you agree with the author's opinion of gratitude? Why (not)? (Please answer within 30 words.)

   _____

   _____

5. Translate the underlined sentence in the first paragraph into Chinese.

   _____

Ⅴ. 写作（满分30分）
在实验室中，科学家们常常用动物做试验。有人认为这样做对动物太残忍，他们建议用计算机模拟相关的条件来进行模拟试验。对此你是怎么看的？请写一篇短文，记述以上现象并发表自己的看法。
词数要求：120～150词。

_____

_____

_____

_____

_____

Module ⑥

The Tang Poems

📖 要点纵览

高考词汇	acquaintance, bar, part, seed, dynasty, expansion, tolerant, Persian, Arab, Buddhism, astronomy, altitude, specialist, share, advance, failure, suffering, corruption, merchant, irregular, realist, reflection, mental, alcohol, long-term, disorder, channel, prove, appeal, glance, upwards, surplus, approve, sponsor, expense, launch, damp, barrier, shabby, caution, literary, bench, preview, departure, carriage, merry, chorus, arbitrary, cater, homeland, enterprise, correspond, anniversary, donate, update, decorate, whichever, zone, independence, imagination, typically, reflect, surgeon
常用短语	as far as, trade with, at the same time, hand in hand with, mark the beginning of, think of…as, take hold of, deal with, face to face, lose one's sense of, raise funds for, be addicted to doing, approve of, a chorus of, take on, cater for, have association with, correspond with
实用句型	1. It is…that / who… 2. have difficulty (in) doing sth
交际用语	1. learn sth by heart 2. I'm hopeless at names. 3. off the top of one's head 4. on second thoughts 5. Fire away!

◆ 高考词汇

1. acquaintance

n. 1) [U] 相识；了解 (+ with)；2) [C] 相识的人，熟人

He has some / little acquaintance with the Japanese language.

He has a wide circle of acquaintances.

He is not a friend, only an acquaintance.

➡ 常用短语：

gain acquaintance with 得以认识

have a nodding acquaintance with sb / sth 点头之交；略知一二

have a slight acquaintance with 对……稍有了解

make sb's acquaintance 结识某人

on further acquaintance 进一步了解后

> **·········· 拓 展 ··········**
>
> acquaint *v.* 使认识，使了解，使通晓 (+ with)
>
> acquaint oneself with 熟悉，通晓，摸清
>
> acquaint sb with 把……通知/告诉某人
>
> You must acquaint yourself with your new duties.
>
> My assistant should be able to acquaint you with all the details.
>
> be / get acquainted with 认识 (某人)，熟悉 (某事)
>
> I am already acquainted with him.
>
> 注意：acquaint 用于被动语态中，过去分词 acquainted 已经失去了动作的意义，相当于一个形容词。例如："我是去年认识他的。" 不能译作 "I acquainted him last year." 或 "I was acquainted with him last year." 第一句是语态错误，第二句混淆了状态和动作。这句话只能译成 "I got / became acquainted with him last year." 或 "I made his acquaintance last year."

2. part

n. 1) 一部分，部分；2) 部件，零件；3) 本分，职责，作用

v. (使) 分开，(使) 分离

Parts of the book are interesting.

Our workshop turns out parts for generators.

If everyone does his part, the project will surely be a success.

What part did you play?

The clouds parted and the sun shone.

> **····· 拓 展 ·····**
>
> partly *adv.* 部分地
>
> It was partly my fault.

They parted in London.

➡ 常用短语：

for the most part 在很大程度上

in part 在一定程度上，部分地

play a part in 在……中起作用

take part in 参加

辨 析

part, divide, separate

part 指把密切相关的人或物分开，如：part gold from silver。

divide 指施加外力或自然地把某人或某物由整体分成若干部分，如：divide the candies / the students。

separate 指把原来在一起的人或物分开，如：Separate those two boys who are fighting, will you?

3. expansion

n. 1) 扩展，扩张，膨胀；2) 扩大物，扩展部分

The industry in this country has just undergone a period of rapid expansion.

The suburbs are an expansion of cities.

拓 展

expand v. 1) 展开，张开 (帆、翅等)；2) 使膨胀，使扩张；扩大，扩充；3) 详述

The eagle expanded its wings.

He is thinking of expanding his business.

I refuse to expand any further on my earlier statement.

4. tolerant

adj. 1) 容忍的，宽恕的；2) 有耐性的，(对冷、热等环境条件) 能耐的

She was tolerant of different views.

Of all the girls she was the most tolerant.

Some plants are tolerant of extreme heat.

5. share

n. 1) 一份，份，(分担的) 一部分；2) (工作、费用等的) 分摊，分担，贡献；3) 股份，股票

v. 1) 均分，分摊，分配；2) 分享，分担，共有，共同使用

I have done my share of the work.

The young engineer had a large share in modernising the factory.

She's put all her money in stocks and shares.

The money was shared out between them.

My wife shared with me in distress.

拓 展

tolerance n. 容忍，忍受，宽容

tolerate v. 忍受，容忍，宽恕

In ordinary living there can be some tolerance of unpunctuality.

Our teacher never tolerates cheating on exams.

6. failure

n. 1) 失败；2) 失败的人或物；3) 破产；(农作物) 歉收；4) (机器的) 失灵，故障；(身体器官的) 衰竭

Failure is the mother of success.

He was a failure as a teacher.

The drought caused crop failure.

She died of heart failure.

➡ 常用短语：

electricity failure 停电

end in failure 以失败告终

failure of eyesight 视力减退

risk failure 冒失败之险

真 题 解 析

Words _____ me when I wanted to express my thanks to him for having saved my son from the burning house. (2004 上海)

A. failed　　　　　　B. left　　　　C. discouraged　　　　D. disappointed

解析：fail 表示"使失望，有负于"，words fail sb 意思是"(因惊讶、生气或激动) 说不出话来"。答案为 A。

7. reveal

v. 1) 透露，泄露，揭露；2) 展现，显示

The survey revealed that the house was damp.

Neither side revealed what was discussed in the meeting.

The open door revealed an untidy kitchen.

8. launch

n. (船的) 下水；(航天器的) 发射；(新产品的) 投产或投放

v. 1) 开办，发起，发行，使开始从事；2) 发射；3) 使船下水；4) 积极投入，展开

A new space launch centre will be built in this area.

The launch of their new saloon received much media coverage.

The company is launching a new model next month.

The miners launched a strike.

He's launching his son on a career in banking.

A test satellite was recently launched in this country.

The lifeboat was launched immediately to rescue the four men.

She wants to be more than just a singer and is launching out into films.

9. correspond

v. 1) 一致，符合；2) 相当，相应；3) 通信

Your account of events corresponds with hers.

Does the name on the envelope correspond with the name on the letter inside?

The American Congress corresponds to the British Parliament.

Have you been corresponding with him?

拓 展

corresponding *adj.* 相符的，相当的，类似的

correspondingly *adv.* 相符地，相当地，对应地

correspondence *n.* 关系，联系；通信，信件

Imports in the first three months have increased by 10 percent compared with the corresponding period last year.

The new exam is longer and correspondingly more difficult to pass.

There was no correspondence between the historical facts and John's account of them.

She has a lot of correspondence to deal with.

◆ 常用短语

1. hand in hand

hand in hand 的含义是：1) 手拉手；2) 联合；3) 并进地，联系密切地

They walked away hand in hand.

The two firms work hand in hand.

Dirt and disease go hand in hand.

2. think of…as

think of…as 意思是"认为……是，把……看作"。

I think of him as a kind man who is always ready to help others.

类似的短语还有：look on…as，regard…as，consider…as，treat…as 等。

3. take hold of

take hold of 的含义有：1) 抓住 (= catch / get / seize hold of)；2) 吸引

Take hold of the rope and I will pull you out.

The music took hold of her slowly.

拓 展

与 hand 有关的其他短语有：

at hand 在附近，在手头，即将发生

by hand 用手工

from hand to hand 转手，传递

give sb a hand 帮助某人

Hands off! 请勿触摸！

Hands up! 举起手来！

on the one hand…on the other hand 一方面……另一方面

拓 展

think of 的其他意义及相关短语：

1) 考虑，关心；2) 想起，记起；3) 对……有某种看法

think well / highly / much of 认为……好，对……评价高

think ill / lightly / little of 认为……不好

Everyone thinks highly of Cong Fei.

Most people think ill of the opinion that parents give their children whatever they want.

辨析

take hold of, get hold of

take hold of 有"抓住"的意思。

get hold of 除了有"抓住"之意外,还有"与某人取得联系"的意思。

I took hold of her hand and gently led her away.

Here, get hold of this for a minute.

Make sure your friends know where to get hold of you.

4. deal with

deal with 的含义有:1) 处理,对待,对付 (某人);2) 与……打交道;3) 涉及,关于

How would you deal with an armed burglar?

You deal with an awkward situation very tactfully.

They try to deal politely with angry customers.

I hate dealing with large impersonal companies.

The next chapter deals with verbs.

This book deals with an important issue.

辨析

deal with, do with

这两个短语都有"处理,对付,应付"之意,但 deal with 中的 deal 是不及物动词,可与 how 连用;而 do with 中的 do 是及物动词,只有与 with 连用时才可表达上述含义,且常和 what 连用。deal with 还可表示"谈论,涉及到;与……相处"等意思,而 do with 无此用法。

5. take on

take on 的含义有:1) 呈现;2) 承担

The chameleon can take on the colours of its background.

Her eyes took on a hurt expression.

He is unwilling to take on heavy responsibilities.

真 题 解 析

We are trying to ring you back, Bryan, but we think we _____ your number incorrectly. (2006 浙江)

A. looked up   B. took down

C. worked out   D. brought about

解析:take down 在这里是"记下,写下"的意思。答案为 B。

拓 展

与 take 有关的其他短语有:

take along 随身携带

take away 拿走,带走,夺去,解除,消除

take down 记下,写下

take in 接受,包含,领会,欺骗

take out 拿出,取出

6. fire away

fire away 意思是"开始提问，开始说话"。

—I've got a couple of questions for you.

—All right, fire away.

Fire away, ask me anything you like.

7. (on) second thoughts

(on) second thoughts 意思是"经重新考虑，继而一想"。

Second thoughts are best.

I said I wouldn't go, but on second thoughts I think I will.

综合训练

考试时间：45分钟   满分：100分

I. 单项选择（共15小题；每小题1分，满分15分）

1. —Hello, could I speak to Mr Smith?
   —Sorry, wrong number. There isn't _____ Mr Smith here.
   A. /   B. a   C. the   D. one

2. It was in the United States that I made the _____ of Professor Jones.
   A. acquaintance   B. association   C. recognition   D. acknowledgement

3. I couldn't help _____ the incident that had taken place with the headmaster.
   A. speaking   B. sharing   C. saying   D. telling

4. —Why was Professor Wang unhappy recently?
   —Because the theory he insisted on _____ wrong.
   A. proved   B. proving   C. being proved   D. was proving

5. Margaret asked me to repeat _____ telephone number _____ second time so that she could write it down.
   A. the; the   B. the; a   C. an; the   D. an; a

6. Reta _____ two hours every Sunday afternoon to spend with her grandparents, because they were too old to look after themselves.
   A. set out   B. set up   C. set aside   D. set off

7. These problems may lead to more serious ones if _____ unsolved.
   A. making   B. remained   C. keeping   D. left

8. You'd better cut your hair short. Our school does not approve _____ long hair.
   A. of students wearing   B. students to wear
   C. students wear   D. of students wear

9. I remember my little niece often asked questions that children _____ would ask.
   A. twice so old as she
   B. twice as old as her age
   C. older twice than her age
   D. twice her age
10. —Are there any tickets left?
    —Sorry. There are _____, if _____.
    A. few; any   B. a few; some   C. some; few   D. any; some
11. He might have been killed _____ the arrival of the police.
    A. except   B. but for   C. with   D. for
12. Tom was caught _____ yesterday and he _____ not to drive that fast again.
    A. speeding; was cautioned   B. to speed; was cautioned
    C. speeding; warned   D. to speed; warned
13. Don't interrupt me, John. _____ you force me to tell you the truth at the moment?
    A. Might   B. Must   C. Should   D. Would
14. Tom, _____ to the hospital — your father suddenly fell ill and was rushed to hospital.
    A. hurry   B. hurrying   C. to hurry   D. hurried
15. It is in the city _____ you're going to pay a visit to _____ this kind of beer is produced.
    A. /; that   B. where; that   C. that; where   D. that; which

II. 完形填空（共20小题；每小题1分，满分20分）

Many a young person tells me he wants to be a writer. I always __1__ such people, but I also explain that there's a big __2__ between "being a writer" and "writing". In most cases these individuals are dreaming of wealth and fame, __3__ the long hours alone __4__. "You've got to want to write," I say to them, "not want to be a writer."

The __5__ is that writing is a lonely, private and poor-paying affair. For every writer kissed by __6__ there are thousands more whose longing is __7__ rewarded. When I __8__ a 20-year career in the US Coast Guard to become a freelance writer, I had no prospects (前景) at all. What I __9__ was a friend who found me my room in a New York apartment building. It didn't __10__ matter that it was cold and had no bathroom. I immediately bought a __11__ manual typewriter and __12__ a genuine writer.

After a year or so, __13__, I still hadn't got a break and began to __14__ myself. It was so hard to sell a story that I __15__ made enough to eat. But I knew I __16__ write. I had dreamed about it __17__. I wasn't going to be one of those people who die __18__: What if? I would keep putting my dream to the __19__ even though it meant living with uncertainty and fear of failure. This is the shadowland of __20__, and anyone with a dream must learn to live there.

1. A. advise   B. encourage   C. tell   D. warn
2. A. step   B. advance   C. distance   D. difference
3. A. and   B. but   C. not   D. for

4. A. in the room　　　B. at a typewriter　　　C. with a novel　　　D. for a desk

5. A. reality　　　B. thing　　　C. life　　　D. reason

6. A. writing　　　B. readers　　　C. fortune　　　D. others

7. A. never　　　B. always　　　C. sometimes　　　D. only

8. A. began　　　B. found　　　C. left　　　D. put

9. A. had had　　　B. have had　　　C. am having　　　D. did have

10. A. ever　　　B. just　　　C. even　　　D. greatly

11. A. used　　　B. wonderful　　　C. useful　　　D. nice

12. A. felt like　　　B. acted as　　　C. typed like　　　D. performed as

13. A. consequently　　　B. therefore　　　C. unluckily　　　D. however

14. A. scold　　　B. doubt　　　C. beat　　　D. hate

15. A. almost　　　B. partly　　　C. poorly　　　D. barely

16. A. had to　　　B. ought to　　　C. was able to　　　D. wanted to

17. A. for years　　　B. long ago　　　C. since then　　　D. once again

18. A. regretting　　　B. wondering　　　C. dreaming　　　D. depressing

19. A. point　　　B. best　　　C. test　　　D. most

20. A. time　　　B. death　　　C. hope　　　D. life

Ⅲ. 阅读理解（共10小题；每小题2分，满分20分）

A

Having finished her homework, Ma Li wants some music for relaxation. As usual, she starts her computer and goes to baidu.com to download music files. But this time she is surprised when an announcement about protecting songs' copyright bursts onto the screen. The age of free music and movie downloads may have come to an end as some web companies like Baidu are accused of infringing (侵犯) copyright. Lawsuits have been filed against four websites offering free downloads. In September 2005, a Beijing court ordered Baidu to pay recording company Shanghai Push compensation for their losses. Baidu was also told to block the links to the pirated music on the website. This caused a heated discussion on Internet file sharing.

"Baidu's defeat in the lawsuit shows it is not right to get copyrighted songs without paying. Downloaders may face lawsuits or fines," said an official.

Like many teens, Huang Ruoru, an 18-year-old girl from Puning in Guangdong Province, doesn't think that getting music from websites is wrong. She always shares her favourite songs downloaded from Baidu with her friends. When told about the lawsuit, she began to feel a little guilty about obtaining others' work without paying.

However, other teenagers have different ideas. Wang Yafei, a Senior 2 girl from Jinan, Shandong Province pointed out that file-sharing is a good way to promote pop singers. "If I download a song and really like it, I will buy the CD," she said. "So what the recording companies really should concentrate on is improving their music, rather than pursuing file-sharers."

1. Which of the following best describes the passage?

    A. Music on the Internet is of better quality.

    B. Downloading material can be illegal.

    C. It's good to get free music on the Internet.

    D. Baidu is a popular web company.

2. The four web companies were put to court because they _____.

    A. got copyrighted songs without paying

    B. downloaded copyrighted music for people

    C. enabled people to download copyrighted files for free

    D. composed free music online

3. How do some of the teenagers feel while downloading free music after the lawsuit?

    A. A bit guilty.　　B. A little sad.　　C. Extremely angry.　　D. Awfully sorry.

4. What's the advantage of file-sharing for recording companies?

    A. Getting more money from web companies.

    B. Enabling people to download their favourite songs.

    C. Helping improve the music.

    D. Making pop singers more popular.

5. It can be inferred from the text that _____.

    A. web companies are still ignoring the copyright laws

    B. recording companies' music is not as good as that on the Internet

    C. people will have to pay to download music

    D. teenagers prefer CDs with copyright to pirated music

B

"The pen is more powerful than the sword." There have been many writers who used their pens to fight things that were wrong. Mrs Harriet Beecher Stowe was one of them.

She was born in the USA in 1811. One of her books not only made her famous, but has been described as one that excited the world. It was helpful in causing a civil war and freeing the slaved race. The civil war was the American Civil War of 1861, in which the Northern States fought the Southern States and, finally, won.

This book that shook the world was called *Uncle Tom's Cabin*. There was a time when every English-speaking man, woman, and child, had read this novel that did so much to stop slavery. Not many people read it today, but it is still very interesting, if only to show how a warm-hearted writer can arouse people's sympathies. The author herself had neither been to Southern States, nor seen a slave. The Southern Americans were very angry at the book, which they said did not at all <u>represent</u> the true state of affairs. But the Northern Americans were wildly excited over it, and were so inspired by it that they were ready to go to war to set the slaves free.

6. According to the passage, _____.

A. every English-speaking person has read *Uncle Tom's Cabin*

B. *Uncle Tom's Cabin* is not very interesting

C. those who don't speak English cannot have read *Uncle Tom's Cabin*

D. the book *Uncle Tom's Cabin* helped bring about the American Civil War

7. What do we learn about Mrs Harriet Beecher Stowe before the American Civil War broke out?

A. She had been living in the North of America before the American Civil War broke out.

B. She herself encouraged the Northern Americans to go to war to set the slaves free.

C. She was better at writing than using a sword.

D. She had once been a slave.

8. What is the meaning of the underlined word "represent" in the last paragraph?

A. Speak for.　　　　B. Describe.　　　　C. Constitute.　　　　D. Stand for.

9. What can we learn from the passage?

A. Sometimes we needn't use weapons to fight things that are wrong.

B. A writer is more helpful in a war than a soldier.

C. We must understand the importance of weapons.

D. No war can be won without such a book as *Uncle Tom's Cabin*.

10. What do you think of Mrs Harriet Beecher Stowe? She was _____.

A. warlike　　　　B. humorous　　　　C. sympathetic　　　　D. patient

Ⅳ. 阅读表达（共5小题；每小题3分，满分15分）

You don't need every word to understand the meaning of what you read. In fact, too much emphasis on separate words both _____ and reduces your comprehension.

First, any habit which slows down your silent reading to the speed at which you speak, or read aloud, is inefficient. If you point to each word as you read, or move your head, or form the words with your lips, you read poorly. Less obvious habits also hold back reading efficiency. One is "saying" each word silently by moving your tongue or throat; another is "hearing" each word as you read.

These are habits which should have been outgrown long ago. A beginner is learning how letters can make words, how written words are pronounced, and how sentences are put together. Your reading purpose is quite different — it is to understand meaning.

It has been supposed that up to 75 percent of the words in English sentences are not really necessary for expressing the meaning. The secret of silent reading is to find out those key words and phrases which carry the thought, and to pay less attention to words which exist only for the sake of grammatical completeness.

An efficient reader can grasp the meaning from a page at least twice as fast as he can read the page aloud. Unconsciously perhaps he takes in a whole phrase or thought unit at a time. If he "says" or "hears" words to himself, they are selected ones, said for emphasis.

1. What is the best title for the passage? (Please answer within 10 words.)

2. Which sentence in the passage can be replaced by the following one?
   These habits are formed when readers are young and they should have got rid of them as they grow up.

3. Fill in the blank in the first paragraph with proper words or phrases to complete the sentence. (Please answer within 10 words.)

4. What do you think is your bad reading habit? Why? (Please answer within 30 words.)

5. Translate the underlined sentence in the second paragraph into Chinese.

Ⅴ. 写作（满分30分）

目前，越来越多的中国人喜欢英语诗歌。请根据下表，以 "English Poetry" 为题写一篇短文。

特性	1. 遵循一定的节奏和押韵形式； 2. 与其他的文学形式相比，能更好地运用声音、词汇和语法。
历史	1. 历史不长，好诗却很多； 2. 20世纪初，大量英语诗歌进入中国，许多诗歌被翻译成中文。
作用	1. 把不同地方和不同时代的人联系在一起； 2. 成为东西方文化交流的桥梁，有助于人们更好地相互了解。

参考词汇：押韵 rhyme
词数要求：100词左右。

English Poetry

复习检测题 二

第一部分 听力（共两节，满分30分）

第一节 （共5小题；每小题1.5分，满分7.5分）

听下面五段对话。每段对话后有一个小题，从题中所给的三个选项中选出最佳选项。听完每段对话后，你都有10秒钟的时间来回答有关小题和阅读下一小题。每段对话仅读一遍。

1. What does the man ask the woman to do?
   A. To work half an hour.　　B. To work an hour more.　　C. To finish the work.

2. What's the man doing?
   A. Borrowing a book.　　　B. Buying a book.　　　C. Reading a book.

3. What is the total cost for the woman and her daughter?
   A. 120 *yuan*.　　　　　　B. 140 *yuan*.　　　　　C. 150 *yuan*.

4. Where does this dialogue take place?
   A. In a hotel.　　　　　　B. At a concert hall.　　C. In a meeting room.

5. Who will go to Canada?
   A. The woman.　　　　　　B. The woman's brother.　　C. The man and Ken.

第二节 （共15小题；每小题1.5分，满分22.5分）

听下面五段对话或独白。每段对话或独白后有几个小题，从题中所给的三个选项中选出最佳选项。听每段对话或独白前，你将有时间阅读各个小题，每小题5秒钟；听完后，各小题将给出5秒钟的作答时间。每段对话或独白读两遍。

听第6段材料，回答第6至第7小题。

6. How long is the dinnertime at the restaurant?
   A. Five hours.　　　　　　B. Six hours.　　　　　　C. Seven hours.

7. What can we infer from the conversation?
   A. Mr stone will be the first person to arrive.
   B. Mr Bryant will treat his friends.
   C. Altogether five people will join the dinner.

听第7段材料，回答第8至第10小题。

8. What are they talking about?
   A. Seeing a film.　　　　B. Going to night school.　　C. Travelling abroad.

9. What's on at the Odeon tonight?
   A. A horror film.　　　　B. A Western film.　　　　C. A classic film.

10. Why can't the woman go to the cinema tonight?

    A. Because she doesn't like the film.

    B. Because she doesn't like the actor — John Wayne.

    C. Because she has to go to night school.

听第8段材料，回答第11至第13小题。

11. How did Miss Scott hurt her foot?

    A. She fell down from the window.

    B. She fell down from the stairs.

    C. She fell down from a chair.

12. How was her left foot?

    A. Some bones were broken.

    B. It was seriously hurt.

    C. The problem was not serious.

13. What will Miss Scott do next weekend?

    A. Go dancing.

    B. Go to see a film with her friends.

    C. Go to see the doctor again.

听第9段材料，回答第14至第17小题。

14. Why does the woman want the man to read the letter?

    A. She wants him to rewrite it.

    B. She wants him to get a job for her.

    C. She wants to have his opinion.

15. What should the first part of the letter be about according to the man?

    A. Education.   B. Work experience.   C. Job information.

16. What does the man think of the second part of the letter?

    A. It should be shorter.   B. It should be longer.   C. It is quite all right.

17. What will probably happen next?

    A. The woman will post the letter immediately.

    B. The man will help rewrite the letter.

    C. The woman will make some necessary changes to the letter.

听第10段材料，回答第18至第20小题。

18. What's the aim of the language evenings?

    A. For people to see an English film.

    B. For people to learn a language.

    C. For people to watch events.

19. What do the members do on Thursday evening?

    A. They have sports.

    B. They have a language evening.

    C. They have dinner together.

20. If people want to join the club, what do they have to do?

    A. Give their phone numbers.

    B. Give their names and addresses.

    C. Come from a different country.

第二部分 英语知识运用（共两节，满分35分）

第一节　语法和词汇（共15小题；每小题1分，满分15分）

从 A、B、C、D 四个选项中，选出可以填入空白处的最佳选项。

21. _____ killing of so many protected animals made _____ stir among the local people.

    A. /; /　　　　　　　B. The; /　　　　　　　C. /; a　　　　　　　D. The; a

22. It's a programme designed to _____ mainly to 10- to 16-year-old students.

    A. appeal　　　　　B. attach　　　　　C. contribute　　　D. refer

23. Your meaning didn't really _____.

    A. get through　　　B. get in　　　　　C. get away　　　　D. get across

24. Don't _____. You will _____ new customs and different ways of thinking.

    A. lose your heart; apply to　　　　　　B. lose heart; apply yourself to

    C. lose your heart; adapt to　　　　　　D. lose heart; adapt yourself to

25. —You seem to have had that car for years.

    —Yes, I should sell it _____ it still runs.

    A. while　　　　　　B. after　　　　　　C. until　　　　　　D. before

26. In order to _____ a good command of German, she quit her job and went to study in a German school.

    A. require　　　　　B. inquire　　　　　C. acquire　　　　　D. request

27. There is a new problem _____ in the popularity of private cars _____ road conditions need to be improved .

    A. involving; that　B. involved; that　C. involved; where　D. involving; which

28. Enjoying popular songs on the Internet has greatly _____ me the trouble of going to the shops to purchase CDs.

    A. shared　　　　　B. spared　　　　　C. cancelled　　　　D. cost

29. The headmaster of our school _____ by all the teachers and students.

    A. is well thought of　　　　　　　　B. is good thought of

    C. is thought well of　　　　　　　　D. is thought good of

30. I have trouble _____ with changes.

    A. to deal　　　　　B. dealing　　　　　C. dealt　　　　　　D. deal

31. He will come to call on you _____ he finishes his painting.

    A. at once　　　　　B. suddenly　　　　　C. the moment　　　D. immediate

32. The number 2008 is a special number, _____ I think, that will be remembered by the Chinese forever.

    A. which　　　　　B. what　　　　　　C. one　　　　　　　D. it

33. _____ seen smoking here will be fined.

    A. Who   B. Whomever   C. Anyone   D. Whoever

34. —Can I pay the bill by check?

    —Sorry, sir. It is the management rules of our hotel that payment _____ be made in cash.

    A. shall   B. need   C. will   D. can

35. The Chinese government is firmly _____ the practice of power politics between nations.

    A. sticking to   B. opposed to   C. resisting on   D. addicted to

第二节　完形填空（共20题；每小题1分，满分20分）

阅读下面的短文，掌握其大意，然后从每题所给的四个选项中选出最佳选项。

A true apology is more than just acknowledgement of a mistake. It's recognition that something you've said or __36__ has damaged a relationship and that you __37__ enough about that relationship to want it __38__.

It's never __39__ to acknowledge you are in the wrong. Being human, we all need the art of apology. Look back and think how __40__ you've judged roughly (草率地), said __41__ things, pushed yourself __42__ at the expense of a friend. Some deep thought in us know that when __43__ a small mistake has been made, your __44__ will stay out of balance until the mistake is acknowledged and your regret is __45__.

I remember a doctor friend, __46__ me about a man who came to him with __47__ illnesses: headache, insomnia (失眠), stomachache and so on. No physical __48__ could be found. Finally the doctor said to the man, "__49__ you tell me what's on your conscience, I can't help you."

After a short silence, the man told the doctor that he __50__ all the money that his father gave to his brother, who was __51__. His father had died, so only he himself knew the matter. The old doctor made the man write to his brother making an __52__ and enclosing (附寄) a __53__. In the post office, the man dropped the letter into the postbox. As the letter disappeared, the man __54__ into tears. "Thank you, doctor," he said, "I think I'm all right now." And he __55__.

36. A. done   B. thought   C. announced   D. expected

37. A. lost   B. care   C. advise   D. heard

38. A. built   B. formed   C. repaired   D. damaged

39. A. difficult   B. easy   C. foolish   D. shy

40. A. long   B. often   C. much   D. soon

41. A. unusual   B. harmful   C. precious   D. unkind

42. A. ahead   B. away   C. down   D. off

43. A. still   B. even   C. only   D. such

44. A. sense   B. brain   C. weight   D. feeling

45. A. shown   B. explained   C. offered   D. expressed

46. A. asking   B. telling   C. requiring   D. setting

47. A. strange   B. serious   C. various   D. much

48. A. signs   B. reason   C. cause   D. marks

49. A. Whenever   B. Unless   C. Suppose   D. Although

50. A. stole   B. accepted   C. seized   D. wasted

51. A. mad   B. lost   C. abroad   D. dead

52. A. order   B. excuse   C. agreement   D. apology

53. A. note   B. card   C. cheque   D. photo

54. A. joyed   B. burst   C. laughed   D. cried

55. A. should   B. did   C. had   D. was

第三部分 阅读理解（共20小题；每小题2分，满分40分）

阅读下列短文，从每题所给的四个选项中选出最佳选项。

A

The medical world is gradually realising that the quality of the environment in hospitals may play an important role in helping patients get better.

As part of a nationwide effort in Britain to bring art out of the museums and into public places, some of the country's best artists have been called in to change older hospitals and to soften the hard edges of modern buildings. Of the 2,500 National Health Service hospitals in Britain, almost 100 now have valuable collections of artwork in passages, waiting areas and treatment rooms.

These recent movements were first started by one artist, Peter Senior, who set up his studio at a Manchester hospital in Northwestern England during the early 1970s. He felt the artist had lost his place in modern society, and that art should be enjoyed by a wider audience.

A common hospital waiting room might have as many as 5,000 visitors each week. What a better place to hold regular exhibitions of art! Senior who held the first exhibition of his own paintings in the outpatients' waiting area of the Manchester Royal Hospital in 1975 was believed to be Britain's first hospital artist. Senior was so much in demand that he was soon joined by a team of six young art school graduates.

The effect is striking. Now in the passages and waiting rooms the visitors experience a full view of fresh colours, playful images and restful courtyards.

The quality of the environment may reduce the need for expensive drugs when a patient is recovering from an illness. A study has shown that patients who had a view onto gardens needed half the number of strong painkillers compared with patients who had no view at all or only a brick wall to look at.

56. Some best artists have been called to _____.

    A. pull down older hospitals and build up new ones

B. make the corners of the hospital buildings round

C. bring art into hospitals

D. help patients recover from illness

57. Peter Senior is _____.

A. one of the best artists in Britain

B. a pioneer in introducing art into hospitals

C. one of the young art school graduates

D. a painter who sells his paintings to hospitals

58. After the improvement of the hospital environment, _____.

A. patients no longer need drugs to kill their pains

B. patients needn't buy any expensive drugs

C. patients need fewer painkillers

D. patients can take fewer pills each time

59. Which of the following is TRUE according to the passage?

A. Artists in Britain have completely lost their places in modern society.

B. Patients should be encouraged to learn art.

C. Hospitals in Britain should be changed into art museums.

D. The introduction of art into hospitals is of benefit to the patients.

B

Grandma Moses is among the most famous 20th-century painters of the United States, yet she did not start painting until she was in her late 70s. As she once said of herself, "I would never sit back in a rocking chair, waiting for someone to help me." No one could have had a more productive old age.

She was born Anna Mary Robertson on a farm in New York State, one of the five boys and five girls. At 12 she left home and was in domestic (家庭的) service until, at 27, she married Thomas Moses, the hired hand of one of her employers. They farmed most of their lives, first in Virginia and then in New York State, at Eagle Bridge. She gave birth to 10 children, of whom 5 survived; her husband died in 1927.

Grandma Moses painted a little as a child and made embroidery (刺绣) pictures as a hobby, but only changed to oil paintings in old age because her hands had become too stiff (硬的) to sew and she wanted to keep busy and pass the time. Her pictures were first sold at the local drugstore (杂货店) and at a market and were soon noticed by a businessman who bought everything she painted. Three of the pictures were exhibited in the Museum of Modern Art, and in 1940 she had her first exhibition in New York. Between the 1930s and her death she produced some 2,000 pictures — detailed and lively portrayals (描绘) of the country life she had known for so long, with a wonderful sense of colour and form. "I think really hard till I think of something really pretty and then I paint it," she said.

60. According to the passage, Grandma Moses began to paint because she wanted to _____.

    A. make herself beautiful   B. keep active

    C. earn more money   D. become famous

61. Grandma Moses spent most of her life _____.

    A. nursing   B. painting   C. embroidering   D. farming

62. From Grandma Moses' description of herself in the first paragraph, it can be inferred that she was _____.

    A. independent   B. pretty   C. rich   D. nervous

63. Which of the following would be the best title for the passage?

    A. Grandma Moses: Her Life and Pictures

    B. The Children of Grandma Moses

    C. Grandma Moses: Her Best Exhibition

    D. Grandma Moses and Other Older Artists

C

Moving to a new home, perhaps even a new state? Here are some tips for making it a more positive, even fun experience.

Write in a journal

You may have a lot of thoughts rolling around in your head about the move and getting them down on paper can really help you sort through them. Once written down on paper, you can expand on them and even research ways to solve problems.

Do some research

Concern and doubt may turn into excitement as you find out about your new town and neighbourhood. If you have access to the Internet, find out what there is to see and do. Most cities have websites with links to activities, services and places to eat. Schools and park departments also often have websites.

Plan your new room

If you get to visit your new home beforehand, snap (抓拍) a photograph of it. Think about how you'll arrange the furniture you're bringing. Check out online stores for ideas. There are also magazines devoted to ideas for decorating kids' rooms.

Say goodbye

Make a list of those you'd like to say goodbye to, then try to visit each person before you go. Make sure to get their addresses and phone numbers. Take an autograph book and have them sign it.

Once you've arrived

Even with the best planning, everyone can get lonely after a move. So to get through the blues, visit places you researched, try to get involved in activities similar to the ones you were in before, keep writing in your journal, keep in touch with your old friends by phone and mail and send them photographs of your new home and school.

64. The text is mainly intended for _____.

    A. families   B. parents   C. school kids   D. tourists

65. According to the text, before you move away, you may _____.

    A. refer to magazines about how to decorate rooms

    B. send photographs of your new school to your friends

    C. make sure the Internet in your house works

    D. have your numbers written down by your friends

66. The underlined phrase "the blues" in the last paragraph means _____.

    A. blue colour   B. the feelings of being lonely

    C. the good plans   D. the journals students write

D

"Jingle bells, jingle bells, jingle all the way…" there went the popular Christmas tune. With the song in my head, I felt a bit sorry for myself. Instead of rushing back and forth across a freezing school campus, I could have had a cozy Christmas dinner at home or enjoyed the fabulous fireworks lighting up campus at night. But this Christmas would not be celebrated as usual.

One month ago, all six girls in my dormitory (including me) had made detailed plans for a more-exciting-than-ever Christmas holiday. But one day we received an unusual mission— we were asked to organise a party that would be a fund-raiser for mentally disabled children from the hospital. The children would perform on stage while volunteers offered food to the spectators (观众) and collected some money for the organisation.

Naturally, we were supposed to support the idea wholeheartedly, and we did. But wait —the date of the show was set right on Christmas Eve! This meant that all our original Christmas plans would have to be set aside.

However, we took the plunge into preparations for the party. We spared no effort in organising, designing, publicising, making contacts with the potential sponsors, negotiating and so on. We went through thick and thin and finally made it, though with a bit of reluctance.

Finally, Christmas Eve arrived. As I dragged myself into the auditorium after another day of hard work, I detected the notes of a beautiful Christmas song that immediately filled me with happiness. I looked to find the source of the song — it was a group of children singing onstage. Though disabled, they appeared extraordinarily earnest and sincere in front of the audience. Everyone attending was deeply moved by the sight. People wanted to donate some money or show their support. The performers earned recognition and respect from all of us.

At that point, I found all that I had done in the one-month time was worthwhile. And all the volunteers who had been participating in this Christmas party shared the same feeling: the true meaning of Christmas was giving and receiving love from one another.

67. The author thought her Christmas was unusual because _____.

    A. she had a cozy Christmas dinner and enjoyed fabulous fireworks

    B. she had a more-exciting-than-ever Christmas holiday

    C. her experience enabled her to understand the true meaning of Christmas

    D. she rushed back and forth across the freezing school campus

68. Why did the girl believe their hard work was worthwhile?

    A. Because they collected more money than they had expected.

    B. Because the disabled children gave wonderful performances.

    C. Because she had a new experience.

    D. Because she was deeply moved by the children's performances.

69. By saying "We went through thick and thin…", the writer meant _____.

    A. they passed through a crowd of people

    B. they found various people, thin and fat

    C. they overcame great difficulties

    D. they did a lot of things — difficult ones and easy ones

70. What would be the best title of the passage?

    A. Christmas on Campus   B. Help the Disabled

    C. A Wonderful Christmas   D. Get Ready to Help

E

Consumers are being confused and misled by the hotchpotch (大杂烩) of environmental claims made by household products, according to a "green labelling" study published by Consumers International Friday.

Among the report's outrageous (令人无法容忍的) findings — a German fertiliser described itself as "earthworm friendly", a brand of flour said it was "non-polluting", and a British toilet paper claimed to be "environmentally friendlier".

The study was written and researched by Britain's National Consumer Council (NCC) for the group Consumers International. It was funded by the German and Dutch governments and the European Commission.

"While many good and useful claims are being made, it is clear there is a long way to go in ensuring shoppers are adequately informed about the environmental impact of the products they buy," said Consumers International director Anna Fielder.

The 10-country study surveyed product packaging in Britain, Western Europe, Scandinavia and the United States. It found that products sold in Germany and the United Kingdom made the most environmental claims on average.

The report focused on claims made by specific products, such as detergents (洗涤用品), insect sprays and by some garden products. It did not test the claims, but compared them to labelling guidelines set by the International Standards Organisation (ISO) in September, 1999.

Researchers documented claims of environmental friendliness made by about 2,000 products and found many too vague or too misleading to meet ISO standards.

"Many products had specially-designed labels to make them seem environmentally friendly, but in fact many of these symbols mean nothing," said report researcher Philip Page. "Laundry detergents made the most number of claims with 158. Household cleaners were second with 145 separate claims, while paints were third on our list with 73. The high numbers show how confusing it must be for consumers to sort the true from the misleading," he said.

The ISO labelling standards ban vague or misleading claims on product packaging, because terms such as "environmentally friendly" and "non-polluting" cannot be verified. "What we are now pushing for is to have multinational corporations meet the standards set by the ISO," said Page.

71. According to the passage, the NCC found it outrageous that _____.
    A. all the products surveyed claim to meet ISO standards
    B. the claims made by products are often unclear or deceiving
    C. consumers would believe many of the manufacturers' claims
    D. few products actually prove to be environmentally friendly

72. As indicated in this passage, with so many good claims, the consumers _____.
    A. are becoming more cautious about the products they are going to buy
    B. are still not willing to pay more for products with green labelling
    C. are becoming more aware of the effects different products have on the environment
    D. still do not know the exact impact of different products on the environment

73. A study was carried out by Britain's NCC to _____.
    A. find out how many claims made by products fail to meet environmental standards
    B. inform the consumers of the environmental impact of the products they buy
    C. examine claims made by products against ISO standards
    D. revise the guidelines set by the International Standards Organisation

74. What is one of the consequences caused by the many claims of household products?
    A. They are likely to lead to serious environmental problems.
    B. Consumers find it difficult to tell the true from the false.
    C. They could arouse widespread anger among consumers.
    D. Consumers will not buy products they don't need.

75. It can be inferred from the passage that the group Consumers International wants to _____.
    A. make product labelling satisfy ISO requirements
    B. see all household products meet environmental standards
    C. warn consumers of the danger of so-called green products
    D. verify the effects of non-polluting products

第一节　阅读表达（共5小题；每小题3分，满分15分）

阅读下面的短文，并根据短文后面的要求答题。

On October 19, 1959, the first Special English programme was broadcast on the Voice of America (VOA). It was an experiment. The goal was to communicate by radio in clear and simple English with people _____ is not English. Experts said the goal was admirable, but the method would not work. They were proved wrong. The Special English programmes quickly became some of the most popular on VOA. And they still are.

Forty years later, Special English continues to communicate with people who are not fluent in English. But during the years its role has expanded. It also helps people learn American English. It succeeds in helping people learn English in a non-traditional way. And it provides listeners, even those who are native English speakers, with information they cannot find elsewhere.

Today, Special English broadcasts around the world seven days a week, five times a day. Each half-hour broadcast begins with 10 minutes of the latest news followed by 20 minutes of feature programming (特写报道节目). There is a different short feature every weekday about science, development, agriculture and environment, and on the weekend, about news events and American idioms. These programmes are followed by in-depth 15-minute features about American culture, history, space, important people or short stories.

76. What is the best title for the passage? (Please answer within 10 words.)

_____

77. Which sentence in the passage can be replaced by the following one?

But it has played an increasingly important part in more and more areas over the years.

_____

_____

78. Fill in the blank in the first paragraph with proper words or phrases to complete the sentence. (Please answer within 10 words.)

_____

79. What do you think about Special English? (Please answer within 30 words.)

_____

_____

80. Translate the underlined sentence in the second paragraph into Chinese.

_____

第二节　写作（满分30分）

假如你是高三学生张明，你在学校组织了一次"有烦恼向谁说"的调查活动。请用英语给校报编辑写一封信，反映相关情况。内容包括：调查结果（如图所示）、持相应想法的理由以及你对调查结果的看法。信的开头和结尾已经给出，不计入总词数。

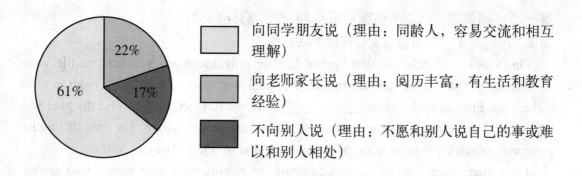

向同学朋友说（理由：同龄人，容易交流和相互理解）

向老师家长说（理由：阅历丰富，有生活和教育经验）

不向别人说（理由：不愿和别人说自己的事或难以和别人相处）

词数要求：120～150词。

Dear editor,

　　I am a Senior 3 student. Recently, we have carried out a survey — "To whom do you go when in trouble?" The results are as follows.

_____

_____

_____

_____

_____

Yours sincerely,

Zhang Ming

总复习检测题一

第I卷（满分105分）

第一部分　听力（共两节，满分30分）

第一节　（共5小题；每小题1.5分，满分7.5分）

听下面五段对话。每段对话后有一个小题，从题中所给的三个选项中选出最佳选项。听完每段对话后，你都有10秒钟的时间来回答有关小题和阅读下一小题。每段对话仅读一遍。

1. What are the speakers going to do?
   A. They will forget about asking Susan.
   B. They will go without Susan.
   C. They will not go at all.

2. What do we know from the conversation?
   A. The woman missed the carnival.
   B. The weather was bad for a fortnight.
   C. The traffic was bad.

3. When will the speakers get to the destination?
   A. At 3:40 in the afternoon.
   B. At 2:20 in the afternoon.
   C. At 2:40 in the afternoon.

4. What is the boy going to do first?
   A. To finish his writing.　　B. To have supper.　　C. To watch TV.

5. What are the speakers talking about?
   A. Their children.　　B. A jacket.　　C. The price.

第二节　（共15小题；每小题1.5分，满分22.5分）

听下面五段对话或独白。每段对话或独白后有几个小题，从题中所给的三个选项中选出最佳选项。听每段对话或独白前，你将有时间阅读各个小题，每小题5秒钟；听完后，各小题将给出5秒钟的作答时间。每段对话或独白读两遍。

听第6段材料，回答第6至第8小题。

6. What is the possible relationship between the two speakers?
   A. Friends.
   B. Salesman and customer.
   C. Husband and wife.

7. What are the speakers talking about?
   A. A girl.　　　　　　B. A bike.　　　　　　C. A birthday party.

8. What do you know about the birthday present?

   A. The man is happy to give it to the woman.

   B. The woman wants to buy a new bike.

   C. It will look new.

听第7段材料，回答第9至第11小题。

9. Where are the speakers?

   A. At home.　　　　　　B. In a hospital.　　　　C. In an office.

10. Why can't the man sleep well?

   A. His cough is particularly bad at night.

   B. He has to work late into the night.

   C. He has a sore throat.

11. Why doesn't the man go to the clinic?

   A. He is having a meeting.

   B. He is too busy to do it.

   C. He can take care of himself.

听第8段材料，回答第12至第14小题。

12. Who are the two speakers?

   A. Shop assistant and customer.

   B. Husband and wife.

   C. Boss and employee.

13. What are the speakers doing?

   A. Checking the things they bought.

   B. Tidying the house.

   C. Shopping.

14. What does the man think is expensive?

   A. Chicken.　　　　　　B. Cream.　　　　　　C. Strawberries.

听第9段材料，回答第15至第17小题。

15. Why is John here so early?

   A. To meet Jenny.　　　B. To prepare for a test.　　C. To see his school once more.

16. What does Jenny say about the test?

   A. It will be difficult.

   B. It will be easy.

   C. It will be surprisingly difficult.

17. Why is John so nervous?

   A. He is afraid of losing the scholarship.

   B. He never attended this course at all.

   C. He didn't work hard.

听第10段材料，回答第18至第20小题。

18. What does the mother do when her son reads a book?

    A. She also wants to read it.

    B. She keeps a close watch on him.

    C. She doesn't want him to read it.

19. What does the son feel?

    A. Happy.   B. Proud.   C. Anxious.

20. What do we know about the son's girlfriend?

    A. She hasn't met his mother yet.

    B. She always criticises the boy.

    C. She doesn't want to see him anymore.

第二部分　英语知识运用（共两节，满分35分）

第一节　语法和词汇（共15小题；每小题1分，满分15分）

从 A、B、C、D 四个选项中，选出可以填入空白处的最佳选项。

21. A terrible thought suddenly _____ me — had anyone broken into the house?

    A. occured   B. knocked   C. attacked   D. struck

22. —She is introducing the new cartoon film.

    —No _____ the children are so fascinated.

    A. wonder   B. question   C. problem   D. doubt

23. When she came out, Mary looked a bit tired because she _____ the house for the whole day.

    A. cleaned   B. was cleaning   C. has cleaned   D. had been cleaning

24. The Gate of Fortune, from _____ top visitors can enjoy a wonderful sea view, will attract lots of tourists.

    A. which   B. whose   C. its   D. where

25. Obviously, he's very disappointed at the way things have _____.

    A. turned up   B. turned out   C. turned on   D. turned down

26. Surely he _____ have forgotten about the wedding! But he has to put business first.

    A. needn't   B. mustn't   C. can't   D. shouldn't

27. If I'd known you were coming, I _____ have got your room ready.

    A. would   B. could   C. might   D. must

28. I no longer have the support of the committee. _____, I have decided to resign.

    A. However   B. Otherwise   C. Therefore   D. Besides

29. This lecture is by no means the most boring. I've attended _____.

    A. better   B. worse   C. the best   D. the worst

30. The criminal was living in Brazil, _____ the reach of the British police.

    A. under   B. over   C. above   D. beyond

31. Mum came to see me from hometown, _____ me a lot of local products.

    A. bringing   B. to bring   C. brought   D. had brought

32. —What's your parents' opinion about your choice?

    —They always let me do _____ I think I should.

    A. when   B. that   C. how   D. what

33. The mother felt herself _____ cold and her hands trembled as she read the letter from the battlefield.

    A. grow   B. grew   C. grown   D. to grow

34. —I reminded you not to forget the appointment.

    —_____.

    A. So did you   B. So you did   C. So I did   D. So do I

35. Hardly _____ to speak when there was a shout from the back of the hall.

    A. has she begun B. she has begun   C. had she begun   D. she had begun

第二节　完形填空　（共20小题；每小题1分，满分20分）

阅读下面的短文，掌握其大意，然后从每题所给的四个选项中选出最佳选项。

At midnight Peter was awakened by heavy knocks on the door. He rolled over and looked at his __36__, and it was half past one. "I'm not getting __37__ at this time," he __38__, and rolled over.

Then, a __39__ knock followed. "Aren't you going to __40__ that?" asked his wife.

So he dragged himself out of bed and went downstairs. He opened the door and there was a man __41__ at the door. It didn't take Peter long to __42__ the man was drunk.

"Hi, there," slurred (嘟囔) the stranger. "Can you give me a push?"

"No, get lost. It's half past one. I was __43__," Peter said and slammed the door. He went back __44__ to bed and told his wife what had happened.

She said, "That wasn't very __45__ of you. Remember that night we had a __46__ in the pouring rain on the way to pick the kids up and you had to __47__ that man's door to get our car __48__ again? What would have happened if he'd told __49__ to get lost?"

"But the guy was __50__," said Peter.

"It doesn't matter," said the wife. "He needs help __51__ it would be the Christian thing to help him."

So Peter went out of bed again, got dressed, and went downstairs. He opened the door, and not being able to see the stranger anywhere, he shouted, "Hey, do you still want a __52__?"

And he heard a __53__ cry out, "Yeah, please."

So, still being unable to see the stranger he shouted, "__54__ are you?"

The man replied, "Over here, on the __55__."

36. A. door   B. clock   C. wife   D. window

37. A. out of bed   B. out of the house   C. down to work   D. into trouble

38. A. complained   B. explained   C. replied   D. thought

39.	A. weaker	B. louder	C. longer	D. angrier
40.	A. stand	B. stop	C. answer	D. refuse
41.	A. standing	B. lying	C. knocking	D. looking
42.	A. remember	B. show	C. realise	D. doubt
43.	A. in bed	B. in surprise	C. at home	D. at work
44.	A. down	B. up	C. inside	D. home
45.	A. nice	B. foolish	C. typical	D. generous
46.	A. hard time	B. quarrel	C. fight	D. breakdown
47.	A. drive to	B. pass by	C. knock on	D. drop into
48.	A. started	B. refreshed	C. united	D. delighted
49.	A. us	B. them	C. the man	D. others
50.	A. mad	B. drunk	C. different	D. dangerous
51.	A. but	B. though	C. and	D. because
52.	A. rest	B. push	C. room	D. lift
53.	A. lady	B. gentleman	C. drunk	D. voice
54.	A. What	B. How	C. Who	D. Where
55.	A. roof	B. bed	C. swing	D. ground

第三部分　阅读理解（共20小题；每小题2分，满分40分）

阅读下面的短文，从每题所给的四个选项中选出最佳选项。

A

A Chinese teenage girl, Fan Yi (Nancy), who had her primary education in the US, recently published her first fairy tale, *Swordbird*. The English fairy tale was listed as the bestseller of children's fiction in the US, *Shanghai Evening Post* reported.

Fan Yi was greatly interested in observing birds ever since she was a little girl. In Florida where she lives, she often watches kingfishers and woodpeckers flying over her house from the small woods nearby. And the inspiration for writing the book *Swordbird* actually came from one of her dreams. At that time, she was studying American history in school and happened to read many articles in magazines about the 911 terrorist attacks. One day, she had a dream in which some <u>cardinals</u> and <u>bluejays</u> were controlled by some black birds and began to fight with each other. When she woke up, she decided to turn her dream into a story and to convey her message for peace to the public.

In order to get her book published in China, Fan translated the entire English version into Chinese.

"It is a learning process. Since I didn't know many Chinese idioms, I had to get help from my mum and dad from time to time. For another thing, a lot of poems in the original story are written in rhyme. So when I translated them into Chinese, I wanted to make sure that they were in rhyme too," she said.

Fan Yi was born in Beijing in 1993. She stayed in Beijing until she finished her first grade of primary school. Then she moved with her parents to the United States when she was 7. Two years later, she started to write her English story.

In February, 2007, the book was published by HarperCollins Publishers. It was selected as the week's bestseller of children's fiction by *The New York Times* soon after it was published.

In future, Fan Yi might write more series for her book. In fact, her second book *Sword Quest* came off the press in January, 2008.

56. The underlined words "cardinals" and "bluejays" in the second paragraph probably refer to _____.

    A. outer-space creatures   B. different kinds of birds

    C. different kinds of planes   D. people from different races

57. Her book was related to the 911 terrorist attacks in that _____.

    A. it was being written when the attacks happened

    B. it expressed her desire for peace against terrorism

    C. they both involved fighting in the air

    D. the attacks were mentioned in her book

58. Fan Yi thinks of the process of _____ as "a learning process".

    A. writing her book   B. writing the poems

    C. translating her book   D. getting her book published

59. Fan Yi started to write her first book at the age of _____.

    A. 7   B. 8   C. 9   D. 10

60. What else can we learn about Fan Yi from the article?

    A. She's believed to be writing more Swordbird stories.

    B. Her Chinese version of *Swordbird* was published in the US.

    C. *Swordbird* was re-published by *The New York Times*.

    D. She's likely to become a professional writer.

B

For years it has been possible to set up cameras to take pictures of cars as they speed along highways, jump lights or drive too fast down the street.

However, even if the pictures are taken automatically (自动地), someone still has to do all the paperwork of sending out fines. But now a British company called EEV has come up with a computerised video system that can do it all automatically.

They suggest that all number plates have a bar code as well as the usual number. The bar codes are just strips of lines like those you see on food packets but bigger. EEV's high speed video camera system can read a bar-coded number plate even if the car is doing over 100 miles per hour. The computer controlling the system could then use the information from the bar code to find out the name and address of the driver (from the car records), print out the fine and send it off automatically. The inventors also suggest that the system should watch traffic to help catch stolen cars.

The new electronic system could be watching everyone that passes the cameras! Many people find the idea that "big brother is watching you" is more of a worry than a few motorists getting away with driving too fast. Besides, some people will be very unhappy to realise that with the new system the police should find out where a particular car has been.

61. The best title for the article can be _____.
   A. People Who Drive Too Fast
   B. Stop People from Driving Too Fast
   C. EEV and the Police System
   D. A New Computerised System for Monitoring Motors

62. The former camera used by the traffic police system is to _____.
   A. take pictures of cars on highways
   B. send fines to fast motorists
   C. catch cars breaking traffic rules
   D. make the traffic system fully automatic

63. The newly-invented system works much better with the aid of _____.
   A. car number plates
   B. car speeding records
   C. bar codes on number plates
   D. print-out fines

64. An additional purpose of the new system is that it could _____.
   A. help catch stolen cars
   B. add code numbers
   C. watch everyone who drives too fast
   D. print out bar codes automatically

65. " '…big brother is watching you' is more of a worry than…" means that many people _____.
   A. are more worried about fast-driving motorists than being watched
   B. find "big brothers" more worrying than motorists
   C. are more worried about being watched than about fast-driving motorists
   D. find motorists more worrying than "big brothers"

C

Naomi Campbell, 38, has never looked so happy — and no wonder. Her five-day community service sentence in New York has served as the basis of a fashion shoot for *W* magazine, the monthly companion to *Women's Wear Daily*, which is regarded as the American "rag trade bible".

W's editorial director, Patrick McCarthy, said the 20-page feature would run in the July issue.

"We're having great fun watching her every day," he said. "It's going to make a great story... Naomi was very keen to do it; she thought it would be a lot of fun."

Campbell has used the short walk from her car to the doors of the Sanitation (卫生) Department's District 3 Garage as a catwalk, each day presenting a new suit carefully matched with must-have sunglasses and handbags.

Her agency, IMG, says Campbell's basic rate is about £25,000 a day.

News that Campbell had used what was supposed to be a punishment — she mopped floors and cleaned toilets — as a promotional money-spinner has angered New Yorkers.

New York lawyer Raoul Felder said that while there was nothing illegal about Campbell's deal, her behaviour had "made a mockery of our system of justice and insulted (侮辱) every hard-working person in this city".

Campbell was sentenced in January to five days' community service after admitting she'd been guilty of throwing a mobile phone at an assistant.

66. What can we learn about *W* magazine from the article?

    A. Its full name is *Women's Wear Daily*.

    B. It's very important to the fashion industry.

    C. Its July issue has Naomi's picture on the cover.

    D. It's a 20-page monthly magazine.

67. Naomi was supposed to _____ in the District 3 Garage.

    A. do some cleaning   B. work as a fashion model

    C. have her car repaired   D. sell fashion clothes

68. The New York lawyer must have thought that their system of justice _____ in Naomi's case.

    A. worked effectively   B. lost its power

    C. proved unfair   D. changed its nature

69. Naomi was punished because she _____.

    A. hadn't paid her debt   B. had made money illegally

    C. had tried to hit someone   D. had damaged her assistant's mobile phone

70. The article mainly tells us that _____.

    A. it's easy for Naomi to make money   B. Naomi received her punishment

    C. it's hard to punish a superstar   D. Naomi used punishment for profit

D

I once brought some foreign friends to visit a Malay kampong (小村庄) a few kilometres outside the city. These friends from Australia were rather interested in finding out how Malay villagers lived. I decided the best way was to take them to an actual Malay kampong where they could see for themselves.

The kampong we visited was a seaside kampong. Naturally most of the kampong folks were fishermen although some were engaged in other jobs.

There were about 30 houses — most of them were wooden structures with atap roofs (用聂帕榈叶盖的屋顶). There were no fences to separate the house — they had a sort of communal garden. Each family had its own small plot of land where they planted flowers or vegetables. They had no piped water supply but depended on wells for their water.

The kampong folks kept ducks and chickens which were allowed to wander freely about the compound (大院). The visitors were surprised that the people in the kampong were so friendly and helpful towards one another. Although they shared communal gardens or compounds, there was no bickering or quarrelling.

Most of the houses were built on stilts and we also found large numbers of coconut trees growing within the kampong. We were invited into one of the kampong houses for some refreshments. Later the visitors took some photographs and walked round the village. We thanked the headman for allowing us the opportunity of visiting the village.

71. According to the writer, _____.

    A. all of the kampong folks were fishermen

    B. most of the kampong folks were farmers

    C. most of the kampong folks earn their living by fishing

    D. not one of the kampong folks was a fishermen

72. Most of the kampong houses were _____.

    A. stone structure   B. made of wood and atap

    C. made of mud   D. made of cement (水泥) and wood

73. The visitors were surprised because _____.

    A. the kampong was so dirty

    B. the kampong folks were so kind and friendly

    C. the kampong folks were always quarrelling

    D. the villagers kept so many ducks and chickens

74. The kampong houses _____.

    A. stood on stilts   B. were built on the sea

    C. were built on tree tops   D. stood on the rocks

75. The kampong the writer and his friends visited _____.

    A. had piped water supply

    B. used sea water

    C. depended on wells for their water supply

    D. had no water supply at all

第四部分　书面表达（共两节，满分45分）

第一节　阅读表达（共5小题；每小题3分，满分15分）

阅读下面的短文，并根据短文后的要求答题。

Winter sports are very popular in European and North American countries. These places usually receive a lot of snow during the winter months.

Skiing and skating become the major sports activities for Westerners during the winter. People from Norway, Italy, the United States, Sweden and Canada all like winter sports.

Winter sports such as alpine skiing (高山滑雪) and skating are very popular because they allow people to keep warm while enjoying outdoors.

People can exercise outdoors in beautiful surroundings: snow-covered mountains and pine trees among endless white snow. Putting oneself into the white world and breathing fresh air, one can relax and forget all worries. Of course, the practice of flying down the hills also excites people.

The Alps in Europe is the most ideal place for skiing. The Rocky Mountains in the Western United States is another good place.

Some people call winter sports "royal sports". That is because of their high cost. These sports always require expensive equipment. They also need high-standard places to be enjoyed.

Winter sports are not popular in China. The southern and coastal areas have no skiing and skating. And the snow-blanketed northeastern and southwestern areas have poor equipment.

But thanks to the efforts of the government, China has caught up with world-class competition in short track speed skating (短道速滑). This is also true for women's figure skating. However, in alpine skiing events, China _____.

76. What's the best title for this passage? (Please answer within 10 words.)

_____

77. Which sentence in the passage can be replaced by the following one?

Taking part in the outdoor winter sports with snow-covered surroundings makes you feel refreshed and carefree.

_____

_____

78. Fill in the blank in the last paragraph with proper words or phrases to complete the sentence. (Please answer within 10 words.)

_____

79. Do you think winter sports will become popular in China? Why (not)? (Please answer within 30 words.)

_____

_____

80. Translate the underlined sentence in the third paragraph into Chinese.

_____

第二节 写作（满分30分）

假如你是李明。今年暑假你应在纽约的叔叔的邀请，去美国度假。到美国后，你的堂妹领你参观了纽约的主要景点，给你留下最深刻印象的是纽约的唐人街（Chinatown）。请用英语给你在国内的朋友刘伟写一封信，记述你对美国的印象，并发挥想象力，描述一下唐人街的景色。

词数要求：120～150词。

_____

_____

_____

_____

_____

_____

第I卷（满分105分）

第一部分 听力（共两节，满分30分）

第一节 （共5小题；每小题1.5分，满分7.5分）

听下面五段对话。每段对话后有一个小题，从题中所给的三个选项中选出最佳选项。听完每段对话后，你都有10秒钟的时间来回答有关小题和阅读下一小题。每段对话仅读一遍。

1. Where are the speakers?
   A. At home.   B. At a shop.   C. At school.

2. What will the man probably do?
   A. Have dinner.   B. Clean the table.   C. Read the notebook.

3. Why is the woman so disappointed?
   A. She won't have a chance to see the play.
   B. The man wouldn't go to the play with her.
   C. There are no good seats left in the theatre.

4. What does the woman suggest doing?
   A. Waiting in the corner.   B. Taking a taxi.   C. Telephoning the hotel.

5. What does the woman mean?
   A. She can help the man.
   B. The machine was just repaired.
   C. The clerk doesn't like to be troubled.

第二节 （共15小题；每小题1.5分，满分22.5分）

听下面五段对话或独白。每段对话或独白后有几个小题，从题中所给的三个选项中选出最佳选项。听每段对话或独白前，你将有时间阅读各个小题，每小题5秒钟；听完后，各小题将给出5秒钟的作答时间。每段对话或独白读两遍。

听第6段材料，回答第6至第8小题。

6. What are they talking about?
   A. Their childhood.   B. Their grandsons.   C. The young's behaviour.

7. How many T-shirts did the boy buy once?
   A. Thirteen.   B. Thirty.   C. Three.

8. How did the man and the woman live in the past?
   A. They wasted money.   B. They didn't have shoes.   C. They didn't have enough clothes.

9. What is the relationship between the man and the woman?

    A. Husband and wife.　　　B. Sportsman and saleswoman.　　　C. Customer and saleswoman.

10. Where is the sporting goods department?

    A. On the 3rd floor.　　　B. On the 4th floor.　　　C. On the 5th floor.

11. What does the man ask about first?

    A. Where the shoe department is.

    B. Where the toy department is.

    C. Where the restroom is.

12. What causes the conversation?

    A. An advertisement.　　　B. A TV programme.　　　C. An article.

13. Who will shop quickly?

    A. Those who know what they want to buy.

    B. Those who have little money to spend.

    C. Those who shop at the cheapest stores.

14. What can we conclude from the conversation?

    A. People spend more time looking than shopping.

    B. People enjoy shopping when they are free.

    C. People buy things easily if time is limited.

15. When is the man's departure date?

    A. The 13th.　　　B. The 20th.　　　C. The 30th.

16. What is the flight number?

    A. 1700.　　　B. 1070.　　　C. 1017.

17. What request did the man make regarding his flight?

    A. He asked for a specially-prepared dinner.

    B. He wanted an aisle seat.

    C. He asked for a seat near the front of the plane.

18. Why is it difficult for us to find someone to repair the broken electric appliances (电器)?

    A. The workshops want us to buy new ones.

    B. The workshops are short of hands.

    C. To buy new ones is cheaper than to fix the broken ones.

19. Why did Mrs White phone the workshop?

    A. Her washing machine was broken.

    B. Her fridge didn't work.

    C. Something was wrong with her TV set.

20. When do you think Mrs Smith phoned the workshop?

    A. On May 20.   B. On May 21.   C. On May 22.

第二部分 英语知识运用（共两节，满分35分）

第一节　语法和词汇（共15小题；每小题1分，满分15分）

从A、B、C、D四个选项中，选出可以填入空白处的最佳选项。

21. —Do you want to go to the movies?

    —_____. I feel like doing something different.

    A. Yes, I do   B. I don't want   C. Not really   D. Don't mention it

22. They are enjoying themselves; _____, they appear to enjoy themselves.

    A. still   B. therefore   C. or rather   D. so that

23. Although they lost their jobs, savings and unemployment benefits allow the young couple to _____ their comfortable home.

    A. come in for   B. look forward to   C. catch up with   D. hold on to

24. Generally speaking, when _____ according to the directions, the drug has no side effects.

    A. taking   B. taken   C. to take   D. to be taken

25. As it turned out to be a small house party, we _____ so formally.

    A. needn't dress up   B. didn't have to dress up

    C. might not have dressed up   D. needn't have dressed up

26. —Do you think an advertisement is _____ help when you look for a new job?

    —Well, it all depends. Anyway, it gives me more of _____ chance to try.

    A. a; a   B. the; the   C. a; the   D. /; /

27. I think your sister is old enough to know _____ to spend all her money on beautiful dresses.

    A. other than   B. rather than   C. better than   D. more than

28. The Double Ninth Festival _____ on October 19 this year, and this is the day of the young to show respect for their elderly relatives.

    A. sets   B. fixes   C. falls   D. lies

29. —Why haven't you asked her to come here?

    —She _____ an important experiment when I found her and she _____ it.

    A. had done; didn't finish   B. was doing; hasn't finished

    C. did; wouldn't finish   D. would do; hadn't finished

30. —Are you sure he is able to do the job well?

    —_____ he would give his mind to it.

    A. In case   B. Until   C. If only   D. Unless

31. Difficulties and hardships have _____ the best in the young scientist.

    A. brought in   B. brought up   C. brought out   D. brought about

32. Which book would you rather _____ tomorrow?

    A. have printed   B. get print   C. have print   D. to be printed

33. There was a reward system in the manners class _____ the politest children would receive a reward for being nice to the rest of the class.

    A. how   B. that   C. which   D. what

34. —What made Susan so depressed? She is in tears in her room.

    —_____ of cheating in the exam.

    A. Suspected   B. Being suspected   C. Suspecting   D. To suspect

35. —What should I do now?

    —I'd prefer _____ if you didn't smoke in front of children.

    A. one   B. that   C. it   D. this

第二节　完形填空（共20小题；每小题1分，满分20分）

阅读下面的短文，掌握其大意，然后从每题所给的四个选项中选出最佳选项。

When someone says, "Well, I guess I'll have to go to face the music," it does not mean he's __36__ to go to a concert. It is something far __37__, like being called in by your boss to __38__ why you did this and did that, and why you did not do this __39__ that. Sour music indeed, but it has to be __40__. At sometime or another, __41__ of us has had to face the music, especially __42__ children. We can all remember father's __43__ voice, "I want to talk to you!" and only because we did not obey him. What an unpleasant __44__ it was!

The phrase "to face the music" is __45__ to every American, young and old. It is at least 100 years old. And where did this expression come from? The first explanation __46__ from the American novelist, James Fenimore Cooper. He said, in 1851, that the expression was __47__ used by actors while waiting in the wings to go on the stage. When they __48__ their cue (提示) to go on, they often said, "Well, it's time to go to face the music." And that is exactly what they did — face the orchestra (乐队) which was just below __49__. An actor might be __50__ or nervous as he moved onto the stage in front of an audience that __51__ be friendly or perhaps hostile (敌意的), especially if he forgot his __52__. But he had to go out. If he did not, __53__ would be no play. __54__ the expression "to face the music" came to mean "having to go through something, no matter how unpleasant the __55__ might be, because you knew you had no choice".

36. A. planning   B. wanting   C. hoping   D. wishing

37. A. wiser   B. more foolish   C. less pleasant   D. more interesting

38. A. ask   B. prove   C. explain   D. show

39. A. or   B. and   C. but   D. then

40. A. listened   B. played   C. faced   D. sung

41. A. every one   B. all   C. few   D. none

42. A. to   B. like   C. for   D. as

43. A. angry   B. sweet   C. quiet   D. loud

44. A. phrase   B. business   C. talk   D. way

45. A. familiar	B. close	C. common	D. usual
46. A. hears	B. goes	C. comes	D. grows
47. A. once	B. certainly	C. still	D. first
48. A. got	B. took	C. made	D. did
49. A. you	B. it	C. them	D. us
50. A. eager	B. anxious	C. unwilling	D. frightened
51. A. might	B. should	C. must	D. would
52. A. phrase	B. lines	C. stories	D. ideas
53. A. there	B. he	C. it	D. we
54. A. Now	B. Then	C. Afterwards	D. So
55. A. activity	B. experience	C. thing	D. performance

第三部分 阅读理解（共20小题；每小题2分，满分40分）

阅读下面的短文，从每题所给的四个选项中选出最佳选项。

A

Today in the West, people can hardly imagine a world without the teddy bear, but actually it did not make its appearance until 1902, when during a four-day hunting, President Roosevelt (nicknamed "Teddy") spared the life of a bear. The incident inspired a cartoon drawn by Clifford Berryman and caused an immediate sensation instantly it appeared in *The Washington Post*.

Following that cartoon, Morris Michtom displayed in New York a bear labelled "Teddy's Bear", which looked sweet, innocent, and upright. Perhaps that's why "Teddy's Bear" made a hit with the buying public. Meanwhile in Germany, the Steiff firm made a toy bear looking more like a real bear cub while the Michtoms' bear resembled the wide-eyed cub in the Berryman cartoon.

In 1906, the teddy-bear-craze was in full swing in the US — especially among ladies and children. Roosevelt even used a bear as a mascot in his re-election bid. The next 25 years saw teddy bear companies springing up in England, France, and other parts of the world. More styles, such as musical bears and mechanical bears, were popularised and produced worldwide. But the outbreak of WWII stopped the fun. The world's workers and factories were needed for the war effort. Some companies closed and never reopened.

In the post-war years, fueled by a desire for washable toys, synthetic fibres were in fashion. Traditional companies could adapt to this change in materials, but they were not prepared to compete against the flood of much cheaper, mass-produced teddy bears coming from the Far East. Even the old, well-established firms got hurt by the blow.

Strangely enough, it was a British actor's book that created a perfect climate for the teddy bear's <u>resurgence</u>. The teddy bear began to regain its popularity, not so much as a children's toy, but as a collectable for adults, which has also increased the value of antique teddy bears. Since 1974, thousands of teddy bears artists have created soft sculpture teddy bear art for eager collectors. Today, teddy bear books, magazines, museums and fairs spread across the world.

Unlike the majority of toys and dolls, the novelties (新颖) of teddy bears always seem to come and go along with the latest children's crazes. The secret of the success in survival lies in the unique face of each teddy bear.

The enchantment (魅力) and the mystique will last forever!

56. What does the passage mainly focus on?

    A. The teddy bear craze in the US.   B. Research on toy-making culture.

    C. Historic development of teddy bears.   D. Rise and fall in toy business.

57. Which of the following statements agrees with the passage?

    A. President Roosevelt refused to kill the bear for the sake of the cartoon.

    B. Teddy bears couldn't be more popular with US women and kids in 1906.

    C. Musical and mechanical bears were designed and popularised after WWII.

    D. Adults are interested in collecting mass-made teddy bears.

58. The underlined word "resurgence" in the fifth paragraph is closest in meaning to "_____".

    A. boom   B. decline   C. promotion   D. recovery

59. Teddy bears are popular with the buyers mainly due to _____.

    A. the influence of President Roosevelt   B. cartoon pictures by Clifford Berryman

    C. the book written by a British actor   D. their lovely images

60. What is meant by the underlined sentence in the last paragraph?

    A. More and more people tend to love cartoon figures rather than real animals.

    B. Teddy bear companies will always be doing well in toy business.

    C. The unique faces and the novelties of teddy bears will always satisfy the taste of buyers.

    D. Booming teddy bear art contributes to the rising value of antique teddy bears.

B

At this busiest gift-giving time of the year, many of us wonder what to do with the unwanted presents we get. Is it all right to re-gift — to give the unwanted presents to someone else?

A gift is a symbol of what a relationship means to us. The best gifts meet the needs or satisfy the desires of the receiver. A gift should be about pleasing the other person, not showing off the taste, wealth or power of the giver. We should give with the other person, not ourselves in mind.

Still, a friend, colleague or family member who knows us well might now and then buy us something that is the last thing we'd buy for ourselves. People in long-term relationships can be surprised at the choices in clothes, music or gadgets (小玩意儿) made by their friends or relatives.

Re-gifting creates a dilemma (窘境) because we don't want to hurt the feelings of the gift-giver, but we also feel it's wasteful not to use something that might benefit someone else.

Re-gifting avoids waste and repays a debt of gratitude we owe to someone else, but it presents the risk that the original giver will be hurt if she or he discovers what we did.

The following are a few guidelines for re-gifting:

- Don't use the gift.
- Re-gift soon, so you don't risk re-gifting to the original giver.
- Make sure that the new receiver doesn't know the original giver or is unlikely to run into him or her.

If there's a possibility that the original giver could learn about the re-gift or if he or she expects to see you wearing the gift, consider asking for permission. Let him or her know how much you appreciate the thought behind the gift. A person who understands that a gift is intended to be pleasing will understand. As long as the person who gave the unwelcome gift doesn't mind or won't find out, you can re-gift with a clear conscience. Besides, you can be sure that at least one of the gifts you've received was given originally to someone else.

61. What's the best title for the passage?
    A. What Is Re-gifting?   B. Dilemmas of Re-gifting
    C. Re-gifting with Care   D. Do You Know Re-gifting?

62. According to the author, the gift that you want to buy for your friend had better be the one that _____.
    A. can benefit someone else   B. you want to buy for yourself
    C. is a necessity for your friend   D. will surprise your friend

63. In the third paragraph, the author wants to tell the readers that _____.
    A. people sometimes get the gifts that they don't really like
    B. our friends usually choose the best gifts for us
    C. we should not buy clothes, music or gadgets for our friends
    D. your best friend should know what gift is the best for you

64. What can we infer from the last sentence of the passage?
    A. The gift you get is the one you bought for someone.
    B. Re-gifting is a very common practice today.
    C. You should re-gift at least two gifts each year.
    D. More than one of your friends will re-gift their presents to you each year.

65. According to its meaning, the sentence "After all, some people like orange and red sweaters, or the complete recorded works of Wayne Newton (a US singer), or fruitcake (which you don't like at all)." should be put at the end of _____.
    A. Paragraph 1.   B. Paragraph 2.   C. Paragraph 3.   D. Paragraph 4.

C

Like many men at some point, I dream about opening a bar. On Friday nights, people will be able to come here and enjoy themselves.

See, I have a gift for business. I am, as my wife Zsa Zsa likes to note, "A man with a million ideas, none of them very good." Speaking of Zsa Zsa, she is fed up with this plain little life I've made for us — too many kids, too many chores, mind-numbing debt. The other day, she said she thought we needed a new family car. "Sure. How about an '87 Lincoln?" I said, and saw my dear Zsa Zsa age about 20 years, and become her mother right before my eyes.

Yes, money is our madness. Last year, we thought we had found a little cushion when I published a book about the life here in suburban America. It sold 12 copies — six of them to my mother. Four other copies went to various aunts and uncles, who used them for martini coasters, then sold them at yard sales. The two remaining copies went to perfect strangers. (I think I owe you dinner, whoever you are. Call me, OK? We'll arrange something.)

When the book didn't take off, I wrote a TV show. Then I penned a short novel based on the earlier TV idea that didn't sell. Currently, I am at work on a set of encyclopedias. In a month, I plan to sell them door-to-door.

Such is the life of a writer — sending off the most personal thoughts possible to his hard drive. I am a writer, but also the breadwinner in my family. I'm at the keyboard at 6:00 almost every morning, hoping to tap out one idea — one that will take us up the hill, to the mountain, to the top.

66. According to the passage, the author's life is indeed _____.
    A. happy   B. easy   C. poor   D. wealthy
67. By saying "Sure. How about an '87 Lincoln?" the author means he _____.
    A. really wanted to buy that car
    B. was showing off their fortune
    C. thought his wife would like it
    D. was joking about their economic situation
68. What was the result of the book the author mentioned in the third paragraph?
    A. He sold it door-to-door.
    B. It didn't sell well at all.
    C. He made a lot of money from it.
    D. It was really a cushion for his family.
69. Which of the following statements is TRUE?
    A. The author has a real gift for business.
    B. The author isn't serious enough about life.
    C. The author is a hard-working writer.
    D. The author's wife is satisfied with their life.
70. The author writes the passage in a _____ tone.
    A. regretful   B. humorous   C. persuasive   D. grateful

D

Very old people do raise moral problems for almost everyone who comes into touch with them. Their values — this can't be repeated too often — are not necessarily our values. Physical comfort, cleanness and order are not necessarily the most important for them. The social services from time to time find themselves faced with a flat with decaying food covered with dust on the table, and an old person lying alone on bed, taking no notice of anything. Is it interfering with personal freedom to insist that they go to live with some of their relatives so that they might be taken better care of? Some social workers are the ones who clean up the dust, thinking we are in danger of carrying this idea of personal freedom to the point where serious risks are being taken with the health and safety of the old.

Indeed, the old can be easily hurt or harmed. The body is like a car; it needs more care as it gets older. You can carry this comparison right through to the provision of spare parts. Never forget that such operations are painful experiences, however good the results. At what point should you stop treating the old body? Is it right to try to push off death by using drugs to excite the forgetful old mind and to activate the old body, knowing that there is little hope? You cannot ask doctors or scientists to decide, because so long as they can see the technical opportunities, they will feel sure to have a try on the belief that while there's life, there's hope.

When you talk to the old people, however, you are forced to the conclusion that whether age is happy or unpleasant depends less on money or on health than <u>it</u> does on your ability to have fun.

71. What does the author indicate in the first paragraph _____.

   A. very old people enjoy living with their relatives

   B. very old people are able to keep their rooms clean

   C. social services could have nothing to do with very old people

   D. very old people prefer to live alone so that they can have more personal freedom

72. Some social workers think that _____.

   A. one should not take risks of dealing with old people

   B. old people should have the idea of cleaning their rooms

   C. personal freedom is more important than health and safety

   D. health and safety are more important than personal freedom

73. In the author's opinion, _____.

   A. the human body can't be compared to a car

   B. the older a person is, the more care he or she needs

   C. too much emphasis has been put on old people's values

   D. it is easy to provide spare parts for old people

74. The underlined word "it" in the last paragraph refers to _____.

   A. whether age is happy or unpleasant

B. the conclusion you have come to

C. one's money or health

D. your talk to the old people

75. The author thinks that _____.

A. the opinion that we should try every means possible to save old people is doubtful

B. medical decisions for the old people should be left to the doctors

C. old people can enjoy a happy life only if they are very rich

D. it is always right to treat old people and push off death

第II卷（满分45分）
第四部分 书面表达（共两节，满分45分）

第一节 阅读表达（共5小题；每小题3分，满分15分）

阅读下面的短文，并根据短文后的要求答题。

Slow down, Multitaskers

Think you can walk, drive, take phone calls, email and listen to music at the same time? Well, New York's new law says you can't. And you'll be fined $100 if you do it on a New York City street.

The law went into force last month, following the conclusion of a recent research that a shocking number of accidents are relevant to people using electronic gadgets crossing the street.

Who's to blame? Scientists say that our multitasking abilities are limited. "We are under the impression that our brain can do more than it often can," says Rene Marois, a neuroscientist in Tennessee. "But a core limitation is the inability to concentrate on two things at once."

The young are often considered the great multitaskers, but a research suggests this perception is open to question. A group of 18- to 21-year-olds were given 90 seconds to translate images into numbers, using a simple code. The younger group did 10 percent better than the older group _____. But when both groups were interrupted by a phone call or an instant message, the older group matched the younger group in speed and accuracy.

It is difficult to measure the productivity lost by multitaskers. But it is probably a lot. Jonathan Spira, chief analyst at Basex, a business-research firm, estimates the cost of interruptions to the American economy at nearly $650 billion a year. The estimate is based on surveys with office workers. The surveys conclude that 28 percent of the workers' time was spent on interruptions and recovery time before they returned to their main tasks.

76. What's the main purpose of this passage? (Please answer within 15 words.)

_____

77. Which sentence in the passage can be replaced by the following one?

People take it for granted that young people are good multitaskers. However, the idea needs to be further proved, a research says.

_____

_____

78. Fill in the blank in the fourth paragraph with proper words or phrases to complete the sentence. (Please answer within 10 words.)

_____

79. Are you a multitasker? What's your opinion on New York's new law? (Please answer within 30 words.)

_____

_____

80. Translate the underlined sentence in the second paragraph into Chinese.

_____

第二节 写作（满分30分）

现在，建设社会主义新农村成为热点话题。请你根据下列提示，以"New Socialist Countryside in the Future"为题描绘一下未来的社会主义新农村的蓝图。文章的开头已经给出，不计入总词数。

参考词汇：义务教育 compulsory education，医疗保障系统 medical care system

词数要求：120～150词。

New Socialist Countryside in the Future

With the efforts and support from the government in many aspects, a new socialist countryside will appear in China.

_____

_____

_____

_____

_____

Module 1

I. 1－5 DACCB　　6－10 ACDAC　　11－15 ABDAB

II. 1－5 CBCAB　　6－10 BACBD　　11－15 CBDDB　　16－20 DADBC

III. 1－5 ACDDB　　6－10 ADDAB

IV. 1. Making their jobs more interesting.

2. Because the modern factory has its complicated machinery that must be used in a fixed way.

3. How to Make the Workers More Productive

4. giving the workers freedom

5. 就提高生产力而言，多样性不是一个重要因素。

V. 1. so good a; that　　　　2. in addition to　　　　3. make an apology

VI. 1. There is no need　　　　2. will have to be punished　　3. that let out

4. needn't have picked him up　　5. with water covering

Module 2

I. 1－5 CBCBD　　6－10 CDABA　　11－15 CCDAC

II. 1－5 BCADC　　6－10 ACDBB　　11－15 DCBCA　　16－20 CBBCC

III. 1－5 CCADC　　6－10 CBADC

IV. 1. Crime Cycles / Crime and Season

2. You are most likely to be robbed

3. In all cases, he found a spring high and autumn high separated by a summer low.

4. （略）

5. 对2,400多个市镇的警局记录所进行的为期五年的调查显示，季节变化和犯罪形式之间有着惊人的联系。

V. 1. dreams / dreamed of becoming　　2. Not having heard from him　　3. by means of

4. what to do with / how to deal with　　5. have similar tastes

6. match her in knowledge of　　7. for some reason

8. appeal to　　　　　　　　　　　9. Not knowing

Module 3

I. 1－5 CCAAB   6－10 DBCCA   11－15 CABDB

II. 1－5 ABDCC   6－10 ABCAC   11－15 DACAB   16－20 ACACB

III. 1－5 CACCA   6－10 CADBD

IV. 1. How to Start a Conversation with a Foreigner / Suggestions on How to Start a Conversation with a Foreigner

2. Observe him to decide whether it is suitable to continue with the talk.

3. chatting with foreigners in English

4. （略）

5. 为了使谈话进行下去，要问开放式的问题，而不要问可以用"是"或"不是"回答的问题。

V. 1. resulted from 2. to have seen 3. burst out crying 4. is made up of 5. have told you

VI. 1. When he and his partner finished the story, everyone burst out laughing.

2. I regret to tell you that your pet dog was knocked over by a car.

3. The couple turned round and walked away without saying a word.

4. They expressed their satisfaction with the job we have done from the bottom of their hearts.

5. As mentioned in his diary, he lost touch with his girlfriend after graduation.

复习检测题（一）

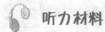 听力材料

Text 1

W: It's already 9 o'clock. I wonder if Tom will come.

M: We were supposed to be here at 8:30. He told me he would leave home at 8:00.

W: Maybe something went wrong with him.

Text 2

M: I want to have this shirt washed and this suit dry-cleaned.

W: OK, sir. Your name and room number, please.

Text 3

M: Did you check the power plug and press the play button?

W: Um, yes, the electricity was turned on, and it was running, but somehow the sound didn't come through.

Text 4

M: Juana, I am terribly sorry. I didn't mean to hurt you. Shall we have a beer and forget the whole thing?

W: OK, we can drop it this time. But don't do it again.

Text 5

W: Did you find the book you needed in the library?

M: It closed before I got there. I had no idea that it closes so early on weekends.

Text 6

M: Thank you very much, Miss Green. That helped me a lot.

W: I am glad I could be of some help, Carlos. Let me know if you have any more questions later.

M: I will. And thank you for giving up your coffee break to help. I know you need one after teaching three classes.

W: Oh, I don't mind. Teaching is what I love most.

M: Well, goodbye and thanks again.

W: You are welcome, Carlos. See you in class on Monday.

Text 7

M: When do you want to leave for that seaside town, Martha?

W: I'm not sure yet. But maybe we should leave on Friday after work. It's a long drive. But I'd rather get there late Friday than midday Saturday. We have only three days off this time after all.

M: How long is the drive?

W: Five or six hours.

M: Say you leave at 4:30 right after work you will be there around 9:00 or 10:00.

W: I suppose so, and we could still have a good night's sleep.

M: What are you going to take?

W: Mostly shoes and T-shirts.

M: You don't think it's going to be a bit cold at night at the seaside?

W: Maybe. I'm going to take a sweater or a light coat, just in case.

M: Hope you have a good time there.

W: Thank you.

Text 8

W: Madison Square Garden. Can I help you?

M: Yes. Do you have any more tickets for the concert on Friday night?

W: Do you mean the Rock and Roll Revival Show? Yes, we still have some $30 tickets left.

M: Great. OK, and is the box office open now?

W: Yes, the box office is open from 10:00 am to 8:00 pm.

M: Oh, by the way, what time does the show start?

W: It starts at 8 o'clock in the evening.

M: And what time does it end?

W: Well, there are four bands, so it'll probably end about midnight.

M: Thanks a lot.

W: You are welcome.

Text 9

M: Hi, Alice, have you made any New Year's resolutions?

W: Just the usual. I'd like to lose some weight, and I want to save some money.

M: Come on! Everyone makes those sorts of resolutions.

W: I know, Henry. Well, I hope I'll get a good job after I graduate this summer. But that's not a resolution. I'm going to work harder. How about you?

M: Hmm. I stopped smoking last June. That was last year's promise to myself.

W: So what do you want to do this year?

M: I want to start getting more exercise. I have to lose some weight, so I'd like to join a health club.

W: I'd like to do that too. Jeff told me he'd like to treat himself to a really nice vacation.

M: Oh? Where does he think he would go?

W: He might go to a quiet beach in Mexico, or go fishing in Canada. He hasn't made up his mind yet.

Text 10

Good afternoon, and welcome to England. We hope that your visit here will be a pleasant one. Today, I would like to draw your attention to a few of our laws.

The first one is about drinking. Now, you may not buy alcohol in this country if you are under 18 years of age, nor may your friends buy it for you.

Secondly, noise. Enjoy yourselves by all means, but please don't make unnecessary noise, particularly at night. We ask you to respect other people who may wish to be quiet.

Thirdly, crossing the road. Be careful. The traffic moves on the left side of the road in this country. Use the crossing for walking and do not take any chances when crossing the road.

Finally, as regards to smoking, it is against the law to buy cigarettes or tobacco if you are under 16 years of age.

I'd like to finish by saying that if you require any sort of help or assistance, you should get in touch with your local police station, who will be pleased to help you. Now, are there any other questions?

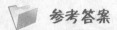 参考答案

1 – 5 ABAAA   6 – 10 ABBAC   11 – 15 BACCB   16 – 20 ABAAB

21 – 25 DCDAC   26 – 30 BDBDB   31 – 35 CADAB

36 – 40 DCDAB   41 – 45 CABCC   46 – 50 DBACB   51 – 55 CDBAC

56 – 60 BDBDA   61 – 65 DBCAC   66 – 70 DABAC   71 – 75 CAABD

76. Say No to Doping / Fighting Against Doping / Olympics and Doping

77. Three.

78. damage a person's health / do great harm to athletes' health

79. （略）

80. 奥运会被看作是对运动员能力的最大考验，也是对公平竞赛精神的体现。

 写作

As we know, when senior students graduate from school, most of their textbooks as well as reference books are thrown away or sold as waste paper, though they are still in good condition and of good value. What a great waste it is!

I suggest that we should recycle these books. On the one hand, recycling them can save a lot of natural resources, which are used to make textbooks. On the other hand, senior students may have made plenty of useful notes on the pages which are very helpful to the later users.

At present, the whole nation is called on to build an energy-saving society. I think it's certainly meaningful for long-term interests. In fact, in Australia and some other countries, recycling textbooks is quite popular, which gives us a good example.

Module 4

I.   1 – 5 DBADC   6 – 10 AABDD   11 – 15 BCDBB

II.   1 – 5 DACBC   6 – 10 ADBBC   11 – 15 DABDC   16 – 20 ABACD

III.   1 – 5 CBBDD   6 – 10 BACDB

IV. 1. Wax Apples Help Keep Doctors Away / The Healthy Fruit — Wax Apples

2. The sweetness of the wax apple depends on its ripeness.

3. good for your health

4. （略）

5. 可以把这种水果切成片，在盐水里腌一会儿，然后和黄瓜片、胡萝卜片一起油炸。

V. 1. My teaching style is similar to that of most of other teachers.

2. Until recently, this remote tribe had little contact with the outside world.

3. He is quite clever but he doesn't work hard. It is the same with his elder brother.

4. Children should experience things for themselves in order to learn from them.

5. In addition to the gold medal, each champion will be given 100,000 dollars.

6. The hot climate there didn't agree with him.

7. The building around the corner caught fire last night. The police are now looking into the matter.

8. I'm more than happy to pick you up at the airport tomorrow.

9. The examiners have given away the answers of the test.

10. The biggest challenge is to respect the traditions but to add my own style. The same is true of my second instrument, the *guzheng*.

Module 5

I.   1 – 5 AADBD   6 – 10 BADDB   11 – 15 CDABC
II.   1 – 5 ACADB   6 – 10 ABDAA   11 – 15 DCADC   16 – 20 BAACA
III. 1 – 5 CBDAD   6 – 10 BBAAC
IV.   1. H5N1 Virus Survives Longer

  2. One of the often overlooked facts about H5N1 virus is that it's more heat stable than people realise.

  3. in the coming summer months / in the warmer season

  4. No, we can't, because experts have already proved that the virus is more heat stable than people expected.

  5. 据了解，自从2003年底在亚洲再次出现以来，H5N1病毒已感染了205人，其中113人死亡。

V.   1. until; an end 2. in which; used to 3. feel like having 4. would be 5. on my doing

VI.   1. It was simply for that reason that I wouldn't tell him the truth.

  2. Before recording, I made sure that there was nobody else in the studio.

  3. The government has banned the use of chemical weapons.

  4. Fresh air is beneficial to one's health.

  5. My candle was almost burnt out when I heard the loud noise made by our plane.

Module 6

I.   1 – 5 DABAD   6 – 10 ADADB   11 – 15 CDADB
II.   1 – 5 CDABA   6 – 10 BDACB   11 – 15 DBACC   16 – 20 AABDC
III. 1 – 5 ACCBD   6 – 10 CBADD
IV.   1. Trying to Walk Straight / What Helps You Walk Straight?

  2. Eyesight helps us correct the direction of walking and leads us to the target.

  3. it is almost impossible for people to walk exactly straight / no one can walk straight

  4. No. It is because of a slight structural or functional imbalance of our limbs.

  5. 这时候，尽管眼睛提醒我们要走直线，但是大脑却听从于旋转中的耳朵，于是我们走的就不是直线了！

V.   1. It was under the tree which was planted five years ago that they met for the first time.

  2. While wandering in the street, he saw two armed policemen get involved in the fight.

3. He threw himself on the ground so that he escaped being killed by the bombs.

4. Chinese scientists have made many breakthroughs in the field of genetic research.

5. The king of the small state was forced to declare war on its neighbour.

6. He worked so hard that eventually he made himself ill.

7. The car was found abandoned near the village.

8. To my astonishment, the door opened of itself.

9. She gave us food and clothing and asked for nothing in return.

10. He demands to be told everything. / He demands that he be told everything.

复习检测题（二）

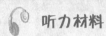 听力材料

Text 1

M: Do you rent rooms by week? You see, I'm not sure whether I'll stay for a whole month.

W: Yes. The rates are higher, though. It's $50 a week but only $160 a month.

Text 2

W: You should have known that it might do you harm if you don't cover your head on such a cold winter day.

M: It doesn't matter. I'm used to it.

Text 3

W: Are there any children in the classroom?

M: Yes, seven are reading at their desks and five are playing on the floor.

Text 4

M: Sam sent me a postcard yesterday.

W: I've got one from Tim but not from Sam...

Text 5

W: What time will you be back?

M: About 5:00, I suppose.

W: Would you please take valuables with you? We might move your luggage because we are going to paint the room. You can get your key to a new room at the reception desk when you are back.

M: OK. I see.

Text 6

W: Hello, George! I wanted to speak to you yesterday, but you weren't at your usual place for lunch.

M: No, I had a free day from the newspaper office because I worked so much overtime last week.

W: Oh, I see. You had a holiday.

M: Well, I stayed at home and looked after the baby.

W: What? You took care of the baby? Whose baby?

M: Oh, it was my sister's baby. She wanted to go shopping in the morning. So I stayed at home and did a lot of things.

W: Oh?

M: Yes. I mended my radio, washed a shirt and some socks and cleaned out the drawers of my desk.

W: I don't call that a holiday. I wanted to ask you to a concert last night. The one at the Town Hall near where we lived.

M: What a shame!

Text 7

W: Lovely weather!

M: Yes, really warm.

W: I've seen you before, haven't I?

M: Well, you may have. I've been here once or twice, for a walk in this quiet park. Do you live near here?

W: Yes. I live in one of those flats over there. What about you?

M: Oh, I'm staying with a family down near the station.

W: Are you on holiday?

M: Well...er... I'm here to improve my English. I'm from Greece, you see.

W: I didn't think you were English, but your English is very good.

M: Thank you very much.

Text 8

M: Have you travelled much in Britain?

W: No, not much. But I travel quite a lot in London every day.

M: What do you think of the London traffic?

W: I think the London underground is OK, because it's fast and comfortable. And I also like your buses, especially for short journeys.

M: But don't you think the buses are rather slow?

W: Yes, I do. Particularly during rush hours.

M: What about London taxis?

W: Taxis often get caught in traffic jams, and besides, they are too expensive.

M: Well, what do you think is the best way to travel in London?

W: Ur... The London underground is, I think.

Text 9

W: Good afternoon.

M: Good afternoon. Have a seat, please.

W: Thank you. I'm interested in the sales manager position you advertised yesterday.

M: Well. Have you been in the sales department for a long time?

W: Yes, for 10 years.

M: Then, why do you want to come to our company?

W: I am in a small company and chances of my future development are slight. Also I enjoy working at different places and meeting new friends.

M: Um, that sounds nice. But your future depends on your performance, not your age.

W: I understand.

M: Now. Please fill out this form.

W: OK. Thanks.

Text 10

It was raining heavily as I walked up the hill towards the station at 6 o'clock on a Saturday morning. At this early hour there wasn't much traffic and there weren't many people in sight. Just as I was crossing the road near the top of the hill, a car came round the corner. It was travelling very fast and the driver was obviously having difficulty in controlling it. Suddenly it went off the road, hit a lamppost and turned over.

At once I ran to the car to help the driver, but he was seriously hurt. A young woman hurried into the station and called the First Aid Centre while I took care of the driver. A number of other people gathered around the car, but there wasn't a great deal we could do. A policeman arrived a few minutes later and asked me a lot of questions about the accident. Shortly afterwards an ambulance arrived at high speed and took the driver away to hospital.

Later, I went to the hospital to see the driver. I was told that his operation had been successful and that he was getting better rapidly.

参考答案

1－5 BACAC	6－10 CABBC	11－15 BCABC	16－20 CBBAB
21－25 DCACA	26－30 DBCAD	31－35 CDCAB	
36－40 CACDB	41－45 ACBAC	46－50 ABCAD	51－55 CDBBC
56－60 ACBDB	61－65 ABCDA	66－70 DDCDB	71－75 DCBAD

76. Ways to Improve Reading Comprehension / Tips on Reading

77. Some prior knowledge will help him get prepared and make his way through tougher classroom texts.

78. Provide the right kinds of books / Buy him the proper / suitable books

79. （略）

80. 为了弄清楚一个词的意思而更为频繁地停顿，则会使他难以把注意力集中在对文章整体意义的理解上。

 写作

With the development of Internet, more and more people tend to send electronic cards instead of paper ones to their friends and relatives when important festivals such as New Year or Christmas are coming. Compared with the traditional cards, electronic cards are more interesting and lively, for you can get not only pictures but also sound and even animations. Besides, it's faster to send an electronic card. There are many websites where different cards are available. If none of these cards is of any interest to you, you can design cards of unique style using Flash or other software by yourself. More importantly, with the popularity of electronic cards, less paper is used for making paper cards, which contributes to the environmental protection.

顺序选修7

Module 1

I. 1−5 BDAAC   6−10 BCCBD   11−15 ABDBD

II. 1−5 DBACA   6−10 BCBAC   11−15 ACABD   16−20 CBCAB

III. 1−5 CDADB   6−10 CDBCA

IV. 1. Blood Types

2. Without enough healthy blood, the body won't get the oxygen and energy it needs.

3. If it's negative

4. They must make sure the person gets the right type of blood because getting blood of the wrong type can make a person sick.

5. 这是一种可以了解一个人的血液中是否含有Rh蛋白质的方法。

V. Dear Li Qiang,

It's already one year since we graduated from No. 1 Middle School. Have you ever thought of seeing all of your old classmates again some day? I'm now planning a get-together of our class.

The get-together is on July 20. We will gather at 10 am. Please come on time. Bring something interesting to surprise everybody if you like. We are all looking forward to seeing you.

The address of the place of our get-together is No. 20 Zhongshan Street. Take the No. 22 bus to get there. You can't miss it.

Please inform us if you can't come. Write to the above address or call me up at 94673413 and leave the message by July 10.

Yours,

Chen Wei

Module 2

I.   1—5 CADCC   6—10 BCBBB   11—15 CABAB
II. 1—5 BAADD   6—10 DDAAD   11—15 DCADA   16—20 DDBCA
III. 1—5 BDCAC   6—10 DCBCB
IV. 1. University students may not be taking the best option.

2. dropped out of university

3. It's possible to succeed without getting a degree.

4. People can make mistakes when they choose what to study.

5. 在英国，大学的录取率是申请者的1/2到1/12不等，这就意味着，在大学最好的专业上竞争激烈。

V.

Chaoyang Middle School

August 1

Dear Liu Ying,

I'm very pleased to learn that you have successfully passed the college entrance exam this year and have been admitted into Peking University with honours. Please allow me to offer my most sincere congratulations to you on this happy occasion.

You have all along been working hard at your studies and excelling in almost all the subjects. Your success shows that only hard work can yield good results.

I take this opportunity to express my determination to learn from you.

Wish you greater achievements in your college years.

Yours,

Li Ping

Module 3

I.   1—5 CCBBA   6—10 DCADB   11—15 AAABD
II. 1—5 DBCAB   6—10 ABACB   11—15 DCCBC   16—20 BCACD
III. 1—5 AADAC   6—10 CDCBD
IV. 1. An Auction of a House

2. So many buyers took part in the auction that the price of the house was soon increased by 20,000 pounds and it was still rising.

3. receive the best care from me / be taken best care of by me

4. Because the old man will be able to live a happy life with the young man's considerate care.

5. 老人深陷在沙发里，心情沉重，这是可以理解的。

V. Dear Peter,

I am writing to ask whether you are able to do me a favour.

I want to have a pen friend, hopefully a girl in her early twenties, and with interests similar to mine. In my opinion, she is someone who is interested in travelling, swimming, playing table tennis or some other sports. Besides, it would be perfect if she has a pet dog as I have kept one at home for some time. With such a pen friend, I hope I can share with her our experiences in travelling, taking care of pets, or whatever we have in common. And I believe I will improve my English and learn more about her country by doing so.

I look forward to hearing from you soon.

Best regards.

Yours,
Li Hua

复习检测题（一）

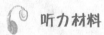 听力材料

Text 1

M: Do you have any particular views on TV programmes?

W: Generally speaking, they are educational except too much violence sometimes.

Text 2

M: I have spent three days preparing for the exam. I will do anything as long as it can let me pass the exam.

W: Do you think that can help? You've been absent from school for over a month.

Text 3

M: I just heard the boat wouldn't arrive until tomorrow morning.

W: Gosh, what can we do to kill the next 11 hours?

Text 4

W: I've been working on the problem for a long time. But I still can't work it out.

M: Take it easy. You might as well do something else now. Maybe you can find some clues later.

Text 5

M: Professor White, I'd like to have your advice on my article.

W: It's good except for some spelling mistakes. What's more, the second paragraph is about another topic. It should be crossed out.

Text 6

M: How much freedom do your parents give you?

W: Quite a lot. I mean I'm allowed out most evenings. On weekdays, I have to be back by 9:30. But on weekends I can stay out till 11:00.

M: What about money? Do you have any pocket money?

W: Yes, my parents give me two pounds a week.

M: Is there anything you'd like to do which your parents won't let you?

W: Yes, I wanted to go on holiday this coming summer with my boyfriend, but they say I have to wait till I am 17.

M: Do you think that's unfair?

W: I don't know...he is very responsible, I mean my boyfriend, even my parents think so, and I don't see how two years is going to make much difference.

Text 7

W: I'm thinking about transferring out of State College into another school in mid-spring.

M: After a year and a half, how come? I thought you like it here.

W: I do, but our Commercial Art Department doesn't give bachelor's degrees.

M: So where do you want to go?

W: I wouldn't mind going to West University. It is famous for commercial art. But I'm feeling it's very selective.

M: But you've got good grades in the three semesters you've been in the State College, haven't you?

W: Yeah. Mostly As and Bs.

M: So what were you worried about? Just ask your professors to write letters of recommendation for you and you'll be set.

Text 8

M: Welcome back! I didn't see you in the maths class on Friday.

W: I wasn't here on Friday. My class went on a field trip to look at some of the different rock formations here in California. Our last stop was Death Valley; in fact we camped there last night.

M: Death Valley! But that's a desert. Wasn't it much too hot for camping?

W: No, not really. It gets hot during the day, but it cools off very quickly at night.

M: Well, did you enjoy the trip?

W: Yes, very much. The desert is nicer than you would think. You really should go and see it some time.

Text 9

W: Hello! Come in and sit down.

M: Thank you. Here I've got a small present for you for Christmas.

W: How nice of you! Let's open it right now. Oh, how lovely it is!

M: This small basket will be just right for candy and some other little things.

W: Where did you get it?

M: It's from China. Two months ago, I went to China with my parents and I bought it for you in Beijing, the capital of China.

W: From China? Thank you so much. No wonder it's so lovely. China's famous for her handicrafts. Let me see what it is made of.

M: It's woven of bamboo.

W: Really? How skillfully it's done! I'll put it right here. Everybody can see it when coming to my office.

M: I'm very glad you like it.

Text 10

It was a lovely spring day. Harry went to a park and took some photos. When he finished, he decided to stay a little longer. All the seats in the park were full, so he lay down on the grass, putting the camera beside him. The sun was so warm that he soon fell asleep.

When he woke up, he found his camera was gone. He told a policeman in the park about it. The policeman told Harry that three other people had lost cameras there that week.

Harry published an ad in the paper the next day. It read, "Bring me your cameras. I will buy them and offer a good price. Come and see me at No. 14, Lincoln Road every Sunday from 9:00 until 6:00 pm."

Two policemen came to Harry's house on Sunday. Harry gave them a piece of paper with the number of his camera on it. At 10 o'clock, a man came with some cameras for sale. Harry picked up an old black camera and looked at the number printed on it. It was his! Then he called the policemen who were waiting in the kitchen.

参考答案

| 1—5 | BCACC | 6—10 | AABBC | 11—15 | CABBB | 16—20 | BCBCA |

1—5 BCACC   6—10 AABBC   11—15 CABBB   16—20 BCBCA
21—25 DBACB   26—30 BCBCD   31—35 ACBBC
36—40 BACDB   41—45 DCDBA   46—50 BDBBA   51—55 BCADA
56—60 BDCCB   61—65 CBADB   66—70 BDCAB   71—75 DADBA

76. Tips That Can Help You Succeed on Campus (in College) / How to Get the Most Out of Your College Education / How to Live a Successful Life in College

77. Don't cut off all social contacts, which are as vital to surviving in college as reading.

78. asking ways /directions

79. （略）

80. 有些教授在讲课时会讨论书中没有但与考试有关的内容。

Traffic in the City

With the development of economy, traffic is becoming one of the greatest problems of a modern city.

One problem is pollution. The waste gases from the exhaust pipes are great enemies to the air. Another problem is crowdedness. Much time is wasted every day due to traffic jams. Furthermore, traffic accidents are real-life disasters. Traffic has become one of the nightmares of people living in cities.

To build highways and bridges only works out part of the problem. Cars and buses should be improved to release less waste gases. Governments should encourage citizens to take public transportation. People should obey traffic rules. Only when we pay enough attention to the problem will it be possible for us to solve it.

Module 4

I.   1 – 5 CCDCB   6 – 10 AADBB   11 – 15 DCCBD

II. 1 – 5 CABDA   6 – 10 BDACD   11 – 15 CCBAB   16 – 20 DBCDA

III. 1 – 5 DCBCA   6 – 10 BADAC

IV. 1. Homecoming Day

2. Watching the football game and voting for homecoming queen or king.

3. homecoming queen or king

4. Because they come to meet their teachers or classmates and have fun.

5. 有些标语祝愿球队好运，还有很多欢迎所有毕业生的标语。

V.   **How to protect Your Eyesight**

As we know, "Eyes are windows of the soul." Everyone understands the importance of the eyes. But now more and more students are getting nearsighted. So how to protect the eyes remains a question. Here are some advice.

First, you should not keep your eyes working for a long time continually. Second, when reading, you should keep the book about a foot away from you. After reading for an hour or two, you'd better have a rest by looking in the distance. Third, you ought to remember not to read in dim light or in the sun. Don't read in a moving bus or in bed. Finally, doing eye exercises will help you keep good eyesight.

In a word, one must form good habits to keep good eyesight.

Module 5

I.   1 – 5 ACABA   6 – 10 DABDC   11 – 15 CDABB

II. 1 – 5 CACDB   6 – 10 ADCBA   11 – 15 CBDBA   16 – 20 DBDAB

III. 1 – 5 BDBAB　　6 – 10 BDCDD

IV. 1. It's about an introduction to a book.

2. To anyone who wants to develop leadership of a child. / To anyone who wants to bring out the leader inside a young person.

3. isn't only for parents

4. A brief introduction / guidance to the second section of the book.

5. 我写本书的目的是：当你尝试开发孩子内在的领导潜质时，为你提供一些实用的方法。

V.　We all feel the stress of modern life. How do we get rid of the stress? How can we live happier? Maybe different people have different ways. My friends Mary Yan, Jack Park and Paul Wilson have their own ways to fight against stress.

Mary says the best way to fight against stress is to do yoga for one hour every morning. She says she does that every day and she never feels stressed.

Jack insists that the best cure for stress is laughter. He says if you laugh for five minutes every day, you will feel relaxed.

Paul's suggestion is to have more sleep. He says people should take a short nap every day for a few minutes, which will help relieve stress.

What's your idea?

Module 6

I.　1 – 5 DBABA　　6 – 10 CCCCB　　11 – 15 CDDAD

II.　1 – 5 DBACC　　6 – 10 ACABA　　11 – 15 DCDBA　　16 – 20 ACBDB

III. 1 – 5 BDBDB　　6 – 10 ABCCD

IV. 1. It's about high school and college students' work as volunteers.

2. They read books to the old people. Or they visit them and play games with them or listen to their problems.

3. who help bring happiness to others

4. （略）

5. 每个城市都有一些俱乐部，男孩儿和女孩儿们可以在那里做游戏或学做手工艺品。

V.　Recently our class has had a discussion about whether we should have computer classes. I think we, the students of Senior 3, should have computer classes. In my opinion, computers are helpful for our study, especially in improving our English. For example, they can improve our English listening skill.

If we make good use of them, computers can enrich our life as well. With them, we can surf the Internet and enjoy ourselves — playing games, chatting, finding and communicating with e-pals, searching for useful information, etc. However, we can't spend too much time on computers, or they will have a bad effect on our study. So at the same time we should learn to control ourselves when using the computers.

复习检测题（二）

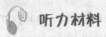

Text 1

M: You look nice with your hair done.

W: Thanks. The hairdresser is a good one.

Text 2

W: I'm tired of eating the same terrible foods all the time.

M: There's nothing we could do as patients.

Text 3

M: Let's go to the store.

W: You go on ahead — I'll come along later.

Text 4

W: I wonder what happened to Betty. I don't see her anywhere.

M: I don't know. She told me she would be here at the play tonight.

Text 5

M: I suppose one reason so many tourists come here is that everything is so cheap.

W: Cheap? Nothing is really cheap in America.

Text 6

M: Hello, Mona, this is Peter.

W: Hi, Peter. What can I do for you?

M: I need directions on how to get to the football stadium.

W: Oh, it's very simple. First, go south on Highway 25 for five miles until you come to a large restaurant called Little Bear. Turn left at the restaurant and continue for a few miles more and you will come right to the stadium. There are plenty of signs once you pass the restaurant and they will take you right to the stadium.

M: Do you think the stadium will be very crowded?

W: Well, the radio announced that all tickets for the game tonight have been sold out. That means you should leave about an hour before the game starts.

M: Thanks for your help, Mona. I'll take your advice.

Text 7

W: Hi, Jack! Have you been to the Grand Theatre?

M: Certainly! It's a wonderful place. If I lived in London, I'd probably go there every week.

W: Yes, I agree. I have already been there four or five times. I'm going to see *Swan Lake* at the theatre this Sunday.

M: Oh, are you? Have you booked a seat?

W: No, not yet.

M: Well, if I were you, I'd book immediately.

W: Is that so? Then let's go and see it together, shall we?

M: What a pity I won't be here! I've already arranged to go to the airport.

Text 8

W: Radio has really changed a lot since we were young. It used to be the major source of fun for the family.

M: Nowadays when you turn on the radio, either you hear music, talk shows or news.

W: Fortunately, you can choose the kind of music you want to hear.

M: Yes, and there are a lot of different points of view when you listen to talk shows. I usually enjoy listening to them. I particularly like it when a caller disagrees with the talk show host. I like to hear how the host will defend his views.

W: Some talk show hosts are very rude to those who have opposing ideas. I really find that terrible.

M: It seems that people only listen to the radio when they are driving in their car.

W: That's true for me, but I know that my husband listens to it while he is working at home.

M: Now that I think about it, I realise that a lot of stores have the radio playing.

W: It's still a useful and pleasant form of communication.

Text 9

M: Darling, I've decided to become a vegetarian. From now on, I will stop eating meat.

W: Why?

M: Because people nowadays eat too much meat and it's healthier to eat less.

W: Is this another one of your crazy ideas? It won't last a week! Last month, in order to lose weight, you decided to jog to work every morning. That only lasted a week because every day you were late for work!

M: That's not the only reason why I stopped! I stopped jogging because I pulled a muscle in my leg.

W: Well, what about the bicycle?

M: What bicycle?

W: Exactly! You can hardly remember you own a bike as it's been locked away in the garage ever since you bought it.

M: That's not completely true! As soon as the weather improves, I'm going to start using it again.

Text 10

When Tom was a small boy, he often could not have breakfast or lunch. He wanted to buy some bread but he didn't have any money.

His father died when he was very young. His mother was often very sick and could not take care of him and his brother, Mike. Both of them had to work to help their sick mother.

Though he was very young, he had a big dream. His wish was to become a great man in the world of films. He worked hard to sing and dance well.

One day a man came to him and asked, "Will you work for my film?" "Certainly!" He answered. And he did his best in it. Many years later, this very boy was among the most famous people in the world. He made many interesting films and was liked by a lot of people.

 参考答案

1－5 BABAB   6－10 CACAB   11－15 CABBA   16－20 CBACA
21－25 BCDAD   26－30 ADBAC   31－35 DAABD
36－40 CBADB   41－45 DACBB   46－50 CADBA   51－55 BDBCA
56－60 DBABD   61－65 ABBCC   66－70 DBCAB   71－75 ABBAD

76. A news report about China's South Pole exploration.

77. No. One of the members had to quit because of serious altitude sickness.

78. Difficult / Impossible to reach.

79. The first group to reach a place is responsible for leading scientific work there.

80. 登上 Dome-A 的顶峰并在上面进行科学研究将会给人类的极地探险事业带来突破。

✏️ 写作

Dear Aunt,

First of all, I'd like to thank you for your hearty invitation.

Nowadays more and more Chinese secondary school students choose to study abroad. But my parents are not sure whether it is good for me to do so. In their opinion, I'm still too young to take good care of myself. As for me, I would like to receive my college education in China and then go to America for further study.

One reason is that I don't think my English is good enough to handle all the courses in the American universities right now. More importantly, the tuition will be a heavy burden for my family. I hope I will do some part-time jobs to help myself complete my post-graduate education abroad when I am older. I hope to show that I am quite independent.

What do you think of my idea? I'm looking forward to your opinion.

Yours,

Li Hua

319

Module 1

I. 1－5 DBADC   6－10 CCABD   11－15 AACCC

II. 1－5 BDACC   6－10 ADAAD   11－15 CABAC   16－20 DAACB

III. 1－5 DCBBA   6－10 CACCD

IV. 1. Beaver Goes to Hospital to Get New Teeth

2. A beaver's front teeth grow continually throughout its life and require constant biting to keep them at a healthy length.

3. are expected to grow back

4. A beaver lost her four front teeth in a car accident. The vets of a hospital treated her carefully and her lost teeth were expected to grow back within three months. Then she would be taken to wildlife recovering centre for a long-term care and sent back to nature.

5. 这一次，一只在车祸中丢掉了四颗门牙的海狸被送往华盛顿州立大学的兽医教学医院接受治疗。

V. As can be seen from the caricature, more and more icebergs are melting, leaving almost nowhere for penguins to live. So the mother and the son penguins have to move into a fridge. Seeing the picture, I can't help thinking what has caused the phenomenon and who is to blame.

In recent years, we may feel that the climate is getting warmer and warmer, which is caused by global warming. In fact, people nowadays have suffered a lot from disasters related to global warming, of which the worst is the icebergs are melting and the sea level is rising. In the future, perhaps many major cities in the world will disappear like Atlantis and we human beings will also be thrown into the danger of total destruction.

Faced with the situation, in the interests of us and our later generations, we must make immediate and continual efforts to stop global warming before it is too late. We can't wait any longer. Do it right now.

Module 2

I. 1－5 CCBBC   6－10 CBCBD   11－15 BAABB

II. 1－5 BCDAD   6－10 BACCD   11－15 BDCDA   16－20 BACDA

III. 1－5 CADCB   6－10 DBADA

IV. 1. Agassi's Changes (in Sports and Life) / Changes in Sports and Life / Change for the Better

2. Eventually, though, injuries and his bad attitude caught up with him.

3. thinking about others / to think more about others

4. （略）

5. 但是，他（阿加西）在职业生涯中的巨大改变可能是他最大的成就。

V. The Celebration of Western Festivals

Now people in growing numbers are beginning to realise that they prefer enjoying Western festivals. A lot of reasons are responsible for this phenomenon. To begin with, the youth are exposed to the international trends, and they are partly influenced. What's more, the Western views have been spread widely. Moreover, people nowadays enjoy the freedom to have a taste of various cultures. In other words, they may celebrate festivals they like besides the traditional festivals in China.

Obviously, this has some effects on our life. For example, some people worry that the Western festivals are to replace the Chinese traditions. Others, however, think the policy of "let it be" will do more good than harm in this field. In my opinion, it is necessary to take some effective measures to prevent the negative effects of the Western festivals.

Module 3

I.　1－5 ACCBC　　6－10 ADAAB　　11－15 ADABA

II.　1－5 DAABC　　6－10 DABCB　　11－15 CDBAB　　16－20 CDACA

III.　1－5 CDCAB　　6－10 CBACB

IV.　1. Using TV as a Reward May Get Kids to Exercise

2. Overweight children may be more inclined to get outside and get moving when their TV time depends on it.

3. change both their exercise and eating habits

4. Too much TV time promotes weightgain not just by keeping kids away from exercise, but also by encouraging them to snack more.

5. 专家认为，日益严重的儿童肥胖问题与他们过多地看电视或玩电脑密不可分，而且这时他们通常都拿着高热量的零食。

V. Health

Health is far more important than wealth. Good health enables us to enjoy our life and achieve what we hope for in our career. On the contrary, poor health tends to deprive us of our interest in everything. How to stay healthy concerns everyone, though we have advanced medicine. When we discuss this, we should bear some fundamental principles in mind.

Firstly, it is very important for us to eat plenty of fruits and vegetables because they can provide us with rich vitamins. We need to keep a balanced diet and avoid food with too much sugar and fat. Secondly, we'd better exercise everyday to keep fit. Finally, we have to get rid of those bad habits that damage our health, such as drinking and smoking.

In conclusion, if we follow the above advice, it's very likely for us to lead a healthy and happy life.

听力材料

Text 1

M: Wow, what a lot of food!

W: Sure, in China we usually have plenty of food on the dinner table during Spring Festival.

Text 2

M: I don't think we can find a better hotel around here at this time.

W: Let's walk a little farther to see if there is another one. I just can't bear the traffic noise here.

Text 3

W: Excuse me, would you mind if I sit here?

M: Of course not. I will move my books.

W: Thanks. I didn't expect so many people to turn up.

M: There will be more coming.

Text 4

W: It's so cold outside that it is impossible for us to go out.

M: Yes, the radio says that it will last a week or so.

Text 5

M: Shall we go to the cinema this evening?

W: Oh, sorry. I'm afraid I can't. I'm seeing my mum off at the airport at 7 o'clock.

Text 6

M: Good morning.

W: Good morning. What can I do for you?

M: I'd like a ticket to London, please.

W: Round trip?

M: No, one way.

W: OK. That'll be 22 pounds.

M: Twenty-two? Last time I took this bus it was only 20.

W: I know. The rate went up this month.

M: Does the bus still leave at 2:15?

W: 2:15 at Gate 11. You ought to be at the door by 2 o'clock, though. The driver usually begins loading 15 minutes before the trip.

M: Fine.

W: Do you want to check in your suitcases?

M: Just two. I'll carry the other one with me.

W: That's good. We only check in two of them anyway.

M: OK. Thanks a lot.

W: You are welcome. Have a good trip.

Text 7

M: What shall we do this weekend?

W: Did you have something special in mind?

M: No, not really. I just thought it might be fun to do something new.

W: Do something for a change, you mean?

M: Yes, something different. I need a change.

W: I usually go shopping and have my hair done during the weekends. And you usually watch the football games on TV.

M: Yes, you often have tea with your friends. And I sometimes play cards with my friends. We seldom do anything together. It's quite unlike when we were first married.

W: Now I've got an idea. Autumn is the best season in Beijing. Why don't we go for a picnic this weekend? You'll invite your friends and I'll invite mine. We'll go together.

M: Good idea! I will see about the car and you can prepare the food. But are you sure you really want all our friends to come along?

Text 8

W: What do you think of the students in our class?

M: I love those children. They are so lovely.

W: They love you too. They said that you were the best teacher that they had ever had.

M: When I first came into the classroom, all the students stood up and looked at me. They all had smiles on their faces.

W: It seems that they began loving you from the very beginning.

M: Right. They are also very active. No one is shy.

W: That is why you became friends with each other.

M: Yes, I think so. I really don't want to leave. But I have to because of my parents.

W: They will miss you.

M: I will miss them too.

Text 9

M: Do you like animals?

W: Yes, very much. I'd like to have a dog for a pet but it's difficult when you live in a flat. Dogs need plenty of space to run around in, don't you think so?

M: I agree. Have you thought of getting a cat?

W: That's a good idea. A friend of mine has a beautiful cat. Maybe he'll tell me where I can get one. Cats are easy to look after and are good company.

M: You are right. They are clean too.

W: Yes, my friend's cat is always cleaning herself. If cats are well fed and loved, they're easy to keep.

M: You should get a small kitten if possible.

W: Yes, I will. I know it's difficult for older cats to settle into a new home. I'm quite excited about having a cat to look after.

Text 10

Today I'm going to tell you something about table manners in different countries. I think you already know that people in different countries have different ways of doing things. Something that is rude in one country may be quite polite in another. For example, in Britain you mustn't lift your bowl to your mouth when you are having some liquid food. And in Japan you needn't worry about making a noise when you have it. It shows that you are enjoying it. But that is considered bad manners in Britain.

In Britain we try not to put our hands on the table at all during a meal. In Mexico, however, guests are expected to keep their hands on the table throughout a meal. But it is in the Arab countries that you really must be careful with your hands. You see, in Arab countries you mustn't eat with your left hand. This is considered to be very impolite. So, what should you do if you visit another country? Well, you needn't worry. You can ask the native people there to help you or just watch carefully and try to do as they do, not as you do at home.

 参考答案

1—5 BCACB	6—10 CCBAC	11—15 BCACC	16—20 ACCBA
21—25 DABAA	26—30 ABABD	31—35 ADBAB	
36—40 CACDC	41—45 CAAAB	46—50 ACDCD	51—55 DBCDD
56—60 DBCAC	61—65 DCBAD	66—70 BCDDA	71—75 CBCAB

76. Courage / Take Courage / What's Courage

77. Courage is standing up for what you believe in without worrying about the opinions of others.

78. being responsible for

79. （略）

80. 勇气就是在事与愿违时保持积极的心态，把失败看作是崭新的开始，而不是结束。

写作

Nowadays, with the development of China's economy and the enhancement of China's status in the international affairs, the Chinese language has become more and more popular in the world. As a result, many countries offer Chinese courses in colleges or universities. Meanwhile, there are an increasing number of overseas students coming to study Chinese and the Chinese culture. What's more, foreigners actively take part in HSK tests. All these are pushing the

"Chinese Craze", which is regarded as a bridge connecting the 5,000-year-old civilisation of China with the outside world.

I'm proud of being a Chinese. In my opinion, language is the main tool for human intercommunication as well as a reflection of its culture. After all, China has made major achievements in all aspects recently, which further strengthen the "Chinese Craze". I'll spare no efforts in learning my lessons and developing skills to make our country more powerful and beautiful.

Module 4

I.   1–5 CACBC   6–10 BCACB   11–15 BDBBA

II. 1–5 ADDBD   6–10 DDAAD   11–15 DCDBA   16–20 CADDA

III. 1–5 DBBAC   6–10 BDDAC

IV. 1. Safe Tips Online / Safe Tips on the Internet (for Young People)

2. It could be someone trying to trick you, some kind of weirdo, or someone really dangerous.

3. you don't know who it's from / you are not sure of it / you suspect it

4. （略）

5. 如果你安排与只(在网上)聊过一次的人见面，记住他们所说的可能与实际不符，所以一定要在公共场所和他们见面，并且要有成年人陪同。

V.   The students of Class 3 had a discussion about whether it is necessary to start learning English from childhood. Some of them think that English learning should start from childhood. As little boys and girls have a very good memory, they can learn a lot of English words by heart. This will help them lay a solid foundation for their future English learning. But others do not agree. They think young children have to learn Chinese pinyin at school. If they study Chinese pinyin and English at the same time, it will be very easy for them to mix them up. This will do a lot of harm not only to their Chinese learning but also to their future English learning. At the end of the discussion, the students did not arrive at any agreement.

Module 5

I.   1–5 CCDCA   6–10 BDCDC   11–15 DCABC

II. 1–5 AABCB   6–10 ACBBD   11–15 ACBDA   16–20 CBCCB

III. 1–5 DABDD   6–10 BAADD

IV. 1. Gratitude / The Value of Gratitude / Practise Gratitude! / Be Grateful!

2. One single serving of gratitude is often enough to open the heart, energise the body, warm the bones, put a spring in your step, start you humming, and make you smile like a baby.

3. something to receive

4. （略）

5. 在实践感恩之前，我们对其一无所知，似乎没什么值得我们感激。

V.　　Among all the living things, animals are our closest relatives. So it is but normal that scientists should use animals to test new drugs and to study certain diseases. Some people feel that it is unkind to use animals for scientific tests because that puts the animals under stress, pain and even death. They argue that modern computers can create environments similar to that of the real human body which can then be used for research and testing. However, I think it is very necessary to use animals for testing because we need a real body environment to see how certain drugs react and what the diseases cause. Not all the conditions can be imitated by computers. But it may be dangerous using a person for such tests. Moreover, there are laws to regulate the use of animals in research. So there is nothing to worry about too much.

Module 6

I.　　1 – 5 BABAB　　6 – 10 CDADA　　11 – 15 BABAC

II.　　1 – 5 BDCBA　　6 – 10 CACDC　　11 – 15 AADBD　　16 – 20 DABCC

III.　　1 – 5 BCADC　　6 – 10 DABAC

IV.　　1. How to Read Fast

2. These are habits which should have been outgrown long ago.

3. slows your speed

4. （略）

5. 一些不太明显的习惯同样会影响阅读速度。

V.　　**English Poetry**

More and more Chinese people are interested in reading English poetry at present. Why do they like it so much?

English poetry often follows special patterns of rhythm and rhyme, and it plays with sounds, words and grammar more than any other form of literature. Despite its short history, there is a lot of good English poetry around. In the early 20th century, much English poetry was brought in and translated into Chinese.

Reading English poetry can bring people from different places and different times together. What's more, English poems can be bridges between the East and the West, which can help us understand each other better.

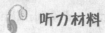 听力材料

Text 1

M: Do you think you could possibly work late?

W: Work late?

M: I'm afraid there's some work we really must finish this evening. I can't possibly do it myself.

W: I suppose so, if you really think it's necessary.

M: Thank you. We'll have to work about an hour's overtime. That's all.

Text 2

M: What can I do if I can't finish reading it in one week?

W: You may come and renew it.

Text 3

W: How much will it cost for my daughter and me to go to Wuhan?

M: That's 100 *yuan* for you and half of the price for your daughter, as she is below one metre.

Text 4

W: Oh, we're just in time. It hasn't started yet.

M: What are our seat numbers?

W: Row 10, Numbers 18 and 20.

M: That'll be a bit further towards the front.

W: Here we are. Those two over there.

Text 5

M: Linda, your brother will go to London for the summer holidays, won't he?

W: I'm not sure. But where are you going?

M: Oh, I got a letter from Ken. He said he will go back to Canada and he asked me to go with him.

W: Really? That's a good idea.

Text 6

W: Soft Rock Restaurant. May I help you?

M: Hello. What time does your dinner start this evening?

W: At 6 o'clock, sir. And we close an hour before midnight.

M: OK. I'd like to reserve a table for four, please.

W: For what time?

M: Around 7 o'clock. A Mr Stone will be there 20 minutes earlier.

W: OK. Could I have your name, please?

M: Yes. Dennis Bryant.

W: A table for four for this evening at around 7 o'clock for Dennis Bryant?

M: That's right. Please let Mr Stone stay and wait if I'm a few minutes late.

W: With pleasure. Thank you then, sir.

M: Thank you. Bye.

Text 7

M: Would you like to go to the cinema tonight?

W: What's on?

M: There is a horror film at the Odeon and there is a Western at the Classic.

W: Yes. Let's go to see the Western. Who's in it?

M: John Wayne, I think.

W: Wait a minute. It's Monday today, isn't it? I go to night school on Mondays. I can't go to the cinema tonight.

M: What about tomorrow?

W: Yes. Tomorrow is fine.

M: See you tomorrow then.

W: See you tomorrow.

Text 8

M: Is there anything wrong with you, Miss Scott?

W: Oh, doctor. I hurt my left foot this morning.

M: How did it happen?

W: I was doing some cleaning at home this morning. When I was cleaning the window, I fell off the chair and hurt my foot.

M: Let me see your foot.

W: Is it serious?

M: No, I don't think so. Don't worry.

W: I can't walk well now. Do you think any of the bones here is broken?

M: Of course not. You'll be all right in a few days.

W: That means I can go to the dance party next weekend, right?

M: Yes, you can.

Text 9

W: Jack, would you please read this letter of application I've just written? I'd like to have your opinion.

M: I'd be glad to tell you what I think.

W: If you don't think it's any good, please say so. I really want to get this job.

M: It looks fine to me. But I have one suggestion.

W: Good. I'm interested in your advice.

M: If I were you, I'd change the beginning. You should write about your education first.

W: Good idea, Jack. What do you think about the second part?

M: Well, I'm afraid it's too short. You should include much more information about your work experience.

W: You're right. I'll change it. How do you feel about the last part of the letter?

M: Very good, I should say. But personally I believe a business letter should end with "very truly yours", not "sincerely".

Text 10

Good morning, ladies and gentlemen. I want to take a little of your time to let you know about the International Friends Club. We're a sort of social club for people from different countries.

It's quite a big club — we have about 500 members at the moment, and we're growing all the time. We organise many kinds of events. We have social get-togethers and sports events. Every day except Thursday we have a language evening. People can come and practise the languages they are learning — you know, over a drink or something. We have different languages on different evenings. Monday — Spanish; Tuesday — Italian; Wednesday — German; and Friday — French. On Thursday we usually have a meal in a restaurant for anyone who wants to come. If you are interested, just give us your name and address, and we'll send you the form and some more information. If you join now, you can have the first month for free.

参考答案

1—5 BACBC	6—10 AAAAC	11—15 CCACA	16—20 BCBCB
21—25 DADDA	26—30 CBBAB	31—35 CCCAB	
36—40 ABCBB	41—45 DABDD	46—50 BCCBC	51—55 CDCBD
56—60 CBCDB	61—65 DAAAA	66—70 BCDCC	71—75 BDCBA

76. History of VOA's Special English

77. But during the years its role has expanded.

78. whose native / first language

79. （略）

80. 它能提供给听众，甚至那些以英语为母语的人，在其他地方找不到的信息。

Dear editor,

I am a Senior 3 student. Recently, we have carried out a survey — "To whom do you go when in trouble?" The results are as follows.

Sixty-one percent of the students surveyed consider friends and schoolmates as their ideal listeners when they have trouble. The reason is that they are in the same age group and have a better understanding of each other. Another 22 percent choose teachers and parents to talk to. They think that teachers and parents are rich in life and educational experience. Nevertheless, there are still 17 percent who don't share their troubles at all. They hold the view that their troubles are none of others' business or they just find it hard to communicate with others.

It seems clear from the response that some students lack communication with others, which can be bad for the development of their body and mind. In view of this, I think, teachers and parents should work hand in hand to change those students' attitude and help them improve interpersonal skills.

Yours sincerely,

Zhang Ming

总复习检测题（一）

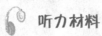 听力材料

Text 1

M: I've already asked Susan three times to come with us and she said no.

W: Forget it then.

Text 2

W: I would have come back a week earlier, but the weather was so bad, we couldn't travel.

M: That's a real pity. The carnival lasted a fortnight and only finished yesterday.

Text 3

M: I'll pick you up at half past ten tomorrow morning.

W: How long will the journey last?

M: It's a three and a half hour drive. And we should give ourselves 40 minutes to have lunch.

Text 4

M: Mum, my favourite TV show is on this evening.

W: But first you must finish your writing.

M: You promised to help me.

W: No problem. But supper is ready now.

Text 5

M: That's a nice jacket. I really like the design — and the colour.

W: It's my son's. He got it as a birthday present.

M: It's a bit large, isn't it?

W: Large? You just can't imagine what a giant he is!

Text 6

M: Hello.

W: Hello, Peter. This is Mary speaking.

M: Oh, hello, Mary. How are you?

W: Fine. Listen, Peter. Do you still have that old bike of Jenny's which she doesn't use anymore?

M: Yes. Why?

W: Well, you know, it's our Laura's birthday next month, and she needs a bike. And I thought that if Jenny doesn't use hers anymore, perhaps I could buy it and paint it and give it to Laura as a birthday present.

M: That's OK with me. Of course I must ask Jenny, but I'm sure she will be glad to help you.

W: That's terribly nice of you.

M: When do you want it?

W: Shall I drop in tomorrow?

M: Fine.

W: And will you ask Jenny?

M: All right. See you tomorrow.

W: Bye then, and thanks.

M: Bye.

Text 7

W: Morning.

M: Morning.

W: But...but how are you today? You don't look very well.

M: I have a sore throat, and I cough, especially at night. So I can't sleep very well.

W: Oh! Have you got a temperature?

M: Yeah, I've got a fever.

W: Um, I think you've got the flu. I suggest you take a day off and go back home to have a good rest.

M: Sounds great. But I have to prepare my speech for the conference. You know, it's only five days from now. And yesterday they asked me for the summary.

W: Did you go to the clinic?

M: I had no time for it.

W: Take good care of yourself.

M: Sure. Thank you.

M: Right. Now, what did I get? Er, I got some cream.

W: OK. Fine.

M: I could only get single cream but I don't think you actually specified what you wanted on the list.

W: Dear! Well, I suppose yes. I can beat it up with some sugar and egg yolk or something and make it thicker. What else have you got?

M: I've got some strawberries.

W: Yeah.

M: But just a few because they were a bit expensive.

W: How much were they?

M: These?

W: Yeah.

M: Mmm. Would you believe 40 dollars?

W: Well, all right. OK.

M: Here you go. Now, ah, the main course. Here we are — chicken. It's quite a big one.

W: OK.

M: Four pounds eight ounces. Does that do?

W: Hmm. Well, I suppose it is the best you could get. What else have you got? Did you get the tomatoes?

M: Yes. They're somewhere down here.

Text 9

W: Hi, John. Why did you come to school an hour early?

M: I want to get a front row seat and revise one more time before the test because I failed this course last term. Why are you here early?

W: I get a lift to school and arrive at this time every day. You seem to be nervous about your lessons. Have you finished your revision?

M: I've been studying day and night for the last week. If I don't get an "A" in this class, I won't get the scholarship. How come you seem so calm?

W: This class is really a review for me. This exam is a resit for me. I have been studying it for two years.

M: Jenny, do you have any idea what the test will be like? Will it be difficult?

W: I would be surprised if it wasn't easy. This is the easiest test to correct for the teacher.

M: I hope so. But I'm still worried about it.

W: Well, cheer up. I wish you good luck!

M: Thanks. I'm going to need it.

Text 10

I don't know what to do about my mother. She is always criticising me — the way I dress, the way I speak or look... I can't even read a book without her interrupting me to ask what it's about and tell me whether I should be reading it or not, and why. And of course every moment of my life away from her has to be accounted for... I try to tell her to stop interfering with my life, but it doesn't seem to help. And I've no one to advise me. My father is dead and I have no brothers or sisters. It isn't as if my mother has any worries; we're well-off and she doesn't have to work, only do the housekeeping. I've now met a wonderful girl who I want to see a lot, but I'm afraid to bring her to the house — when she meets my mother, she won't want to see me anymore.

 参考答案

1－5 BACBB	6－10 ABCCA	11－15 BBACB	16－20 BABCA
21－25 DADBB	26－30 CACBD	31－35 ADABC	
36－40 BADBC	41－45 ACABA	46－50 DCAAB	51－55 CBDDD
56－60 BBCCA	61－65 DCCAC	66－70 BABCD	71－75 CBBAC

76. Winter Sports

77. Putting oneself into the white world and breathing fresh air, one can relax and forget all worries.

78. still has a long way to go

79. （略）

80. 像高山滑雪和滑冰这样的冬季运动能让人们在享受户外活动乐趣的同时还保持温暖，所以这些运动非常流行。

写作

Dear Liu Wei,

When I arrived in New York, my uncle and his daughter, Susan, were at the airport to pick me up. The next day, Susan showed me around some of the city's major landmarks. We went to many places including the Statue of Liberty, the symbol of American democracy and freedom.

However, my best experience was the visit to Chinatown. A Chinatown is a neighbourhood with a large concentration of Chinese. New York's Chinatown is the largest concentration of Chinese in the Western Hemisphere. Chinatown gives you a homelike feeling. There are Chinese shops, restaurants and hospitals. For a brief moment, I did not feel that I was many kilometres away from home. I guess I'll come here more often to drink my favourite green tea.

I'll tell you about the American education system next time.

Yours sincerely,

Li Ming

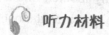 听力材料

Text 1

M: Excuse me, madam. I'd like to choose some flowers for my teacher.

W: Let me see. These fresh roses are very nice.

Text 2

M: Do you mind if I look at your notebook?

W: No, of course not. It's on the dining table.

Text 3

M: Hi, I'm home.

W: Hi! Did you remember to buy the tickets?

M: Well, I remembered; but they were sold out.

W: Oh no. I was really looking forward to it. It's the last night that the play is on.

Text 4

M: Excuse me, could you tell me how to get to the Grand Hotel? I thought it was on this corner but I seem to have made a mistake.

W: Hmm, I'm sorry. Maybe you should try calling them.

Text 5

M: I'm still waiting for the clerk to come back and make some copies of this paper for me.

W: Why trouble him? I'll show you how easy it is to work the machine.

Text 6

W: Look at the young people nowadays. They have everything. They are completely different from us when we were young.

M: You're right. Too much money — that's the trouble. They can afford to buy anything they want.

W: You know my grandson? He went shopping in a department store near our flat, and came back with 13 T-shirts! He only wears them once or twice, and then throws them away. It's a terrible waste of money.

M: But young people don't understand the real value of money, do they? They have too much of it. When I was young, we didn't care about whether clothes were fashionable or not. We didn't buy special shoes to match our trousers. We were just grateful to have any clothes!

W: You're right. But it's not worth arguing with them. They don't understand.

Text 7

W: May I help you?

M: I'm looking for the shoe department.

W: Women's or men's?

M: Uh, children's actually. I'm here with my son.

W: OK, the children's shoe department is on the third floor. And right now we're on the fourth floor. Oh, you'll also find children's shoes in the sporting goods department right over there. See the tennis rackets on the wall?

M: Oh, OK, I see… Now, where's my son? Is the toy department over there too?

W: No, it's on the fifth floor, next to the restaurant.

M: Hmm. Maybe he's in the restroom.

W: Oh, that's on the fifth floor too, just by the men's wear department.

M: OK, great. Thanks.

Text 8

W: I just read an interesting fact. Did you know that people who spend less than 10 minutes in a store are five times more likely to buy things than those who spend half an hour there?

M: I read that article too. But I think if someone runs into a store for 10 minutes, he usually has something to buy.

W: And someone who spends more time there may be just looking around.

M: Exactly. Haven't you ever gone into a store, thinking you'd buy something, and then talked yourself out of it?

W: Yes, I have, especially when I thought I could get it for less money elsewhere, or I really didn't need it at all.

M: Exactly. But if you run in to buy something special and have very little time, you pick it up, pay for it immediately, and then leave.

W: That's very true. Maybe we should learn a lesson from that: Take your time and you'll spend less money.

Text 9

W: This is Swan Travel Agency. Can I help you?

M: Yes, I'd like to make a flight reservation for the 13th of this month.

W: You destination, please?

M: I'm flying to Bangkok, Thailand.

W: OK. Let me check what flights are available. Would you please tell me when you will be returning?

M: Well, I'd like to return on the 20th. By the way, I'd like the cheapest flight available.

W: OK. Let me see. Well, the price for the flight is almost double the price you would pay if you left the day before.

M: Hou much is it?

W: It's only $980.

M: Then let's go with that.

W: OK. That's Flight 1070 from New York City to Bangkok Airport, Thailand.

M: And what are the departure and arrival times?

W: It leaves New York City at 11:35 am, arriving in Bangkok at 1:34 pm.

M: All right. By the way, I'd like to request a vegetarian meal.

W: No problem. Could I have your name, please?

Text 10

It's often very difficult these days to find someone to come and fix your fridge, your TV set or your washing machine if it breaks. Everybody wants to sell you new fridges, new TV sets or new washing machines, but nobody wants to fix them when they stop working. One day I discovered that my washing machine didn't work, so I phoned a workshop. Three days later, a man from the shop came to see what was wrong with my washing machine. But I was not happy and said, "Well, you've finally arrived! I called you three days ago!" The man paid no attention to what I said. He simply took a piece of paper out of his pocket and looked at it. Then he said, "Three days ago? That was May 21, wasn't it? Well, I am sorry, Mrs White. I've come to the wrong place. I'm looking for Mrs Smith's house, not yours. She phoned me four days ago."

 参考答案

1－5 BCACA	6－10 CACCB	11－15 ACACA	16－20 BAAAA
21－25 CCDBD	26－30 ACCBC	31－35 CABBC	
36－40 ACCAC	41－45 ADABA	46－50 CDACD	51－55 ABACB
56－60 CBDDC	61－65 CCABD	66－70 CDBCB	71－75 DDBAA

76. To warn readers not to be multitaskers. / To tell readers about the danger of being multitaskers.

77. The young are often considered the great multitaskers, but a research suggests this perception is open to question.

78. when (they were) not interrupted

79. (略)

80. 最近的研究结果显示，由于人们在过马路时使用电子产品而导致的（交通）事故的数量让人触目惊心，因此纽约于上月开始实施这项法律。

写作

New Socialist Countryside in the Future

With the efforts and support from the government in many aspects, a new socialist countryside will appear in China. There will be more new farmers with the basic knowledge of science, technology, laws and management. Many farming techniques will have been modernised. With the help of scientists, farmers will use the latest technologies to increase agricultural production without harming the environment. As a result, the yearly income of the farmers will be increased and their housing conditions will be improved as well. People in the new countryside will enjoy a clean, tidy and orderly environment. Besides, the government will provide free compulsory education for rural kids and also perfect medical care system for farmers.

As students, we should study hard to be well prepared for the future construction of the new socialist countryside, thus making our country more beautiful and powerful.